DREAM WARRIOR BOOK

DARK WARRIOR ALLIANCE BOOK ONE

BRENDA TRIM

TAMI JULKA

This book spun from the amazing life and unfortunate death of one very important man. John Andrew DeCaprio will always be loved and remembered. Thank you for your love!
We want to send a special thank you to Brenda's husband, Damon Trim, for designing our website.
This book is the beginning of a new journey for us and we want to thank all of our family and friends for joining us on this E-ticket ride!

PROLOGUE

Vampires? Dalton wondered as he lay in an ever-widening pool of crimson, questioning reality and doing a mental inventory. Throat shredded, chest riddled with holes, and too many bite wounds to count. What the *hell* had Jag become? Dalton had never encountered more strength in a man before, and when he had seen the sharp, pointed fangs protruding from his mouth, he knew he was in trouble. One look in those haunting, eerie eyes said it all. Jag was a vampire.

Dalton's limbs were lead bricks at his sides, and he could not lift them to staunch the blood seeping out of the wounds on his neck, stomach, and chest. *Fight this, Elsie needs you!* The rattle with each breath turned the little blood left in his veins to ice. He wasn't going to make it out of this. The drum-beat in his chest slowed and the pain lessened. An image of his wife, Elsie, and her beautiful heart-shaped face swam into his mind. He loved her more than anything and didn't want to leave her. He managed to inch his fingers across the floor and dragged the phone closer.

He dialed and closed his eyes when he heard his wife's

sultry voicemail greeting. He realized he didn't have enough words left in him to adequately warn her of the dangers that existed. "I don't have long...I love you, Elsie...I'll always love you...Bye, baby."

He worried about his wife. Who would protect her from the evils he now knew roamed the night? He wanted to protect her and couldn't. His very soul cried out at the injustice of it all.

*What the...*an all-encompassing sense of peace enveloped Dalton and the most brilliant, white light filled the room. This sense of calm was shocking and at complete odds with his brutal attack. He was dying and it pissed him off.

His eyes slipped closed and his last thoughts were of his beautiful wife the day they married. He saw her long, wavy, brown hair curled with tiny, white flowers flowing around her face. Her clear, blue eyes displayed the depth of her love for him. She held a small bouquet of jasmine and wore a simple, white, strapless dress. She was the most beautiful sight he had ever seen. As he looked into her eyes and they exchanged their vows, he knew he'd love her until the day he died.

He just didn't know that day would come so soon.

CHAPTER ONE

Elsie woke, drenched in sweat with a scream trapped on her lips and her sheets tangled around her legs. Her sister stirred next to her on the queen-sized mattress. She didn't want to wake her and shoved a fist into her mouth, stifling the scream from clawing its way out as the images from her nightmare continued to consume her. No matter how long and hard she fought it, the visions and memories refused to leave her.

It always started the same, with her standing on the cracked linoleum in the long hall of the group home where Dalton had been murdered. She had relived that entire night countless times over the past eighteen months. She squeezed her eyes shut as the images flooded her aching brain for what seemed like the millionth time. An abattoir surrounded her. Blood splatter covered the walls, and there were pools of the crimson liquid congealing on the black-and-white checkerboard floor. She gagged when she saw a lump of bright, red meat on the floor...flesh. Yellow flags and cones lined the walls and floor, amidst the carnage. Her stomach revolted while her body went numb.

In between heaving, she had whispered a plea for help. No one responded and she fell into a heap on the floor. Mindless of the blood she sat in, she gazed at the sight of her husband lying in a pool of blood, his sightless eyes trained on her. His neck had been torn open and shredded. How long she sat there screaming, she didn't know. Finally, a police officer had escorted her away from his body and out of the house where her nightmare became worse when she came up against a mass of news media shouting questions about her husband being the latest TwiKill victim. Her world came to a crashing halt that night. At that moment, a giant black hole imploded into an endless ache in her chest.

Now, eighteen months later, that black hole had grown thorns and pierced her heart. The pain forced her to curl into a ball on her bed. She hated how much power the memories had over her. Joining SOVA had been a way to gain some of that power back. Still, she longed to be a "normal" college student again. *You haven't been normal since you were three years old*, she thought wryly.

Not even thoughts of her childhood could suppress the pain of loss. No matter how much time had passed, Dalton's murder still seemed unbelievable. The police still didn't know who was responsible, and the detectives in charge had been spouting the same bull-shit excuses to the press for eighteen months. They were incompetent and hadn't learned a fraction of what she had within the first forty-eight hours. Not that she was able to tell them what she had learned. She couldn't, or she'd risk herself or her friends' freedom. The instant the police learned the facts of the case they'd all be charged with a crime.

She jumped from the bed and made it to the bathroom where she promptly lost the measly contents of her stomach. It had been the same day in and day out for what seemed like forever. She had been wracked with unending grief, barely able to function.

Sleep was a thing of the past, interrupted by her night-mares. The dark circles under her eyes she could live with, but the muddled memory and irritability were another story. She lived on energy drinks and candy. She couldn't remember the last time she had consumed a full meal because the grief created a barrier in her throat. Between the black smudges and her weight loss, she looked like a zombie. Hell, she felt like one too.

As the stomach spasms stopped, she wiped her mouth, flushed the toilet and prayed for the millionth time for a magic pill that would take the pain away. Sadly, science wasn't on her side with that one.

After washing her face and brushing her teeth, she checked on her sister. Throughout Elsie's life, Cailyn had always made sure she was safe and had what she needed. Despite living two states away, that was no different now with her daily calls and bi-monthly visits. Cailyn was her only remaining family and her saving grace. She loved her more than anything.

Thankfully, her sister hadn't heard her in the bathroom and was still asleep. She didn't need or want another lecture about her lack of eating and weight loss.

Quietly, she grabbed her robe off the back of her bedroom door and made her way into the living room. She stopped by the kitchen first for an energy drink before she plopped down onto the futon with her laptop. She needed to put the finishing touches on a paper before she turned it in on Monday. As she waited for her laptop to start-up, she grabbed her day planner and looked at her work schedule. In order to keep her apartment, she picked up extra shifts to make up for the loss of income. The reality of it was that she used her activities as a diversion from the crushing grief.

Her head flopped back on the futon and she stared at the colorful Mexican blankets that served as one of the reminders of her life with Dalton. Tears gathered in her eyes. Would she ever be free?

ELSIE HUNCHED into her black coat and wrapped her scarf tighter when a breeze found its way down her back. Shivering, she flipped up the collar and pulled her pink beanie down over her ears. It was cold and to add to the misery it had started to drizzle. Springtime shouldn't be this cold, Elsie thought to herself, but that was Seattle for you.

"Let's grab a burrito for dinner since I know your fridge is empty. You need to eat at least one meal today," Cailyn said as she linked her arm through Elsie's and they headed down the street.

"I do try and eat, you know. I just can't get anything down, but before you go all maternal on me again, I will try," Elsie replied, contemplating an umbrella to cover them. Since coming to live in Seattle, where it seemed to rain constantly, she had become accustomed to being damp like the rest of the city.

They hurried down the street and talked about what assignments Elsie had remaining before she graduated from college next month. Time had crawled by since Dalton's death and Elsie still couldn't believe her Bachelor's degree was within reach. She didn't want to go down memory lane again today and focused on the fast food restaurant. Cailyn held the door for her and they walked inside. Warm, greasy, cumin-scented air hit her as they entered the establishment.

Her stomach growled. She was hungrier than she realized. She removed her jacket and shook off the moisture then turned to contemplate the menu.

Cailyn leaned into her side and her warm breath hit her cheek as she whispered in her ear, "El, your high beams are on and there are two gorgeous guys who have noticed."

Heat suffused Elsie's cheeks. She had on an unpadded bra and it provided no protection under her skin-tight Henley. "Oh God, and I'm mostly nipple too," she whispered back.

"You aren't wrong about that, sis. Doesn't mean they aren't enjoying the show."

A deep, masculine groan had Elsie's blush intensifying. She glanced out of the corner of her eye and spotted a trim waist encased in tight, black, leather pants. Controlled by an unknown force, she was drawn to the sight and turned to appreciate the man more fully.

Her eyes followed the ropes of muscle up his abdomen and broad chest, locking with the bluest eyes she had ever seen. Electric currents ran underneath her skin as he devoured her with his gaze as if she were a gourmet meal he intended to savor, slowly and thoroughly. Her stomach clenched with need. His full lips pulled in an erotic grimace. He was the sexiest man she had ever seen.

An unbearable ache bloomed in her core, followed by a strange pull. She wanted to perform sexual acts with this man that were illegal in some states. A wanton sex-fiend had just awoken, wanting this strange, sensual man and it was decidedly unsettling. Hell, who was she kidding, she was terrified.

An odd fluttering and pain in her chest took her breath as guilt assailed her. She shouldn't have these thoughts. In her mind and heart, Dalton was still her husband, and she was betraying him with these urges. She made vows to be loyal and love her husband to the day she died and that was what she was going to do. There would never be anyone else for her.

She lowered her head and rubbed her temples, hoping to erase the image burned into her retinas. It was not right to ogle this hot guy. Flustered, she pulled her jacket back on and rushed to the counter, sputtering out an order for God only knew what food. She chanced a glance back to her sister. Cailyn, thankfully, was oblivious to Elsie's desire for Mr. Blue Eyes. The last thing she wanted was for her sister to question her.

"Someone has an admirer," Cailyn half-sang, bumping her shoulder against Elsie's.

"Shut up. I do not," Elsie hissed under her breath.

"You've been out of the game too long. He is absolutely checking you out." Elsie gritted her teeth as she listened to Cailyn.

"He is hot," Elsie snuck another peek of Mr. Stunning Blue Eyes, "and an opportunity waiting to happen."

Elsie's eyes widened when she noticed he was hard everywhere. Wow, his leather pants left little to the imagination. One word ran through her mind...huge. She felt that desire and pull once again.

"Not going to happen," Elsie declared, a kernel of shame blossoming alongside her guilt. She wasn't this person. Turning away, Elsie thought of her vows and love for her husband, dead or not. The second her order was ready she raced from the establishment without a backward glance.

ZANDER WATCHED THE FRAIL, human female hurry from the

restaurant. Something about her was familiar, but all he could focus on was how beautiful and intriguing she was. The cupid bow of her lips had thinned as she fled the establishment. The image struck him as wrong. She should always smile, and her lips would look best wrapped around his cock. He berated himself for obsessing over the female. Yes, she was sexy and held his attraction in a way no female ever had before, but he'd never had sex with a human and didn't plan on starting now. Besides, he didn't care for one-night stands and that was all he could ever have with any human.

Humans were fragile beings, unaware that all legends of myth and fantasy were no myth at all. As the vampire king of the Tehrex Realm, it was his duty to enforce the Goddess' edict and protect humans from the demons and their skrim. That job didn't leave room for much else.

He shook his head at the fact that he was tempted by the female, and was surprised at how difficult it was to stop from following her tantalizing honeysuckle fragrance. Sure, he could have sex with her and erase himself from her memory, but he wanted more. He was tired of having empty dalliances. He was one of the few in the realm who still held high hopes of finding his Fated Mate. The fact that his thoughts lingered on the female belied those beliefs. She was a human and not the one for him.

Put her oot of your mind, dumb arse! The order fell on deaf ears as desire consumed him.

Like an addict, he replayed every moment from the second she had entered the establishment. The cold left her face flushed, and her nipples had strained enticingly against her top. His keen hearing had picked up the conversation between the two females and she wasn't far off about their size, but he found them positively perfect.

With one glance, his heart had raced in his chest, sweat had beaded his brow, and static electricity zipped under his skin. His fangs had painfully shot into his mouth. For an instant when their gazes locked, his soul stirred. The enigmatic female had controlled his body at that moment, and he had to close his eyes, lest the glow reveal his true nature.

Her sweet, honeysuckle scent had set an inferno ablaze in his veins. His shaft had hardened the moment the tendrils reached his nostrils. The urge to get naked and sweaty with her had become irresistible. So much so, that a groan had slipped past his lips. A fucking groan, of all things.

He'd never hear the end of it from Kyran, who was, at that moment, chuckling softly beside him. Not that his twisted brother had much room to talk, but Zander had never lost his focus. For the first time in his seven hundred sixty-five years of existence, he was struggling to control his mind and body.

ZANDER SHOOK his head at his warriors. He had come to Confetti after encountering an enchanting human, seeking release. The problem was, no one appealed to him. He wanted what his mamai and da had shared.

Happiness. A true and lasting love. Completion.

He wanted to find his Fated Mate.

That wasn't going to happen anytime soon, seeing as the Goddess had not blessed any couple since he had become vampire king over seven centuries ago. He had tried so hard to please the Goddess and had made strides never before seen in the Tehrex Realm. He had initiated and formed the Dark Alliance and established the Dark

Warriors, the realm's first army, but still, the curse continued.

"I need a female so bad it's not even funny. If it weren't for their hair-scorching breath, I'd grab that sexy little fire demon," Orlando said, grabbing Zander's attention.

Shoving aside thoughts about what he couldn't change, Zander scanned the crowd. He was looking for Lena, one of his few preferred partners. He heard she was there and tonight he needed to ease the ache.

"You afraid of a little heat, O? Can't handle the flames?" Rhys teased.

Orlando threw a pretzel at Rhys, "Fuck off, dick-head."

A delectable, honeysuckle scent teased Zander's senses, taking him to earlier that night. He had been obsessing over the human for the past several hours when it dawned on him that she had been all over the news eighteen months ago after her husband's murder when every reporter in the area showcased her misery.

"Orlando. Do you remember the case where a group home counselor was murdered aboot a year and a half ago?" Zander asked, redirecting the conversation.

"Huh? Oh, uh, yeah. Why? What's up?"

"Just curious. Kyran and I ran across the widow tonight," Zander replied.

"She seems like a pleasant girl. Hasn't given the department any problems. Did she say something?"

"Nay. We didna talk to her. Skirm were responsible, aye?" Zander wanted vengeance for the beautiful female. He may never be able to have her, but he would do this for her. There had been an old pain in her clear blue eyes that he hated to see.

"Yeah, their magic was all over the body and scene. Why?" Orlando asked, his eyebrows scrunched and mouth twisted. Zander understood his warrior's confusion. There was no reason for him to scrutinize the case.

"Did you locate the ones responsible?" Zander sipped his scotch as he looked around for the provocative scent.

"No. Santiago and I didn't take the case. We didn't see the need. You know how hard it is to discover one particular skirm," Orlando said, a crease marring his forehead.

"I want you two to take the case and uncover the one responsible. Re-open it if necessary," Zander ordered. His warrior was smart enough not to question him and nodded his agreement. "Good, now has anyone seen Lena?"

Orlando chuckled and slapped him on the shoulder. "No, Liege. I've been too busy talking shop with you."

Another wave of honeysuckle reached him and his body responded to the delectable fragrance, hardening in his pants. And damn, if his fangs didn't shoot out of his gums. He ran his tongue over the teeth that had become recalcitrant and was stunned he had this reaction. It had to be because he hadn't had sex in months.

He continued his search for Lena, scanning the large dance floor. Numerous colored lights and lasers bounced from the steel rafters on the ceiling and down onto the stained cement. He didn't see the human's heart-shaped face among the crowd of gyrating, sweaty bodies. He scanned both bars. She wasn't there either. He rested his arms on the back of the chairs next to him and looked toward the hall of private rooms. Nothing.

He shook his head and reminded himself he needed to look for Lena, not the human. That didn't stop him from opening his senses and telepathy. He picked up nothing of the human in the club. The scent hadn't come from her. He felt a bone-deep disappointment at that. But, why?

New voices brought his attention back to the table.

Orlando was off with a female and his brothers, Kyran and Bhric, had joined them. He hadn't realized how pre-occupied he had become. Normally, he was aware of everything going on around him. He couldn't afford to be so distracted, not with his position. He straightened in his chair and berated himself for not being more vigilant.

"No, you're a douche-bag. An entire coven of witches wouldn't be able to fix the mess your escapade with her would create. You would ruin the poor girl. Thank the Goddess for not gifting cambions with a vampire's ability to erase human memories. You'd leave the entire human female population of Seattle empty shells. Stay the hell away from the staff at my hospital," Jace snapped at Rhys.

Zander wondered what he had missed. Rhys smiled and threw his arm over the back of the chair next to him. Trouble was brewing behind the cambion's kaleidoscopic eyes.

"Hmmm...vampire abilities. Hey, Bhric, I have an idea that I think you'll like," Rhys proposed as he sat up straighter, excitement in his every move.

"Do share," Bhric smiled broadly as he leaned forward, folding his thick arms on the paint-splattered table. Zander wanted to smack the back of his brother's head for encouraging Rhys. They all knew better.

"It's hard to be with human females because they notice differences about me when I fuck, so I say, we double-team the humans and you erase—"

Horror washed over him at what his warrior was proposing. "Absolutely no'! No vampire will use their power over the human mind so you can tup them. With the way you guys go through females, we would be exposed by dawn. There are plenty of willing females in the realm," Zander interrupted before this conversation escalated any further.

The problem was, the idea was out there and he could tell both males were churning it. He growled low in warning, "Doona even think it, arseholes. I mean it." He pondered enacting a law prohibiting his subjects from using their mind control in such a manner on humans. Such abuse of power went against his beliefs. The realm and its supernaturals were better than that. They were protectors, not predators, of humans.

The sound of glass breaking caught his attention. He noticed that each of his warriors had gone into battle-mode. Across the bar, an imp was arguing with a sea demon. The pesky little demon had grabbed the transformer talisman from the sea demon, and he was now a fish-out-of-water, literally, gasping for air. Females began shrieking at the sight of the large fish. Zander shook his head. Imps were notoriously mischievous demons, but they meant no harm, and thankfully, sea demons were fairly mild-mannered.

He turned away from the scene as Bhric began grumbling. "Stupid little fuckwad had to go and scare the females. Speaking of fuckwads, have we received confirmation of a new archdemon, *brathair*?" Bhric asked as he threw back another shot.

Zander met his brother's gaze. He had suspected for months there was a new archdemon in town. It was to be expected after they had killed the last one, but he had the feeling whoever Lucifer sent this time was more powerful with better skill. They had been encountering skirm who were trained in combat and on organized patrols. No doubt the patrols were designed to discover the location of their compound. "Nay, dammit. The Valkyrie and Harpies deny any knowledge. There is only rumor and conjecture."

"Och, it would be good to know what we are facing and

give Killian a chance to work his magic on the computer and gather some intel," Bhric said.

"That it would. But, for tonight, put it oot of your head, *brathair*. Find a lass, or ten. The war will still be there in the morning, unfortunately," Zander responded as he spotted Lena returning from the restroom. He had found his partner for the night. He crooked his finger at her. "Lena, join me, it's been too long since I've seen you."

"Of course, *mon couer*," she purred as she sashayed to his side. He looked into her dark-brown eyes, eagerly grabbed her hand and sat her across his legs. His erection returned with force. He paused in his caress of Lena's arm when he realized the honeysuckle scent was coming from her. He picked out slightly astringent notes that told him it was a bottled fragrance as opposed to the natural tones of the human's. "You smell different tonight. Is that a new perfume?"

"*Oui*, it is. I thought of you when I bought it. I was hoping to find you here tonight. I have missed you, *mon ami*. I see you are eager for me," she whispered in his ear and started caressing his inner thigh and erection.

Inhaling deeply, he closed his eyes and enjoyed the feel of her soft hands caressing his body. It amazed him the incredible effect the perfume had on his libido.

Lena tilted her head slightly, exposing her neck to him. The movement stirred her perfume. *Mmmm, addictive.* He ran his teeth over her throat, anticipating sinking his fangs into her neck as he sunk his cock into her heat.

He downed the rest of his scotch, stood up and pulled Lena up against his chest. Lowering his lips to hers, he relished the gentle slide of her soft lips against his.

"Backroom, now," he ordered.

CHAPTER TWO

Zander led Lena down the long hallway. He refused to take her back to Zeum with him. His bed was reserved for his Fated Mate. He had designed and hand-carved it with the guidance of his mate's soul, and would never sully it with other females. For the past century, he had used the private rooms in the back of Confetti for his liaisons.

Even through the loud thumping music, his preternatural senses heard Lena's heels clicking on the stained-concrete floor, and the passionate moans and sounds of skin slapping skin through the doors they passed. With the erotic sounds surrounding them, anticipation thrummed through his blood. He opened the last door on the left and ushered her into the small, dimly lit room.

The cement floor was covered with a plush, black rug, silencing her heels. The walls were the same burgundy color as the hall and the only furniture in the room was a black, leather couch that rested along one wall.

She reached for him, but he stilled her hands. He

needed fast and hard right now for the physical release his body craved, not the leisurely exploration he knew she wanted. Plus, he didn't want to be touched by her. He had her tight, blue shirt and black bra off before she could blink. Her ample breasts pressed against his chest as he pulled her into a deep kiss, exploring her mouth with his tongue. With one hand he captured her wrists and held them behind her back, pushing her breasts further into his chest.

Leaning back, he latched onto one breast and suckled her pert nipple into his mouth, squeezing her other dusty-rose peak with his free hand. Her nipples elongated with his attention and she arched into him, moaning. She began to sweat, releasing more of the honeysuckle scent. Damn, he loved that perfume. He wanted to buy a vat of it and bathe daily in it. His lust had never been driven so high, taking him to the edge.

She wriggled her hands free, and he shuddered when she ran her hands under his fitted, black t-shirt. Much to his dismay, the shudder was not from pleasure. Nope, no touching. He recaptured her hands and inhaled deeply, taking in the honeysuckle.

He turned her back to him and unzipped her black mini skirt letting it drop to the floor, leaving her in lacy, red panties. He refused to step back and admire the view. His need was too high. He slipped his fingers into her panties and found her slick and wet for him. She was always ready for him. He placed her hands on the back of the leather couch. "Doona move your hands. Bend over, now."

She knew to comply with his demands without hesitation, which is one reason she was one of his partners. He pushed her panties down her long, lean legs. She wavered on her feet as she stepped out of her underwear. He stepped back and unzipped his leather pants, freeing his cock. She spread her legs and bent over the sofa, exposing her slick channel to him. She looked back over her shoulder at him, "Come. I need you inside me, Zander. I ache."

He palmed his cock and stroked it. Damn, that felt good. "You want this?" he taunted. He didn't want Lena to think his need meant she held any power over him. It wasn't about Lena at all tonight. In fact, he was highly disconcerted by the knowledge that it was one hundred percent about a bewitching, human female.

"Always. Fuck me. Now, *mon Cher*." She arched her back presenting a better view of her wet pussy. He didn't need to be told twice and stepped up behind her with his feet apart, bracing him. Without a thought to further foreplay, he slammed into her core. She cried out, but he gave her no quarter as he began a punishing rhythm.

"You like that, Lena? You want me to fuck hard and fast?" he demanded.

"Mmmm, *mon coeur*, yes," Lena hissed. She pushed back and into him so he could go deeper. "Goddess, Zander, harder. *Mon grand*, don't stop!" Lena flipped her long, blond hair over her shoulder, exposing her throat to Zander.

Losing himself in the carnal pleasure and increasing his pace, his fangs slowly descended. He was famished, yet, as he bent over her back, intending to bite her and feed, his fangs scrambled back into his gums. He cursed. They'd been doing this for a year and a half. *Ignore it.*

Not wanting to go over thoughts of his lack of ability to feed or consume any blood, he straightened and the scent of honeysuckle reached him again. His fangs once again lowered. Never slowing his thrusts, he prepared to bite into her flesh, only to have his fangs hide once again. Before he could become distracted by his feeding issue, she climaxed, pulsing around him. The fragrance of her perfume intensified once again, and he joined her in release.

Even before his orgasm waned, he realized the anxiety that had plagued him of late had resurfaced. Now, added to that, was a yawning sense of emptiness and dissatisfaction. The sexual release had not helped. And he still hadn't fed, which was becoming a critical issue.

A peculiar warmth rustled within his chest and he realized it was his Fated Mate's soul. All of the Goddess Morrigan's subjects were born carrying a vital part of their mate's soul. It was exactly the reminder he needed right now.

He withdrew from her, stuffed his softening penis back into his pants, zipped up and pulled down his shirt. Lena smoothed her hands over his seed staining her thighs, "I'm hungry and was hoping this time I could have a bite, *mon cher.*"

His body shivered in revulsion. Misconstruing his shiver for a sensual response, Lena sauntered closer to him. "Besides, I need you again. I want to ride you."

"Nay, lass, no' this time. I have an emergency, and you know I never let any female feed from me," he bit off, unable to keep his agitation from his tone. He didn't want to hurt this female, but he knew he could never be with her again. He turned and left the room.

He staggered as his mate's soul pulsed painfully and a bloody image flashed in his mind. This same image had been haunting him nightly for far too long. For the thousandth time, he wondered about the dead male and what his role was in the war. The male appeared human, but something told Zander he was immortal. He had to get out of this club and clear his mind before he went mad.

ZANDER LAY ON THE GOLD, silk duvet that covered his large, king-sized bed, but sleep continued to elude him. The discomfort he had been experiencing had become a piercing ache in his chest. He rubbed at the pain and stood to pull on some jeans and a dark-blue t-shirt before he padded into the living room of his large suite. He flipped on the television and went into the kitchen area. After he set a pot of coffee to brew, he turned to the fridge. He was hungry but not for food. He needed blood. The thought sent a flutter through the tightness in his chest. He grabbed an apple and crossed back into the living room.

He plopped down on the dark-brown, leather sofa and turned on CNN. His thoughts drifted to the previous night and his encounter with Lena and his peculiar reactions. Her perfume had driven him mad, but he was repulsed by *her*. The heavy clomp of boots interrupted his thoughts. He expanded his senses and picked up the sound of Santiago and Orlando headed his way.

He didn't read their thoughts to determine why they were darkening his door before they knocked. "Enter," he called out.

Orlando opened the door and peered around the wood panel. "Good afternoon, Liege. Can we speak with you for a moment? The matter is urgent."

Orlando took a few steps into his rooms followed by Santiago, who shut the door behind him. His warriors were tense as hell and he immediately tried to tune into them but was only able to pick up conflicting thoughts. Something about the widow, concern for the realm, attraction to the female, at least on Orlando's part, and shock all bombarded his mind.

They were setting his jittery nerves on edge. He stood and began pacing, a nervous habit of his. "Is this aboot the counselor's murder?" he demanded.

Orlando began wringing his hands and shifting from foot to foot. "Yes. We looked into it as you asked, and, well..."

After several moments of allowing the male to find his words, his patience snapped. "Spit it oot, already." He looked to Santiago for answers but the male kept his mouth shut and his lower lip gripped between his teeth.

"The widow is pissed about how the department has handled her husband's murder investigation. She threatened to give the news reporters her side of the case," the male paused and met his gaze squarely. "And, more importantly, I believe she knows about skirm," Orlando said

Zander stopped in his tracks and turned to face his warriors. "How the hell does she know aboot them? What does she know?"

Orlando shifted restlessly. "I'm not certain of what she knows, or how she knows it, but she mumbled about their existence under her breath, unaware I could hear her."

A scenario like this was precisely why Zander had assigned Orlando and Santiago to the human police department. It was his duty to protect the Tehrex Realm and keep it secret. He used his best warriors to keep a lid on information and stop it from leaking out. He'd had a suspicion about the case involving the murder of a group home counselor. It didn't sit well with him that this had gotten out of hand. On the upside, he now had an excuse to pay the female a visit. Excitement thrummed through him. "Is it possible you misunderstood what she said? Tell me exactly what she said."

Orlando cleared his throat, "After I informed her of the change in detectives on her husband's case, she began ranting and raving about how SPD had mishandled the case and placed the community at risk by allowing a dangerous killer to run free without even looking for him. I believe her exact words were—"

Zander cut off what was going to be a lengthy dialogue. "Och, I doona want to hear how she thinks SPD is incompetent. What did she say aboot skirm?"

"After I told her Santiago and I were going to dedicate all of our energy and resources to finding the person responsible, she said, and I quote, 'Detective Trovatelli, there is nothing you can do to make this better for me and I don't believe for a minute that you will be able to find who did this. You don't have the first clue as to where to start. This will be an exercise in you chasing your tail.' Then she mumbled under her breath, 'If you only knew about what stalks the night.' I was stunned, to say the least, Liege."

THE FEMALE'S temerity brought Zander's ardor roaring back. It was somehow sexier coming from such a powerless creature. Focusing on the issue at hand, he addressed Orlando, "Interesting indeed. I wonder where she is getting her information. When are you meeting with her? I will need to be there to handle this." The difficulty he had with causing her any harm was overshadowed by the fact that he was going to see her again.

Santiago jumped in and answered before Orlando. "Certainly. We set up the meeting with her at her house tonight to accommodate you. And, I discovered her sister is currently visiting from San Francisco so she will be there too."

Orlando crossed his arms over his chest. "You are only

planning to erase her knowledge of the Tehrex Realm, right? I don't want you to hurt her. She has been through enough and deserves better."

Bluidy hell, if Zander didn't know better, he'd say that Orlando was smitten. Regardless of Zander's obsession, this was a great reminder to stay away from the female. Orlando was far better suited for the human. He refused to acknowledge the ache that bloomed in his chest.

"I doona have to explain my plans to you, Orlando, but rest assured, I willna hurt her. I will be ready by sundown. You're excused," he motioned them to the door. When the warriors reached the hall, Zander called their attention again. "Oh, and plan for enough time so we can pick up dinner on the way to her house."

They both gave him a what-the-hell-are-you-thinking look. He waved his hand, and a burst of his power slammed the door on their confused faces.

Elsie peered through her peep hole and saw three huge, good looking men standing on her small stoop. Detective Trovatelli with his white-blonde hair sticking out in every direction, reminding her of Guy Fieri, stood there holding up his police badge. She opened the door but left the chain in place. Not, she told herself, that it would stop these men.

Their bulging muscles rippled under their button-down shirts, and their aura screamed don't-fuck-with-me, which should have frightened her, but she felt no fear. Rather, she felt safe with them, as if they would always protect her. She wasn't sure where the sense of security came from given that she didn't know them and one of them she'd never even met. She was not naïve enough to think a badge made them harmless.

"Hello detectives, how may I help you?" she asked.

"Mrs. Hayes, Detective Reyes," Trovatelli motioned to a familiar man with warm brown eyes and a shaved head, "and I wanted to go over the case with you again. And this is our colleague, Zander Tarakesh. He has specific skills that will be beneficial in Dalton's case."

Her heart stopped when she looked over at Zander. The detectives were good looking, but...Zander was something else altogether, with his sharp, masculine features and silky, shoulder-length, black hair. His broad, muscled shoulders seemed to take up all the space outside, and power poured off him.

To say he was gorgeous was an understatement. She was thrust out of her body the moment she met his captivating, sapphire-blue eyes. Something about his intense gaze was familiar. It took several embarrassing moments of ogling the guy before she realized she had seen those eyes a couple of nights ago when she and her sister had picked up burritos for dinner. Shockingly, her reaction to him had been the same.

Arousal, hot and insistent, coursed through her to pool in her core. She hid her torso behind her front door to hide how her nipples had hardened. It was unsettling how rapidly she lost control of her body as she began aching for this man. And, it was a stab to the gut that she was drawn to this stranger. Her black hole throbbed painfully, making her sick to her stomach. Guilt and shame warred for dominance over the desire in her mind, and conflicting emotions lashed her.

Her sister and friends had told her that it had been over a year and she needed to move on. That was impossible to do when, for her, Dalton was hardly cold in his grave. She made a promise to avenge Dalton if it was the last thing she ever did, and nothing would stand in her way. There was no room for anything or anyone else. She pushed aside her physical symptoms and held her vows to Dalton close to her heart. She loved him and always would.

CHAPTER THREE

Zander was shaking. He was standing on the cracked, concrete step outside Elsie's apartment. Elsie...her name was delicate like her appearance. Both were at odds with how she had been scrutinizing him. He wondered what was running through her mind and before he knew what he was doing, had tuned into her thoughts and almost staggered from the grief and loss that hit him.

Humans with their short life spans loved more fiercely and tended to hold on with all they had. This female was no different. Zander, on the other hand, knew nothing about intimate relationships. He had sex with females, but there was nothing deeper than meeting his body's physical demands. That made him a crass bastard, but his Fated Mate's soul had never allowed anything else. He wasn't able to turn his back on that sacred presence.

Sweet honeysuckle brought his attention back to the female before him. Oddly, he wanted to erase the pain from this female. She had suffered horribly, and he found he loathed her sadness. This was a first for him, well, another first. It was bad enough that he desired the human, but now he wanted to give her affection and comfort.

Suddenly, Orlando turned around and placed both hands on his shoulders. "Relax, Liege. You're all over the place. We can't minimize the risk she poses without you," Orlando whispered, too low for her to hear. Zander was shocked by the statement. He hadn't been aware that his emotions were so unstable. He needed to remind himself that the empath picked up everything he was feeling and he needed to keep better control.

Zander nodded his appreciation. He heaved a heavy sigh that carried the weight of his agony. His cock ached for a taste of this female, and his heart wanted to reach out to her all the while his head was arguing she was too fragile. He feared her human status but still wanted her. Not one part of his body was in agreement with another.

"Is everything ok?" Her sultry voice struck the match of his desire, heating him further. He glanced back over Orlando's shoulder as the warrior turned back around.

She stood in baggy jeans and a soft, pink sweater that hid her bare skin from his gaze. She smiled at whatever Orlando said back to her, and his world rotated on its axis.

Her sweet honeysuckle scent rushed his senses. It wracked his body with a need for her body and her blood. But, something clicked into place and, for a moment, it didn't matter that she was human or that she had belonged to someone else. He was going to have her. He couldn't keep her but, by the Goddess, had to be inside her before she died.

He ignored the twinge the thought of her death caused, too consumed by the intensity of his desire for a frail human, when he had never had an inkling of attraction to any human before this.

He was unnerved by his body's uncontrollable reactions. At that moment, his cock was hard as granite and only getting harder as he slowly perused Elsie's lean runners build, full, kissable lips, and perfect, pert breasts that were pressing enticingly against her pink top. He marveled at the lust coursing through his veins, and his inability to control any aspect of it.

Not that he wanted to control any part of it. He wanted the out-of-control passion to consume them both. Normally, he was in complete control and had never experienced such sensations. He gazed at the luminescence of her pale, peaches-and-cream skin and nearly came in his trews. Ravishing.

"Everything is fine, just tired from working long hours," Orlando replied smoothly. "Can we come in?"

"Sure," she agreed.

The door closed and he heard the female disengaging locks. He followed Orlando and Santiago into the small dwelling. As he passed her small frame, he noticed her pupils dilate and heard her heart racing as if she was being pursued by a rabid wolf. Her arousal was unmistakable. It was more than a bit disconcerting that he was jealous that it might be directed towards one of the other males.

Unable to resist, he reached out for her hand. The moment their skin touched he was transported to another plane. Electrical tingles hurtled through his system, and his seed rushed into his shaft. He took a deep breath to calm himself down. It was counter-productive. Her intoxicating honeysuckle scent was thick with her arousal. He was close to losing control, but his worry about her fragile body being able to handle the sensations running through her body kept him in check.

"Elsie," he murmured as he bent his head and brought

her hand to his mouth for a kiss. The kiss was gentle and too brief for his liking. He was a ravening beast who wanted nothing more than to devour her.

"'Tis a pleasure to officially meet you. Orlando and Santiago told me aboot your case. Between the three of us, we will find who did this and make sure they pay," he vowed.

He heard her sharp intake of breath and caught her confused and wild thoughts. She wanted him as badly as he wanted her, but there was so much turmoil. He forced his fingers to relax and let her go.

She met his gaze again, a pretty blush staining her cheeks, and finally replied, "It's good to meet you, too. We, uh, my sister and I saw you and another guy in that restaurant last night, didn't we?"

"Aye, you did. I remember it vividly." The way her nipples strained against her top was forever seared into his mind. The recall was enough to have his shaft thickening further. Much more and he may take her right there. Good thing he liked living on the edge, he thought, closing the door.

She flushed, making her even prettier. "Please have a seat and make yourselves comfortable. This is my sister Cailyn," she pointed to the bright green futon and the female standing in the threshold between the small kitchen and living room.

He noted the crowded apartment and the meager furnishings. While it was apparent Elsie didn't have much money and lived simply, he saw that she was proud of what she had and kept her space neat and clean.

He turned his attention back to her sister. They shared some features, but Elsie was, in his opinion, the better looking sister. He extended a hand.

"'Tis a pleasure, Cailyn." He shook her hand and gestured to Santiago. "We brought dinner with us. I hope you like Thai."

ELSIE SILENTLY WATCHED as they set out food and chatted with her sister. Dinner? These weren't typical police officers. She had barely been given acknowledgment before and now they show up acting as though they were long lost friends. Her spine stiffened, she had learned enough in the past eighteen months to know she couldn't trust anything.

A warm palm landed on her shoulder. She looked back at Zander and met his sapphire blue eyes. That one simple touch was an electric shock, followed by a searing sensation as desire scorched her. She thought her body had been long dead, but he brought it back to life.

By no means was she a virgin, but the only man she had ever been with was Dalton. And, while satisfying, they hadn't had a very adventurous sex life. With Zander, she wanted to do wicked things.

Her inner-sex-fiend wanted to lick every inch of his body and ride him into exhaustion. It was all so confusing. She stepped away from him, needing space. His touch was too distracting.

"You are no' eating, lass. Sit, and I will get you some food." His Scottish brogue was delicious. There was just something about a guy with an accent.

"No, thanks. Are you always this bossy?"

"Aye, I am," Zander replied with a smile that lifted one corner of his mouth. Elsie couldn't help but smile back and stare at his lips, starving for a taste.

She was attracted to this man, despite the fact that he

looked to be capable of snapping her neck with two fingers. He was tall, about six and a half feet, and built like a heavyweight champion.

If she had to guess, she'd say he was black-ops or something similar with his fierce demeanor. There was an intensity about him that would bring grown men to their knees, yet she was inevitably drawn to him. What happened to all the training Mack and the others had given her?

Thoughts of Mack brought reality and guilt to the forefront. She would never be with this sexy, enigmatic man no matter how badly she wanted to. She was a widow, and her heart still belonged to another. She could not, would not, open herself up to anyone ever again. To allow herself to become vulnerable to the pain of loss again was unthinkable. Besides, her heart was in pieces, and they all belonged to Dalton.

Detective Trovatelli broke the tense moment by laughing. "I know what you're thinking. We know this is unprofessional, but we also know that you have been through so much in the past year and a half and, well, we are trying to make up for your bad experience with our department. After meeting you earlier and reading through Dalton's file, we feel as if we know you. Believe it or not, you matter to us. It's not just about the investigation. So, you've inherited new friends," Trovatelli winked at her.

"Some of us are better than others. You'll learn that I'm full of awesomeness. I like action movies, but am not opposed to chick flicks, and I make one mean margarita. No need to thank me for blessing you with my friendship, your stunned silence is thanks enough," he finished with a smile.

She let out a shaky laugh. The guy may be good-looking, but he was extremely presumptive. And yet, her instinct had told her when she eyed them on her stoop that these were people she could trust. Still, it was tough to embrace them with such open arms.

Before she could respond, Santiago snapped back, "You're such a jackass. More like he's full of shit. I'm the awesome one." Their banter put her more at ease. She appreciated a smart-ass.

"Ignore him, he's jealous," Orlando retorted.

"Both of you are delusional. They are children at best most days, but they mean well," Zander teased them and winked at her, too. His wink did things to her she refused to contemplate.

None of these men were like any she had ever encountered. "You guys aren't right, are y—"

A loud screeching meow cut her off, followed by Detective Trovatelli muttering, "Fucking Rhys." Her smile widened as he pulled his phone from the front pocket of his black slacks. Not a ring tone she would have pegged for a big, tough guy like that.

"You must have a thing for cats," she smirked.

Zander and Detective Reyes laughed heartily, causing Detective Trovatelli to look up from his phone. He ruefully shook his head. "A colleague of mine enjoys messing with us by changing our ring tones. He's rather annoying, but I do have a soft spot for cats."

Goes to show you couldn't judge a book by its cover. His Cheshire-cat grin held a private joke, and she wondered if she would ever know what that was all about. She shook her head. For now, she would give them her trust. After all, she was skilled with a blade and could protect herself.

"What are the next steps detectives?" she asked, wanting to make sure they had a plan and weren't blowing smoke up her ass.

"First, call me Orlando, and this bonehead is Santiago,"

Orlando gestured to his partner. "And second, we have questions for you, but later. Let's eat then we can talk about the case."

She had no idea what to think about these guys. Not only was she inexplicably drawn to one of them, but she felt an innate kinship to them all, and it was disturbing. She wasn't one to believe in fate or instant anything, but those beliefs were challenged by the easy camaraderie with these fierce men.

CHAPTER FOUR

Elsie dumped her uneaten food in the trash. It had been more months than she cared to admit since she had last eaten a full meal, and tonight had been no different. The anxiety of the upcoming conversation was killing her. She had to tread carefully. These men may seem invincible, but they had no idea of the monsters out there. They wouldn't stand a chance against the vampires that had killed Dalton and preyed on the innocent.

"What did you want to talk about?" she asked.

"We know this has been difficult for you and are truly sorry for your loss," Orlando said as his emerald green eyes held her gaze, somehow grounding her.

The sincerity in his voice told her that this man knew of gut-wrenching pain. That comforted her in a way she needed, and the tension in her body eased.

"We are following the leads involving the children from the group home. What can you tell us about them?" Santiago asked.

With those words, she felt far more compassion and

caring from these men than she had from anyone involved in the case. It was the genuine concern of a friend. Which made the situation mean even more. They meant what they had said about being friends now.

She had to pick her words carefully. There was so much she wasn't able to share with them. They'd think her crazy if she told them about the existence of vampires. Finding and eliminating them would have to stay with her and other SOVA members.

"I can't tell you much except that they were all troubled, but looking into them is a waste of time. Obviously, I want the thing responsible for Dalton's death to pay for what it did, but I don't believe there is anything you can do," she told them honestly.

"We will do everything we can to help you, but understand that at after so much time has passed, leads are lost, and it becomes much more challenging. Now, that does not mean we won't put all of our efforts into finding out who did this. I can promise you that no stone will be left unturned," Santiago assured as he walked over to crouch near her chair. He reached out and squeezed her shoulder. His smile was genuine and comforting.

"Of course, you are already giving me excuses. No surprise there. And here I thought you guys were going to be different," she countered and crossed her arms over her chest.

She had been foolish to think their approach would be any different. In reality, there was nothing they could do to either find the vampire responsible or deal with it.

"Hey now," Orlando chided. "We aren't giving you excuses. We will find the answers—"

Zander cut Orlando off. "Elsie," he murmured. Her name leaving his lips was a sensual caress with his Scottish accent. "I give you my word that I will put every resource at my disposal, of which there are many, and find the culprit. Your husband will be avenged." She shivered at the sincerity in his voice, and it was impossible not to believe what he said.

Her sister joined the conversation. "El, don't be so hard on them. Hear them out before you jump to conclusions," Cailyn urged, as she played hostess to the men taking up space in her house. She loved her sister and was grateful she was taking care of her as usual.

"You're right, Cai. This is your chance, detectives, don't blow it. You won't get another one," Elsie informed them. She wasn't getting her hopes up, she knew the score, but she wanted to see them try. Something that had been lacking thus far.

Zander sat across from her, watching her intently. His presence was so unnerving that she got up and poured a glass of wine. She both hated and relished the effect he had on her. Elsie didn't *want* to want him, but it was there, none-theless. Maybe it was because she had never been the focus of someone's attention so fully.

"Thanks for not putting pressure on us," Orlando teased. "We'll start with questions that you've been asked in the hopes that fresh ears can glean new information. Phone records revealed that Dalton called you shortly before he died. What did he say?"

It was easier to hold back the tears when she focused on the orange blanket hanging on the wall as she revisited that night. "I didn't speak to him. He left me a brief voicemail message saying," she swallowed the emotion that choked her, "that he didn't have long and he loved me."

"Is there anything else you can remember about the message?" Santiago added.

"Just that he was tired and sounded out of breath. His tone was sad...he was saying goodbye to me. I know that now," Elsie murmured as she choked back the tears. Talking about this still brought her to her knees. It always would. That vampire stole her life.

Orlando reached out and grabbed her hand, squeezing it in comfort. Shocked, she looked up at him. Understanding and acceptance met her gaze. "Did anyone have a reason to want him dead?"

"No, Dalton didn't have any enemies. He was a stickler for the rules, but he was fun and easygoing, as well. He had an open heart and mind that the children in the home responded to and respected. This killing was the work of evil."

"There isna doubt that this act was evil. His death should no' have happened," Zander declared.

The vehemence in his tone had her head swiveling in his direction. She met his eyes and for several long seconds as he captivated her. It felt as if he were looking through to her soul.

Orlando's voice broke the connection, and she took a deep breath she hadn't realized she was holding. "Had he behaved any differently in the days leading up to his death?"

"No, nothing different. Dalton went to work that morning like usual." If she had known he was never returning to her, she would have kept him home. At least made love to him again.

"This question is tough and I don't ask it to be insensitive, but I have to ask," Santiago qualified. "Is it possible he was having an affair? Or you? A jealous spouse or boyfriend or girlfriend would have the motive to harm him."

Red dotted her vision as her anger quickly boiled out of control. She stood up and balled her fists. "How dare you come into my house and accuse my husband of having an affair," Elsie yelled. "You know nothing about us. Neither of us had an affair. You are no friends of mine. Get out of my house," she spat, itching to pull her knife from the sheath in her boot. They might not turn to ash, but she could do some damage.

Santiago stood and placed his hands up, palms out in a gesture of peace. While Zander closed the distance between them and took her shoulders in his big warm hands. "Elsie, Santiago, while only doing his job, spoke out of turn. He knows, as do Orlando and I, that there wasna any cheating. Please understand that asking is part of leaving no stone unturned."

Cailyn sidled up to her side and wrapped her arm around her waist. "El, honey, take a deep breath. These nice gentlemen have no idea how much you and Dalton loved each other. You accused them of not doing their job so don't get angry when they do it."

She had her head down, not wanting to meet anyone's stare as silent minutes passed. Cailyn and Zander were both right. The question touched a nerve that set her off like a firework. Finally, she saw reason and lifted her head.

"I'm sorry. You're right, of course. That is a sensitive subject for me. I hate that people always assume there had to be something like that when there is no other explanation. There are things in this world that defy explanation and are capable of evil for no reason," Elsie replied. More than anything, she wanted to confide in these men about vampires. SOVA needed strength like theirs.

Zander's hands tightened almost painfully. "Not everything is at it seems. Doona risk yourself. You are now part of us."

Orlando peered over Zander's shoulder smiling broadly.

"Yeah, for better or worse, you're part of the family now. We're a motley crew, but we'd do anything for you."

She was helpless but to return his smile as the sense that her life had changed irrevocably settled in her gut. It was unnerving and had her clenching in response until she realized the feeling of tragedy that usually accompanied her predictive episodes was absent. It was a nice change to the usual doom and gloom.

HOURS LATER, Zander's steps never faltered as he hit the landing of the grand staircase of Zeum, searching for his siblings and Dark Warriors. Thanks to modern technology, automatic shutters descended before dawn, and covered the large picture-windows, protecting the vampires from the sun. No longer were his kind relegated to the rooms in the basement during the daylight hours.

He spotted Rhys crossing the grand foyer, heading into the war room with a bottle of wine. He must've stopped by their massive wine-cellar in the basement.

"Where are the others?" he barked, causing the warrior to jump.

Rhys twisted toward the staircase in a graceful move. Ready to fight any threat. The bottle of wine was a deadly weapon in his capable hands. His stance relaxed once he caught sight of Zander. "Goddess, Liege, you need to make some fucking noise. I think Kyran, Breslin, and Bhric are in the media room and I'm joining Gerrick in the war room now. What's up?"

"Is that wine for you and Gerrick? A nice, cozy, little interlude?" Orlando teased, as he walked up behind Zander.

Zander scowled at the warrior. Normally, he enjoyed

Orlando's humor, but he was wound tight from the unspent lust being around Elsie for hours had caused. Not to mention, there was a new threat to them which was complicated by the fact that Zander lusted after a member of the vigilante group. He was able to glean pieces from Elsie's mind about SOVA. He was still shocked that the little fireball was part of such a group.

"Awww, O, jealous we didn't include you? You're welcome to join us, but get your own bottle."

"Dickhead. There has been a development that holds implications for the entire realm." Orlando retorted all semblance of his good nature had vanished.

"Grab Gerrick and join us in the media room, now!" Zander's pulse leaped, and his tension increased. His muscles were wound so tight they may snap.

"Yes, Liege." Rhys nodded his acknowledgment and disappeared into the war room.

Zander headed down the hall beneath the twin staircases and entered the kitchen, which was empty at that time of day. He was thankful for that because he didn't want to share this information with anyone outside his inner circle. The alliance council and the entire realm needed to be told given this news affected them all, but right now he had too much he needed to sort through.

Past the kitchen was the enclosed patio, but he saw no one lingering there, either. His gaze slid over the lime-green cushions on the wicker sofa and landed on the tiled floor. He recalled the blood, sweat, and tears that went into the hand-cutting of each tile that now formed the intricate design of the Triskele Amulet in the center of the floor.

He heard his siblings talking down the hall in the media room. He entered the room and rolled his eyes at the sight of Breslin and Kyran sitting on one of the black, leather sofas, arguing about their card game. Bhric sat in an overstuffed chair next to them. The scotch was sitting out on top of the well-equipped bar in the corner. Which one of them was hitting the bottle this early in the morning? His money was on Bhric. It seemed his brother had been using alcohol, and other substances, with increasing frequency over the past few decades. One glance at the end table next to Bhric confirmed his suspicions. The ice hadn't had time to melt in the tall glass.

A flat-screen television took up one entire wall and was tuned into ESPN. He picked up the remote off a Louis XVI cabinet and muted the volume. That grabbed his siblings' attention. Only then did they realize he had entered the room followed by Orlando, Santiago, Rhys and Gerrick.

Bhric took in the scene quickly and grabbed his titanium *sgian dubh* from his ankle holster. "What's up, *brathair*? Are we under attack?"

"Nay, we are no' under attack. We have a situation." He stopped and gathered his thoughts. "Orlando and Santiago took a case at my behest and we have discovered there is a new threat. We need to determine what we do aboot it, if anything."

Gerrick pulled his lips into a thin line, making the scar that stretched over the left side of his face stand out. "What kind of a threat? I can deal with any threat easily. Tell me who it is, and I'll kill them."

Zander rebelled at the thought of any harm befalling Elsie. "That approach willna work. The case involves the human female whose husband was murdered eighteen months ago. 'Tis a death sentence to kill a human...and, I canna tolerate even a slight toward her."

Orlando chimed in, "To clarify, Elsie doesn't pose a threat. She may know about vampires, or what she thinks are vampires, but she would not disclose that to anyone, or she would have told us. The bigger threat comes from SOVA. Having a bunch of humans trying to kill supernatural creatures is a disaster waiting to happen."

"Okay. Back up and explain more," Breslin said.

Zander sat down on one of the sofas and leaned forward with his elbows resting on his knees. "Orlando is right. Elsie doesn't pose a direct threat. That much was evident from her thoughts. She willna tell anyone aboot skirm for fear of being seen as insane. She blames her husband's death on vampires, but what she doesna know is that it was skirm. She has become involved in a vigilante group called SOVA or Survivors of Vampire Attacks, and they hunt at night. From what I was able to glean, they've been fairly successful in their mission to eliminate *vampires*. The humans involved in this group are all victims that have survived encounters with skirm."

"Och. I assume the risk is in them killing a real vampire and thus exposing the existence of the realm," Kyran threw out as he tossed his cards on the table.

"Aye, that would be the concern. Use caution when handling this situation. I willna tolerate Elsie being harmed in any way and we canna eliminate humans for being rash. They seek justice for a wrong done them. How many of us wouldna do the same thing? We need to learn who is involved and include their territories on our nightly patrols. I willna have more innocent humans killed on my watch." Zander needed a reprieve from his ruminations about Elsie. He wasn't thinking straight and developing a more effective plan at the moment seemed like an impossible task.

Thankfully, his sister began plotting for him. "Why don't we erase their memories of their encounters with skirm? That would take care of it."

"That isn't going to work, Bre. We have no idea how widespread this group is. We can't assume the group is restricted to this area. If this is global, there would be no way to get to every member. It would be easier to put an ad in the paper," Santiago replied sardonically.

Breslin's face fell. "Oh, I hadna considered that. What can we do then?"

Kyran had been eyeing him intently. "I say we follow this group. They may have uncovered the skirm lair. Skirm canna sense humans like they do us, and won't take as many precautions around them. I volunteer to follow Elsie," his brother said with a sly smile.

Zander's objection was immediate and vehement. "Nay, you willna follow her. I will be the one to do it."

Kyran's smile spread. "This is the female you got sprung for the other day, is it no'?"

Zander scowled. He fell into his brother's trap. All he thought about was Kyran seducing her and introducing her to his dark desires. That thought made him so angry he reacted without pause. "I did not get sprung over her," he gritted out.

"Aye, *brathair*, you did. Everyone in the restaurant heard how attracted you were to the human."

Everyone laughed which did nothing to diminish Zander's desire to punch his brother.

"Our Liege attracted to a human?" Orlando teased. "No wonder you wanted Santi and me to take her case. You wanted an excuse to see her again—" Orlando's reply was cut off as he ducked out of the reach of Zander's punch.

"Enough," Zander barked. He wanted to deny their claims, but the words would be a lie, and he refused to lie to his warriors. "The only information I was able to learn from Elsie is that she works with someone named Mack." He had no idea if it was a male or female. He didn't care for how much she seemed to rely on this Mack. "I will ask Killian to do his magic on the computer and see if he can discover who this Mack is, as well as, anyone else involved with SOVA. I suspect it may take some time. In the meantime, no one will follow Elsie without my direct order. Now, get some rest."

He stalked from the room, ignoring their ribbing. He was more unnerved than they could ever make him by his undeniable desire for the female. The Vampire King should never consort with humans.

CHAPTER FIVE

Elsie finished texting Mack and placed her crappy cell phone on the table. She hated canceling another patrol, but her sister was still visiting, and there was no way Cailyn would understand or allow her to do something so dangerous.

Elsie loved her sister, but part of her was itching to be out there with Mack. Her phone chirped, indicating she had a message. She picked it up expecting to see a reply from Mack and was shocked to see it was Orlando.

It had been a few days since they had taken her case and she had yet to calm down. It wasn't Orlando, or even his partner, that had her on edge, but their friend Zander. She cursed and sent a reply.

"What it is?" Cailyn asked from where she stood, gazing into the empty fridge.

"It was Orlando. He said they have some news and will be here in a couple of minutes." She wrung her hands as a thousand different things ran through her head at once. At the top was that there was no way they found the vampire responsible. They wouldn't be alive if they had.

"I'm sure it's good news," her sister reassured.

"That would be nice. I have wanted to hear that whoever had killed Dalton was going to pay for so long," she admitted.

The doorbell interrupted. Elsie opened to see Orlando's emerald-green eyes full of mirth and hiss two sidekicks. She wondered at her easy friendship with these men and was forced to acknowledge that some people clicked the moment you met. She clicked with these men. Her heart kicked at the sight of Zander. He was even more gorgeous than she remembered.

Giving herself a mental head shake, she stepped back and invited them in. They each carried bags. She tilted her head curiously. "I thought you said you had news? It looks like you guys are going to a birthday party."

They all laughed. "Good one, Chiquita," Santiago murmured as he hugged her close. Being so readily accepted was magnificent, but she had to wonder if they'd do so if they really knew her. If they knew she was a freak who had premonitions of death and hunted vampires at night.

Zander pulling her into his arms stopped all coherent thought. He smelled utterly male and magnificent. "'Tis great to see you again, Elsie." She flushed as he kissed her cheek. His formality struck her as old school. She imagined he was better suited for chain mail and knighthood. The intimate note to his kiss, however, had her stepping out of his reach.

Orlando claimed her attention before she gained footing. He wrapped his arm around her shoulders holding out one of the bags in his hand. "Because we know you have no food, El, we brought some grub. We also brought tequila and chick-flicks. We're going to have a girls' night." He air quoted the last, causing laughter to bubble up her throat. It may have still felt odd to be so chummy with them, but they knew how to put her at ease. "I may even let you paint my nails," Orlando teased.

Cailyn laughed and hugged the men. "With as good of a cook as my sister is, you'd think she'd have some food in her house."

"Shut it, Cai," she snapped. Zander shifted a sparkly, silver, gift bag to his other hand, catching her attention. She paused. What girl wasn't tempted by a shiny gift bag? No, she was more curious about what they had to share. "I appreciate the food and stuff, but I need you to tell me the news first." She braced her nerves with her hands on the back of a kitchen chair. Had they already discovered who or what had killed Dalton? That would be impossible she reminded herself.

She busied herself with emptying the contents of the bags Orlando and Santiago had brought in while she listened to them update her on the investigation. After reviewing all the evidence, they had found some blood on a pen they believed belonged to the perpetrator. It had useful DNA on it that they compared to a corpse they had discovered in a dumpster. She sat in stunned silence as she digested the information.

She hadn't believed the kid they had found was responsible until they told her about his fake fangs. Every vampire she'd ever killed had turned to ash when she pierced their heart. Now she couldn't help but wonder if that didn't happen when their heart was removed. If that was the case, then she had a name for who destroyed her life. Jag. And she couldn't take any of her anger out on him now. He was dead.

She grabbed plates and silverware from her kitchen cabinets and set them next to the food. She expected to feel better with the news, but the same pain and heartache pierced her as before. Nothing of her torment had changed. For all these long months she told herself that she would feel better and begin to heal when the culprit was identified and killed. It was devastating to learn that it made no difference. Her suffering was never going to end. In fact, it was so much worse because now she was left without the ability to exact vengeance of her own.

Regardless, she was so thankful they had been assigned to the case. She gained not only answers but what she suspected were lifelong friends. Life went on, regardless, and she would, too.

She glanced around and realized that no one was eating and the lighter mood was gone. She wanted it back. She was tired of being sad. "Eat you guys. Put in one of your movies, Orlando. You know, I never would have pegged you for a chick-flick-kinda-guy." She smirked at the blonde-haired hottie. "I'm going with the drink-'til-you-drop plan, anyone with me?"

She turned from the table and headed back to the refrigerator where she pulled out the Limeade and other key ingredients for her passion-inspired margaritas. Her neck tingled with awareness. Someone was watching her. She cocked her head to the side and noticed not only her sister watching her intently, but Zander's eyes had yet to leave her. She felt the censure in her sister's glare and the erotic heat from his.

"Stop," she hissed at Cailyn.

Cailyn placed her hands on her hips, "Then eat before you drink. You haven't had much food since yesterday."

"You know I try to eat, Cai. If you thought getting that information from Orlando and Santiago was going to magically make me eat, sleep, and be fucking merry, you were wrong," she snarled. No one understood what she went through and she was tired of trying to make it okay for others.

"It's been well over a year since he died. You don't sleep, and you've lost a ton of weight. You need closure. You can't survive like this," her sister replied as she rounded the counter and grabbed her shoulders.

"You know what Cai? Closure is a myth. The most insidious myth ever created. I haven't forgotten about him, or stopped loving him. Nothing can make his murder any less traumatic or tragic. There is no magical cure to erase the memories or the blood. My emotions aren't a dry-erase board that can be wiped clean. It wasn't your husband and best friend that was ripped from your life, so get off your fucking high-horse!" she sobbed and fell into her sister's arms.

A large, hot hand settled on her back. "Why doona you have a seat, I'll make you a drink." She lifted her head as the deep timber of Zander's voice sent goose bumps coursing down her spine. When she met his gaze, the emotions she saw reflected there floored her.

"That would be great, thank you." She walked over and settled into one of the chairs at her kitchen table. Cailyn helped Zander, giving her space to regain her composure. Still, no one was eating, and the tension in the apartment could be cut with a knife. That didn't work for her. Not tonight.

She took a deep breath and leaned back in her seat. She threw her hands up in exasperation. "For crap's sake, people, lighten up and eat."

Orlando and Santiago chuckled and headed over. "You

don't have to tell me twice. I'm as hungry as Cailyn. Can I make you a plate?" Orlando asked.

An animalistic noise sounded in the apartment. Was Zander growling? As he approached her, she lost her train of thought. It flew right off the track, and the heat that she felt before was now a blazing inferno. She wasn't ready for what she saw in his eyes, didn't think she ever would be. Her devotion to Dalton produced guilt far too potent to ignore.

He prowled up to her and set the shiny bag in her lap then propped his hands on the arms of her chair. His hair brushed her cheek when he leaned over to whisper in her ear. His breath was a lover's caress against her cheek. She had to change her imagery. He wasn't her lover, and never would be.

"For you, my sweet, Lady E. I hope these bring a smile to those luscious lips of yours," Zander vowed.

She sat stunned as he again kissed her cheek. He hovered, waiting for her to lift her head. Chicken that she was, she shook her head and kept it downcast. He stood over her for a few more seconds before he straightened and picked up a plate. She lifted her head and watched as he began piling it high with food, envying his healthy appetite.

She met her sister's questioning gaze and shrugged then turned her attention back to the shiny bag. "Thank you for the gift, but you shouldn't have," she murmured.

"Nonsense. 'Tis nothing. The drinks are ready, but I agree with your *puithar*. I'd feel better if you had something in your stomach before you drink. Can I get you some food?"

The let down from their news still sat in her stomach like a stone. Her purpose in life had been to hunt down and kill the vampire who had killed Dalton, but now that was gone. "Just a drink, please. I promise to eat, but I need a drink," she explained when she caught sight of his stern expression.

Feeling awkward with the bag sitting in her lap, she peeked into it and pulled out green tissue paper, revealing several small boxes. A musky, oak fragrance wafted from the bag. It was Zander's masculine scent, and it drove her crazy. Her skin felt tight, as a zing ran through her body. Her head swam. Where was that drink?

She clutched the paper, fighting a warm rush. If she wasn't mistaken, he was quite interested in her. She glanced over at him, and the lust was back in his eyes. It slammed into her, and she blushed furiously. She was in uncharted territory. She and Dalton had been high-school sweethearts, and she was not familiar with how to handle the situation.

Choosing to ignore Zander, she picked up the first box and lifted the lid. They were all boxes of gourmet chocolates. Yum, she loved sweets. Before she indulged, she met Zander's gaze and felt an odd constriction when his eyes revealed nothing. She stood on shaky legs and took the three steps to stop in front of him. She had to crane her neck to look up at him.

"Do you give all your friends expensive candy? If so, I'm glad we became friends. Thank you." She stood on tiptoes and stretched her arms around his neck, hugging him. Every muscle in his body tensed and she worried she had offended him until he softened and clasped her back. Zing!

Her sister cleared her throat, rather loudly, behind her. It was surprisingly difficult for her to let go of Zander. She released him and tried to turn, but was unable to move. Zander still had hold of her. She looked into his eyes and murmured, "You have to let me go now."

One corner of his mouth lifted along with one of his eyebrows. "Do I? I'm no' accustomed to following orders.

Typically, I'm the one giving them," he laughed, winking at her as he loosened his hold.

He picked up the plate of food he had set down, and she smacked his arm. "Well, aren't you Mr. Bossy Pants?" she teased and smiled then turned to her sister and took the drink she was holding out to her. "Thanks, sis. And, I promise I will eat. In fact, I plan to start with these chocolates."

She sipped her drink and retrieved a box. She popped one into her mouth. Delicious. Chocolate and tequila, her favorite combination. She drank and watched the men interact with her sister for several minutes.

Orlando stopped next to her and picked up her empty glass. "Would you like me to refresh that?" A man after her own heart and he didn't even gripe at her about eating.

She beamed at him and replied, "Yes, thank you." A pleasant buzz was humming in her system thanks to her empty stomach.

She grabbed her chocolates and went to the living room. A salted vanilla caramel was calling her name. "Mmmm," she moaned as she ate it, closing her eyes and enjoying the candy. They popped open when the cushion next to her dipped. Zander had joined her on the futon. A quick glance around told her Cailyn was talking to Santiago on the other side of the small room and Orlando was in her kitchen. All of a sudden, her apartment felt even more cramped.

Distracting herself from his presence, she picked up a honey saffron and lavender chocolate and took a bite. Not as good as the caramel. She tucked her legs up under her, sitting cross-legged and turned toward Zander. "You mentioned giving orders. What do you do?"

He set his fork down and put his arm across the back of the futon. "I head up a large...corporation. We deal with safety and security. What aboot you? The other evening you only mentioned being a student. Do you work as well?"

She took a bite of a peppercorn chocolate. Ugh, she placed the uneaten portion back in the box. She didn't want to be rude, but that tasted awful. Where was her beverage? "Orlando, where is that drink?" He was handing it to her as quickly as the question left her lips. She took a healthy swallow and washed out the flavor. Peppercorn and chocolate were a horrible combination.

"I'm a waitress at Earl's. It's close to UW, and the schedule works with my classes," she answered, picking up more candy.

ZANDER WATCHED Elsie eat another caramel. The way she voiced her pleasure and closed her eyes was maddening. He clenched his fist and gulped his margarita. He needed to cool down. A bath in a tub of ice may do.

"You like those," he observed.

What had possessed him to bring her chocolates? It was simple to glean her love of candy from her thoughts during their last encounter, and he was compelled to purchase her the best in the area. Dear Fates, he was flirting with a human. It was mistake and he needed to stop pursuing her. He didn't need the problems that came along with her kind.

"Mmmm, these are incredible. My favorites are the salted vanilla caramels. The others are...unique. But, I could live on those caramels alone," she moaned in ecstasy as she ate another.

She had a drip of caramel on her lip that he wanted to lick off. He ached to taste various places on her delectable body, too. That was not helping to calm his raging erection.

His fangs shot down for the hundredth time since entering her apartment, which only made matters worse.

They ached to sink into her flesh to taste her life's blood. It was an urge his beyond his control. Too many months had passed since he had been able to feed properly, and he desperately needed blood. The revulsion he would see in her eyes stopped him from acting.

"You will have some every day then," he declared, ignoring his better judgement. Truth be told, he would buy the damn store to see the joy on her face.

Elsie finished her second drink and was waving her cup at Orlando. She already had the warrior wrapped around her finger as he jumped to refill her glass. And she called him bossy.

"Uh, I hate to tell you this, Mr. Bossy Pants, but you can't say that. And, you definitely can't buy me some every day," she smiled, patting his cheek.

His eyebrow arched imperiously, and he took on the challenge she unknowingly issued with her words. "Doona be so sure aboot that, lass. I have powers beyond your imagining," he whispered in her ear.

She laughed out loud at that. "Oooh, I have powers beyond imagining. What, can you leap tall buildings in a single bound? Oh, or do you have x-ray vision?" She threw her head back and laughed at that. The mirth in her expression was breathtaking. He sat up straighter knowing he had brought her happiness.

Her sister strolled over and sat between him and Elsie. She grabbed up the empty candy box and huffed, "Wow, El, you could've saved one for me. It is so good to hear you laughing again. And, I will help pay for the candy if it gets you eating."

The sight of Elsie sticking her tongue out at her sister

brought the blood right back to his groin. "Sorry, biz-nitch, they were too good to stop eating. Like Lays potato chips, you can never only eat one." She was tipsy and fun when she had a bit to drink.

"Funny, I don't have that problem with Lays. It's John I can never get enough of," her sister tossed back.

Elsie broke into a bout of laughter then stopped and gaped at Cailyn. "I can't believe you said that in front of all these guys."

Santiago settled his bulk on the floor and leaned back against the wall. "It's no big deal. We're family now," the bald detective declared.

Elsie smirked. "In that case, I need another drink, Cabana Boy," she called to Orlando.

"Sure thing, cupcake. Always at your service," Orlando said and bowed before her with a flourish. There was no doubt that the warrior liked her, and she seemed to like him, too. Jealousy had Zander wanting to punch his friend.

A knock at the door interrupted. Zander opened his senses and noted it was Gerrick and Jace. He watched Elsie's superb ass sway as she rose and walked to answer the door. He wanted to take a bite out of that tasty flesh. And, his fangs were back. They wanted to sink into the vein running up her inner thigh. He cursed under his breath, willing them to retract.

"Um, may I help you?" Elsie asked, confusion on her face.

Gerrick rubbed his free hand down his chin, clearly uncomfortable. "Yeah, Orlando sent us a text and told us to bring this over," he said and gestured to the box in his hand.

"I've got this, El. Here's your drink. Go back and join Zander and your sister." Orlando pushed her back into the apartment.

"You had better start explaining, or else," she exclaimed with her hand on her hip.

Orlando began talking, and for once he was grateful for the insouciant warrior. It eased the tension. "Honey, I cannot watch the Mariners on that dinosaur you call a TV. Plus, our Blu-ray won't play in your ancient VCR. And, I can't let you paint my nails without the proper chick-flick playing," he teased Elsie and bumped her hip with his.

"You assume I will allow any of you back into my house. I don't need a new TV. Mine works perfectly fine." He braced for a battle between Elsie and Orlando. He already understood how stubborn she was.

Orlando chucked her chin lightly. "Ouch, that hurts. I thought I was irresistible. Think of this as being on loan for my viewing pleasure."

Elsie flipped her hair back on her shoulders, causing her curls to bounce before they settled over her back. The honeysuckle scent hit him again, making him want this human beyond all reason. She was going to be the death of him. "Like I'd let you watch sports on my TV. No, it's perfect for Food Network," she retorted. "Snap to it, would ya? I want to watch that movie you promised."

Saucy wench. He may have just fallen in love.

CHAPTER SIX

Cailyn gaped at the hot men who seemed to have taken over her sister's little apartment and life. Despite how most of them were beyond domineering, she was mesmerized by the gorgeous one with the beautiful, amethyst eyes and long, black hair. Something stirred in her chest and reached for him. A fantasy about undoing his long braid and running her fingers through it as he pleasured her body popped into her head. Surely, she wasn't that drunk. She'd only had two drinks. Having such thoughts was so unlike her.

"Jace, Gerrick, this is my sister Cailyn," Elsie introduced the two new guys as they carried a TV between them. Gerrick was frightening, and it was hard for her not to stare at the scar on his face, so her gaze remained trained on Jace with his captivating amethyst eyes.

Jace smiled slyly and set the box down. He reached a hand toward her and murmured, "It's nice to meet you as well, Cailyn. Orlando didn't warn me how beautiful you and your sister are. I suspect he was hoping to keep you for himself." He laughed when Orlando began punching him and cursing at him. Cailyn watched Jace and wondered at the feel of his full lips. Would they be soft when he kissed her?

Her sister plopped down next to her and heaved a sigh as the guys went about setting up the electronics. Cailyn saw right through Elsie's feigned annoyance. Her sister had not smiled so much since before Dalton died. She grabbed Elsie's hand and squeezed it. "They are something else, aren't they?" she asked her sister.

"Yes, they are. Delicious eye candy," Elsie muttered, and they fell into a companionable silence, watching the men work.

Cailyn found she was helplessly transfixed by Jace's bulging biceps as he hefted the TV out of the box and helped mount it on the wall. The muscles in his arms rippled under his dress shirt. And, damn, his chest flexed, straining the buttons. She prayed some of them would pop off and give her a peek. His chest tapered into a perfect V at his waist. Her gaze traveled down his pants, which he filled out nicely in the front. Righty. Her mouth watered. She wanted a view of the back, too, and almost asked him to turn around. She slammed her lips back together before the words flew out. She didn't want to embarrass herself or her sister.

She tapped into her ability and tried to listen to his thoughts. It was surprisingly difficult for her to pick up on anything. She only caught snippets, enough to determine that he was a doctor and was anxious to get to the hospital where he worked.

Without conscious thought, fantasies of them intimately entwined played through her mind. A peculiar energy raced through her bloodstream as she obsessed over this stranger. No matter how hard she tried to pry her eyes away, they didn't budge. She had never seen such a handsome man. Thoughts of her boyfriend, John, finally penetrated her lust-driven brain.

She stood, needing to get out of the room. It was one thing to fantasize about other men, but she was perilously close to acting on her desires. Her fingers itched to run across his copper skin. As long as she was involved with John, or any other man, indulging was off limits.

THEY HAD PLACED the TV on the wall when the most delectable aroma hit Jace. An enticing, cinnamon scent mixed with a hint of sultry, feminine heat teased his senses. He flared his nostrils and drew in a deep breath. His body hardened as he became unbearably aroused. This time, unlike previous encounters with females, his arousal was not accompanied by anger, shame, hopelessness, and unbearable thoughts of his past.

No time to make sense of everything, his cell phone vibrated with a text message. "I have to get to Harborview. Catch you guys later. I'm on patrol with you and Rhys tomorrow night, right, Santi?"

"Yeah. You okay?" Santiago asked, his eyebrow drawn together. Jace hoped the wolf shifter didn't get a whiff of Jace's arousal.

"Yeah, there's just an emergency at the hospital," Jace responded, as he made his way to the front door.

"Ok, see you later. Thanks for the help."

"Sure. Elsie, Cailyn, it was great to meet you. Hopefully, I'll see you again soon," he called to the two females. He allowed himself one last look at Cailyn. He had been covertly stealing glances at her since he arrived. She was stunning with her light-brown hair and hazel eyes. And then there were her big, full breasts. They way her flesh overflowed from the v-neck sweater should be outlawed.

He scrambled out the door and gulped down the fresh air once the door shut behind him. It wasn't enough as the image of Cailyn was imprinted on his mind forever. Disconcerted by the arousal, he scrambled for the nearby bushes. Anger coursed like lava through his veins as he lost the contents of his stomach. It was always the same.

EXCITEMENT RACED through his veins as Zander impatiently wiped the rain from his eyes. He missed her already. It had been several hours since they talked. He shook his head in disbelief. Him, sitting and talking with a human. He was a man of action and struggled to sit through council meetings when they ran long, but he loved every second of being with Elsie. He had never enjoyed anything more in all of his seven hundred sixty-five years and wanted to be back in that apartment with her.

He had learned so much about her. They couldn't be more different. She loved to cook where he didn't have the first clue as to how to boil water, let alone make something. He had cooks for that.

Elsie touched everyone around her for the oddest reasons, and he suspected she liked the physical contact. He was more comfortable with several feet of space between him and those around him, except where she was concerned. He wanted her as close as possible.

Zander could use someone like Elsie to help him run the vampires. There was this aura about her. She went out of her way to make sure each of them felt welcomed, and had their needs met. The only thing he gave was orders. It would go a long way with his subjects and warriors if he focused on them as individuals. That was impossible for him given the burden of ensuring the safety of humans and supernaturals.

The differences between them highlighted everything he needed in his life, as well as her fragile, human nature. She was vulnerable and easily killed which made her determination to get vengeance for what happened to Dalton frightening. Zander knew Elsie wasn't going to let that go until she had eliminated every skirm. He forced back his anger over that before it led to him doing something irrevocable. He hadn't experienced this fear since his parents were killed. He loved her tenacity, but it was a double-edged sword.

Orlando's voice brought him back to the matter at hand. "What do we do about SOVA? You didn't manage to get any new information from her and Killian hasn't been able to find anything out."

None of them had any idea how difficult making these decisions were. Zander took a deep, calming breath. Honeysuckle had his body as tight as a bow-string. His blood rushed through his veins, and his heart raced. He had never felt so alive, and he wanted to lose himself in Elsie's delectable heat so badly his balls hurt.

He couldn't stop the smile that spread across his lips and transformed his sharp patrician features when he heard her tiny snore. It seemed absurd that he found even that endearing.

"We are going to have to follow her and the others when they hunt. 'Tis the only way we will be able to gather more information."

Zander paused and considered the female who had

captured his attention. Elsie was remarkable, and he almost lost it at her sounds of pleasure over the caramels. He imagined dripping caramel all over her body and slowly licking up every drop, paying special attention to her perfect, rosy nipples. He would lap it from her sex until she was screaming his name.

He shuddered with repressed desire. Not being able to have Elsie was more torture than spending hours in the sun. He closed his eyes as he held his breath and regained some composure. His eyes opened to meet his warriors' curious stares.

He ignored the questions he saw there. He didn't have the answers. "Get to your patrols and keep an eye oot for the SOVA members," Zander ordered.

"Liege, are you joining us tonight?" Gerrick asked.

"You ask me he's staying right here to ogle Elsie. It's what I would choose to do if I could. The skirm are hard to pass up, but—" Gerrick smacked Orlando on the back of his head, cutting off his ribbing.

"Santi, Gerrick, you guys join Rhys downtown. Orlando, stay here with me. I need to enter her dreams to see if I can get information on SOVA. As you pointed oot, Orlando, we don't have the information we need. You will protect me while I dreamwalk with her." Ignoring his desire to ravish Elsie, he watched Santiago and Gerrick disappear into the shadows.

"I want her to trust us and confide in us. I will be there as much as possible, but you need to get closer to her since I canna be there during the day. And, Orlando, by closer, I doona mean that you tup her. That is something I willna tolerate. She mentioned her sister is leaving tomorrow, so my guess is that she will be meeting with SOVA soon. Hopefully, we will find out who their members are. If they are out patrolling for skirm, we need to keep them safe and ignorant of the realm," he expressed to Orlando.

"That will be my pleasure. I like Elsie. She's spunky," Orlando responded readily.

Zander bit back the jealousy that comment inspired. He had no reason to have such feelings. He never planned to take the relationship further with Elsie, no matter how much the desire beat at him.

Anxious to be near her again, he leaned back against the evergreen, closed his eyes and accessed his dreamwalking powers. Within moments, he was inside her mind and was immediately stunned. She was dreaming about making love to him. He hadn't expected to encounter that. Shocked by the erotic nature, he forgot to cloak his presence. He wanted to be inside her sensual body.

He would lose control if he went anywhere near her. "I canna do this, 'tis too much," Zander choked out on a whisper.

Intending to take one last look, he became transfixed by the sight of her breasts as they jiggled, and the desire to leave died. Need and a vast number of virginal emotions consumed him. Before he could form a coherent thought, he felt his shaft enveloped by her tight sheath and was pounding into her body from behind. He had lost control of his dreamwalking for the first time in his existence.

His fangs shot out from his gums with a hiss, as his lust for her blood rivaled his lust for her body. He could not recall a time in his life when he had felt stronger bloodlust. His eyes fixated on the pounding flow of blood through the main artery in her delectable neck. He could lean forward and take a sample, and she would never know. He clenched his jaw shut, refusing to give into that desire. But, he was unable to stop his cock from thrusting into her heat. Nothing had ever felt so good.

He reached around and grabbed her breasts. Her rosy nipples pearled in his hands. He pinched and pulled, eliciting a moan from her. "Oh, Zander, yes. Dear God, don't stop," she cried out. The way she pleaded his name sent him into a frenzy.

It didn't matter to him that he was not physically with her. Spiritually, physically, and emotionally, he had never experienced anything more satisfying. The connection between them was tangible. He forgot that she was a fragile human and grabbed her breasts and slammed into her molten core. Her walls began to tremble and spasm. She was close. He gave her breasts and nipples one last squeeze and ran his hands down the silky planes of her abdomen.

Elsie's skin was smooth, and he caressed the slight roundness of her stomach before trailing his fingers lower. He was touching and making love to Elsie. His hands shook with emotion as he worshipped her body. His fingers grazed her closely shorn mons and easily found the engorged nub at the apex of her thighs. It throbbed beneath his fingers. He wished they were awake and experiencing this skin to skin. He was beyond the moon that this fiery, little female wanted him despite the fact she had rejected any thought of a relationship.

Her body clenched his shaft tightly, and he groaned in pleasure. "Careful, *a ghra*, I want this to last. You bring me to my knees and unhinge me. Goddess, you feel incredible."

"Oh, yes. Zander...I'm close..." He knew what she needed. He pinched her clitoris and rolled it between his fingers and she detonated.

Elsie cried out her pleasure. Zander stilled and clenched

his teeth against the spasms surrounding his cock. Not yet. He wanted that again.

He continued to tease her flesh and brought her down only to withdraw and slam back in. "No, it's too much. I can't," she protested while she met him thrust for thrust.

"Yes you can, *a ghra*, I want that again," he growled as his hands explored her back and the round globes of her fine ass. His movements became frantic, and he chastised himself. Get control, he admonished. Savor her. Show her how good it can be. Doona rut on her like a rabid animal.

He slowed his movements, but her passion was too high. "Mmmm...no, harder. Please," she begged.

A beast took over his body, one that was intent upon having all of her. He bared his fangs as he pounded into her and lowered his head to her neck. A much needed moment of clarity struck. She feared vampires and wouldn't like being bit by one.

He kissed and sucked her neck and roved his lips to nip at her ear. Her breathing was erratic, and her walls began to clench his cock. She was getting close again, and he couldn't hold back much longer.

"Zander," she attempted to turn around and look at him. With one hand, he grabbed her hair, holding her head in place so that she wouldn't see the glow from his eyes or his fangs. She arched and moaned. He nudged her legs with his knees, so she was spread wider for him. He sank impossibly deeper, and a groan slipped out. "You...are so...beautiful," he said hoarsely while he continued his frantic pace.

He would not come before she gave him another orgasm. His free hand rubbed across her buttock and hip and curved around. His fingers slid through her slick channel. He rubbed and pinched her clitoris, sending her tumbling into another orgasm.

Eyes squeezed shut, Elsie was screaming his name, over and over. It was enough to send him over the edge.

"Fuck. I'm coming...Elsie," he shouted as he pumped his seed into her hot, little pussy.

His release continued and showed no sign of waning. Pain tore through his back, scorching his skin. He arched and tried to see what it was even while his release continued. Pleasure and pain surrounded him until he knew nothing else.

"Holy crap, are you still coming? Damn, I love this dream...It's...oh, shit, I'm going to cum again," Elsie gasped.

Hell yes, he reached up and cupped her face as he poured everything he had into her and growled against her lips, "Give it to me, give it all to me," and ground himself against her ass. That was all it took.

After Goddess only knew how long, their orgasms ended and they collapsed to the bed. He was heavy and probably crushing her, but his body wasn't moving. He rolled to the side taking her with him, careful to keep from rolling onto his burning back.

"That was incredible," he breathed as he traced circles on her arms and kissed her neck. He glanced down and was stunned silent. There was an iridescent Celtic cross behind her left ear. It couldn't be...

"This isn't real," she murmured.

"What?" he replied too sharply. It had been more real than Elsie realized. Irrevocably real.

"Dream," she reminded him. "This is a dream."

"Felt more real to me than any encounter I've ever had." Zanders powers slipped away and he woke, sitting in a stupor with his back resting painfully against the evergreen.

Elsie was his Fated Mate!

CHAPTER SEVEN

Elsie drove through the entrance to Mt. Pleasant Cemetery with Cailyn to visit Dalton. It was their wedding anniversary, and she needed to be close to him. That day was the second anniversary without him, and her black hole hurt. After her erotic dream about Zander the night before, she was racked with guilt. And, it didn't matter that it wasn't real, she had betrayed Dalton.

She gazed out the windshield at the beautiful landscaping. Mt. Pleasant was forty acres, located atop a hill in the middle of the historic Queen Anne district in Seattle, and was home to the largest variety of mature trees in any cemetery on the west coast. The sprawl of gravestones interspersed with the trees created a calm and peaceful atmosphere, even though it was a place full of death.

She parked on the street close to Dalton's gravesite. All those months ago, she had been guided as if by an invisible hand to this particular spot. Stone angels topped the marble headstones. Each enormous angel had outstretched, black wings and stood sentry at the entrance to this particular section of the cemetery. She exited her car and waited for her sister. She grabbed the flowers from Cailyn and walked across the sprawling lawn.

She traced her fingers across one of the exquisite black wings of Dalton's angel. Goosebumps raced across her skin. There was leashed energy beneath the stone. She couldn't explain or describe what she felt, but her sister had agreed. Neither of them understood why certain objects felt different to them, but they had learned at a young age to keep their abilities and odd experiences to themselves. She shook off her brooding. Dalton's angel stood amongst these powerful protectors.

"I love these headstones. The first time I saw them, they spoke to me. They reminded me of Dalton and how he looked out, and ultimately gave his life, for those kids." Her black hole pulsed painfully in her chest. She missed him so much, and it was made all the worse today because she had betrayed him.

She knelt in the damp grass over Dalton's grave. She took the flowers and placed them in his vase. "I love you, D. I miss you so much. I was able to get new detectives assigned to your case. They told me that Jag did this to you and that he is dead now..." she broke off and let the tears flow.

Her sister crouched next to her and smoothed the tendrils of hair from her face that had escaped her ponytail and handed her a tissue. She wiped her eyes. Cailyn was always taking care of her. It warmed some of the ice from her heart. Her sister was the one she went to when she had been called a 'freak' and teased at school. When Elsie's first boyfriend had dumped her, they shared a gallon of chocolate ice cream.

"I'm so sorry that you are going through this. I wish I could take your pain away," Cailyn cooed.

Elsie put her arm around Cailyn and hugged her tight. "I love you, sis. Thanks for being here for me."

"I wouldn't be anywhere else. We're all that we have now." They sat like that, with one arm around each other, in silence, for some time. Her arm fell to her side when Cailyn crouched, making kissy noises.

"Come here, kitty, kitty," her sister crooned. She looked over and noticed a beautiful, white cat approaching Dalton's burial plot. The animal was pure white but for one black spot on one of its front legs. They laughed as it rolled over and exposed its stomach for attention.

As they petted the cat, it dawned on her what seemed familiar about it. "Look at the eyes on this cat. The intense, green color reminds me of Orlando's eyes." Picking up the cat, she stroked its soft fur. The cat curled into her chest, purring loudly.

"This little guy has no collar, I wonder where he belongs. He doesn't look malnourished or anything," Cailyn speculated as she reached over and stroked the cat's head.

They both scanned their surroundings, searching for its owner. There wasn't another soul in the place. Was it homeless? She hadn't seen it in the cemetery before. Unfortunately, she had stuff to do and didn't have time to look into it, so she set it down with a final pat on its head.

She stood up and watched the cat run into a stand of trees at the outskirts of the grave sites. She turned to her sister and blinked against the tears welling in her eyes. "As much as I don't want you to go, we'd better get you to the airport."

Her sister wiped her cheeks with her thumbs. "Hey, none of that. I'll be back in a couple of months for your graduation."

THE DAY ZANDER had waited for his entire life had finally occurred, yet it brought no peace. He was going out of his mind. Images from his dream with Elsie tortured him relentlessly.

His connection to her grew by the minute, and through that bond, he sensed her conflict. She shifted from grief and sadness to guilt and shame and back again with dizzying speed. He surmised that Elsie was agonizing over the passion she not only welcomed but had instigated in the dream.

Discovering one's Fated Mate was a day to celebrate. Especially considering there had been a mating curse in the realm for seven centuries.

Zander had been given the biggest blessing in the realm, yet there were no parties, no big announcement, and no celebration. The Goddess had not blessed a single soul with their Fated Mate for seven hundred and fifteen years. This was huge news, and he wanted to share it with his subjects and give them the hope they had longed for, but fate was biting him on the ass.

He had been given a human as a mate, and was honored, but also worried about her vulnerability and fragility. And then there was the fact that his mate was involved with a vigilante group that hated what she believed were his kind. The cherry topper would be that his enemies killed her husband and she refused to even entertain the idea of a romantic relationship with anyone.

Frustration beat at Zander. He hated not knowing anything, yet was trapped by the sun. Unable to tolerate anymore, he sent Orlando to his mate's apartment.

The warrior informed him that he had followed her and

her sister to her late husband's grave. That explained the grief. Zander ordered Orlando to shift and stay close to her. Now, he was pacing his rooms, waiting for an update. When his frayed nerves were ready to snap, his cell phone rang.

He snatched it off the coffee table and slid his finger across the screen to answer Orlando's call. "Where is she now? What's going on? Is she alright? Does she need anything?" His breathing was erratic with his anxiety. Anxiety. Another emotion he had not experienced before yesterday. The past twenty-four hours had proven to be a rollercoaster of varying emotions. It was exhilarating.

"Liege, she is fine. She just dropped her sister off at the airport. Talk to me. I don't understand why you are so hung up on this human. Sure we need to get a handle on SOVA, but this seems like there is something more," Orlando said.

Zander heard the hustle and bustle of the airport through the phone. He took a deep breath. News of his Fated Mate wasn't something he wanted to share over the phone. "Get back to Zeum. I'm calling a meeting in thirty and I need everyone here."

He may not be able to tell the realm, but he had to inform his siblings and warriors. He'd need their help keeping his mate safe until they mated. Any apprehensions he had about her heritage and questionable pastime, he would mate with her. She carried part of his soul as he did hers and he would finally be whole. And, Goddess willing, he would be able to win her heart.

ELSIE WATCHED her sister rush through the automatic doors of the Southwest terminal at Sea-Tac. She missed Cailyn already, but swore she was not going to call her sister more than once a day. Tempted to ask Cailyn to return, Elsie shook her head and reminded herself that she wasn't calling her sister to come back before her graduation in June.

Elsie had been a burden for Cailyn for too long now. Her pain wasn't something she shared with Mack or the others at SOVA. With them she shared the bond of surviving a vampire attack, but the pain of loss was Elsie's alone.

Put your big girl panties on and do what needs to be done, she told herself. She looked over her shoulder and signaled before she pulled away from the curb. A man in an SUV wasn't paying attention and cut over from the outer lane at the same time, nearly hitting her. She slammed on her brakes and swerved. Her palm slammed down on the horn, and it blared as she cursed the man who continued as if she didn't exist. Her car shuddered as she pressed the gas.

"No, no, no, you piece of shit," she cursed her car and heaved a sigh of relief when the clunker picked up speed rather than dying on the freeway. One crisis averted.

That brought her around to the disaster she had created in her dreams. Maybe that was a bit dramatic, but she did feel guilt and shame for her desires. She wasn't a fool. That was her subconscious at work, acting out what her body began craving the moment she laid eyes on Zander.

There was no denying she felt a connection to him. He was easy to talk to and was a great listener. It wasn't only the fierce lust, either. Zander was a friend now. In fact, she had opened up to him and Orlando in ways she had only done with Dalton and Cailyn. *A friend with benefits,* her inner-sex-fiend purred. Her black hole grew talons and pierced her chest wall. She was a mess.

CHAPTER EIGHT

Zander turned away from the maps he had been pouring over as his warriors joined him in the war room. He looked them over as they each took a seat at the large wooden conference table. They were dressed in their typical head-to-toe black leather. Each of them exuded a deadly aura that could crush any being under their combat boots before they knew what hit them. Determination rode the warriors hard. They wanted to do their job and eliminate the risk to the realm. That was far more complicated now than it had been before.

Cutting right to the chase, he pulled his shirt off and turned his back to them. Ever since his mate mark had appeared, it had been a minor irritant on his back. That discomfort had only increased since his dream with Elsie. He wondered why, and searched through some realm documents that Killian had uploaded onto their protected website. It was shocking to learn that the mark would become more and more painful the longer a mating was delayed. He understood his mate was in no position to finalize their union, and he was prepared to deal with the pain. He was happy to endure the pain. He had found his Fated Mate and eventually, his soul would be complete.

The reaction to his revelation was instantaneous and chaotic with everyone talking over one another. His sister's gasp snagged his attention. "Your mark is so beautiful. Is it painful? The red, angry-looking welts seem like they'd be uncomfortable."

Zander thought about the pain that seared through him at the moment of climax. "'Twas painful but for a moment. Now 'tis an exquisite reminder of how verra fortunate I am."

Bhric stood and crossed to his side and reached out a hand, slapping him on the back near his mating brand. "I canna believe that the Goddess has given us the first Fated Mate in over seven hundred years. 'Tis a new beginning for the realm. Tell me *brathair*, who is the lucky female?"

Zander turned around and faced the room. "The human female, Elsie Hayes." Orlando's mouth dropped open and anger crossed his features before the warrior schooled his reaction. Interesting.

"When did you bed her?" Orlando gritted out.

Zander met his glare. "Watch it, welp. Doona forget who you are speaking to. I called you all here to tell you and to enlist your help keeping her safe. The situation is complicated. She isna aware of what she is to me."

"I am more than happy to keep my new sister safe," Breslin offered as she waved her fingers, flames bursting from their tips. Still as awe-inspiring, Zander mused, as it was when she was three years old. Like it was yesterday, Zander recalled how Kyran lifted a tearful Breslin into his arms as other blessings were bestowed on their parents' funeral pyre. Shocking everyone, Breslin spread her pudgy, three-year-old hand and called a flame to her palm. She threw the flames to the bodies so lovingly arranged, surprising everyone with her power and control at such an early age.

Santiago grunted his approval, interrupting Zander's memory, as he slid his ammo clip back into his Glock and jumped into the conversation, "I'll help you with that, too. If rumors are true, skirm will be able to see her mark when she patrols for them. It will set her apart from other humans."

"I didn't see anything different about her. Maybe it was Lena, Liege. Weren't you with her?" Orlando asked.

"You walk a dangerous line, shifter," Zander warned. "Elsie carries my mark, plain as day to any supernatural. And, the rumors are true. 'Tis an iridescent mark below her left ear. Skirm will see it, without doubt."

Kyran rubbed his hand down his face. "I am still in shock that Fated Mate blessings have begun once again."

Gerrick jumped out of his chair, causing it to hit the floor with a loud bang. Zander glanced at the warrior and noticed his hands clenched into fists at his sides, anger darkening his eyes and his chest heaving. "Zander's mate is not the first. There was another!" he roared.

Zander gaped at Gerrick's outburst. What was he talking about? There had been no mates for over seven centuries. As the king of the vampires, he would have heard if there had been. "What the hell are you talking aboot? Explain, now."

The room was engulfed in silence as everyone watched Gerrick clench and unclench his fists at his sides. It was obvious the warrior was struggling to deal with the words that had escaped his lips. Zander was incredulous. It was difficult to remain quiet while Gerrick found his words. Questions and scenarios tore through his mind, but he refused to give them a voice. The entire realm had become so bitter and angry about the lack of mates that, after three hundred years, most had identified it as 'The Mating Curse.' It didn't seem plausible to Zander that there had been a mate previously.

As much as he wished numerous times for the blessings to resume over the centuries, it hadn't and their population had suffered. Most supernaturals became fertile only after they had sex with their mate. Every species underwent changes with mating. For Zander, as a vampire, his orgasms extended to last several minutes after intercourse with his Fated Mate.

He jolted as he realized he had undergone that change from sharing dream-sex with his mate. And, Goddess, how the prolonged orgasm had driven not only him, but his mate, to new heights. Diverting his thoughts from what was sure to cause his balls to ache more, he considered the larger picture. Without mates, these changes didn't occur, leaving most of the realm incomplete and infertile. Hence, the decline in the realm's birthrate.

His silent ruminations derailed the moment Gerrick broke the silence. "I found my mate four hundred years ago. My family had moved from London to Draffen, and I met Evanna there. She was a vision with her long, silky, blond hair, fair face and green eyes. I was in love immediately. I thought of little but Evanna. We snuck to the loch every chance we had and spent every spare moment together. She was an incredible sorceress and taught me many spells. She also helped me to gain better control of my ability to travel back in time. When we shared our first kiss, everything escalated quickly and she was soon out of her corset and shift..."

Gerrick fell silent for several moments and finally met Zander's gaze. He was nearly knocked on his feet at the pain he saw in those ice-blue eyes. He hoped to never experience whatever it was that Gerrick had endured. "I don't recall the pain, but afterwards, she pointed out our marks. We were terrified and kept it a secret for many weeks. The realm had begun to talk of a mating curse and I feared she would be taken from me." The warrior's gaze took on a faraway look as he recalled that terrible time in his life.

"A fortnight after learning we were mates, my greatest fear came true. It was a warm spring day and I had been working for hours with my parents doing chores, anxious to get to my Evanna. By the time I reached her, she and her entire family, had been killed by skirm." Zander detected anguish in Gerrick's tone. It was impossible to ignore Zander's own fears of losing his mate before he completed the mating. He longed to hold his mate and have his soul rendered whole. He didn't want to become the tormented, hollow male he saw before him.

"Through my red haze of rage, I called up my power and was able to travel back longer than I ever had before...but it was not enough time to save Evanna. She was already gone when I arrived. I tried to stop the slaughter of her father. That day, I learned that my travels are limited to one trip. I also learned that there is a price to pay when traveling back in time. Aside from having to live with failing my mate, I was permanently disfigured. Her soul torments me daily," Gerrick thumped his fist against his chest as a tear slid from the corner of his eye.

Zander was utterly speechless. What Gerrick had said did not seem possible, but there was no denying that he was telling him the truth. He wanted to go to the Goddess to obtain the answers he and Gerrick deserved. So many questions filled him, but the most pressing was why she would do such a thing to mates. Why make them suffer so greatly?

He met Gerrick's solemn gaze. "I doona know what to

say to you. I'm sorry doesna cover it. Before I found my Elsie, I wouldna have understood the shadows in your eyes. Now, I can understand completely what that loss must have done to you. The thought of losing Elsie, or of never having her, shreds my heart in my chest."

"I vow to you that I will do everything in my power to protect Elsie, and any other mate, from harm," Gerrick promised.

He admired the strength it took for Gerrick to continue on with such determination after such a tremendous loss. He didn't think he would be able to. "Thank you."

Each of the warriors and his siblings offered their protection, as well as, vowing to seek vengeance for what Elsie had suffered. The Goddess gave Elsie to Zander, but she also gave the realm a queen, one they had already embraced. Elsie signaled a turning point for them, she symbolized their hope.

GOING OUT OF HIS MIND, Zander looked at the clock for the millionth time. It was after seven in the evening. Surely, Orlando had had enough rest by now. As soon as Zander concluded the afternoon meeting, the warrior had requested a few hours to rest since it had been a couple days since he had last gotten any sleep. Zander took the time after the sun set to go out and run some errands.

He glanced at the clock again. It had been over three hours. Elsie's distress was driving him crazy. Orlando was an immortal shifter and a Dark Warrior, enough with nap time. He had to go check on her and didn't trust himself to go to her alone.

Strapping on his concealable weapons, he hurried from

his rooms and burst into Orlando's. "Get up! I must go to her! Her anguish is killing me. I need to see her and you are going with me."

"What the hell, Liege? I asked for a few hours of sleep," Orlando grumbled as he sat up and rubbed his eyes.

"You've had three hours. Get up! I canna hear her exact thoughts with this much space between us, but I am certain she plans to go on patrol tonight. We must intervene."

"With all due respect, going there at all right now would be a bad idea," Orlando said. He glared at his warrior, ready to drag him, kicking and screaming, if he had to.

"But," Orlando hurried to continue, "I can see you're not going to listen, so give me five minutes. I certainly don't need my beauty sleep, seeing as I'm already devilishly handsome." Orlando flipped off his comforter and stretched as he unfolded to his six-foot-one-inch height.

What the hell had the male done to himself? "What in the Nine Circles of Hell happened to your hair? That isna right. Shite, you doona look like a grown male, you look like you havena passed your stripling years."

Zander struggled to understand why a male would shave his balls in such a manner. When he was young, he couldn't wait to be a full-grown male, in every way. And, he sure as hell had never had a desire to make any part of his body resemble a young lad.

"I have one word for you. Manscaping. The females love it."

He looked ridiculous, stupid male. Shaking his head, he tossed the warrior his clothing. "You have so much to learn, lad. I want to leave, be downstairs in two," Zander threw over his shoulder before he pounded down the stairs.

～

ELSIE SURVEYED her surroundings as she watched Mack-endra park her motorcycle along the curb. As she removed her helmet, Elsie recalled when Mack found her. It was shortly after Dalton had been killed, and Mack had seen her on the news. She hadn't listened to the woman until she pulled down the neck of her charcoal-grey t-shirt, revealing several horrific bite-marks.

Elsie was consumed by the sight of the injuries to Mack-endra's neck and arm. The ink started on the right side of her neck and wound down to a full sleeve on her right arm. A great-white shark, its jaws wide and dripping blood, was tattooed near a bicep injury. She had been speechless as she played 'Where's Waldo', trying to find the scars amongst the intricate designs.

Mack's whiskey-colored eyes may have been deter-mined, but they held more compassion and understanding than Elsie had seen from anyone. She had classically good looks with her short, spiky, black hair, round face, and olive complexion.

"Hey Elsie. How was your visit with your sister?" Mack called out, bringing her back to the present. She focused just as Mackendra was unzipping her leather jacket to reveal a t-shirt that said 'it's irony you dumb bitch.' The woman typi-cally wore snarky t-shirts that brought even more attention to her big, full breasts.

Why did it seem like everyone had bigger boobs than Elsie did? Probably, because they did. Sigh. And, Mack was beautiful. The sleeve of ink made her fierce, but also added to her beauty.

"The visit was too short, but good. I always hate to see her go. Shall we?" Elsie asked as she motioned to the quiet park. It was an hour or so past dusk and most people were home having dinner with their families.

They walked and chatted about what she had missed while her sister was in town. Apparently, things had been busy. Mack had killed two vampires. It seemed that there had been more vampires lately.

"Hey, I wanted to ask you if you've ever heard of a vampire not turning to dust when they die," Elsie asked Mack as they headed off.

"As far as I know, all vampires turn to dust when they are stabbed through the heart. Why?"

"Well, the new detectives assigned to Dalton's case said they found the kid responsible in a dumpster, missing his heart."

"That doesn't make any sense. Did he have fangs? Did they mention if his eyes had that charcoal ring?"

"They said he had fake fangs, but of course, they had no idea they were real. They never mentioned…" Elsie trailed off as they hit pay-dirt and ran into two vamps.

"Oh look, Paul, dinner. And, this one here is marked. Maybe she belongs to a Dark Warrior," one said, pointing at Elsie.

The other vamp made a comment Elsie missed as she pondered what he was talking about. Mack had too many tattoos to count and she didn't have any. Neither of them belonged to anyone. Well, Elsie would always belong to Dalton, but he was dead, thanks to a vamp. Her thoughts fractured as the pair attacked.

Elsie pulled the knife out of her boot and dropped to the ground, rolling away from the one charging toward her. She threw her hand back, slashing at his legs and missed.

She jumped to her feet and they circled one another. He lunged and she didn't see his fist until it landed on her cheek. Pain immediately exploded across her face and her vision blurred for a few seconds. Instinctively, she ducked and dodged more blows he sent her way. Her vision cleared and she got back into the fight with gusto. She allowed anger to course through her veins when she realized that she was going to have a massive bruise.

She danced around, striking out at every opportunity, but after several minutes, she was tiring and he was landing every blow. Her side ached. Heaving, she would have to get closer or risk running out of energy. She turned and he wrapped his arms around her, squeezing with his preternatural strength. She heard Mack cursing her opponent, but couldn't respond as she couldn't draw in a breath. Now, her side ached for an entirely different reason, she just hoped her rib wasn't cracked. She cradled the knife close to her chest and squirmed to a better position, hoping to end this fight.

"That was a mistake. You're mine now," the vamp breathed in her ear. "I'm going to have fun with you before I drain you." He lowered one hand to the zipper on her pants and she had a moment of supreme panic. There was no way she was going to let him touch her. The bright flash of fire followed by the smell of smoke distracted the vamp holding her and she twisted around, plunging her knife into his chest. His eyes flew open in shock right before he burst into flames, turning to ash a second later.

She turned to Mack who was sweating and swearing as she kicked the pile of ash at her feet. Elsie stood there, bracing her hands on her knees as her face throbbed and her heart raced while she struggled to draw in a full breath. The fight hadn't lasted that long, but she ached all over. Elsie's cell vibrated, startling her, and she pulled it out of her pocket, checking the screen. It was Orlando.

She flipped the top. "Hello."

"Hey, El. I've been calling you, what's going on?"

"Sorry, I'm out with a friend." She could hear her heart pounding in her ears and she held her breath, waiting to hear what he was going to say. Surely, he wasn't aware that she just killed a vampire. She looked around, but saw no one. She shook off her paranoia.

"Well, we are at your house with chick flicks, hoping you're up for company. I still didn't get that pedicure." The tension broke and she laughed, noticing that Mack was eyeing her curiously. "Come home, Zander has more presents for you."

Zander? Presents? "Okay. Be there in twenty minutes."

"What was that about?" Mack asked, clearly suspicious.

Jacked up with adrenaline and mixed feelings about seeing Zander again, she glanced sideways at her friend through the swelling around her eye. "It was one of the detectives on Dalton's case. We've become friends, believe it or not. He wants to watch a movie, and honestly, after this fight, I could use it."

"You need to watch it. Cops are ignorant of what's really out there and would throw you in lock up for murder if they knew what we did. And you look like you just got in a fight. What are you going to tell them?"

"I'm always careful and will think of something, Mack. You taught me very well," she reminded her friend as she laced her arm through Mack's and limped back to her car.

CHAPTER NINE

Elsie winced as the bright light from the car behind
her made her eye hurt even more. She hadn't yet
concocted a story to tell Orlando and Santiago
when she saw them. As police detectives they weren't likely
to let the matter slide. And, then there was Zander. To make
matters worse, the swelling had spread and her face
throbbed insistently from the pain. Every breath she took
was a stab to the side, convincing her that she had, indeed,
cracked a rib. If she was smart, she would stop hunting
vampires, but that wasn't going to happen. Mack and SOVA
had given her life purpose again and she wasn't about to
give that up.

She parked her car and looked into her rearview mirror.
Mack was right, she looked like she had gone ten rounds in
the ring. Her cheek was already a deep purple and her eye
was nearly swollen shut. She had no makeup, not that there
was a way to hide the injury. She'd better come up with
something fast.

She looked over and saw Zander's intense blue eyes and
serious expression as he approached her car. She took a

moment to admire the blue cotton t-shirt straining over his gorgeous, muscled chest. She opened her door and climbed out of the car, finding him right next to her. Orlando gasped from behind Zander and Zander's body had gone rigid.

"What happened?" Zander said through gritted teeth. Elsie began to sweat and her mind went blank.

She blinked up at him and opened her mouth only to close it. She couldn't tell him the truth and for some reason she didn't want to lie to him either. "My friend and I were, uh, kickboxing and I didn't duck fast enough." That was close to the truth, she hadn't ducked fast enough. Zander eyed her suspiciously and she quickly turned to glance at Orlando.

"You need to stop kickboxing, cupcake. Clearly, you're not very good at it and if you don't watch it, you'll get seriously injured," Orlando chastised.

She half-laughed and walked to her front door. "Come on in," she invited after unlocking the door.

Zander's gaze slowly trailed down her body, causing a searing heat to take her over. "Aside from the bruises, you look tired. How did you sleep last night?" He paused next to her and grasped her hand, bringing it to his lips. The kiss released electrical tremors, and his words caused blood to flood her face. Her words froze in her throat. Could he know she had dreamt about making love to him last night?

"I slept okay," she stammered.

Zander's expression said he knew every dirty detail and he wanted it for real. Oh God. "I brought you more chocolates, as well as, other surprises." He remained in place, despite the fact, that they were crammed face to face in the narrow entryway.

Orlando slapped her on the shoulder, breaking the connection. "You gonna make me stand out here all night? I brought tequila and you favorite energy drinks," he crooned as he waved a bag in her face. The man already knew what she liked and they just happened to be two items she couldn't afford this week, and wanted desperately.

She couldn't resist teasing him. "Uhhhhh, yep I am," she replied, shutting the door in his face.

She was laughing when Orlando called out from the other side of the door. "Damn, that hurt. Fine, I'll leave and take these," she could hear the rattle of bottles, "home with me."

She opened the door and grabbed the grocery bag then shut it again. At that, Zander burst out laughing. She looked over at him and nearly collapsed. Laughter had transformed his sharp patrician features. Simply gorgeous.

Orlando was talking as he opened her door and walked in the apartment. "I'll let that one slide, El, but know that my feelings are fragile and you might hurt them."

"Uh-huh," she said dubiously. "So what movies did you bring this time?" She limped toward the living room and felt both sets of eyes watching her closely.

Zander set down several bags and a large, white box with a big, purple bow on top of her coffee table and helped her to the futon. Zander sat so close to her that their thighs touched. She wasn't sure what to do. It wasn't necessarily inappropriate, but it was intimate. It was everything she didn't want, especially after her dream. He reached up and gingerly touched her cheek. The touch was light and it was funny how her cheek didn't hurt at all right then. Time for a distraction.

"Fetch me a drink," she beseeched Orlando.

"Anything you want, cupcake. I believe Zander brought goodies, too." Orlando said as he headed into her kitchen.

She doubted she could eat anything, her stomach was a

roiling mess, but she was curious. "What did you bring this time?" she asked Zander.

Zander's masculine voice rumbled with his Scottish brogue. "I brought bon-bons, *a ghra*," something about that word tickled her memory, but she was unable to chase down the thread. "My *piuthar*, Breslin, assured me females liked to watch TV and eat the ice-cream treats, so I brought some."

She couldn't help it. She laughed and immediately clutched her side. His look turned dark and landed on her hand. She lowered them to her lap. "I'm not sure what pju.ər is, but I'm going to guess that it's your sister or your mom. That idea is old-fashioned, women *doona* sit around eating bon-bons anymore. Not that I believe they ever did."

The way his eyebrows creased and his brow furrowed was adorable. He shrugged and reached over the side of the couch. He opened the white box and handed her two pillows.

"It wouldna be the first time my *sister* was wrong. No' that I'll tell her that, she'd kick my arse. Here," he said as he handed her the softest creation she had ever touched. "I remembered what you said last night aboot no' being able to sleep and hoped these would help."

The ice around her heart melted a fraction. How did he know how to say exactly the right thing? "I can't believe you remembered that, of all things. I don't feel right about accepting gifts from you."

"I remember everything you told me and I only want to help. You've been through a lot tonight and need to rest," he said, propping the pillows on the side of the futon.

"You can't tell someone to rest. It doesn't happen that way." Boy, he wasn't kidding when he said he was used to giving orders. That didn't change the fact that the pillows were calling her name. She laid her head down and it was like lying on a cloud. They were so soft they cradled her face without causing more discomfort. She knew she needed to shower and clean the dirt and vamp dust off her body, but she was too comfortable at the moment.

Zander laid one of his big, strong hands on her shoulder and mesmerized her with his hypnotic sapphire-blue eyes. It registered somewhere in her muddled brain that he had picked up her legs and draped them across his lap, but all she was able to think was sleep. "I believe it does work that way, my sweet. You are, after all, resting comfortably now."

He was right. She had relaxed into the pillow and was content to remain there. Her body was exhausted from lack of sleep and the adrenaline from the fight had worn off, leaving even more fatigue behind. Still, she didn't know these men that well and was uncomfortable lying there. She tried to sit up, but he stopped her.

"Let me up," she argued. Despite her vulnerable position, she wasn't truly afraid. She should be frightened. He scowled more than he smiled, had more muscles than the Hulk and was intimidating. Hell, most often he looked as if he could tear you apart and not break a sweat. Yet, there was something intangible, something she couldn't explain that made her believe he would never harm her.

His face softened as one corner of his mouth curled up. "Nay, I am rather enjoying this. 'Tis something I've never done before and it willna end yet." He closed his eyes and took a few deep breaths and said, "I will never harm you. Relax and settle that tired body back doon...please." He added the last with reluctance. It was obvious he was unfamiliar with saying please.

"There you go again, Mr. Bossy Pants." She wondered how a man could be so overbearing in today's society. He was domineering and controlling and she was shocked that she found it attractive. "What haven't you ever done before?"

"Och, I've never catered to anyone but my siblings."

"Not even a girlfriend?" She couldn't believe she had asked him that. It was none of her business and it implied an interest she wanted to keep buried and hidden.

"Nay, not even," he murmured, running his hand over her calf.

She curled her legs into her body. "Whoa there. I like you, but we're just friends. Hell, I barely know you." She may lust after the man, but that didn't mean she wanted more. Or, did it?

Zander kept his eyes locked on hers and she noticed one of his eyebrows arch toward his hairline. "I canna deny my attraction to you, but I willna push you. I willna jeopardize the gift of your friendship for any reason. Now, tell me aboot your day. It looks like it was pretty exciting."

His voice has ticked up at the end. Was he implying anything? No way had he known about her encounter with the vampires. Her heart began pounding in her chest at the suspicion in his voice. Paranoia was becoming her best friend.

"I didn't do much. Took my sister to the airport and did some work on my final papers then, as you know, didn't fare well in my kickboxing with my friend, Mack."

"Tell me aboot this Mack. Mack is an interesting name." His hand tensed on his leg and there was obvious irritation in his tone. Did he think Mack was a guy? Was he jealous? The idea thrilled her more than it should.

She smiled at the gruff Scotsman. "Mack is short for Mackendra," she drew out the name. "Aside from my sister, she is my best friend."

Orlando's return stopped any reply. "Madame," he

bowed and presented the plastic cup. "I combined a little of your energy drink with the margarita. Tell me what you think."

"Why thank you, Jeeves." She took a sip and her eyes rolled back in her head. "Mmmmm, that is so good. I can't believe I didn't think of doing that. Put on one of those comedies you brought, please." She had to stop the conversation from going back to Mack. Her patrols with SOVA weren't something she was free to discuss. Best to avoid anything remotely related to it.

"Sure, any preferences?"

She propped the pillow against the arm of the futon, sitting more upright. "No, I don't care. I haven't seen any of them yet." Zander's hand reached out to her feet and he unlaced her tennis shoes, slipping them off her feet. She wiggled her toes and felt his fingers trace lightly over the tops of her socks. It was as if he couldn't stop from touching her and she silently acknowledged that she liked the attention. It had been so long since she had sat and cuddled with someone. It was harmless enough to allow this small intimacy.

Zander pulled out a box of those yummy caramels. All she could manage were a couple. Next, he tried the clam chowder he brought with him, but that was also a no-go. When she was unable to eat that, he grabbed her spoon and finished the chowder for her. The sight of him eating from the spoon she had used reminded her of all the dirty, dirty things he did with that tongue in her dream. Don't go there, she chastised herself.

Orlando finally selected a movie and put it on, then brought the rest of the caramels and bon-bons to the futon. They settled in and watched Melissa McCarthy do her thing in yet another great movie. She laughed and gasped at the pain it caused.

"Are you sure you're okay?" Zander asked, tracing her sore rib.

"It's just soreness from the kickboxing earlier," she prevaricated. He nodded and held her gaze for several seconds. Her chest warmed and she felt a pull towards him that was impossible to deny.

Apparently, Zander felt the same pull as she noticed his hands twitch several times. There were even several times that he reached for her hand, but he stopped himself. The movie ended and she realized she'd watched Zander more than she had the television.

She stood and stretched, careful of her injuries. "Thank you for stopping by. I need to head to bed. I have an early class."

Zander lifted her hand and brought it to his lips for a lingering kiss. His mouth was warm and sensual on her skin. He met her eyes and the connection between them flared. He laid his desires bare for a split second before he shuttered his expression and stood up. She appreciated his consideration given how guilty she was feeling over her emotions. "Sweet dreams, *a ghra*." His sexy smile had her hoping for a repeat of last night.

"You need to take up a different sport, cupcake," Orlando teased. She flipped him off, shutting and locking her door behind them.

Moments later, she heard a noise at the door. Figuring that one of them had forgotten something, she opened the door and was surprised to see the white cat from the cemetery on her stoop. That was beyond odd. As she looked around the parking lot, the hellion scampered in and jumped up onto her futon. He wasted no time and made himself right at home by kneading his claws, finding a comfortable spot to lie down.

"You are a mystery and a cute little thing, I'll give you that," she muttered as she shrugged her shoulders. She had no idea how he found her, but she didn't have the heart to throw him out.

She sighed and went into the bathroom to shower and change into her pajamas. When she returned to the living room, her furry friend was purring peacefully like he belonged there. Her life had become so strange. The Twilight Zone had nothing on her.

ZANDER WASN'T a patient male and it was difficult to give his mate the space she needed. He wanted everything and wanted it right now, but would never turn his back on the one thing that she could give him. Her friendship, he was learning, was as important as the rest. The truth was the concept of a friendship with a female was foreign to him. The females in his life consisted of his warriors, his sister, or the occasional bed partner, not friends.

His father had told him that being blessed with a Fated Mate involved intense bonds. What he hadn't expected was to care so much about her opinion of him. He wanted her body and soul, but none of that meant anything without that magnificent heart of hers.

After ordering Orlando to shift and remain with his mate, he made his way home, recalling how Elsie had chastised him for bossing her around and put him in his place. No creature had ever dared speak to him in such a manner. Most were too afraid of him, as they should be. Elsie was the only one who would ever get away with it.

With Orlando by her side, he was able to check in with the warrior telepathically. Each time she woke, Orlando told him that his mate went through a ritual of throwing up and crying, before she did a half hour, or so, of school work then went back to bed. It turned out to be a long night of worry.

He knew nothing about humans and wondered what effects not eating and not sleeping had on her. For an immortal, it was of no consequence, but for a human, it couldn't be good. He questioned the Goddess yet again for giving him a human mate. Despite his dissatisfaction with the situation, his Elsie was now essential to his survival. And, the little minx was worming her way into his heart.

Orlando returned to Zeum when Elsie left for her class. Orlando had informed him that she had an hour class before her shift at the restaurant. He hated the thought of her waiting tables for twelve hours straight when he knew she hadn't had more than a few hours of sleep and probably hadn't eaten anything, either.

He was unable to sit still, needing to see her. When he went searching for Orlando, he saw an update in the war room that he and Santiago had been called to a homicide. In an effort to keep busy, he checked in with his warriors on patrol. Next, he dealt with the paperwork and reports on his desk. Once all the menial tasks were done and there was nothing pressing on his plate, he was at a loss. The compulsion to be near her was driving him crazy. Dinner it was.

CHAPTER TEN

Zander tapped the leather-wrapped steering wheel of his Jag as he considered all that had happened in the past several days as he drove south. His strength had been tested in ways he had never expected. Sure, he had fought countless enemies over the centuries and won, but he doubted that he was strong enough to keep from claiming Elsie. He reached deep for the strength to resist. He didn't want to do anything that would cause him to lose her forever.

That precious part of her soul that he carried and protected reminded him why he must put his desires aside. She was far too important. He laughed at himself as he considered his obsession. Stalking her wasn't kingly behavior, but he was unable to stay away. His hands shook as he pulled into a parking space. She was close enough that he opened his mind, searching for the now familiar thread of her thoughts. He hated how anxious she was about fitting in enough shifts before rent was due.

Impatient to see her, he exited his car and headed into the pub. The heavy scent of greasy food, sweat and stale alcohol didn't drown out her sweet, honeysuckle fragrance. It instantly caught his blood on fire. His body coiled and his erection strained to claim her. Unruly bastard. After wrangling with his fangs and controlling the glow from his eyes, he approached the hostess, using glamour to ensure he was seated in Elsie's section.

He'd never before had to fight for control over his body. He had always been in charge, giving the orders, providing direction, and making the difficult decisions. And, he'd always done this without a second thought. Now, he felt like a mindless creature controlled by his cock and this unending desire for a mate he feared he would never have. If he was unable to have his mate, he knew he would become an empty shell of a male, and his life would hold no meaning. Not to mention, he would die of starvation. The Goddess was either a sadistic bitch or brilliant.

Watching his mate sneak into the back with fatigue etched on her bruised and battered face was a slap of cold water that doused his ardor. He wanted to take care of her, should be the one providing for her. He wanted to lavish her with luxuries and give her everything she had ever desired. She deserved to be cherished like the queen she was.

His breath left him when she returned from the back. Tonight, she wore a tight, black sweater that had a deep V-neck, giving him a glimpse of her cleavage. She was stunning. She moved with grace and greeted her customers with smiles and patience. Once again, her sweet scent wrapped around him. He had to close his eyes against their glow and press his lips firmly together to hide his fangs. The musical sound of her voice soothed and enflamed him as she spoke to the customers at the next table and took their orders. He opened his eyes and his lust heightened as he watched her nibble her lip as she wrote. He wanted some of that tasty treat.

The swish of her movements as she walked toward the computer to enter the order had him remembering how her hips had moved under him in the dream-sex they shared. With a groan, he covertly adjusted his erection. Goddess, he needed her. Her beautiful, heart-shaped face and sensual, full lips had him yearning to touch and taste them. His loved the small spattering of freckles across the bridge of her nose. The gentle clearing of a voice had his eyes snapping open. There she was and suddenly, his world settled into focus.

Her lips stretched into the most beautiful smile he had ever seen. "Why am I not surprised to see you here tonight? You alone?" she asked, looking around for Orlando or Santiago, no doubt.

"Aye, I'm alone. I was hungry," he took her in from head to toe, "and I wanted to see you. You look stunning as always. How has your day been, *a ghra*?"

She sighed and glanced over her shoulder. "I'm just glad my boss didn't send me home when he saw my face. I can't afford to miss a shift, rent is due next week." He was determined to find a way to support her and relieve some of this stress. "You keep calling me *ah hraw*. What does that mean?"

He held her gaze for a moment before he spoke, not sure how she was going to feel about this. "*A ghra* means my love."

He watched her reaction to his words and dipped into her thoughts. He couldn't help the slow grin that escaped when she thought about how she loved his accent. He focused on that rather than her fear of anything between them.

She cleared her throat, "So, what can I get you?"

He reached up and ran a finger along the back of her hand. He felt her shiver in response. He held his tongue. *You, naked in our bed* almost slipped out. Instead, he said, "I'll take a Black and Tan and whatever you recommend for dinner."

"What happened to Mr. Bossy Pants? Letting someone else make decisions for you? This must be uncharted territory for you," she smirked.

"You're the only one I've ever given the privilege." He enjoyed how her eyes widened and her pupils dilated.

"I don't know what to make of you, Zander." A customer at another table called for her attention. She looked over her shoulder and held up a finger indicating she needed a moment then turned back to him. "I'll put in your order right away."

"Take your time," he said before she turned away. "I plan to enjoy the view." He knew she had heard his words by the pretty, pink blush that stained her cheeks as she lowered her head before rushing off.

He was good to his word and enjoyed watching her move comfortably around the restaurant. The mating compulsion had him standing up too many times, to take the heavy tray from her. Instinct was difficult to deny and he must have looked like an idiot. The delivery of his food was a much-needed distraction from his obsession, although, he was disappointed that she wasn't the one to deliver it. He sipped his beer and smiled down at the Irish nacho fries and the Hot Chipotle burger she had ordered for him. His little mate had a sense of humor, but joke was on her, he liked spicy food.

She approached his table, putting a little extra sway in her hips. She stopped next to his chair and cocked her hip. "Everything ok with your order?"

One of his eyebrows winged to his hairline and he smiled. He liked this game. "Perfect."

She snorted prettily. "I doubt that. I told Rodrigo to spit on your burger."

He loved how she teased him and seemed comfortable with the rapport. "Too bad it wasn't your spit," he winked at her, yearning to take her into his arms. Their eyes locked. The minute hitch in her breath had his heart pounding in his ears. She felt their connection, too. A smile curved his lips as her mind began detailing what she wanted to do with him. He felt the little control he had mustered slipping away.

"I, uh, have to go check on orders," she stammered before she hurried to the window of food.

As much as he wanted to stay, he needed to leave. He waited to stand up, willing his erection to lessen. No such luck, it wasn't going anywhere. He zipped his jacket closed and threw down all the money from his pocket, which turned out to be several hundred dollars, as her tip, then headed her way.

She was at one of the computers. He grasped her hands and leaned in to kiss her bruised cheek. "I will see you tomorrow night." Leaving her standing there with her mouth agape, he headed for the exit.

He would join his brothers on patrol and hopefully relieve some pent-up frustration until her shift was over. Then he planned to watch her from the trees near her apartment.

From Vampire King to stalker, how the mighty had fallen.

~

BLOOD DRIPPED from Zander's arm as he gripped a skirm by his hair. He punched the shit out of the guy, and damn, did it feel good. He hated these motherfuckers. They had robbed him and those he loved of so much, and he'd be damned if he allowed them to take any more. He kicked out hard and was rewarded for his efforts by a cry of pain. Gerrick and Rhys had joined Zander and his brothers in the fight.

"Get those sons of bitches!" Kyran yelled. He was on the ground and a skirm had his teeth locked on one of his calves.

"Two got away," Zander grunted, punching the scumbag he was holding in the kidney. The guy had spun around and ripped into his forearm. The second the venom reached his bloodstream burning pain almost put him on his knees.

"Arsehole," he cursed, slipping his *sgian dubh* between the skirm's ribs. He released his hold as the skirm flashed on fire, becoming ash.

He looked over and saw that Gerrick had punched his enemy in the head one last time before grabbing the titanium blade from the small of his back. Quick and efficient, he pierced the guy through the heart. A sweep of Gerrick's boot scattered the remains and as the ashes of his kill were swept away in the breeze, the sorcerer took off running, muttering a tracking spell which would allow them to follow the trail all skirm left behind.

Rhys dispatched the minion he held and began running after Gerrick. "C'mon, let's follow the baby-poop-road," the cambion threw over his shoulder. Zander cracked a smile at the irreverent warrior's description of the magical path the spell illuminated. Fucking Rhys.

"Goddess, this shite burns", Bhric complained as he examined a bite wound on his shoulder. Zander could attest to how painful the injuries were and how they left scars. The one on his forearm didn't need stitches, but right now, hurt like hell.

Skirm bites took longer to heal because of the demon venom in their saliva. Normally, supernaturals healed at an accelerated rate, the exceptions being wounds made by silver and skirm bites.

"We all have injuries, but have no time for that now. Let's go," Zander lifted his arm to show a huge tear of his flesh where the skirm had ripped into his arm. "I can't wait until the scientists can figure out how to counteract this venom."

"Och, you're like wee *bairns*, with all the crying. That's nothing. Stop bitching and start moving, Jace will bandage your boo-boos when we get home. Dawn is coming arse-holes, so hurry the fuck up," Kyran snapped back as he limped down the alley towards his Denali. Zander knew the guy liked pain, but damn, he had a hunk of flesh hanging off his calf. He shook his head, glad Kyran was on their side.

YANKING a makeshift belt fashioned from a scarf through her belt loops, Elsie cursed the emptiness and the painful ache of the black hole that tortured her constantly. She poked at her visible ribs, grateful that her sister wasn't there to scold her. She had lived on energy drinks and little else for longer than she could recall.

Her thoughts went to Zander while she did her hair and applied the only make-up she typically wore, mascara. He had come into her life like a whirlwind and drove her to the point of insanity. Her body reacted every time she so much as thought about him. If she saw him or heard that sexy Scottish accent of his, forget it, she was done.

His gruff exterior was misleading. At first, she thought of him as an autocratic jackass. Correction, he was an autocratic asshole, but he was one of the most thoughtful and giving persons she'd ever met. Not only had he given her gifts, he had left her an obscene tip two nights in a row. Now, she had more than enough money for rent that month, as well as, the next two. Everything he had done was making her life better in some way. He wanted more from her, yet he had never pushed her on the subject. Guys like him were rare and he was slowly and methodically chipping away at the ice surrounding her heart. It was scary and overwhelming.

She didn't want to want him. She'd made a vow to Dalton to love him forever. Hell, she had joined SOVA to exact revenge on that being taken from her. She'd been using the guilt her desire evoked to keep the distance between her and Zander, yet, her will was slowly crumbling, and it broke her heart.

Shaking her head, she pulled on her black boots and left her apartment. There was too much running through her head and hoped she could force it out before she encountered any skirm. Being this distracted on patrol wasn't wise. She jumped into her beater and headed to meet Mack.

A loud ringing had her fumbling through her worn, black backpack to answer the call before it went to voicemail. The night Dalton was killed had left her with a phobia of voicemail messages. She grabbed the phone and quickly flipped it open. Placing it to her ear, she rushed out, "Hello."

"Hey, cupcake, how's it going? I stopped by with a key lime pie. Where are you?" She smiled at Orlando's familiar voice. She could imagine him running his hands through his white-blonde hair, making it stand up. They had become close; he was the brother she never had.

"I'm actually on my way to meet a friend. Next time."
She hated lying to the men who had become her friends.
Keeping secrets felt wrong, but it was for their safety.

"Is your friend single? I don't mind joining you guys."
She had to laugh at his response, so magnanimous of him.

"She is single, but not your type at all. She would eat you
for breakfast, buddy. Besides, no boys are allowed. It's girls
only tonight."

"You don't know what you're missing. Have fun, but be
careful and don't do anything stupid. I'd hate to arrest you,"
he teased.

"I'm more than capable of taking care of myself. And,
don't forget that you are my get-out-of-jail-free-card. I'll call
you tomorrow." She flipped the phone closed and tossed it
on the passenger seat.

Her car sputtered and coughed out a cloud of black
smoke as she sped through the next stop light. The wheel
started shuddering under her palms. "Don't you even think
of dying on me right now," she yelled at her car. Saying a
quick prayer, she kept motoring along. The shimmies over-
took the car next and it seemed as if the whole thing would
fall apart. Slowing her speed didn't help matters and when
she tried to speed up, the car jolted and a loud clanging
noise sounded before the engine died.

"No, no, no. Not right now," she pleaded. She tried to
maneuver the vehicle across the lanes of traffic to pull over.
After pissing off most of Seattle, she made it to the side of
the road and turned the key, trying to start it again, but the
car didn't make a noise. "Shit!" It was well and truly dead.
She laid her head down on the steering wheel and looked
out into traffic. What was she going to do now?

Mack was waiting for her at the park. Good thing she
used to take the bus daily and knew the schedule. There was

a bus she could catch. As she climbed out of her car and glanced back, she realized a piece of her engine was lying in the street. The hunk-of-junk was literally falling apart, but she'd worry about that later. Right now, she had to get to Mack.

CHAPTER ELEVEN

Forty-five minutes and three bus transfers later, Elsie climbed off the bus a few blocks from the park where Mack was waiting. She flipped up her collar against the cold wind and mist. The familiar sensation of a million, tiny ants crawling restlessly under her skin had her fingers flexing over her knife as she scanned the area. There was a vampire near, but she had no idea where he was.

Her stomach suddenly lurched and her heart twisted in her chest. Vertigo struck and she swayed on her feet. It was a feeling she had learned to identify all too well. As she waited for the premonition to hit, she realized it wasn't merely a vampire. Something was going to happen to someone she loved.

She waited, steadying herself on a nearby tree trunk. No vision came, only a deep sense of menace. Her ability had never given her exact details, but it always identified the person tragedy was about to strike. She considered texting Mack and calling her sister, but didn't have her phone in her pocket. Any further thought was sidetracked when a rancid odor drifted on the breeze. The vampire was hiding in the bushes behind her.

Not wasting a minute, her feet carried her further into the park. She veered toward the trees on her left. Lowering her head, she snuck a peek back to see if the vamp was following her. Nothing yet. Unwilling to risk the confrontation endangering any innocent, helpless people, she continued on her path. Soon, she heard the crunch of leaves beneath heavy tread.

Her heart began racing and her palms sweated from her anxiety. The threat was breathing down her neck, despite the fact that the vampire was still yards behind her. At the first evergreen, she chanced a full look at what she was facing and her heart kicked up at what she saw. Two vampires were strolling unhurriedly toward her, confidence in their stride. Their eyes had the same eerie charcoal circle, and she wasn't surprised by the fangs that gleamed in the moonlight when they smiled.

She shuddered and headed into the wooded area. She stopped in a small clearing and rolled her shoulders trying to displace the tension as she waited. She didn't have to wait long.

One of the vamps with greasy blonde hair lowered his head slightly and adopted a feral grin. "You shouldn't have come in here little girl. Run now, we love a good chase. And, be sure to scream, screaming turns us on."

She cocked her head to the side and considered her options. "Nah, I don't think I will, but you may want to consider it yourself," she declared as she pulled her knife from her boot.

The black-haired vamp appeared cleaner and a bit saner, laughed loudly. "You're brave. It'll be fun to watch you crumble."

The greasy-blonde vamp charged toward her before the other finished talking. She backed up toward some big boulders, wanting something safe at her back. The thing moved fast and its claws scraped against her forearm as she turned and ducked. Her knife hand slashed out, catching him low in the side. Black bloomed across his side and she blanched. She had never seen one bleed and it made her pause, the vile odor making her gag.

Her inattention was a mistake as blondie managed to wrap his arms around her waist. Terror sank claws into her gut. She yanked against his hold, but she couldn't escape his tight grip and he was squeezing her sore rib. If she didn't get free, she wasn't coming out of this clearing. She fought harder, yanking and thrashing wildly. Black hair stalked toward her and the large trees looming overhead intensified her fear, causing her fight-or-flight instinct to hit overdrive.

She began kicking out at his legs and tugging with her arm. "Oh, hell no! I won't let this happen." There was no doubt in her mind what he meant to do to her. And, she wasn't going down easily. She clawed at the young man's hand, to pry it from her arm. The guy's grip was like a vice. Trying to unbalance him, she threw her body forward and kicked. She aimed for his groin, but missed.

"Ah, ah, ah," he crooned.

"Ugh!" Nothing was working, so she screamed for all she was worth. It may seem like she was in the middle of nowhere, but she knew all too well that there were homes and businesses close by. Surely, someone would hear her.

A hand clamped over her mouth with more strength than she would have thought. Without thinking, she bit into the flesh covering her face until she tasted foul, rotten blood. Her mouth watered and she knew her weak stomach would hurl any minute.

Her head snapped back when black-hair back-handed her, adding to her injuries. She shook her head to clear the stars. The side of her face was on fire with pain. The swelling was back and she could have sworn a baseball had hit her cheek and was now lodged under her skin.

"This is much better," grease-ball murmured in her ear.

She was in major trouble and struggled in earnest. The tearing of her shirt echoed loudly as she thrashed in his hold. She twisted hard and felt her bones bend and heard a pop in her shoulder. She screamed out in pain, but wasn't giving up that easy. Trying to ignore the pain she picked up her legs, unbalancing his hold. She fell in an unceremonious heap to the ground, quickly crawling away.

"Damn, you're fine. Good thing we're in no hurry," black-hair leered at her exposed bra, giving her a smile that made her skin crawl and raised the hairs on the back of her neck. "I'm going to take my time and sample *all* of you," he promised, evil leaking from his words.

"Leave some for me," blondie said, looking his fill.

The vampires eyed her throat and flashed their teeth at her. Black-hair lunged toward her this time and instinctively, she raised her arm to protect her neck. Razors cut into her flesh as his fangs sank into her left forearm. His face was so close to hers, she smelled his stench and clearly saw the peculiar ring around his eyes. There was no life behind those evil eyes.

Using every ounce of strength she had, she brought her knee up and connected with his balls, yanking her arm free from his jaws. She went flying out of his grasp and threw out her hands before she hit the ground. The sound of a twig snapping underfoot echoed, followed immediately by intense pain radiating from her right wrist up her arm. That arm could no longer hold her weight up and her face met the ground.

She refused to meet the same fate as Dalton. "You aren't going to kill me, asshole. I've been killing slime like you for the past eighteen months!" This would end no differently.

Pushing up to stand on shaky legs, adrenaline flooded her system and she shut out the pain. She assumed a fighting stance with her body bladed, knees bent, and her good fist awkwardly poised in front of her, ready to strike out. Blood dripped to the dirt from her forearm. She cried out and ran toward her attacker.

"I'm verra concerned about Zander," Bhric divulged as they picked their way through the park where Elsie was supposed to meet Mack.

Kyran listened to his brother, his worry for Elsie escalating. She hadn't arrived yet and Zander had called Kyran, telling him that Elsie was heading their way, but he and Orlando had lost her. That boded ill given her proclivities to go searching for skirm.

"He has been worse since meeting his Fated. He hasna been feeding properly and now he is withering before our eyes." Bhric looked to Kyran, worry on his face. "He might be the most powerful vampire in the realm, but even he canna go withoot blood that long. I havena ever seen him like this. I doona remember what he was like when mamai and da were killed, but this is bad."

Kyran remembered all too well everything about the time their parents had been massacred. It was something that haunted him daily. They left the open area behind and headed into the trees.

"I do remember what he was like then, and I can say he is far worse now. The worst part is, we canna do anything aboot it. This situation is shite. And, Elsie seems to be doing far worse than him right now. From what Zander and Orlando have shared, I'm worried about her, too. She is mortal—" A muffled scream cut off Kyran's reply. He snapped to attention, opening his preternatural senses and flaring his nostrils. Blood. And, skirm.

"Feel that?" Bhric whispered. His brother reached under his black, leather jacket and his hand came back shinning. Kyran slipped his own titanium *sgian dubh* free and held it at the ready. "That had better no' be *brathair's* Fated they are attacking. If our Queen is harmed they will rue the day they were born," Bhric promised as they followed the magical aura and located two skirm, struggling with their victim.

Kyran winced as the female went flying and a distinct, cracking sound echoed through the clearing. The sound of female cries, along with the echo of her bones breaking, sucked Kyran back in time seven hundred fifteen years.

Thud,

Thud,

Thud.

A menacing laugh followed by a wet, tearing sound, thick and obscene, something out of a nightmare.

"Please doona hurt me," a whispered gurgling plea. He glanced up to find his mother's throat torn out.

Another scream jolted him out of his haunted past. An innocent female needed their protection. "You help the female, I'll take care of them," Kyran instructed, before he used his ability to sift. Between one blink and the next, he was crouched behind one of the attackers and had plunged his blade into the skirm's chest. The guy flashed then turned to ash.

In the next heartbeat he was wrapping his arms around the skirm who had her pinned down and yanking him off her. He hated that the human female needed to have a mind-wipe on top of her other injuries. A red haze filled his vision as he thought of what the skirm had clearly planned to do to the female.

"Prepare to meet your maker, in hell," he promised.

ELSIE'S HEAD SWAM. Black spots danced in her vision and nausea rose in her throat. That last lunge had been a mistake. The black-haired vampire side-stepped her at the last second and wrapped his arm around her throat, throwing her to the ground. Her head smacked hard on the ground. She swallowed back the bile as he ripped her bra open.

"No," she pleaded.

"Oh, yes," he hissed as he grabbed her breast and squeezed. She pushed against his chest to no avail, eliciting a smile from the creep. Crap that hurt, it felt like he was going to squeeze her breast from her body. His fetid breath washed across her aching cheek. A flash of fire caught the corner of her vision. She turned to try and see what had happened.

She knew that flash. The greasy-haired vampire had been killed. Mack must be there to save her. Relief washed over her.

Suddenly, the weight left her and she opened her eyes to see a large man dressed in black leather behind her attacker with his arms wrapped around his chest and throat. She rubbed her eyes. It wasn't Mack and her fear resurfaced as she realized she wasn't necessarily being saved.

Another similarly dressed man, only much bigger, approached her with his hands out in an I-come-in-peace gesture. "'Tis okay, lass, we're here to help. We willna hurt you." Elsie heard the man's words and was speechless. He sounded like Zander. The large man crouched in front of her, repeating his assurances, but she struggled to respond.

Her head throbbed, her cheek pulsed with pain and she was laying there with her shirt wide open, exposing her. She tried to cover up, but was unable to move. She looked into his intense, amber eyes and knew she was safe. There was no question, these men would protect her.

"Bugger, 'tis you...holy shite," the large man breathed. "Are you okay, Elsie? We mean you no harm."

How did this man know who she was? She prayed he was related to Zander like she suspected and wasn't some nutcase stalking her. She tried again to speak to him, but all she managed was a groan of agony.

She stared at the hand he extended to her. "I'm Bhric and the other one over there is my *brathair*, Kyran. You're injured and need a hospital."

He helped her sit up and braced her back as her head swam dizzily and throbbed painfully, causing her to swallow back bile. She wondered if she would pass out from the pain. She cradled her right arm to her chest, as adrenaline flooded her system, keeping her upright.

"Unh...I think...you're right...something is wrong," she gasped out between breaths, "I hurt...everywhere." She held up her left arm and winced from the pain of the movement.

She closed her eyes and took several deep breaths. "How do you know...who I am?" She watched him expectantly as another fire flashed in the periphery of her vision. This time she didn't bother to turn and see what had happened. Kyran had killed the black-haired vampire.

"We know you because we are Zander's *brathairs* and a close friend of Orlando. They talk aboot you often," Bhric said.

She didn't trust them completely, despite her instinct telling her they were there to protect her. A mistake like that could be fatal for her. She wanted to get to a hospital, but did she trust them to take her? She could see the headlines, 'Stupid Co-ed Gets Into Car With Strangers Moments After Being Attacked, Found Dead In Ditch.'

As the shock slowly wore off, her level of agony increased. "Yeah, I need to get to a hospital. Can I borrow your cell phone to call Orlando? He can get an ambulance to me faster than calling 911. I'm not sure where mine is. I may have left it in my car when it broke down."

"We can get you there faster than an ambulance could respond." Bhric wrapped his arm around her waist and helped her stand. Her legs wobbled and threatened to collapse. His arms tightened, helping her to remain standing.

Haunted grey eyes came into her line of sight. "Bhric is right. We need to get you to the hospital. Will you let us help?" She hadn't realized Kyran now stood well within her personal space. She looked down and saw that his hands were at the ready like he anticipated her passing out. Smart of him because she felt as if she'd topple over any moment.

She swayed on her feet as she glanced from one to the other. Kyran placed a hand on her shoulder and Bhric twined his arm around her back.

"Yes," she uttered, wanting the pain to end.

"We will have you to Jace in no time and he will fix you up in no time," Kyran encouraged.

Gritting her teeth against the pain, sweat broke out on her forehead. Gonna hit the deck any second now. What was it about Zander and his friends that made her feel like she belonged with them? Pain muddled any thoughts of reason.

Bhric took his iPhone out of his pocket and dialed a number. "Orlando, we have a situation." She listened as Bhric quickly told Orlando about the attack on her and their subsequent intervention. Her vision blurred again and everything went dark.

CHAPTER TWELVE

Cold fluid flooded Elsie's veins as the nurse pushed the last of the morphine into her IV. Within moments, her head went fuzzy and the pain eased. She wanted to curse as her upset stomach worsened.

"The pain is better, but I feel sick," Elsie muttered to the nurse.

The middle-aged woman patted her hand. "That will pass. I gave you another medication called Zofran and that takes a few minutes to take effect."

"Thanks," she responded and closed her eyes, trying to take deep breaths. The nurse was right and soon enough, she was floating. Best cocktail ever!

Bhric and Kyran were quietly talking to each other across the room. The sound of their thick brogue distracted her and it was comforting to know they stood sentry in the corner. Zander and Orlando and their friends had gone above and beyond for her. She had never met more caring, or gorgeous, men in her whole life.

She turned her heavy head and squinted at them. "I appreciate everything you've done for me, but you guys don't have to stay. I'm sure you have something better to do than babysit me until Zander and Orlando get here."

"We wouldna be anywhere else right now. 'Tis an honor to make sure you are safe and well cared for," Kyran bowed to her. Actually bowed, like a knight from medieval times.

She giggled. What was up with these guys? They were so old-fashioned, like Zander. "I love your accent. Between that and the bowing, you would think you guys were from another time, another century. You know, like that guy from Braveheart. But, Zander is far scarier than that guy, and way sexier, too." Her mind kept jumping around. "You guys are *huge,* too, with such big muscles, but you don't scare me. I feel like I'm floating. I wonder if Dalton is an angel now that he's dead. Do you think he can fly? Or float? I miss him," she sighed. Her black hole pulsed hotly. Too bad the morphine couldn't take that pain away, too. She closed her eyes against the awful ache.

A warm hand grasping hers brought her eyes open. Bhric stood by the side of her bed, looking down on her. "I think a verra powerful figure looks out for you. But, doona fash aboot that. Rest now, lass, you're safe."

She wanted to ask more about this 'powerful figure', but her eyes slipped closed and she allowed sleep to overtake her.

ZANDER STOOD outside the door to Elsie's room, aware that his eyes had darkened to obsidian with his anger. Someone had hurt his mate, and they would feel his wrath. He had known something was wrong, he had felt her anger, fear, and pain, but hadn't acted quickly enough. He had failed to protect her and the sting of that was like nothing he had ever experienced. He was incensed at the Goddess, and Fate, for causing his mate to suffer. They had put her through enough. She didn't need this, as well.

He needed to calm down before he went to her side. Taking deep breaths was a mistake as it brought a huge lung-full of her scent through the door. Despite his best efforts, he was unable to force his thoughts away from her scent and what it stirred in him. Not even recalling why she was lying in the hospital cooled his ardor. He prayed to the Goddess that he was stronger than his desires, or they were both in trouble.

Shaking fingers gripped cool metal and twisted. The door latch gave way and he was brought close to his breaking point as he was enveloped by her sultry scent. His mouth watered, his fangs shot out, and agony surged through his gums. His cock hardened painfully and he hunched over, gripping his thighs. That was only exacerbated by the pain radiating from his mate mark on his back.

And, he needed to feed. He had been unable to feed for too many months, despite his numerous attempts. His fangs had refused to descend around other females, making feeding impossible. Bottled blood was rejected by his body, as well, and they had resorted to the least effective method infusing him with blood via an IV. Only now, he realized that all that time, his body had been reacting as if they had completed the mating. Fully mated vampires were no longer able to feed from anyone except their Fated Mate. It was perplexing. Sure, he had seen news footage of Elsie after her husband's murder, just as everyone else in Seattle, but he hadn't met her until a little over a week ago.

Now, he had to clamp down on his every instinct. It was like a beast clawing at his insides. The blood rushing through her veins was a siren's call. He glanced up and was unable to tear his gaze away from the slow, steady pulse beating in her neck. He should leave. It was a risk moving any closer to her, but like a moth to a flame, he quickly made his way to her side.

Tears pricked his eyes. He was the Vampire King, he didn't cry, but the sight of his mate with bruises marring her body, bloody bandages on her arm, and various monitors connected to her, brought forth emotions he had only experienced one other time in his life. His anger renewed at who had done this to her. The archdemon and his skirm would pay with their life.

He reached over and tenderly touched her injured cheek with his fingertips. His desire exploded at the contact. He reached deep for the control not to sink his fangs into her beautiful throat, while he claimed her body. Her soul twined around his, drawing comfort. The need for her had never been so intense. He had almost lost her and wanted to join with her in every way to reaffirm that she was alive....and his. It was crucial that he do so soon.

Going outside his comfort zone, he reached out for help. "*Brathair*, one of you will need to step in if I canna resist. Her blood calls to me."

ELSIE WAS BROUGHT out of her sleep by a seductive voice that caressed her in places she thought had died. Her eyes blinked open in a muddled haze. It was difficult to tell if she was awake or dreaming. Some part of her was aware she was on heavy medications, but everything halted as she was captivated by a sinful smile. A gorgeous man ran his hand lightly over her injured cheek.

"Zander," she breathed. He cradled her face in his large

palms and she relished the feel of his flesh against hers. Her entire body tingled with an erotic current that caused wetness to pool between her legs, and her nipples to harden against the cotton fabric of the hospital gown. Only he could elicit that kind of response from her. Which astounded her given the weighed down, disconnected feeling caused by the morphine.

The emotions that crossed his face sharpened his Patrician features, and stole her breath and her words. She wanted to understand what he was thinking and feeling. She wanted to take away the pain she saw and explore the desire she saw banked there. Sadness overcame her, as she remembered that having a relationship with him wasn't in the cards for her.

That didn't change the fact that his sapphire-blue eyes held a mystery she felt compelled to unravel.

ONE LOOK FROM HIS ELSIE, and Zander knew he was lost forever. She owned him heart and soul. He needed her in his life, bonded to him as his Fated Mate, yet his fear had never been greater that he would have to live without her. He had thought his greatest hurdle was his acceptance of her being human, and her getting over the loss of her husband.

Now, this incident had further cemented her hatred of vampires. How could she ever embrace his world that was filled with such violence? Would she see him as the same creature that had attacked her and took the man that she loved from her?

He gazed at her beautiful face and grabbed her up in a fierce hug. "You scared the life oot of me. You will never again be without protection." He wanted to forbid her from patrolling all together, but wasn't ready to tell her what he was. Wasn't ready for the questions that would elicit.

She hugged him back. "I'm in a little bit of pain here, Mr. Bossy Pants. Lighten the hold, please." He gentled, but didn't let go of her. "Hey, it's ok, I'm ok. What did I tell you about giving orders? You can't simply say I will never be without protection. I don't need a bodyguard. If my car hadn't broken down, I would have been perfectly safe with Mack."

He pulled back and smoothed her hair. "I remember what you said. And, like I told you, giving orders is what I do. I will be providing protection, either me or one of my... employees. Now, how are you feeling, *a ghra?*"

"My pain was much better before you squeezed me." He reluctantly placed her back against her pillow. "Dr. Jace gave me some good drugs. By the way, I wanted to ask why you've been leaving me obscene tips." She went off on another train of thought before he could respond. "It's so good to see you. I feel safe now." Her soft voice was a balm to his soul. She relaxed further as the humming of the machine signaled she was receiving another dose of pain medication. Thank the Goddess for modern medicine. It killed him to see the pain in her eyes.

He slid one hand from her cheek to her throat, stopping at her pulse and left it there, while the other gently rubbed her hand. He struggled to retract his fangs so he could talk to her, and prayed that his eyes were not glowing with his desire.

When he had gained a modicum of control he continued. "My tips were no' obscene, lass. I wanted to make life easier for you. I saw how hard you were working and know the loss you have suffered."

"Are you kidding me? It made *everything* easier. Hmmm, your touch is nice. It warms my chest and soothes the pulsing black hole. Oh, and, it makes me all tingly, I love it. Christ, your eyes are gorgeous. The color is unlike any I've ever seen," she cocked her head to the side, taking in his countenance. He couldn't help but puff out his chest. His touch eased his mate's pain and she liked his eyes.

"In a world hardened by war and bloodshed, you bring meaning. You are the sunshine to my grey skies." He felt the connection blaze between them. The Goddess' creation of Fated Mates put the human notion of soul mates to shame. There was nothing else like it in this realm, or any other.

Her eyes flared and her pupils dilated. The scent of her arousal drowned out the smells of the hospital and put him to the test as his body hardened.

"Flatterer," she accused. Her eyes finally traveled away from his face and stopped at his groin. Her gaze was a torch, burning his ardor. "Is that leather you're wearing? Beats the scrubs the doctors wear. And, you make me feel so much better than their medications. You know the TV show, about doctors and nurses that is set here in Seattle?" Her stream of consciousness escaped without pause, making him chuckle. "You are so much hotter than Dr. McDreamy. Holy shit, you are *YUMMY* in that soft leather. These are the softest pants I have ever felt."

He bit back a curse as she caressed his thigh. He had never been so close to orgasm with such little contact. Her eyes drifted partially closed, but displayed her lust and drug-induced fatigue. The latter should have cooled his desire, but it didn't diminish it one bit.

"You're my Dr. McYummy. I could eat you up. My face is numb, am I drooling? I think I need a bib...and dry panties," she whispered the last under her breath, but of course, he heard every word. The drugs were obliterating her inhibitions and she was saying anything that came to her mind. His mate may hunt skirm, but this showcased her innocence. It was refreshing and endearing.

He smiled, careful to keep his throbbing fangs hidden, while his shaft stiffened further inside his pants. "Och, you're going to unhinge me with your touch," he whispered.

Her cheeks reddened with her embarrassment. "Oh no, I didn't say that out loud, did I? Oh God," she buried her face in her hands.

He pried her hands away and bent over, placing his lips to her skin. His eyes closed at the soft feel of her against his lips. He breathed deeply of her sweet, honeysuckle fragrance. Delicious. "You are wrong aboot one thing, *a ghra.* Your skin is infinitely softer than my pants, and you are the sexiest thing I've ever laid eyes on. I could drink you in for centuries and no' get enough. Everything will be okay. I'm going to take care of you from now on." The vow escaped his lips and he refused to take it back.

Her eyes widened with surprise. "Wow. This has to be a dream. You are so gorgeous and no one like you has ever told me I'm sexy. I'm dreadfully average. Yep, definitely dreaming. I like this dream..." she trailed off, closing her eyes.

He bit back a groan, hearing her thoughts. His mate had an erotic imagination. Without the grief and guilt hanging over her, she allowed herself to think about the wicked things she wanted to do to him. He couldn't wait to get her in his bed. "I canna survive this," he intoned.

THAT DEEP, masculine voice dripped down her spine,

leaving warmth in its path that set her blood afire. She loved Dr. McYummy's, accent. Guilt over her thoughts rose and receded. This was not Dalton and she should've been castigating herself. Instead, she headed in a decidedly naughty direction. A direction she would be riddled with remorse over later, but for now the drugs stripped her bare.

She took a deep breath and on her exhale, fully embraced the fantasy. She wondered if Zander had any tattoos she could nibble on. She imagined lifting his shirt over his head then tossing it to the floor so she could run her hands across his broad, muscular shoulders. She pictured a beautiful, Celtic cross tattooed somewhere on his muscled body.

She ached to suck his full, lower lip into her mouth. Feel his heavy breaths fall against her lips before she slipped her tongue into his mouth for a passionate kiss. He was a take-charge kind of man, and she imagined him doing that. His kiss would be explosive. He would not simply explore the depths of her mouth, he would plunder and stake a claim.

She longed to run her hands down his sculpted chest, feeling the power radiate from him. A power that would embrace her as she reached around and caressed the fine globes of his ass while he pounded into her tight sheath. She had never let go of her desires like this before and it was liberating. Her inner-sex-fiend was strutting around the room, tail high, begging for him to mount her. She doubted she would ever get a leash on it again.

Glowing pools of desire awoke something in her soul. Their eye contact intensified, but neither person spoke a word, as she continued mentally caressing his body. Her hands itched to run down his arms as she nibbled and sucked his nipples, feeling them pearl in her mouth. Would he like her to bite them? Her mouth watered at the thought.

A sudden urge, to bite him hard enough to break skin and take his blood into her mouth, overcame her. She was lost in the passionate fantasy and was grateful that when her guilt rose again, it quickly fizzled away, leaving her free to continue.

ZANDER WAS unable to form a coherent thought, let alone use any of his powers. Not that he would have dreamed of stopping her fantasies. It wasn't real, but his body was sizzling everywhere her hot, little mind had wandered as if it were. When she imagined biting down on his nipple, a rough sound escaped his clenched jaw. He had fisted his hands at his sides to keep from touching her. His eyes remained glued to her beautiful, blue orbs.

He shuddered when she reached out and caressed his shaft through his leather pants. He knew he should tell her to stop, but he loved it, wanted it, needed it. He was going to explode soon, yet his hand still refused to move. Her grip tightened on his erection and his balls drew up tight. The base of his spine tingled with impending orgasm. He wasn't the only one breathless from her touch. She was panting while she whispered "so big." Unable to stop himself, he softly ground his hard cock against her hand, showing her how big.

"Careful, *a ghra,* that may go off in your hand. Och, but you feel so good," he murmured, as he marveled at her beauty.

"That's the point, I think. And, I love the lust in your eyes. They're glowing," she whispered, gripping his shaft harder through the material.

That was all it took. He lost control and came hard in his

trews. He dropped his head to his chest as he panted and his seed shot from his cock. Despite the fact that she was unaware this was real, her eyes darkened and she rubbed him harder. His orgasm continued. It felt good, so good that he swore he left his body and their bond intensified.

His mate had brought him to climax and he was never going to be the same. This was what he had waited for the past seven hundred years. The sense of rightness was overwhelming. He had better come to terms with her being human and find a way to win her over soon because there was no going back for him. He was irrevocably hers.

"Holy shite," he whispered, shocked about what he had experienced. This was the most incredible and satisfying sexual encounter of his life and there had been no skin on skin contact. The mating compulsion had the need to be inside her, claiming her, clawing at his insides. He both thanked and cursed the Goddess for his fortune. He had received a small taste of his mate and he wanted more, so much more.

"Wow, I think I came with you on that one. I love this dream and I don't ever want to wake up. Real life is full of too much pain," she said as her eyes slipped closed.

She may not realize it and may even fight it, but, eventually, she would be his. He always got what he wanted.

CHAPTER THIRTEEN

Z ander listened to Elsie's inner battle and watched her drift off to sleep. She was telling herself that she'd had her fun and it was now time to remember her vows to Dalton. Her loyalty was a blessing and a curse. One thing was clear to him. He would not be mating her anytime soon. She wasn't ready. Not only did she have to find her way through her grief and guilt, but she hated vampires and hunted them for vengeance. Needless to say, they had a few hurdles to overcome.

He was falling for her and couldn't imagine his life without her. He marveled at the dynamics of a mating. Already, he needed her emotionally and physically. He wanted to confide in her and seek her opinion on realm matters. More importantly, he'd been unable to feed from anyone and his weakening body demanded he proceed with the mating. He refused to force her into something she didn't want, but the realm needed him at his best. Thousands relied on him to battle the demons and keep them safe. Rock and hard place slammed into each other, trapping him in the middle.

One step at a time, he told himself. For now, he enjoyed their combined arousal, which was as thick as pea soup in the room. He used his telepathy to ask Jace to bring him some clean scrubs as he recalled the reason he needed to change. The interlude with Elsie had been intense and erotic.

"Bugger, Zander, I thought she was going to rip your pants off and tup you right here. She sure had a grip on your nob. I bet she is no' a wilting flower in the sack," Bhric teased.

His brother was playing with fire and he was too keyed up at that moment. "Fuck off, *brathair*," he warned. "If we were no' in Jace's hospital, I would rip you to shreds for disrespecting my mate. Doona *ever* speak of her in that manner."

Everyone fell silent as his command and anger pulsed hotly through the room. The absolute certainty that he would harm anyone, including the siblings he'd raised as if they were his children, was frightening and bespoke of the bond between mates. He wondered how much stronger it would be when they completed the mating.

"You're right, I apologize. I forgot who she is. It hasna been but a day since the mating curse was broken. It willna happen again," Bhric promised.

His brother was right. Everyone was adjusting to the news, not just him. The energy he had expended throughout the day and evening was taking its toll and he staggered from his weakness, catching himself on the edge of the bed. He needed to obtain her blood. Sooner, rather than later.

Jace entered the room quietly, clearly wary of the varied emotions. He tossed Zander the clean scrubs and a plastic hospital bag for his dirty pants. "Hey, guys, how long has she been out? Do I want to know what happened in here?"

Zander went into the bathroom and responded to Jace while he took off his combat boots. "The medications you gave her made her believe she was dreaming and she found my leathers very soft. Let's just say the touch of a mate is a verra powerful thing," Zander informed him. "She has been asleep for aboot five minutes. Now, tell me what her injuries are, aside from the wee bite there on her arm," he said through the door as he removed his soiled leathers and quickly donned the scrubs.

Jace cleared his throat and pulled at the stethoscope around his neck. The hesitation had Zander sweating. This wasn't going to be good. "She has several serious injuries. Her right radius and ulna are fractured from the fall. I will be setting and casting those breaks. She also has a concussion and a zygomatic fracture on her left cheek, which I plan to heal. Otherwise, she'd be heading for surgery to correct it. And the bite under those bandages is not so little. The venom permeated the surrounding tissues and her human body is having a hard time fighting it. Aside from a few loose teeth and assorted bumps and bruises, that is it...from the attack."

Jace paused and met Zander's gaze, "What those skirm did to her," the warrior snarled and took several deep breaths before continuing, "is one more reason they need to be eliminated. I still can't believe she goes out hunting them. The most pressing issue here is the weight she has lost and the negative effect this is having on her overall health. She needs to begin sleeping, eating, and regaining weight now, or there will be severe consequences. Her frail system can't handle much more."

Zander shoved his hands in his pockets and walked over

to the side of her bed. "This creates a wee complication." He spoke to Jace but his eyes never left Elsie's face. "You see, I need her blood. As you know, the IV infusions you've been giving me have no' been helpful. Now that I know she is my Fated, I realize that the feeding problems began when I saw her on the news. With her at risk, I canna afford to be as weak as I am, but I canna last much longer without her blood. You will do whatever it takes, Jace, to see her healthy."

Jace rocked back on his heels and sucked in his breath through his teeth. "I can fix what's broken in her body, but I can't make her eat or sleep. That's up to her alone, but, as for blood, we can safely take a pint tonight without causing harm. You will need to be sure and feed her a big steak later. Also, I suggest that she quit working. Waitressing will be near impossible with a broken arm and she needs to focus her energy on healing."

Zander's movements stilled and he reached over and brushed hair from her face. She sighed and turned into his touch. His heart stuttered. "She will no' take that well at all. She's fiercely independent and stubborn," he said with affection.

MASCULINE VOICES PENETRATED the thick fog that had Elsie trapped. They were talking about her, but she was unable to make sense of what they were saying. She fought the effects of the drugs. The haze cleared as she blinked her heavy eyes open. Brilliant, green orbs came into focus.

"Hey, cupcake. How are you feeling? It's so good to see those beautiful, blue eyes shining back at me," Orlando cooed. She noticed the tight brackets of tension around his mouth and how his hair stood out all over. She could imagine he had been plowing his hands through it as he waited for her to wake up.

It took a couple of attempts to get her rusty voice working. "I'm, ugh, it's starting to hurt again." Her head throbbed almost as much as her arm and cheek. She turned her head to look around, wincing at the pain it caused. The pain diminished at the sight of Zander standing on the other side of her bed next to Jace. From the corner of her eye, she realized Kyran and Bhric were still standing sentinel.

Turning her attention back to Zander, she saw he had scrubs on. She had dreamed he wore leather pants and she was exploring the spectacular body beneath. The residual zing in her blood told her it had been one hell of a dream. She would much rather be back there than lying in the bed in so much agony.

Memories rushed back about why she was in pain and a sudden thought struck her. "How is it that Kyran killed those guys who attacked me?" she asked, suspicious and curious about how much they knew. Did they know about vampires? Was she in trouble for killing them?

Orlando grasped her uninjured hand, stealing her attention. "I'm not sure what you remember, but you passed out at some point. Kyran managed to subdue your attackers while Bhric got you to safety, but we can talk about that later," Orlando grasped her uninjured hand.

Nausea churned in her gut. "I passed out? Oh my God. I could've been another TwiKill victim," she breathed, careful to use the media terminology. Her relief was potent that they didn't know she was involved with SOVA or killed vampires.

Zander placed his large palm on her cheek and gently turned her to face him. "*A ghra*, doona fash over this. You have much healing ahead of you. We are here and will keep you safe."

"Speaking of safe," Jace said, stepping into her line of vision. Zander moved over for Jace to do a quick review of her vital signs. He injected another dose of medication into her IV, which quickly took effect. "This should take care of your pain, but let's talk about your injuries."

She met his odd amethyst eyes and cut to the chase, "It helps immensely. Now, what I wanna know is will I need surgery?"

Jace took his pen-light out of his lab-coat pocket and checked her eyes, ears and throat. "No, you won't need surgery. There are several fractures in your right wrist and forearm that I will set and cast. You will be in a cast for six to eight weeks while it heals. Your left cheekbone is badly bruised, but not broken and I need to stitch the bite on your arm." She was surprised that her cheek wasn't broken, given the sharp stabbing pain.

He sat down and made eye contact. She cocked her head and tried to focus. The drugs were affecting her concentration again. They were more powerful than she thought. Dizziness assailed her and she decided it best to close out the world. Warm palms settled on her face and she sighed as the pain lessened even more. She wondered what drugs she'd been given this time.

Jace's soothing voice had her eyes fluttering back open. "You will need to take antibiotics. Saliva carries countless germs and the last thing you need on top of everything else is an infection." His pause made her heart race. "I understand you are a waitress. Given the severity and types of your injuries, you will not be able to work while you are in a cast. It will extend from below your elbow and will cover your palm leaving only your fingers free, and, until you come back for me to put a hard cast on, you will need to wear a sling to keep it immobile."

"Whaaat?" This had to be a joke. This could not be happening to her, shit just kept piling up in her life. Overwhelmed, she sobbed into her hands. "I have to work, you don't understand. I have bills, lots of them and I'm all alone now. I lost Dalton and my car broke down tonight so I don't even have transportation now. Without my job, I won't have anything. Oh God, I am going to be homeless." She grabbed the sheet and covered her face as the tears streamed down her cheeks.

The bed shifted and the sheet was tugged out of her grasp. She glanced through bleary eyes to see Zander on the edge of her bed. He cupped her face. "*A ghra*, you are no' alone. You know I willna allow you to become homeless. I am going to take care of you," he declared. There he went issuing those orders. She heaved a sigh, he didn't get that life didn't work that way. And, no way was she going to allow this man to pay her bills and take care of her.

"That's not going to happen. I take care of myself," she informed Zander tiredly.

She noticed the irritated look cross Zander's features, but Orlando sat on her other side and grabbed her attention. "Stop that, cupcake. None of us will allow anything to happen to you," he said pointing to Bhric and Kyran. "You haven't met everyone at Zeum but none of them would stand for it. Remember what I said?"

His image was blurred by her tears. "You've said a lot. You talk more than any woman," her breath hitched.

Orlando's hands tightened minutely, "Haha, very funny. You are part of our twisted, little family now. You've worked your way into our hearts and we are all here for you, whatever you may need," he promised. She pondered having more than her sister and Mack in her life. Having them claim her as family was miraculous and she couldn't deny wanting to belong with them.

"The family part might not be so bad. I'd fit with twisted. Although, you can be annoyingly dictatorial," she teased Zander who responded with a smirk. "Dalton and my sister are all I have had since my parents died three years ago. Aside from Mack, I thought all I had now was Cailyn. You may regret this, eventually. I'm stubborn and difficult, or so Cailyn says."

"You doona say," Zander teased as he winked at her, caressing her cheek. "Put it oot of your mind. Each of us has issues, stubbornness we can deal with. You are going to take our help and after I get you home, you *will* start eating and sleeping."

She rolled her eyes, but grinned. "*Doona* think you can give me orders just because I'm in pain and on drugs, Mr. Bossy Pants."

He clutched his chest as if stricken. "I'm back to that infernal name. What happened to Dr. McYummy?"

Her cheeks heated with embarrassment and she placed her head in her hands. "Oh God," she groaned. "Tell me I didn't say that out loud."

"But, that would be a lie, cupcake. Besides, I'm enjoying your embarrassment too much," Orlando playfully ruffled her hair. Zander's hand tightened over hers.

Jace cleared his throat, drawing her attention. "I hate to be the bearer of more bad news, but I'm sure this won't come as a shock. I'm one step away from keeping you in this hospital because of your weight loss. You need to listen to Zander and eat. You can't afford to lose anymore." She shrank back into the bed from the severity in his tone. She knew she had lost too much, but hearing it from a doctor, brought it home. Her chin lifted, she refused to be seen as weak, and nodded in acknowledgment.

"I know it's not an excuse, but my life hasn't exactly been a cakewalk lately. I will do better," she promised.

He inclined his head in response, a silent understanding of how hard life had been for her. "Okay, now comes the hard part, let's set these bones. And then, I'll need to take some blood."

DIZZINESS ASSAILED Elsie and she clung tighter to Zander as he carried her to her front door. Blood loss and morphine was not a good combo. At least the pain was gone, for the most part. It had been excruciating when Jace had set her broken wrist. A cry had escaped her the moment he grasped the limb, eliciting a snarl from Zander. The sound spoke of violence and retribution. She had gritted her teeth against any other reaction and clutched his hand, holding him to her. She feared that if she let go, he may attack his friend for causing her pain, despite the fact that it couldn't be avoided.

She was grateful for these new-found friends of hers. She hated to think of how this night would have ended for her without them. Mack wouldn't have made it to her in time. In fact, she needed to call Mack and check in with her. Her friend was likely worried to death.

She looked to her front door and confusion buffeted her. Why were Santiago and another guy with gorgeous light-brown hair waiting outside her apartment with a leather couch and matching chair? Seriously, the new guy had hair women paid tons of money for, with multi-colored high-lights. "Um, what is going on? And, who is he?"

"Hey there, *Chiquita*. How are you doing?" Santiago gave

her an awkward hug, since Zander refused to loosen his hold, and kissed her bruised cheek. "This is Rhys, and O said he can't sleep on your old futon, so I brought him a couch-bed to cushion his hemorrhoid-ridden ass." It wasn't so much Rhys' hair that caught her attention now, but his odd-colored eyes. The only term that came to mind to describe their color was kaleidoscopic. They were mesmerizing, and thankfully, full of mirth and mischief.

She furrowed her brows and looked at Orlando. Her brain was sluggish, but memories of her attack had her heart racing. "We aren't leaving you alone after what happened today," Orlando informed her.

Relief had her sagging further against Zander. "I'm so glad I don't have to tie one of you to the futon to keep you from leaving. I can't be alone tonight. I saw what he wanted to do to me in his eyes and..." She shook as the reality of how close she had come to being raped and murdered sank in.

Suddenly, the image of the two vampires being killed by Kyran returned with a rush. There was no mistaking the way vamps flashed on fire and turned to dust. That wouldn't have happened if they didn't know about the horrors that stalked the night. Vampires could only be killed with titanium weapons, according to Mack, and Elsie believed her friend. She had been hunting them far longer than Elsie. She panicked, could they know about her involvement with SOVA?

Regardless, they had saved her, and for that, she was grateful. She met Bhric and Kyran's gaze and put all of her gratitude into her words. "I would be dead right now if not for you guys. I owe you my life. I don't have much, but when I'm feeling better I want to cook you dinner." They bowed at their waists like knights. These were the oddest men. They looked as if they could tear anyone to shreds and not lose any sleep, yet had this regal bearing that spoke of honor and loyalty.

Bhric spoke quietly. "We were only doing our duty." He straightened and his lazy smile had her lips tilting. "But, we willna turn down a home-cooked meal."

"You guys are so weird," she said. They must not know about SOVA, or they would be handcuffing her, not making plans with her. She lifted her head and kissed Zander's cheek, then wiggled in his arms. "Let me down, please." He let her slide down his torso and her eyes flew wide when she felt the unmistakable evidence of his arousal brush against her hip. She flushed and fumbled with her keys.

Her equilibrium was non-existent at the moment and she staggered. Before she hit the pavement, strong arms wound around her and Zander held her against his chest as he opened her door.

"Thanks," she told him and shuffled into the apartment.

She watched while the others quickly removed her old futon and brought in the new, leather furniture. She was exhausted and wanted nothing more than to go to bed, but she had promised to eat something. She would choke down a sandwich then take more pain pills and sleep for a year.

Zander reached around her and pulled items out of the bags Rhys had set on her table. He opened a Styrofoam container full of gyro meat and cut it into small bites. "Here, you need to eat and drink this juice before you can rest. You lost too much blood." She noticed the tension around his mouth and jaw and wouldn't dare argue with him, even though she wasn't all that hungry.

"I can't ever thank you enough for all you've done. And, now you're sitting here feeding me as if I'm an infant. I do have one good arm." She tried to take the fork from him and he held it out of her reach.

"Doona fash over me. 'Tis good to see you eat," he murmured against her cheek before kissing it. She had a bond with Zander that was intimate and different than anything she'd ever experienced. She couldn't think about that right now so she focused on eating what he fed her.

Several minutes later, she was shocked when she realized she had eaten most of the food, despite the fact that it tasted horrible. Her gyro meat was much tastier and she wasn't tooting her own horn. This stuff was dry and bland.

She turned her head and listened to the guys banter while they sat on her new furniture and ate. She barely recognized her apartment. Dalton wouldn't recognize it, or her life. Both had been completely transformed. A flat-screen adorned the wall between her colorful Mexican blankets. A small cabinet beneath it held her new Blu-Ray player and movies. Now, the futon she had picked out years ago with Dalton was being hauled away and replaced by a toffee-colored, leather sleeper-sofa and matching chair.

She jumped up and raced to her bedroom as her black hole pulsed painfully. Overcome with grief, she needed to be alone. Would this nightmare ever end?

CHAPTER FOURTEEN

*Z*ander had yet to subdue the emotional upheaval from seeing Elsie lying broken and bruised in the hospital bed. When his mate had thanked his brothers, saying she would have been dead if not for them, an invisible razor had sliced his insides to shreds. He was appreciative of his brother's intervention, but it was his job to protect her, and he had failed.

He stared longingly at her closed bedroom door. Her muffled sobs wrecked him. He couldn't bear her grief. An irrational pang of jealousy and hurt coursed through him over her feelings for Dalton. It didn't help that he was driven, beyond comprehension, by the mating compulsion. Hell, he still felt electricity burning under his skin from holding her in his arms.

He had fed her and now, he had to leave and get away from her tantalizingly, sweet scent before he gave into his desires. Every moment close to her made his need grow. He stalked out of the small apartment. He wanted to be alone, but his brothers followed him out. No one was leaving him alone in his agitated state.

"I need to go by Confetti and feed before we head home," Bhric indicated as they made their way to Zander's car.

Kyran bypassed the Jag, walking straight for his Denali. The SUV's interior lit when he unlocked the doors. "You got this right, Bhric? I'm heading to Bite. I'll catch you back at Zeum," Kyran said before he opened the driver's door and climbed in.

Kyran had been going to the seedy brothel for too long and Zander hated it. Something cold and remote descended over his brother after each visit, and it was becoming increasingly difficult to reach him. Zander watched a piece of Kyran's heart and soul die with each escapade. He feared that one day Kyran would be unreachable. But, Kyran wasn't his main concern at the moment. He had more than enough on his plate.

"I wish he'd stop going there. There are plenty of females at Kill's joint who would love to hook up with one of the vampire princes," Bhric said as he headed to the passenger door.

"Here," Zander tossed his car keys to Bhric, "you drive. I'm going to drink the blood Jace took from Elsie and until I understand the effect my mate's blood has on me, I doona want to be behind the wheel." His heart leapt in excitement.

"Should be interesting," Bhric chuckled and unlocked the doors.

The moment he was in the passenger seat of his car, Zander ripped open the small, soft-sided cooler that held the key to his survival. "Fucking Rhys," Zander cursed, shaking his head at the plastic cup embellished with tiny, black bats included in the bag. At this point he didn't care if he drank it from a baby bottle. He needed her blood, now.

He trembled as he brought the straw to his lips. His body

went taut as he took his first sip of his Fated Mate's blood. He jolted with a rush of the strongest energy he had ever felt. His skin tingled with little currents running from his head to his toes. His cock stiffened and his orgasm hit before he blinked. Holy. Fucking. Goddess. He took a second sip and his vision sharpened even more. He heard a mouse scurrying several blocks away. Supreme satisfaction settled in his heart. Bhric laughed and backed out of their parking spot.

It was good to be king and drinking his Fated Mate's blood. One drink and he was addicted to not only the taste of his mate's blood, but the power boost it provided him. He had always felt strings tethering him to the Goddess and the earth, but they paled in comparison to the life-line Elsie had become for him. That bond he had previously felt became an unyielding bond to the one female he would never be able to live without. He savored every sip of the succulent blood.

He contemplated licking every drop from the cup, but was sidetracked when a new awareness blossomed as her blood flooded every cell and altered him fundamentally. His mate's blood was a GPS beacon. At that moment, he discerned that Elsie was west of his location, approximately nine miles, and was stationary. Incredible!

He looked down and smiled. "Thank the Goddess I carry extra clothes. I need to change before we go into the club," he reached around and grabbed the extra leathers on the back seat.

Bhric chuckled, "Apparently, the legend about a mate's blood is true. 'Tis good the realm didna see their king just now. The look on your face when you busted a nut would have shocked the most stalwart female. It was brutal and savage. Pure ecstasy, I'm jealous. Not that I want my mate."

Zander enjoyed the way his brother's gaze turned contemplative. He would love to see the effects a mate would have on someone like his brother, who enjoyed females too much and too frequently. Zander had never found gratification from random couplings, which was why he had only been with three females over the past two centuries. Nothing had even come close to the fulfillment he had found with his human mate.

The fact that she was human mattered less and less, except it made him fear for her safety. But, oh what she made him experience...

Bhric pulled into the parking lot, and Zander quickly changed his pants. With a spring in his step, he followed his brother into the club. The fact that Elsie was at home grieving over her dead husband marred his joy. She was attracted to Zander, but was fighting the mating compulsion with everything she had. Fear of never being able to claim Elsie haunted him, but he refused to give up. He would claim his mate or die trying. He imagined all the different ways he would claim her, spiking his arousal again.

Zander stood at one of the bar tables thinking of Elsie and chastised himself when Lena came up behind him, wrapping her arms around his waist. He had been distracted by fantasies of his mate and his body recoiled when Lena trailed her hands down his hard abdomen to cup his erection. His body screamed out against the contact.

"Looking for me, I see, *mon amour*. Mmmm, hard as always. I can't get enough of you, either. Come with me, I have a treat for you," she purred. His erection deflated and her lovely smile quickly turned into a pout.

No other female would ever touch him intimately again. For once in the past few days, his body and his mind were in accord. Both refused to respond to any but Elsie. And now,

Lena's honeysuckle perfume made him sick, the slightly astringent notes made his stomach roil.

"Nay, Lena. 'Tis for my Fated Mate and I willna be going to any room with you, or any other female, ever again. I have found my heart and soul, the one made for me." He didn't want to be cruel to Lena. After all, they had been having sex for two-hundred years, but he truly had no feelings for her. Now that he had experienced a real connection with Elsie, he could not imagine going back to the empty sexual encounters that had comprised his life.

Lena's surprise was evident as her eyes flew wide. Her mouth gaped as she tried to respond. When she did, her anger and disbelief were obvious in her tone. "If you've found your mate, why has there not been a proper announcement about the curse being lifted? And, why are you here prowling the club?" Her dark-brown eyes turned to his shaft and she reached out to stroke him.

"No, I believe that you are mistaken, *mon tresor*. I'm the one for you. You have to know that, feel that in your heart like I do."

His shaft did not react to her attention or words. Not even a twitch. In fact, his flesh was crawling inside itself to get away from her touch. He gently brushed her hand away. "Lena, I'm sorry, but you are no' the one for me. 'Tis a true miracle, the Goddess has blessed me with my Fated Mate."

She narrowed her eyes but gentled her voice. "I'm sorry, *mon coeur*. Your news took me by surprise. I'm happy for you. I'm upset that we will not be together again, but I want to see you happy. I would do anything for you." His instincts rang with alarm at the calculating look in her eyes.

Shaking his head, he responded to her. "I havena made an official announcement. My mate is not in a position to complete the mating right now. She has been a target of the skirm. I canna put her in the spotlight and at more risk. My Dark Warriors are helping me to keep her safe." He clenched his fists against his fear and anger. "This war with the demons and their skirm is far more dangerous than it's ever been. The announcement will be made when we are ready to move forward with the mating." Not wanting to be so close to her, he took a step back, placing more space between them.

"*Dieu*, she must be human if they are helping you protect her. I would have thought the Goddess would have given a vampire mate to the Vampire King. But, never mind that. Tell me how I can help. You know females, especially human ones, are different creatures and require special handling, *n'est-ce pas*? I assume she knows nothing of Tehrex Realm, or the war and world, she is about to rule. I could be her guide to the supernatural. Your Dark Warriors are great for sex, but this is not a job for them," Lena remarked, a mischievous gleam in her eyes.

Not going to happen. He held any further thoughts and feelings close to his heart. Telling anyone, let alone Lena, that Elsie fought the skirm nightly, was a bad idea. And, he was not about to entrust his mate to this female.

"I appreciate the offer, Lena, but I have everything under control. I doona need your help. I may no' know much aboot females, but I'm certain having someone that I have fucked in the past, befriend my Fated Mate, isna a good idea. Besides, I have her soul to guide me." He turned from her and took his leave of the club entirely.

Putting the exchange with Lena out of his mind, he thought of Elsie and how devastated she had been. She had lost her car and job in one night. He had vowed to take care of her and there was at least one thing he could do for her before sunrise. He jumped into his car and headed back across town.

ELSIE ROLLED over in bed and groaned. Pain shot up her arm. It had woken her several times during the night, and she was exhausted. She had papers to write and new challenges to compensate for. Better get to it. She sat up and flung her feet over the edge of her bed. Her body felt like it had been run over by a semi. She needed an energy drink and a pain pill, pronto.

Dutifully, she grabbed the sling from her nightstand and carefully put it on. Getting her arm into the contraption was a teeth-gritting experience. She stretched as much as was possible and stood up to retrieve her medication and swayed on her feet.

After she regained her balance, an envelope on the floor by her bedroom door caught her eye. What was that? Pulling her broken arm close, she bent over and picked it up. The letter felt heavy in her hand and had an odd lump in the middle. Something slid into a corner when she tilted it. Her curiosity peaked and she tore it open. Her jaw hit the floor. Inside, she found two pieces of paper, a note and a car title, along with a car key.

"For the love of Buddha! A car!" she screeched. And, not just any car. According to the title, it was a Jaguar XKR-S. She rushed to her window, breaking the metal mini-blinds in her haste to check her parking spot. It was Zander's fabulous, metallic-grey convertible that he had driven her home in the night before.

It glinted in the early morning sun. With shaking hands, she opened the crumpled letter. The elegant, masculine script reminded her of the Renaissance time period and she felt the familiar zing course through her body as she read the note.

"I considered giving you an armored tank to keep you safe, but the sleek design of this car reminded me of your sensuous body. It can handle curves almost as well as I can. And, the supple, leather interior made me think of your soft skin. I canna express how sorry I am that I wasna there to protect you. Always yours, Z"

She was flabbergasted. She had no idea how long she stood there staring at the note, before her mind started working again. He was apologizing for not protecting her. He blamed himself for her injuries. And, he had given her a car. An expensive car!

She threw open the bedroom door and stormed over to a sleeping Orlando. "What, in the name of all that is holy, is wrong with Zander? He gave me a car? Who does that shit? I can't accept this, it's too much. No one gives a gift like this without expecting something in return. You have to tell him to come pick it up right now," she shrieked. She didn't give a shit if she was being rude or waking him up, this was too much.

Orlando rolled over and blinked open tired eyes. She could have sworn his eyes were glowing emerald. Her mind stuttered at the half-lidded, heated gaze he shot her way.

"What is it with you two waking me up? I do need sleep, you know," Orlando grumbled, breaking the spell as he sat up. When the sheet fell to his waist, she prayed he was clothed beneath the covers and turned her head in case he wasn't. Now, if he were Zander she'd be praying that he was naked as the day he was born. And, may even tear the sheet away. She couldn't seem to get her mind out of the gutter lately.

"Ah," Orlando muttered, "I see you found the envelope. First of all, no one tells Zander no. And second, are you crazy? It's a kick-ass car, accept it. He gave this to you with no strings or expectations, El. He is truly worried about your safety."

She turned her head and swallowed at the intensity in his stare. "We all are. And, trust me. he can afford to give you this car. He only has twenty others and that doesn't include his collection of motorcycles. Besides, for him, it is the equivalent of you buying me a cheeseburger."

He stood gracefully and walked toward her. She noted that he was wearing black boxer-briefs. She refused to acknowledge the erection that filled his underwear. Men always woke up with morning wood, right?

"But—"

"No, stop right there." He cut her off as he grabbed her chin, forcing her to look up at him. "You need a car, he had one to spare. You owe him nothing. This subject is done. The car is yours, period. Now, be a good girl and grab me one of your energy drinks, the one in the white can, not the nasty blue one."

She hated to admit defeat, but she knew when she had been beat. Besides, she desperately needed a car. And, what a car it was. "Kiss my ass, Orlando. You get me one. I have a thank you note to write," she demanded as she walked to her desk in a huff. His chuckle followed him to the fridge.

She searched through her drawers and found her nicest stationary. How did you thank someone for such an extravagant gift? She grabbed the energy drink Orlando brought her and popped the top. "Thank you, Cabana Boy," she smirked up at Orlando.

"Why I let you boss me around, I have no idea," he

called over his shoulder, before shutting himself inside the bathroom.

Staring back at the blank page, she considered everything. Zander's words caused flutters in her belly and warm tingles to spread through her body. She had never received such a provocative letter. Thoughts of skin and leather brought back her fantasy from the night before. Her guilt reared its ugly head, followed by a sense of betrayal. Still, she could not resist Zander.

"I have no words to express how grateful I am for such an extraordinary gift. It is way two expensive, but I have been advised to accept it. Besides, I know you'd order me to anyway, Mr. Bossy Pants. So, thank you. I plan to take it out for a spin and will tell you how it handles the curves. Always, Elsie"

She was not as eloquent with words, but she hoped her reply would relay her heartfelt gratitude.

CHAPTER FIFTEEN

Climbing into her car, Elsie lamented the loss of Zander's intoxicating scent. It had been three weeks since he had given her his car and she had become addicted to the earthy, masculine scent. It was way better than the smell of a new car! It aroused her and made her feel wanton. It made her think of hot, uninhibited sex. Her stomach tightened, and to her surprise, her groin moistened, readying her for the man who left his smell behind.

She wasn't ready to be with another man, but she had reasoned that there was no harm done, she was not actually sleeping with Zander. She did sneak out several times a day to drive to the corner store and was glad to find that the sharp edges of the black hole that had once consumed her entire being had dulled.

Familiar ire rose as her thoughts slid from Zander to her current situation. She had been forced to quit her job after her attack. Oh, she had gone in the next day, and several days after that, and tried performing her duties but the cast made it impossible and she was forced to admit defeat.

Consequently, Zander and Orlando, along with their

friends, had been helping her pay her bills. Over her rather boisterous objections, they had given her a check that would support her comfortably for three years or more.

The fact that the check was written from a charity, ultimately made her agree. Elsie's Hope had been formed by Zander and his sister, Breslin, in Elsie's honor to assist the families of murder victims. No other gesture had touched her so deeply, not even the fabulous car. Sure, she appreciated the car and other gifts, but this was a legacy she could help them leave behind. Something that would help countless other victims and she planned to pay back every cent they had given her.

Her cell phone rang and she fumbled in her purse. "Hey Mack. How's it going?" Mack had been a great support for Elsie since her husband had been killed and Elsie had missed doing patrols with Mack, but she was more of a liability with her cast than an asset.

"Hey girl. It's good. How are you feeling? How's the arm? I still can't fucking believe that you were attacked and I wasn't there to help. I promised you when you joined me that I would always have your back." Elsie could hear the anger and self-recrimination in her friend's voice.

"Mack. It's not your fault. It was those vampires. I was preoccupied and you taught me better than to allow my guard down." She contemplated telling Mack she suspected that Zander's brothers knew about vampires and she should recruit them for SOVA. She opened her mouth, but the words remained stuck. She wasn't entirely certain what was stopping her. They'd be an asset to have on their side. Especially Kyran, he had taken out two vamps without breaking a sweat. With them, they could rid the city of this threat with ease.

"Well, I'm glad you're okay. Before you know it, you'll be

back out there. Don't forget, our job as survivors is to take out the evil that preys on the innocent. That's the reason we survived. We can't stop until every last vampire goes up in flames. They are a plague on humanity and need to be exterminated. It's our mission. Nothing else matters." Having been victimized twice by these vampires, Elsie couldn't agree more. Being injured and unable to help right now really chapped her ass.

"I saw the doctor today and he said that my bones are healing nicely. Few more weeks and I should be back out there with you."

"Don't rush out too soon. The last thing I want is for you to injure yourself again. Don't worry, the rest of us are all still out there killing the bastards." All Elsie did was worry. She hated the thought that there were people out there being hurt and killed because there were vampires roaming the streets.

ELSIE LOVED the electric chopper she had purchased to help with her dinner preparations. The cast made it impossible for her to chop the veggies without it. Cooking was cathartic for her, and she hadn't prepared a full meal since Dalton died. It felt great to be in the kitchen again. And, she was glad to be cooking for her new friends. It was the least she could do for them.

"Put down that margarita and make yourself useful," she told Orlando. "I need the cornbread taken out of the oven. Then, you can pour me a margarita. I have to stir this roux, constantly."

Orlando came up behind her and looked over her

shoulder into the pot. "Who's the bossy one now? Mmmm, this smells great so far."

"Wait until you taste it." The black hole throbbed as she whisked her roux, thinking of Dalton and how much he loved her cooking. "This was one of his favorite meals, you know."

He put his arm around her shoulder and gave her a one-armed embrace. "I'm sure he loved everything you made. He loved you very much."

She gripped his hand where it rested on her shoulder. "I will always cherish the love we shared. A part of me is in that satin-lined box with him. I know I'm young and everyone keeps telling me that I have my entire life ahead of me, but it feels like the grief will never end."

"I know it's hard for you to accept, but you will have love again. It is your fate to have extraordinary love and happiness. Don't close yourself off to that."

The smell of burned flour reached her nostrils. "I hope you're right. Shit, the roux, it burned. Great, now I have to start over."

A comfortable silence descended over the kitchen as she hummed, cooked and drank. The sun set and darkness descended. She was wondering when the others would arrive right as there was a knock at the door. She watched them all file into her apartment and her heart skipped a beat when Zander walked in last, closing the door behind him. Their eyes locked on one another and she couldn't move. Time stood still.

She heard Rhys call out, "I brought some *hey juice,* so the party can now begin!"

She began placing the dishes next to the plates and utensils on her table and turned to Rhys. "You've been holding out on me. What, exactly, is *hey juice*?"

Rhys walked over to her and placed his large, muscular arm around her shoulders. "Well, sweet cheeks, *hey juice* is my top-secret mixture of the finest ingredients. Best part is, about twenty minutes after you drink it, I guarantee you will be rubbing on me saying 'hey baby' and begging to experience my... magnificence," Rhys said, waggling his eyebrows comically.

She burst out laughing, slid out of his embrace, and shook her head. "I sure hope women are smarter than that."

"Damn, bro, she put you in your place," Orlando laughed.

Zander walked up with a tall, voluptuous brunette who had Bhric's amber eyes. She was stunning. "Elsie, 'tis my sister, Breslin. She keeps us all in line." She exchanged pleasantries with Breslin, but was hyper-aware of Zander's presence. He towered more than a foot above her five-foot-four inch height.

He brushed up behind her, sending her up in flames. "The food is ready. Get it while it's hot," she croaked out. The man had a seriously devastating effect on her, and his clear desire unnerved her.

Everyone clamored to fill their plates and began eating. All the while, Zander was never far away from her and used every excuse to touch her. A brush of a hand here or a clasp of a shoulder there. It was driving her crazy.

She spent most of the evening fighting the heat that pooled in her stomach and resulted in moisture dripping from her core. She was inexorably aroused as his scent permeated her nostrils. It was tiring how her body waged its battle with arousal and remaining coherent. She didn't want to sit there like an idiot drooling over a good-looking man. *Get over yourself. I want some of that fine ass!* Her inner-sex-fiend taunted.

Zander pulled her onto his lap in the leather chair and whispered in her ear. "You look good enough to eat. I think I'll have you for dinner. Stop denying what you want," he murmured the order.

Their eyes locked and she finally managed, "I've told you, Mr. Bossy Pants, you can't order me around." He caressed her thigh and she allowed it. It felt too good to stop him.

She turned her head and smiled at the banter in her small apartment. Feeling his eyes on her, she was struck by the desire to kiss Zander, but they were surrounded by friends and his family. Not the time to share their first kiss. The sexual tension had been building between them for the past few weeks and when they finally did kiss, she had a feeling she wouldn't be able to stop.

She stood and went to get her plate. "So, when are you going to take me to this club you guys keep talking about?" she asked joining the conversation. Everyone looked to Zander as if waiting direction. She rolled her eyes. No wonder he gives orders and expects to be listened to.

Zander grinned, making him look even sexier, and responded, "Anytime you want. Say the word, *a ghra.*"

"Maybe we can go this weekend," she said as she settled on the couch next to Orlando and dug in. The food was delicious, just the right amount of spice and garlic. "I think I'll try some of that *hey juice.*"

She got up to get her drink when a hand on her arm stopped her. Zander handed her a glass of Rhys' concoction and she sipped it cautiously. Hmm, strong, but fruity and good. She imagined it would only take one glass of this to give her a good buzz.

"Thank you," she told Zander before turning to Orlando.

"Why haven't you told me about this club? You have been stuck on my couch for weeks and haven't been out once."

"I wasn't about to leave you alone. You couldn't possibly stay out of trouble without me here," Orlando teased her.

She laughed and a boisterous round of ribbing ensued. At some point, Zander gave Orlando one look and he stood up, allowing Zander to take the seat beside her. He took her hand in his and entwined their fingers. She couldn't help but laugh. The man didn't even have to use words to give his orders.

She was distracted by the soothing circles he rubbed with his thumb. It grounded her and settled her roiling emotions and stomach. She finished her food while enjoying this odd, but wonderful family. There was no doubt that this group of men, and Breslin, had indeed taken her in. She leaned back and settled her side more fully against Zander. It was nice to be close to his masculine warmth. Why did it feel so right?

ZANDER SILENTLY ORDERED everyone to leave Elsie's apartment. He couldn't take the torment any longer. Between his aching cock, his need for her blood, and the ever present pain in his mate mark he was close to losing it. She had been sitting next to him on the couch for hours and he could smell her arousal. Her anxiety rose until he smelled her fear as Orlando left last and closed the door. She turned to him and he placed his finger over her mouth stilling her words.

"Nay, doona think right now. I want you and you want me. Be with me," he pleaded.

He watched indecision cross her face and saw when her

lust won out. He wanted to shout in triumph, but wisely kept to himself. He didn't want to give her any reason to stop this.

"I'm scared," she admitted. "I've never been with anyone but—"

He cut off her response by lowering his lips to hers. The jolt of electricity that zapped him when they connected was exhilarating. He moved his mouth over hers, licking and coaxing hers open. The moment she parted her luscious lips, he delved deep, his tongue sliding sensuously against hers.

His mind blanked and all he could think was how badly he needed his mate. She was soft, her curves fitting perfectly against him. Her soul stretched and slid against his in an erotic caress. Being bombarded from the inside, as well as, out, nearly robbed him of his sanity and had him tearing her clothes from her body.

He trailed his mouth to nibble her pulse pounding in her neck and regained some composure. Her rich, earthy honeysuckle scent drove him on. He pulled her shirt aside and kissed her collarbone. Such delicate bones, so fragile. He wrapped his arms around her waist and tugged her into his lap.

"I always thought I'd stay faithful to Dalton, but now, all I can think is that I want more." She looked down and her cheeks tinged with pink. "What does that make me?"

He gripped her chin between his thumb and forefinger, making her meet his gaze. "You are perfect. And alive. He wouldn't want you to die with him. He will always be a part of you, a part of us. Doona allow the ghosts of the past to dictate your future."

He swiped at the tear glistening in her eyes and kissed her lightly. The moment the tension left her shoulders he deepened the kiss. He kept his ardor in check and made this kiss slower with less of the frenetic energy. She wrapped her arms around his neck and began to loosen up.

He trailed his hands down to rest on her hips. "What do you like, *a ghra*? What turns you on?"

He enjoyed the blush that tinted her cheeks. "Oh...I, uh...I don't really know. The usual, you know."

He chuckled and ran his hands across to her pert ass. It took a nanosecond of contact and he was ready to rip her clothing from her body again. He buried his face in the crook of her neck to hide his glowing eyes and fangs then began raining kisses on her sweet, velvety-soft skin. She shivered in his hold.

"I doona know what the usual is, Elsie." He had no idea what humans enjoyed. He had never been with one. The usual for him involved his fangs and what some thought of as rough sex. "You'll have to be specific with me. I give the orders, but I want you to tell me how to please you. I want to do this right." He wanted to be gentle with her. He wanted to make love to her and explore and savor every inch of her sultry body.

"Surely, you have been with a woman before. I can't believe that a man as good looking as you has never been with a woman," she told him as she arched into his embrace. He leaned down and sucked her breast into his mouth through the fabric. The flesh tightened and lengthened in response. He growled when her moan escaped.

He slid his hand under the fabric of her shirt and continued the sensual torture. "I have been with my share, but none of them has been you, lass. You are verra different. With you I have a connection that I have wanted for longer than I can recall. I want to know how to please you."

She ground her crotch over his erection, making him

moan. "I can see you like this, *a ghra*." He trailed his hand to her neglected breast and guided her movements with the other.

"Yeah, that's nice, but I want to touch your skin." She tugged his shirt over his head and tossed it to the ground.

"Your turn," he murmured and the rending of fabric echoed in the small room. Her eyes flew wide and he claimed her mouth again before the words left her mouth. She was soon squirming in his lap, driving him crazy.

Their tongues clashed together and he removed her bra while the room heated another degree. His hips rose as hers descended and the friction nearly robbed him of his seed. It was difficult to hide evidence of what he was, but he refused to let her see, she couldn't accept it, yet.

"How do you do this to me? I've never been like this before..." Her words trailed off when his hand skimmed her bare breast. He reveled in how responsive she was to him. He bet he could make her orgasm by suckling her breasts alone.

Her sounds of pleasure were matched by his. His hands were everywhere, exploring every silky inch and his mouth followed. Touching, tugging, tasting. Her hands fisted in his hair and clutched him close as if afraid he would pull away.

"Touch me, *a ghra*, I need to feel you," he implored as his hands went to her button. The sound of the zipper descending was loud and she stiffened in his arms. The sweat beading their bodies made her shiver. She panted on his lap and he felt her stiffen. He entered her thoughts and saw that she wanted to take things slowly between them, but didn't want to disappoint him. He needed to stop now or he would be going further than she was comfortable with. The first thing his mother taught him was that he should never push a female for more.

"What's wrong Zander?"

"Nothing is wrong. Everything is right. I'm rather old-fashioned and would like to take things slow. I hope that is alright."

"Slow is good. You're old-fashioned and I'm new at the whole dating game. We're a perfect combination," she said with a smile that spoke of her relief.

They had made more progress than he expected and held that close to his heart. He had waited over seven hundred years to have her and could wait a little longer.

CHAPTER SIXTEEN

"Where the hell are you? We're heading to Club Confetti and you're going, too. Time for that fun you were talking about," Orlando demanded when Elsie answered her phone.

Excitement built at the thought of finally going to the club the guys had talked so much about. She was reluctant to admit that she was anxious to see Zander again, too. It had been a week and she had been super busy with school papers at night, but when she had free time during the day, he wasn't able to see her. She would have been nervous that he'd lost interest in her, but Orlando had explained that Zander was busy with his business.

"I was at the grocery store, buying food for you. I'm tired of you complaining there is never anything in my house. Tonight might not be the best night. My friend, Mack wanted me to stop by now that my cast is off," she said, nervously checking her rearview mirror. She was anxious to go out with them, while, at the same time, she wanted to get back out on patrol with Mack. Thoughts of patrol made her wonder if she should broach the subject of vampires with Orlando.

"I'm at your apartment. Get your sweet-ass home. You're going out with us. Breslin even picked up some clothes for you to wear tonight. And, Zander is going to meet us there. Said he was eager to see you tonight."

And, just like that, her desire ignited and she no longer wanted to take it slow. It was unreal the mere mention of his name made her lust go wild. "Oh, alright, twist my arm. I'm pulling in right now." She grabbed the groceries from her trunk and raced to her front door.

He pulled the door open before she reached her stoop. "I'll trade you," he took the bags and handed her a box. "Tell me more about Mack and why haven't I met her?"

From behind the bathroom door, she gave him a brief rundown of how she met MacKendra careful to keep out any reference to SOVA. She pondered how to bring up the subject of vampires as she lifted the lid and saw a new iPhone in a sleek, black case. It had a raised, silver, Celtic cross on the back. Beautiful and it had to be from Zander. The guy was always giving her gifts. He was persistent, she'd give him that. She pressed the button and saw a text message waiting.

"I look forward to dancing with you this evening. I haven't stopped thinking of you since the other night. If you ever need or want me, I'll always be one touch away. Your Z."

With flutters in her belly, she typed a reply.

"You continue to amaze me. Deeper indebted to you, I only hope I can find a way to repay everything you have done for me. I look forward to dancing with you. Until later..."

Setting the phone aside and saw that Breslin had given her a designer dress and shoes. The dress was a gorgeous rose-gold that had a lustrous, metallic-bandage construction. It was tailored with a flattering cross-front bodice and low-V neckline. She tuned out what Orlando was saying on the other side of the door while she eyed the clothing.

The shoes were a pair of six-inch-platform sandals that had a glittery snake-print. Only celebrities wore designer clothes like this. They probably cost more than she made in a month. She slid into the dress. It fit her like a sensual glove and the shoes made her legs look a mile long.

Even without her hair or make-up done, she felt like a supermodel. She had never worn anything so exquisite before. Nor, had she ever felt sexier and she was anxious to see Zander's reaction. Thinking about that was dangerous. He said he wanted to take it slowly, but she was ready to explore every luscious inch of him. She may not be experienced and may fumble through things, but she wanted him too much to allow that to matter anymore.

She set about doing her hair and makeup and refocused on her discussion with Orlando.

"So, Mackendra told me something that I wanted to ask you about since you are a big, bad detective."

She heard his laughter before he responded. "I am big, but I'm not bad, cupcake. I can hear the worry in your voice. What did Mackendra tell you?"

"Well, this may sound crazy, but she said that vampires are real and they stalk the city at night."

"Wow. Not what I was expecting you to say. Do you believe her?" The nervousness in Orlando's voice caused her to smear her eyeliner across her temple. Wetting a cotton ball so she could fix the disaster on her face, she hesitated in her reply.

She wiped at the black smudge and replied, "I have been through enough to not dismiss what she said outright. I saw that guy's fangs and felt them sink into my arm. And, they both had unbelievable strength and speed when they attacked me. I wasn't strong enough to fight them both off and would have been killed if Bhric and Kyran hadn't been there that night. I'm...not sure what to think."

"So, you believe vampires exist."

"Yes I do, and I question if there could be more creatures out there that we are unaware of. I never did buy the TwiKill bullshit the media reported. What about you, O? What do you think?" she asked pushing him to answer, as she stepped out of the bathroom. She reveled in the way his emerald eyes bulged, his body went taut, and his mouth dropped open. Confirmation, she looked as good as she felt.

"I think you look un*fucking*believable! And, we're late, let's go," he croaked.

FALLING OFF THE BAR SEAT, Zander's shaft stiffened and his fangs shot down the instant Elsie walked in with Orlando. Every nerve-ending in his body came to life. She was a gorgeous faerie with her petite frame, long brown hair, and Scottish-loch-blue eyes. The rose color of her dress enhanced her peaches-and-cream complexion and the lights reflected off her glittery high-heels. Stunning.

Each step she took drew every eye in the club. Thankfully, he had asked Killian to keep supernaturals whose differences were obvious out of the club tonight. It was one of the reasons it had taken so long to arrange a night for her in their club. Hangouts for those with features that clearly set them apart from humans were few and far between. He owed Kill big for this, but it was worth it to see his mate in that dress.

Her hips swayed like a pendulum as she walked next to Orlando and he wanted to tear apart every male lusting after his mate. Who could resist her mile-long legs in those come-fuck-me heels? His black, Armani pants were unable to hide his obvious desire. As she approached the group, he shut his eyes against the lust glowing brightly behind his lids. Luckily, she was busy greeting his siblings and warriors. Goddess, but he wanted to caress every inch of her gorgeous body. He remembered exactly how soft and sensual she felt in his arms. He longed for a full taste of her and wasn't certain how he would make it through the evening without taking her body and blood, claiming her at long last.

Lena sidled up behind him. "*Mon coeur*, I can help with that. Come, let's go to our room," she purred, reaching around to stroke his erection.

He had been so engrossed in ogling Elsie that he had not heard Lena approach. His mate made the world around him vanish. As the vampire king, and leader of the Dark Warriors, he could not afford such distractions. He closed his eyes to reign in his temper as she stroked his now flaccid cock through his pants. Elsie's soul was clawing in his chest wanting to tear into the female. He not-so-gently removed Lena's hand from his groin.

"Lena, I told you, I have found my Fated Mate, and there willna be another for me!" He turned abruptly before he said or did something he would regret, and walked toward his destiny.

∾

ELSIE WAS LAUGHING with Rhys as he offered her some of his

hey juice when she felt a pull from across the table. "I'd love some of that *hey...*" she trailed off, drawing out the last word the moment she locked eyes with Zander. Her heart skipped a beat.

She couldn't take her eyes from his perfectly-chiseled features. His countenance screamed aristocracy, power, and ruthlessness. He was tall, even in her heels she had to look up at him. He had to be six and a half feet tall easily. He had black stubble across his square jaw and his full, luscious lips were tilted at the corners as if he knew her thoughts. She looked into his piercing, sapphire-blue eyes and blushed at how he was undressing her.

He was definitely the most gorgeous man she had ever seen. Normally, she disliked long hair on men, but his shoulder-length black hair was fitting. It flowed freely around his broad shoulders, mesmerizing her. Her entire frame trembled as she read what was in his eyes...sex. And, not just any sex, but wild, uninhibited, can't-walk-the-next-day sex. Exactly what she wanted.

She craned her neck as he stopped so close to her, she felt the heat emanating from his body and she went up in flame like dry tinder. Silence descended over the group, intensifying the moment.

"Shit, I hope my mate eye-fucks me like that when I finally find her," Santiago murmured so low that she questioned if she heard him correctly.

"Yeah, I'm on the edge and need to find a female soon. The sexual tension between them is as thick as I am at the moment," Rhys groaned. That one was unmistakable.

From the corner of her eye she noted that Kyran hit the backs of both their heads. "Shut the hell up, you arseholes. Show some respect."

Her curiosity about the men's comments was short-lived

when Zander enveloped her hand and kissed her knuckles, letting his lips linger a moment. "Nine circles, you look absolutely ravishing. And, I am starving for you."

She blushed at his words and closed her eyes as the lilt of his accent washed over her. The timbre of his voice caressed her body. It was a full-body caress. Sensual and promising. She had no right thinking like that, but no one had ever looked at her like this man did. In fact, no one had ever worshipped her like this. The desire in his gaze had her nerves back on edge.

"Thank you, but I can't take credit, it's the dress and shoes. Breslin did a great job of picking this out." She forced herself to break contact and turned to Breslin. "Thank you for the fabulous clothes. I have never owned anything this exquisite."

Breslin smiled, "You are verra welcome." The woman leaned close and whispered in her ear. "I hoped it would drive my *brathair* mad with how he wants you and I was right." Elsie flushed and was caught in the trap of Zander's sapphire-blues as she reached for her drink.

"I would normally be angry at my *puithar's* interference, but this time I couldna be more thankful."

"You look fantastic, as well. Of course, I am partial to your leather pants but these..." she ran her hot gaze over his body. "I'm sure you are aware how sexy you are."

"I almost wore my leathers, but I havena been able to think straight when I put them on. I keep recalling what it felt like when you were in the hospital and rubbed my... trews." It hadn't all been a dream. Oh God, had she actually been rubbing on him? She flushed with embarrassment and buried her face in her hands, wanting to crawl in a hole.

He grabbed her hands from her face and kissed each of

her fingertips. Her cheeks were hot and she knew they had to be cherry-red. He pulled her against his chest. "Never fear, my Lady E, I enjoyed every minute of it and your words incited a passion I have never experienced. A passion I crave every moment," his breath whispered hotly against her ear, causing shivers to race through her blood, followed by a burning heat.

"I rather like being called Dr. McYummy. You can eat me up any time you want," he growled, licking the shell of her ear.

"No fair," she breathed, hoping to regain composure before her panties flooded. She stepped back and put some space between their bodies. The situation was heading places they couldn't indulge in at the bar. "I thought that was a dream, but you can eat me up any time you want. If you're real lucky, I may return the favor." She met his eyes and felt the breath leave her body. No one had ever looked at her with such raw yearning and she didn't know how to respond.

She finally looked away from that unsettling gaze and searched the bar, for what, she did not know. Numerous women, who were far better-looking than her, were ready to swoop in and devour him. *Back off, bitches, he's off limits.* That was uncalled for, and she was mystified by her jealousy. "Sorry, I assumed too much. I can see that there will be no shortage of opportunities for you here. There are countless women vying for your attention as we speak."

"I'm no' the one who is wanted. I have counted no less than twenty males who have stripped, tongued, and tupped you in their minds, every which way from Sunday, since you walked in that door." He was so close that she felt his breath across her lips as he spoke. Her mouth watered.

"You couldn't be more wrong," she replied and suddenly, she needed space. "Excuse me. I need to use the restroom." She had to collect herself.

He placed his hands on her waist and turned her in his grasp. "Of course, *a ghra,* the lasses room is over there." He extended one strong arm over her shoulder and pointed the way before his hands settled back on her hips.

She shivered as he squeezed her possessively and his fingers skimmed her lower back. She forced herself to walk to the bathroom, when every fiber of her being wanted to turn around and ravish him.

Her heart was pounding at the walls of her chest in an unfamiliar manner. She wasn't a virgin, and yet, she had never experienced arousal so insistent and all-consuming. Her inner-sex-fiend was doing a happy dance in anticipation of a night of primal sex.

Recalling how thick and large his erection had felt beneath her, she entered the bathroom. The intense desire was disconcerting, to say the least. She had never considered herself wild, but at the moment, she was anything but civilized. She walked to the sink and washed her hands, using a damp cloth to wipe away the sweat that covered her décolletage.

A gorgeous woman entered the bathroom and stood behind her at the mirror. The woman was tall with long, silky, blond hair, large breasts, and the face of a supermodel. *What is it with these women and their big boobs?* The woman even had perfect skin. She couldn't detect one pore on her lovely face. She instantly disliked her and it had nothing to do with her beauty. Her instincts were going haywire.

"I couldn't help but notice you were with the Dark Warriors and *my* Zander. We haven't met, I'm Lena." She took out a tube of lipstick and applied the pale-pink color to her bee-stung lips as she made eye contact with Elsie. "*Mon tressor* is quite the specimen, *non*?"

Now she understood why she hated this woman. She was staking claim on Zander. Her heart fell to her stomach when she wondered if Zander had moved on in the past week and that was why he had avoided her. She hadn't asked if he was seeing anyone new. "I'm Elsie. I don't know any Dark Warriors. I'm here with my friends."

Lena straightened from the mirror and adjusted her skin-tight sweater. "Oh yes, Elsie. You must be the one Zander started the human charity for. He is so giving to those of a lesser station."

This bitch was cray-freakin'-cray! How dare she look down her nose at me? Didn't she know slut-gear was out? "Not that this is your business, but Zander has been spending a lot of time at my place. Funny, he's never mentioned you. Is he your boyfriend?"

Lena pasted an innocent smile on her face, but Elsie wasn't buying it. This bitch was bad news. "*Oui*, Zander is mine. I'm glad he's done giving you your two minutes. I plan on taking him back to our private room. He can never get enough of me and it will be hours before we return. What he does to me...truly mind-blowing," her smile turned calculating. "You're nothing more than a charity case, certainly not something he'd mate with. Zander would never be attracted to a lowly serf like you."

Her hackles went up and she felt a surge of malice. "Oh, he's far more than attracted. And, something tells me he won't be up for you anytime soon. My guess is you will have to wait," she was unable to keep the disgust off her face as her gaze roamed Lena from head to foot, "indefinitely."

Where had this possessiveness come from? She had to leave the restroom before her nails dug into that flawless face. Turning sharply on her heels, she strutted back to Zander and the others. *Lowly serf, my ass.*

CHAPTER SEVENTEEN

Zander sensed the fury rolling from Elsie's body as she stomped up to the group and snatched Orlando's drink from his hand. Downing it in one gulp, she muttered, "I needed that more than you. Psycho-bitch back there wants to mate Zander or some shit. What kind of place did you bring me to? More importantly, can you get me another drink, please?" she asked a speechless Orlando then turned to Zander.

His body rippled with desire, she was the most beautiful sight he had ever seen and it overshadowed what she'd said. Eyes glittering with barely contained anger, irritation flowing beneath her skin. So damn sexy!

"I met your girlfriend, Zander, and I'm afraid I wasn't nice to her. I don't know what came over me. The words flew out of my mouth. When I thought of you inside that *thing* in there, I lost my mind, and I have no idea why. Why didn't you tell me you had a girlfriend? We got very intimate the other night," she hissed, waving her hands, speaking with her entire body.

She wasn't making any sense so he read her scathing

thoughts. She believed he belonged to another female and questioned his integrity with all his flirting and sexual innuendos. She was wrong and making incorrect assumptions, but her mind was too chaotic for him to determine who was responsible. Before he could correct her, she continued her litany, "Go find your woman. I don't even want to be around you right now."

She turned her back on Zander and put her palm out toward him, a clear indication she wanted nothing to do with him at the moment. Little did she know he was going nowhere, there were things to set straight. Elsie ignored him and kept her back to him. "Can someone explain who the Dark Warriors are, please? Orlando?"

He grabbed her by the arm and turned her around to face him. He saw her irritation rise. He needed to calm his mate. Between the guilt, anger, lust, grief, and now this jealousy, she no longer knew which way was up. But, he did revel in the fact that she had possessive feeling toward him. There was hope for them, yet.

He cut off what he had no doubt would be a reprimand from his feisty mate. "Listen to me, *a ghra,* I doona have a girlfriend." He lowered his head until their faces were scant inches apart, her heavenly breath falling softly against his lips. "There is no other female for me. 'Tis you I want. To be verra clear, I want to learn every inch of your alluring body, while I explore it with my tongue for hours, before I sink into heaven. I know we are taking it slow, but I wouldna have another female."

He was pushing the envelope and he knew it, but he couldn't stop now. It didn't help that every breath he took brought her honeysuckle scent into his aroused system. She stood staring at him with her mouth open, clearly stunned silent. The dilation of her pupils, the deepening scent of her arousal, and her racing heart were what ultimately urged him on.

He stepped closer to her and she gasped, her thoughts turning sensual. He allowed a carnal smile to cross his lips when she imagined him feasting on her body. He relished her fantasies about him.

Even though he was ready for full-throttle, she was not. "Lass, I doona want to make you uncomfortable, but know that when I am around you, I lose all good sense. Never doubt that you are it for me."

She shook her head and her long, curly, brown hair danced around her shoulders with the movement. "That woman was convinced that you were hers. There is a reason she believes that so ardently. Don't worry about me."

She turned to the rest of the group, "Come on Santi, I know you're itching for some relief, so go get 'em. Show me those skills with the ladies you are always bragging about." She motioned Santiago to the throng of women nearby, and threw down the second shot of tequila that Orlando had brought to her.

Zander understood she was on edge and wanted to alleviate some of the tension, but when she grabbed some *hey juice* from Rhys and threw it back, he realized she was drinking too much too fast. He tried to read her thoughts again to discover who placed this wedge between he and his mate, but heard the same chaos. He wanted to throttle someone for upsetting his mate when the evening had begun with such promise.

"Oh, and Zander, I just wanted you to know, this lowly serf appreciates all you have done." What was this about a lowly serf? She was the Vampire Queen. He may have wanted to change her fragile human state, but that had nothing to do with him believing she was less than him or anyone else. He could lose her to anything from a cold to a car accident before they fully mated. Just the thought had him breaking out in a sweat.

His mate had no idea of the grasp she had on his heart. How she controlled him. "Oh, my Lady E, I love your sharp claws. I doona know where your ideas came from, but from where I stand you are a queen." Little did she know how true that statement really was. He bowed down, reaching out to grasp her hands, "Dance with me."

She couldn't hold back her laugh. "Bad idea, I've got two left feet. I'd probably fall and ruin this dress and I really like it. I'm fine here with the liquor."

She waved him off, but he grabbed her hand before she could down another drink. She had much to learn, his mate. His body would implode if he didn't get closer to her. Placing the drink on the table, he lifted her out of her chair and tucked her close to his chest. Where she was meant to be. Goddess, she felt so right.

He leaned down to whisper in her ear, "I would rather you take hold of me, instead." He canted his hips so she felt the erection that was itching to get to her. "That, lass, is for you. Now, you will dance with me."

He smiled at the roll of her eyes, but didn't pause to allow her to deny him. She pouted as he led her to the dance floor, grumbling about, "Mr. Bossy Pants." His saucy mate began dancing as a path in the crowd opened up for them. She was feeling cocky from the alcohol, letting inhibitions fall. His heart raced as he watched her move sinuously to the pounding beat of the music. He didn't know why she felt she had two left feet. She knew exactly how to move her body. He could imagine her writhing beneath him in pleasure.

His mark pulsed painfully at the thought of completing

the mating. It was getting to the point that it was almost unbearable. He wondered how much worse it was going to get. He had to believe they would eventually complete the ritual and bind their lives together, but doubt was an insidious creature that had wormed its way in and worsened right along with the pain.

His eyes glued to the pulse pounding in her throat, amplifying his needs. His fangs elongated, again, and his eyes glowed with his desire. Little Zander wanted to play. The little minx turned her back and taunted him. He hardened and lengthened while she rubbed her ass against his groin in a very, suggestive manner.

Control lost, he grabbed her up and brought his lips crashing down on hers.

ELSIE WAS ON FIRE. The moment Zander claimed her mouth, her body went up in flames and she melted into his arms. The hard press of his mouth was dominant and skilled, seeking her capitulation. The feel of him licking her lips made her heart race. She opened her mouth and he plundered her depths. Unable to hold back her pleasure, she made a sound in the back of her throat and wrapped her arms around his neck. Her fingers slid into his hair and she practically climbed up his body. She needed more.

She kissed him back with as much fervor as he had kissed her. She nipped and bit at his full, lower lip. The growl that came out of him was electric. The alcohol had freed her and she shoved aside any doubt. She wanted this kiss and was going to take it. She had suffered enough in her life. It was high time for her to get something out of it. And, she wasn't about to pass up this hot guy. Their tempo

changed and became less frantic, more of a leisurely exploration. She wanted urgent and crazed but he teased her
with the slow pace, making her dig her fingernails into his
back.

He grabbed her up against his body, her feet left the
floor and she tried to rub against him. She nearly ripped her
dress so she could wrap her legs around his torso and align
her core with the massive erection prodding her belly.
Apparently, she wasn't all that attached to the dress. It was
difficult to remember that they were on the dancefloor of a
crowded bar, but somehow modesty got through to the
wanton creature she had become. She lowered the leg that
had lifted and wound around his hip, wondering if she had
flashed the room her panties.

She pushed against his chest, needing space, but he
didn't budge. He was breathing as hard as she was and
stared deeply into her eyes. It was as if he saw straight to her
soul, causing a warm flutter to spread from her chest
outward. The emotion in his eyes seared her to the bone.
There was so much there and it frightened her. She didn't
think she could be everything he seemed to want, no
woman could.

A flash caught her attention. She cocked her head to the
side. His eyes seemed to glow under the dance lights. "You
are no' getting away. We've just gotten started. We're going to
dance. Come here."

She was coming to like this side of him as she realized
his demand had settled her chaotic emotions. "I told you,
Zander, you can't—"

His lightly kissed her, cutting off her words, "I can and I
will, *a ghra*." He gave a sharp shake of his head when she
would have retorted. One sway of his hips was all it took to
coax her back into dancing. He moved against her and she

couldn't help but move to the music with him. She knew she was taunting a tiger, unfortunately that didn't stop her.

She enjoyed the rush of power she felt when she thought of making this big, strong man weak in the knees for her. She had never felt more sexy and sensual, dancing against him. Peeking over her shoulder at his groin, she realized she couldn't push him too far, or he would be making a rather impressive appearance.

She smiled at him, mesmerized by the way the lights played in his sapphire-blue eyes. Their bodies continued their sensual dance. They were making love with their dance and she had to put some distance between her and the extremely, large bulge in his pants or it wouldn't just be a dance. He wanted her and she could tell he was fighting that desire. With his penchant for expecting to have his orders followed she imagined this was hard on him.

She was grateful for his restraint because with the jealousy and possessiveness and her inexperience with men, she was in over her head. Like a savior, Breslin joined them, ending the possibility their clothes were going to go flying. Unfortunately, Breslin's presence did nothing to diminish Elsie's arousal. She needed to cool down and fanned herself as she met Zander's eyes.

"I havena enjoyed myself this much for more years than I can recall. I'm going to drive you home, *a ghra*. You've had too much to drink. At least, that is my excuse, because, I doona want this time with you to end."

HONEYSUCKLE ENVELOPED ZANDER as he sat on Elsie's sofa. He closed his eyes, inhaling slow and deep. He had given up trying to gain control of his body. It was a futile effort. From the moment she walked into the club, his cock and fangs had developed a mind of their own. And, they were in agreement. They wanted to sink deeply into his female's delectable flesh. The mating compulsion was drawing her to him, but she was reticent. Her body wanted him, no doubt, and he would push the issue, but he wanted her to come to him. There was so much that could go wrong and cause her to shut him out.

The one thing he was certain of, he needed to tell her the truth of him and the world he belonged to. Someone with her integrity and intelligence would not respond well to lies or prolonging such an important secret. Besides, she was a member of a vigilante group that battled what they believed were vampires and he needed her to know the difference. But could he bare his vulnerabilities? Could he risk it all?

Yes, he would risk everything to gain the love of his mate. He had no other choice, but he would make sure she was unarmed when he told her.

Zander voiced his inner thoughts to Orlando. "I'm going to tell her aboot me, the realm, all of it. I canna keep this from her any longer. I willna have our relationship continue with a lie, she would never forgive or accept me."

Orlando coughed and spewed the beer he had been drinking all over the front of his fitted sweater. "Liege, have you lost your mind? One, she is drunk. Two, she still grieves for her husband. And three, she is a human who prowls the night killing vampires. She will freak the fuck out over this news. You need to give her time."

"I have given her time, and have barely survived on the small amounts of blood Jace procured for me. I canna go on like this," he raked his hands through his hair and hung his head. "And, neither can she. The mating compulsion is affecting her just as much. I can hear her thoughts, torn between wanting to shred my clothes and being frightened of what she is feeling. You doona understand this, yet, but the mating makes you mindless with need. These emotions will drive her insane. I willna sit by and watch my mate suffer any longer. 'Tis my duty to provide for and protect her."

He appreciated Orlando's concern for his mate and knew the warrior had Elsie's best interests at heart, but this wasn't up for debate. "I'm doing this, and I would like for you to remain here and help me. Och, as much as I have hated your closeness to her, you guys have developed a friendship and she may be more accepting with you present."

Like air hissing out of a tire, Orlando sighed in defeat. "This entire situation blows. I get what you're saying, but you might regret this. I have been with her from the beginning, and will not abandon her now."

Zander fisted handfuls of his hair, wishing there was an easier path for them. "I will regret this if I doona tell her now. I pray she will eventually accept me."

CHAPTER EIGHTEEN

Wrestling with the dress, Elsie finally managed to reach the zipper. She swayed in her tiny bathroom, still buzzed from her drinks at the club. Thoughts rattled around in her head. Questions about Zander and the emotions he evoked in her. The dance they had shared kept playing through her mind wreaking havoc on her libido. Her yearning for him was overpowering. *Get a grip!*

He and Orlando were waiting in her living room. She had insisted Orlando leave Confetti with them as her buffer. She didn't trust herself alone with the irresistible Zander. Plus, she was on edge. From Mackendra, to Zander, to Lena, the entire day had brought an endless stream of questions and confusion. Man, she needed another drink.

She could hear the hushed conversation between Zander and Orlando. Zander's sexy baritone sent shivers down her spine. That man played her body like a fine tuned instrument. Needing as many barriers as she could put between them, she threw on her granny-panties and her favorite, flannel pajamas. She hoped her appearance wouldn't reveal how she was truly feeling at the moment, which was aroused and ready for a night of unending passion.

Finally, she exited the bathroom, hiding there all night wasn't an option. Zander was clearly not leaving anytime soon, and Orlando had all but moved in with her after her attack. She noticed they were huddled close to each other and took a seat in the chair. Her buzz was wearing off and she was getting a headache. "O, can you get me a Monster, please? I can't seem to move another muscle."

"How about some water? A Monster will keep you up all night."

She jumped from her seat. "Okay then, I'll get my own. Would you like anything, Zander?" *Me, naked, and spread on my bed.* She cursed herself and stormed into the kitchen.

Zander followed her into the kitchen. His gaze was intense and disturbing. "I'd like a great many things, *a ghra.*"

His closeness and innuendo were unnerving. Not to mention, how delicious he smelled. An eternity passed as she lost herself in his beautiful, blue eyes. She memorized the way the lighter-blue color starburst out from his pupils. The deep, sapphire-blue morphed to...glowing, bright-blue. Huh? "What's wrong with your eyes?" she blurted.

Dread crossed his gorgeous face, but was gone before she blinked. "I will explain that, but please, come sit down, Elsie. I have something to share with you."

Total buzzkill. Quickly sobering, she skirted around the hulking man and plopped down onto the couch. Her heart was beating like a scared rabbit from her panic and fear. What did he have to tell her? That Lena was his girlfriend? That he knew she hunted vampires? That he thought she was crazy for believing other creatures existed?

He sat next to her and picked up her hand. He played

with her fingers and palm. "This is difficult and I know you're no' going to like it, but I beg you to please hear me oot." She watched his face scrunch up as he struggled with his words for several minutes.

"You are correct. Vampires are real. In fact, other beings, such as shifters, sorcerers, imps, cambions, and so many more, exist as well." He looked up and met her flabbergasted gaze. "We are members of the Tehrex Realm."

Of course vampires were real. She had killed several of them over the past year. Although, she'd never encountered any of the other creatures he'd mentioned. Her rapid breaths huffed through her ears as his words sunk in. But, he had said *we*, meaning *he* was part of something. She wouldn't ask, didn't want to know. If he was a vampire that would make him her enemy. She quickly thought about her knife that was safely tucked under her pillow. Her fingers itched to wrap around the comforting grip.

The words flew out of her mouth anyway. "What do you mean by, *we* are members of the Tehrex realm? What are you? Do you kill people, too?" Shaking with fear, she looked to Orlando, seeking protection. He looked worried and uneasy. What did he have to do with this? It struck her that he wasn't surprised by Zander's words. Was he a vampire too?

Zander swallowed thickly. "I am a vampire, and nay, I doona kill people. Vampires are not the same as the creatures you have been hunting." He held her gaze with brightly glowing eyes. His eyes really did glow. Her heart broke as the truth sunk in, he was her enemy. Mack would be so disappointed in her. No matter what, she didn't want to kill this man, well vampire.

"You and your cohorts in SOVA doona have the correct information, lass. The Tehrex Realm, and the stratum of beings that exist within it, were created by the Goddess Morrigan. Many centuries ago, a demon attacked our leaders and started a war. I became the Vampire King when my father was killed. Many humans have been killed by the demons and their skirm. The vile creatures who harmed you, and killed Dalton are skirm, *no'* vampires. Skirm are your enemy, not me or mine." He took a deep breath. She watched him closely. He didn't look anything like the vampires, or skirm, if he were to be believed, she'd been fighting. His eyes were a beautiful blue with no charcoal ring. He didn't seem crazed and she hadn't seen fangs in his mouth. All vampires she had ever encountered had fangs.

As if hearing her thoughts he continued speaking. "Skirm are mindless creatures controlled by the demon that turned them. They doona have retractable fangs like vampires. Skirm drain their victims when they feed. Vampires need blood to survive, but doona kill. I eat, sleep, breathe and have a beating heart, exactly like you." She would have been more bothered by the fact that he had clearly answered her thoughts, but her sister had that ability.

Her head swam with too much information as he continued talking. "For the most part, supernaturals are good creatures. Of course, as with humans, there are always exceptions. Skirm, however, lose all humanity when they are transformed. One of the first changes I made after the war was to form the Dark Warriors. Orlando, Santiago, and all of the others you have met are a part of this group. They protect humans, as well as, creatures of the realm."

Her hands shook as she set her drink on the floor. "I don't even know what to say. Are you going to kill me now that you've told me this?"

She hated how desire burned through her when he

gently took her hands and clasped them between his large palms. How could her body still want this man, thing, whatever the hell he was? It made her sick to her stomach.

"*A ghra*, you are in no danger. I would never harm you. You mean more to me than you can imagine."

"How can that be? Nothing I thought I knew about you is true. You aren't even a man. What are you, Orlando? You've been awfully quiet. Are you a vampire, too?" She played through all her interactions with these two men. How did she miss this?

Orlando's voice brought her head up. "It's easier if I show you what I am. But, promise me you won't freak out and run off screaming like a girl," Orlando pleaded.

Elsie glared at Orlando. She opened her mouth to deliver her scathing reply, only to have her jaw drop open when he slid his fingers into the waistband of his pants then pushed them, along with his boxer briefs, to the floor in one sinuous move. His shirt followed suit. She knew that Orlando was fit, though she had no idea how well-defined and muscular his body was. He was a good-looking man, but did nothing to arouse the craving in her that Zander did.

She liked the druidic-tribal tattoo on his left forearm. Her gaze continued down and she noted that he was well-endowed. She stared at the floor, ignoring the fact how uncomfortable she was. She didn't know what she was about to encounter and to top it all off, Orlando was standing there naked. She had no desire to see all his bits and pieces. He was like a brother to her.

"Elsie, look at me," Orlando commanded.

"What do..." her response died when Orlando's body wavered. It was difficult to see what was happening through the bright light that emanated from him. The light was so bright she had to squint, but he appeared to be changing shape. His face shrunk, along with his limbs and body. Skin rippled along his back and fur sprouted. Actual fur covered his entire body. Before she blinked, he was on all four legs and had become the white cat she had first met at the cemetery.

She was cemented to the sofa, utterly speechless. She had allowed that cat into her house countless times. She was stunned. She had suspected there were other creatures roaming the night besides the evil vampires. Well, evil skirm, if Zander was to be believed. Orlando's body wavered again. Blinking against the bright light, she saw his form began to expand and grow. The fur remained white while he transformed into the largest snow-leopard she had ever seen.

He had to be at least five feet high on all fours, and over seven feet from head to tail. She noticed that no matter what shape he took, his eyes remained that familiar, bright, emerald-green. She realized his patch of black fur was in the same location as the tattoo on his arm.

"Oh my God! Orlando, is that you? Do you understand me?" She gaped as she stared at the most beautiful animal she had ever seen. The snow-leopard strode carefully to her side, obviously not wanting to scare her and nudged her leg with his nose. Her hand hesitantly reached out and her fingers stroked his fur briefly. It was as soft as silk. She yanked it back, wondering what was going on around her.

Zander's voice was gruff and guttural when he ordered, "Shift." She heard the emotion in Zander's voice and couldn't allow herself to be swayed by how upset he was.

The snow-leopard backed away from her, shifting to human form. She watched as Orlando calmly pulled his pants on and then sat on the couch, her mind whirling.

"I'm a feline shifter and can take the form of any cat.

And, yes, I can understand you, but I can't respond. Are you okay, El? You're white as a sheet. Please say something," Orlando pleaded.

"I'm abso*fucking*lutely not okay. I don't even know where to begin. I knew there were other creatures out there, but I had no idea people could change into animals. And, to see it with my own eyes," she shook her head, confused. "Are you like a werewolf who kills people? You say vampires aren't evil that what I have been fighting is skirm. How do I know you are telling me the truth? I know what I've seen. What I've lived through."

"No, I'm not a werewolf and, honestly, we take offense to the term. We prefer to be called shifters. El, I've been living with you for weeks now. You know me. I am no more evil than you. I hunt the bad guys, supernatural and human, alike," Orlando reassured.

"Lass, we are no' the creatures you believe. We are still the same males you have come to know. I hate to see that fear in your eyes. None of us would ever hurt you," Zander replied. He reached out to stroke her cheek and she flinched away from him.

"I can't believe this. It's difficult to simply trust what you are saying. For over a year now I have been killing what I thought were vampires and now I'm supposed to believe they weren't the same as you." She struggled to accept the reality they presented. She felt betrayed by all of them. They had been lying to her and keeping an enormous secret this whole time. Could she ever trust them again?

She had begun to feel like she was a part of a family again, but now she didn't know what was real and what wasn't. "I need you both to leave and don't send any of your guys to my apartment. I need to be alone right now." They both sat, staring at her and when they didn't move she yelled, "Leave, now!"

SHARP CLAWS SHREDDED Zander's heart into pieces in his chest. He never truly believed his mate would reject him, but that is exactly what she had done. His biggest fear had come true. He had a new appreciation for the pain she referred to as her black hole, for he had developed one of his own. He was jealous of the red, chenille blanket she had wrapped around herself as she curled up in the chair. It should be his arms comforting her. His chest she curled into. Her eyes screamed she hated him and wanted nothing to do with him, ever again.

He turned to leave when her tears started, but found it impossible to go out the door. "I know 'tis a lot to take in. You're hurt and angry that we didna tell you this sooner, but understand that our mission is to keep humans and the Tehrex Realm safe. Your mission with SOVA posed an unknown threat that I was obligated to evaluate before arming you with information that could harm countless innocent beings. We all love and care for you. That was never a lie. I will be here if you need me." He shut the door, leaving his heart in the hands of his Fated Mate.

ENOUGH CRYING, Elsie chastised. Call your sister. Cailyn would know what to do. She always knew what to do, she was her voice of reason. Grabbing the cell phone Zander had given her, one more reminder that the creatures of her nightmares had infiltrated her life, she called her sister.

Cailyn answered on the second ring. "Is everything okay? What's going on?"

She felt guilty about calling past midnight when she heard her sister's groggy voice. "I'm not hurt, at least, not physically. I need to talk to you. I'm sorry for calling so late, but this can't wait."

She heard the rustling of sheets and imagined Cailyn sitting up in bed. "You know you can call anytime, day or night. Now tell me, what's wrong. Your thoughts are all jumbled. I can't make sense of anything."

"What I'm about to tell you is going to sound crazy, but trust me, it's real." With a shaky voice, she told her sister what she had learned from Zander and Orlando about the creatures of the Tehrex Realm and the skirm who had killed Dalton. She purposely left out how she had been hunting skirm with SOVA for over a year.

"So, you're telling me that you actually saw your friend, Orlando, change into that cat from the cemetery. And then, he turned into a giant, white leopard? Unbelievable." Elsie heard the awe in her sister's voice.

"That's all you have to say? Unbelievable? This is a big deal, Cai." How could her sister be so calm, when, once again, the fabric of her world was crumbling?

Cailyn released a heavy sigh and adopted her mother-tone. "First of all, it's three in the morning, and I'm half-asleep. Second, these men, or whatever, have gone above and beyond in their support of you. They have given you an expensive car and enough money to live comfortably for years. They have never harmed you in any way and it's obvious they care deeply." She wasn't wrong about any of that, but hello, they weren't human.

"You, yourself, said you would be dead if not for Zander's brothers saving you from that attack. For me, all that matters is how they have given you their love, support and friendship. They have made your life better and made you smile again. I don't care what they turn into, or what they consume, as long as it's not you. Is it weird? Yes. But, is it the end of the world? No. My heart tells me they are kind and caring," Cailyn paused then gentled her voice, "What is your heart telling you? Are you really worried about Zander being a vampire? Or is this about you wanting him?"

Elsie's instincts screamed that these warriors were not malevolent beings, but it was difficult to see beyond the actions of the evil creatures who took Dalton from her. She had to admit that maybe she had wrongly associated Zander and the others with skirm. She didn't even want to acknowledge that her sister had a point with her wanting Zander.

"I do not want him," she denied vehemently.

"El, anyone could see the raging hot chemistry between you two. It nearly incinerated the two of you. You may have loved Dalton, but what you have with him is something altogether different and I think that scares the shit out of you. Don't let your past haunt your future."

"I knew I needed to call you for a reason. You have a way of putting everything into perspective. I may not like what you say and I'm going to keep my head safely in the sand over that last part. But, you're right, Zander and Orlando and the others have always been good to me. I'm sorry for waking you. Go back to sleep. I'll talk to you later today."

"Don't overthink everything, El. I love you, goodnight."

She had a lot to contemplate before she would be comfortable around her friends again. It struck her that she did still think of them as friends. More than friends for one of them. What a mess.

CHAPTER NINETEEN

Thoughts of Zander had haunted her for two days. His sexy smile, the tight fit of his white, Armani shirt and the way his black slacks hugged the best ass known to man. Well, not man, but vampire. Fire coursed through her blood and ignited desire low in her abdomen. She had felt a connection to him from the moment she first saw him. Did knowing he was not only a vampire, but the Vampire King, change how she felt about him? Her logical mind said yes, they were two different creatures and not compatible, but her aching body screamed that it didn't matter one bit. In fact, her body was begging for him to sink his fangs into her throat and take anything he needed. A yearning that disturbed her greatly.

She had reacted to Zander's revelation poorly. Despite her conflicting emotions and disbelief, she missed her friends. She wanted to see them again. Talk to them. It had been lonely in her apartment. The only thing that had kept her company was her turmoil.

The ring of her cell phone intruded, and she scrambled to grab it from her trusty, leather backpack. She considered having voicemail pick up Orlando's call when she saw his name, but, the truth was, she wanted to talk to him. "Hi, Orlando, I'm glad you called," she rubbed her hand nervously up and down her thigh. Her throat tightened with emotions.

"I called because Santiago and I have had a development in the criminal case. Okay, so that's just an excuse. I miss you. We all do." She knew so little about these beings.

She wondered why Orlando and Santiago worked for the police and Jace for Harborview. Zander had said it was their mission to keep humans safe. What did that mean? Would they be willing to partner with SOVA? How would Mack take this news? Her hatred for vampires was so deep that Elsie doubted she'd take it well. She knew she'd have to tell Mack at some point, but wasn't looking forward to that conversation and had been avoiding her.

She stood and paced the floor as she cleared the lump from her throat. "I miss you guys, too. You've helped me so much, and I treated you terribly when you revealed who you are. I understand why you kept it a secret and why you need to. Obviously, people wouldn't handle the news well. They'd be afraid and some would hunt you down." If she were honest, she would have been a part of that ignorant group. "And, I'd bet the government would want to study you. Oh, Orlando, I'm so sorry for kicking you and Zander out of my apartment."

"There's no reason for you to be sorry. But, we never left. We've been keeping watch over you outside your apartment. We wanted to make sure you remained safe."

She smiled. She should've known they would continue to watch over her. It warmed her heart knowing they cared so much, and could forgive her behavior. But, that is what family did. They forgave each other and embraced your crazy. "Do you guys want to come over? I'm making enchilada soup."

"You know it, cupcake. I'll bring Mexican martinis and the gang."

"And, make sure Zander comes with you. I owe him an apology, as well."

THREE MARTINIS IN, Elsie was relaxed and laughing. She guessed she had hurt Zander, since he hadn't shown up with everyone else. She never intended to hurt him and felt terrible about it. His piercing, blue eyes and sexy smile continued to haunt her. Ever since learning what he was, she had a million questions and wanted to learn all about him. What did his fangs looks like? Did his eyes glow, or had she imagined that? Did he feed from women? And, why did the mere thought of him sinking his fangs into another woman's neck set her teeth on edge and make her want to kill someone?

Zander's scent tickled her nose. She whirled, her glass hit the linoleum floor and the shards scattered like roaches scuttling in search of a dark corner. She couldn't move, and not because she would cut her feet if she did. His delectable scent had enveloped her and her body heated, readying for his penetration. Her reaction was insane.

They stared at each other from across the counter. She'd been so lost in her own head, she hadn't heard him arrive. "Zander. I'm glad you came. I owe you an apology. My behavior was appalling and I hope you can forgive me."

When he remained silent she blabbered on, "Let me clean this up and then I can get you a bowl of soup and a martini." She smiled widely at him.

"*A ghra*, I have missed you terribly. Doona move." She gasped as he reached across the counter, picked her up, and brought her into his chest. "Orlando, clean up the glass and get me a drink and a bowl of my lass' soup."

She smirked at his familiar domineering attitude. "I can see that Mr. Bossy Pants is back. And, can I just say, holy shit, you're strong."

The sexy rumble of his laugh vibrated from his chest against hers. "'Tis Dr. McYummy to you, lass."

The cold knot in her stomach eased. "I'm glad you came, Dr. McYummy. I have wanted to talk to you. I'm so sorry for what I said. I had been operating under certain assumptions for so long that I was blinded by my ignorance. I needed to process what you said." She had the urge to nestle closer into his chest, but wasn't sure how he felt and didn't want to be rejected so she wiggled in his arms until he put her down.

Zander took her by the arm and led her to the couch. He sat down and pulled her onto his lap. She resisted the urge to squirm in his lap, already feeling how happy he was to see her. "I knew it would be a lot to take in, but I couldna go on without you knowing the truth of me. Let's no' dwell on the past, but move forward. I canna say how happy I am to be here right now. You look beautiful." He nuzzled her neck and placed a tender kiss behind her left ear. A zing traveled from the point his lips touched through her body.

She was breathless from the touch of his lips. God, how she wanted this vampire. "Thanks. You look gorgeous, too. But, you probably hear that from women all the time."

His hands ran up and down her arms. "All that matters to me is what you think. In my seven hundred sixty-five years, I havena wanted anyone like I want you," he husked, causing her to shiver.

How was it that his voice caused her to clench with need? Her eyes remained glued to his lips while he spoke. *Did he say he was seven hundred sixty-five years old? For Gods sakes, he looks like he's in his thirties!* The difference in their ages should turn her off, but it didn't deter her one iota. Nothing stopped her from imagining everything she wanted him to do to her. The bright, blue glow of his eyes distracted her from his mouth.

She wasn't caught long, as his hiss forced her gaze back down to his mouth, where she saw his white fangs peeking out from his full lip. She gulped down the drink Zander had been given to stop herself from discovering what he tasted like, everywhere. Five minutes with him and all she could think about was hot, sweaty sex. She was weak and pathetic.

IN HEARING his mate's thoughts, Zander used his telepathic abilities to tell the others to leave her apartment. He wanted privacy with his mate.

He turned her in his lap so she straddled him. The position brought his groin in contact with her center. He cupped her cheeks in his palms and brought his lips down across hers. She froze in his embrace. He rubbed his hands up and down her back, calming her. Slowly she relaxed and moved her lips against his.

He pressed kisses across her mouth to her neck and back. When he returned to her lips, she opened for him and he deepened the kiss, careful to keep her in the moment. She took over and became aggressive in her exploration of him. He nearly lost his seed at the slip and slide of their passionate kiss.

She tensed and looked around her apartment. "Nay, *a ghra*. I sent them home. I wanted you all to myself tonight."

Her eyes wild and uncertain, she gulped and nodded. "I see that. You assume I want to be alone with you," she teased him.

He tugged her closer. "I know exactly how much you want me."

She laughed nervously and settled her hands on his shoulders. She held his gaze and he saw her vulnerability laid bare. The fact that she trusted him was huge progress and his world began to settle into place. He knew they had a ways to go, but there was once again hope. He ran his hand up her side and paused beside her breast, hands shaking from his nerves. He brought their mouths together again and kissed her slow and thoroughly.

She was quickly becoming crazed. He fought it and kept his leisurely pace. She bit his lower lip, "Kiss me like you mean it."

His eyes blazed before he capitulated. He didn't want her thinking. He wanted her wild and uninhibited. He wrapped one hand in her luxurious hair and the other grabbed hold of her breast. He squeezed her nipple through her sweater while he feasted on her mouth. She arched her back, pushing her breast further into his hand and ground against his erection. Her heat seared him through their jeans.

He groaned into her mouth and grabbed her ass as he stood with her. He pulled her tight against him and let her feel how much he wanted her. A breeze told him he was so aroused that the head of his cock was out and ready to play. He began walking to her room. The movement rubbed them together, making her shudder. She stiffened in his arms and he wondered if he was pushing for too much.

"Bedroom?" he asked and pulled back to gauge her response.

Her eyes were wide and he realized she had tensed not because he was pushing for too much, but because she was ready to climax. "Hurry, oh god, don't you dare stop. I'm so close," she screeched.

He kept moving and made sure to hold her tightly to him. She whimpered as he settled her on her feet. "Doona worry, I'm only getting started," he promised.

In seconds, Zander had Elsie naked on her bed. He had to pause and take in his fill. She was simply beautiful with her swollen breasts and panting breaths.

"You're not naked, yet," she complained. He was surprised at what an impatient little thing she was and had continued the erotic play without him. She was squeezing her breasts and pinching her own nipples. Perfect, pert nipples. Her hands began to move lower across her abdomen. Naughty, little thing. He leapt onto the bed and grabbed her hands.

"My turn," he croaked. His balls had drawn up tight to his body, ready for release at the sight of her. Heaven stared back at him as he looked down between her beautiful legs. She had the most luscious, shaved pussy he had ever seen. The scent of her arousal drew him like a bee to honey.

He shifted his body down the bed and laid his torso between her legs. His aching cock was pressed into the mattress. Unable to wait, he dipped his head to taste her sweet nectar. Licking his lips, he tasted her juices and attacked the engorged nub, begging him for attention.

He ran his hands up her legs, pushing them wider, and saw her throbbing clit, which tempted him to sink his fangs in. He licked and nipped at her intimate flesh. Her soul entwined with his and enhanced his desire and pleasure. Nothing his father had ever told him prepared him for the experience of being intimate with his mate. It was explosive and brought him to his knees.

He thrust his tongue into her tight channel and pushed as deep as he could, allowing his fangs to scrape her flesh. He was rewarded with her cry of pleasure. He removed his tongue and lapped at the spot that needed him most. He increased his speed and inserted his finger deep into her core. She threaded her fingers into his hair, grabbing fistfuls. Spasms clenched, indicating she was close. He intended to give her as many orgasms as she could handle, before the night was over. He withdrew his finger taking her slick cream with it.

She whimpered, "Zander, oh, god, don't stop. I'm...so, close...please."

"You never have to beg, *a ghra*. Och, you are so verra tight and wet. My cock aches for you. You are mine." He would give her whatever she wanted and re-inserted his finger, then another, and then thrust both deep inside as he sucked and licked her clitoris. Her hands released his hair and traveled down to his shoulders, coming dangerously close to his mate mark. Fire exploded across his back, the pain nearly taking his breath. He sucked hard on her core as he tried to gain control over the impulse to bite her flesh and force her to complete the blood exchange, binding them forever.

Shoving his needs aside was difficult, but he managed by focusing on her. "You taste so good," he murmured. He continued his ministrations and was soon rewarded with her cries of bliss as he felt her shatter, followed by the clenching in her channel. It was all he could do not to replace his fingers with his cock and thrust into her heat. He watched her face as she came and was awed at the beauty of her pleasure. "I love the way you look when you come."

She was gasping for breath when she reached out for him. She pulled him up to her for a kiss. Soft, silky lips met his. He opened her mouth and slid his tongue along hers, taking advantage. He thought he'd explode the moment she slid her tongue into his mouth, licking his fangs. He held back as much as he could to allow her to explore them freely while kissing him passionately.

Her hands roved his body and he loved the feel of her hands on his skin. Had never experienced anything more erotic. Her touch slid down his torso. She pinched and nipped his nipples as she passed them. He bit his lip to stop his orgasm. It was too soon. He wanted her to explore every inch of him.

She unbuttoned his pants and when her hand finally encircled what it could of his hard cock, he couldn't stop the primal sounds that escaped his throat. He brought her mouth back to his and nipped her lips with his fangs and prayed for the strength to stave off his imminent orgasm. How embarrassing would it be for him to come from a mere moment of her touch, but she undid him so completely.

He felt like a young lad who was about to tup for the first time. For him, these sensations were completely new. All of his previous sexual experiences had only been a physical release, and had never been accompanied by such intense emotions. He was overwhelmed by caring for her so deeply, needing this physical connection, and being scared it may end too soon. Nothing had ever felt as good as he did at that moment.

He thrust his hips as she gripped him firmly and

pumped up and down his hard shaft. "My god, you're gorgeous. And, huge! I don't know if you'll even fit."

He smiled at her words and savored her gasp, his fingers working her clitoris, once again. Little did she know, he was made for her, and would fit perfectly.

He felt her slick syrup drip from her core to coat his hand, and had to hold back from sinking into her heat and losing himself. She thrust her hips against his hand and increased her grip on his cock in response to his deep, husky entreaty. She was nearing orgasm again. "That's it, lass, take what you need. You are hot and so verra wet."

"Holy crap, oh yes... like that...come on, baby." She screamed out his name as she came. That was his undoing. He couldn't hold back anymore and thick ropes of his hot seed jetted onto her hand and stomach.

"Goddess, you undo me, Elsie," he cried out, continuing to stroke her, as his orgasm continued.

They were both gasping for breath and their hearts pounding after her shattering release. "Oh, my Lady E, you are truly incredible," he murmured as he worshipped her breasts. She arched her back, forcing more of her breast into his mouth. He loved this side of his mate, she was downright wanton.

She began to squirm under his hand. "Stop, it's too much. And, how the hell are you still coming? Is that a vampire thing?"

He was afraid of answering because it had not been that long since her rejection of whom and what he was. He took the chance. "Aye, 'tis because of my vampire heritage," he said, dancing around the mating issue.

She pressed against his body. "Hey, I'm not complaining. Especially, given that you stay erect to satisfy my every desire. Mmmm," she reached up, wrapping her arms around his neck and sinking her fingers into his hair. He had never felt closer to any female.

"I have been hard and aching for you from the moment I saw you in that restaurant all those months ago. And, *a ghra*, I will always be able to make love to you and feast on your flesh for hours. That is only one of the benefits of being with a vampire," he smiled mischievously, revealing his fangs.

"You're stunning," she breathed.

CHAPTER TWENTY

What had she done, Elsie thought. The guilt and betrayal she felt was like a mass of tar in her hair. Warm, sticky, and impossible to remove. The more she fingered it, the more it gunked-up her insides. She needed a scalpel and acid to get rid of it. A few martinis and an undeniable attraction to a vampire, and she had gone against the vows she made to Dalton years ago. She jumped up and grabbed her robe off the door, sliding her arms into the fabric.

She had made a mess of everything, but it shouldn't surprise her. They had been heading in this direction for weeks. She watched as Zander stood up and reached down for his jeans. Her loins clenched and her core spasmed at the sight of his bared flesh. She couldn't stop the blush that stained her cheeks as she remembered what they had done. For God's sake, she had screamed his name. She had never had that kind of an experience before. She loved Dalton, but what she felt with Zander was no-where near what she did with Zander. Zander made her mindless with lust and desire. Wanting him with abandon like she did made her guilt so much worse.

His gaze darkened even further. "I like the way you scream my name, lass, and I canna wait to make you scream while I'm inside you. Your screams were verra passionate." Her blush deepened and she cringed in embarrassment.

She had hoped to avoid this conversation forever, but, apparently, he was having none of that. She had never actually talked about sex, either before, or after, the fact. She did it and then cleaned up and moved on with her day. "So, is the ability to read minds one of your vampire powers? You didn't go into details of what you can do. And, can you please put on some clothes? I find it impossible to have a conversation with so much of you on display."

He chuckled and stepped into his pants. She silently amended that statement she liked it better when they were off. She prayed he didn't read her mind and take them back off. She was driving herself crazy and hoped to hide it from him a little longer.

"Aye, I can read the minds of mortals, and I can communicate telepathically with supernaturals." She followed him out of the bedroom. He had a gorgeous Celtic cross branded on his back, reminding her of the one on her phone. Something fluttered in her chest as she stared at the beautiful image. She'd heard from some fraternity guys at school that being branded was painful and had to guess that something that big must have been excruciating.

She sighed when he turned back to face her. "So, you can hear everything I think. I must say, that is disturbing. Can you not do that? There are thoughts I'd like to keep private. What made you get a brand on your back rather than a tattoo? Are vampires able to be tattooed?" She sat down on the couch, pulling her legs up under her.

He sat on the couch a few feet away from her. "I could stop reading your thoughts, but I doona want to. You are loyal, brave, and passionate. The cross is a family mark. I didna have this branded into my back. The Goddess had a hand in it appearing. And to answer your question, aye, vampires can be tattooed, but we need to use a special ink infused with silver dust. 'Tis the only way for the ink to remain in the skin."

"It is odd to think of a Goddess interacting with her subjects like that. For me, God is a spiritual element, nothing so tangible. Why do you use silver?"

"Silver is one of the substances that leaves scars on our skin. Silver can be lethal to supernaturals. In fact, it only takes a thin silver chain to immobilize us. Skirm venom is the only other substance that leaves marks."

"I'm not surprised the skirm venom does that. I remember how much it hurt, burning into my skin," she responded, caught by the way he was playing with her fingers.

"'Tis getting close to dawn, lass, and I doona want to be caught in the sun. I *will* see you soon." He leaned down and kissed her lips, softly. She was a deer caught in headlights, paralyzed by glowing, blue passion.

"Verra soon," he breathed into her ear.

ELSIE SAT in the large SUV, relaxing after the hellaciously-long graduation ceremony. It had been a long, extremely difficult road for Elsie and today was bitter-sweet. She had started this journey with Dalton four years earlier, but he would never see her finish it. She was a phoenix rising from the ashes of her grief. A new life awaited her, one that she hadn't imagined, with new and exciting friends.

For weeks, she had fought the love affair she knew Zander wanted with her, yet, she had let down her guard, given into the demand that had been riding her and had ended up in bed with the vampire. The vampire king had been consuming her thoughts and she couldn't wait to see him. She hated that the graduation was held during the day and Zander hadn't been there.

Elsie focused on her surroundings as they headed to Zeum to celebrate the end to her college career. She needed to close her jaw as Orlando drove through the iron gates to their compound. She craned her neck this way and that, taking in the twenty foot stone walls. They weren't as garish as they could've been with the deciduous trees and shrubs surrounding everything. And, it was all perfectly manicured. They had to have several full-time gardeners to take care of it. She couldn't fathom having that kind of money.

When the enormous home came into view, it reminded her of the English countryside. The house was grey stone and stucco with massive columns flanking the entrance and countless windows. She spotted several other buildings on the property, each of which looked bigger than most houses. Zander and Orlando had told her they lived together and she wondered who lived in what house.

These people had more money than God, she thought wryly. She guessed if you'd been alive for over seven hundred years, you'd have time to accumulate that kind of wealth.

"Why do you guys call this place Zeum?"

"Breslin battered us until we finally gave in and she named it after her favorite carousel in San Francisco,"

Orlando replied and smiled as he met her gaze in the rear view mirror.

"This place is unreal and it goes on forever. You would never know this was back here."

"That's the idea. We don't want anyone being able to see it. We have strong cloaking and protection spells. It appears to anyone, human or supernatural, like fifty heavily-wooded acres along Wolf Bay," Orlando relayed as he parked next to a pair of beautiful, black, double-doors. Elsie's gaze traveled over them and took in the intricate Celtic symbols carved into their wood surfaces.

They were greeted by what Orlando called their major-domo, who opened her door. She climbed out as the handsome, young-looking man, dressed in a tailored suit, bowed deeply. "Angus at your service, lass. Anything you need, doona hesitate to ring me." His black hair shone in the overhead lights and his pale-green eyes sparkled with mystery and she liked him immediately.

Elsie wasn't sure what etiquette dictated in this situation and realized she was in way over her head. "Thank you," she muttered with a slight bow of her head. She felt like she was at a five-star hotel and was slightly overwhelmed as Orlando led her through the door. She glanced back and saw that Santiago was leading a shocked Cailyn into the house. Their eyes met and she knew that Cailyn agreed that they were two ducks out of water here. The wealth these guys had was simply beyond her comprehension.

"This place is unreal," Elsie murmured to Cailyn as they entered the home. The luxury was breath-taking with the brown, marble flooring in the entryway and rich wood covering the walls.

"Look at that crystal chandelier, Cai. I feel like I'm inside Buckingham Palace."

Cailyn turned in circles, taking it all in and replied, "I know, right. It's breathtaking. Can you imagine how long it would take to clean that alone?" Elsie found that Zeum was warm and inviting, despite its opulence and grandeur.

Angus chuckled, "The chores never end, but it helps to have a little magic up your sleeve."

She scanned everything around her and snagged on the gorgeous creature with his hand on the rich, mahogany balusters of the main staircase. Zander was scrumptious in his sweaty, white, tank top and navy-blue, track pants. She noticed he had a tattoo on his right forearm that matched the one she had seen on Orlando and Santiago. How had she missed that before? Probably because she spent most of her time admiring his ass.

She blushed at the bent of her thoughts. Needing a distraction, she glanced over and saw that Bhric and Kyran were dressed similar to Zander, and, they too, had the same tattoo on their right forearm. In fact, all of Zander's Dark Warriors, including Breslin, had this tattoo. It was a tribal design merged with druid symbols and she made a mental note to ask what it meant later.

At the moment, she was fixated on Zander and the sweat running down his shoulders. She wanted to lick every bead of sweat from his chest and abdomen, following the trail below his pants. She recalled how big he was. What would he feel like when he took her? She did a mental head shake, reminding herself that he could read her thoughts.

"Och 'tis good to see you. I have missed you, *a ghra*. And, I would love for you to lick the sweat from my body," he said as he descended the stairs and embraced her, meshing their lips in a tender kiss.

She flamed with embarrassment. "Stop reading my mind, Mr. Bossy Pants." Helpless to resist touching him, she placed her hands on his chest. "It's good to see you, too. Your home is beautiful," she said as she craned her neck to look up to him.

"You call this a house? This is a hotel, for God's sake. I can't believe Orlando has stayed at your crappy apartment as much as he has the past couple months," Cailyn observed. "If I were him, I would've made you stay here."

"Who's up for some champagne?" Rhys winked at Cailyn. "You haven't had my *hey juice,* sweetcakes, but that'll come later."

As Rhys led her sister down a hall, Zander placed his hand at the small of Elsie's back and followed suit. "Oh, my," Elsie breathed, as she entered a gourmet-kitchen that could've been right out of her dreams. "The gourmet meals I could make in here. You have two refrigerators and I think your pantry is bigger than my apartment," she sighed and walked around touching every surface with reverence. She didn't need to see the rest. This was, hands down, her favorite room in the house.

She rounded on Zander and glared at him. "How could you guys make me cook for you in my crappy, little apartment? It took me all day using the two working burners I have, but to cook in your kitchen would have been heaven."

He wrapped his arms around her waist and murmured against her ear, "I like your apartment, especially your bedroom." She recalled what they'd done on her bed and swatted his arm and stepped away from him, suddenly hot.

She crossed the room and through the windows, over one of the long, granite countertops, she saw an enclosed patio with a circular, Celtic design embedded in the tile floor. A sense of home, of belonging, and of loyalty surged through her the moment she saw it. These guys took their Scottish heritage seriously and she loved it. The pop of a cork had her turning around as Breslin shoved a crystal flute filled with bubbly in her hand.

"To Elsie," Breslin announced and held her glass in the air. Everyone followed suit and cheers resounded.

"Okay, 'tis time to get ready. C'mon, I want to be the first to give you your present," Breslin told Elsie, grabbing her free hand.

Gerrick grumbled, "What makes you so special that you get to give Elsie her present now? Shouldn't her mate go first?"

"Because, I can. Stop pouting, and get ready. All of you need to be ready to leave as soon as we're done," Breslin retorted, herding Elsie and her sister to the main staircase. Elsie had no time to consider Gerrick's comment.

Her head swiveled this way and that as she absorbed each and every detail of the house on her way upstairs. Her jaw dropped when she walked into Breslin's lavish suite of rooms. Yeah, these people had money. Except, they weren't people. They were supernatural creatures. And, she was in their home with her sister, completely vulnerable to them.

The blade she had strapped to her thigh before leaving her apartment, the one she never left home without, seemed paltry. She shook her head, it was difficult to unlearn nearly two years of training and forget everything she'd been taught and she had to remind herself that these beings were nothing like the ones she hunted and killed.

"Breslin, I think your room is bigger than my apartment. Every piece of furniture I own would fit in here. Do you get lost on your way to the bathroom?" She sat down on one of the couches and sighed.

Breslin waved off her comments and picked up the large box from the antique, mahogany coffee-table in the living room of her suite. "A house is a house, no matter the size, or furnishings. What makes a home truly magnificent is the family that fills it. And, you are both members of this motley crew of ours. And, by the way, I expect to get to take you shopping soon. I've always wanted a *puithar*," she winked at Elsie who couldn't help but respond by grinning broadly.

"Now, I dinna know what you wanted for graduation, so I bought you something that I would have chosen for myself." Breslin crossed to her and handed her the gift, sitting beside her. Feeling dazed, Elsie met her sister's eyes. Cailyn smiled at her reassuringly as she sipped from the crystal flute of champagne.

Enjoying the attention, Elsie excitedly tugged the end of the gold, loopy bow and lifted the top. "Oh, wow! It's *so* beautiful, thank you." She pulled out the fabric and held it up, taking in the entire dress. It was stunning. It wasn't anything she would ever buy herself. Hell, she could never afford anything like this, but she loved it.

"Are you sure this is me? It's strapless and well," she took stock of her chest, "I have no boobs to hold this up." Breslin had given her another dress made for a supermodel, a busty supermodel.

"El, you have great boobs, I have told you this for years. They aren't as big as mine, but then you are skinnier than me. I would give up these boobs to be fifteen pounds lighter," Cailyn cupped her breasts and smirked at Elsie.

"Doona fash over such silly worries. Your breasts will fit this dress fine. This bandage style is made for a thinner build. I couldna wear this myself, because I am too curvy. And, Cailyn, you doona need to lose any weight. You're both like wee faeries compared to me. Put in on, Elsie, you'll see. And, I have a great dress that will accent your large bosom nicely, Cai. We can all drive the guys crazy tonight." Breslin beamed, her bubbly personality was infectious. And, the woman was crazy. She had the most perfect body. She reminded Elsie of a personal fitness trainer. There wasn't one ounce of fat on her muscled body.

She met her sister's excited gaze as they listened to Breslin rifle through a closet that was the size of a bedroom. Her sister hopped up and went to join Breslin. She was astonished that her sister was so comfortable with this new world. But, then, Cailyn could read thoughts. That was reassuring and Elsie relaxed, it was her night and she was having fun. She felt safe regardless of the fact that she didn't understand anything about the creatures she was with.

Suddenly eager to drive Zander crazy, she pulled out the strapless dress. It was a shadow color and tightly fitted to the body with ribs down the length of the dress. It was embellished with bands of sequins crossing around the bust, which would enhance what she didn't have. Would he find her lacking? She wanted him to see her as beautiful and alluring.

Cailyn's squeal of excitement was jarring as she came running out of Breslin's closet. "Oh my God, I love it! I wish John could see me in this dress. I wouldn't make it out of the house. He'd have it off and we'd be going to town. Maybe I'll send him a selfie." She noticed her sister was holding up a racy, little, red dress that she swore had to be a shirt on Breslin's tall frame. No way was that covering any of the important bits.

"Can I wear your black heels tonight? " Cailyn asked as she bounced over to her.

Elsie contemplated the shoes she had on, as well as, the new pair Breslin had given her with the dress. The new heels were only about four-and-a-half inches so she had no problem giving her sister the six-inch torture chambers she had on. "Sure," she slipped them off and handed them over.

"Now, you need smoky, sexy eyes and Zander would love your hair up," Breslin declared, flipping containers open on her dressing table. Who needed this much make-up? She'd not seen so much in one place outside of a department store. She felt like the customer and Breslin the makeup artist as she sat obediently and Breslin set about fixing her up.

She blushed at the thought of Zander liking her hair up, wondering what it would feel like for him to sink his fangs into her throat. The thought was not in the least bit repulsive, as she had expected. Rather, she found it titillating and exciting. She needed to stop thinking risqué thoughts as familiar heat stole over her body.

"Cai, that dress looks outstanding on you. Very sexy. Good thing you have that diamond ring on or men would be all over you. I still can't believe you agreed to marry him. I remember when you said you'd never be tied down. But, I'm so happy for you."

Elsie embraced her sister, "Tonight, we're also going to celebrate your engagement to John," she held up her crystal flute. "To a night we'll never forget." Elegant chiming filled the room as she, Breslin and Cailyn inaugurated the night.

CHAPTER TWENTY-ONE

E lsie lost her footing as she descended the stairs, and tumbled into strong, sexy arms. Apparently, she was unable to ogle Zander and descend stairs simultaneously. Her embarrassment died quickly when she realized she was in the arms of the most gorgeous creature she had ever seen! She stepped out of his arms before she lost all decorum and fell on him like a slavering dog.

He wore a charcoal-grey, cashmere suit that was tailored to perfection. The pants cupped him nicely and his obvious erection was huge. She remembered what that felt like rubbing against her. She dragged her eyes from his groin and the entire world came to a stand-still when their eyes locked. She felt a zing barrel through her body.

The way his eyes widened and took on a glow told her that he must also have felt the magnetic pull. He grabbed her hand, tugging her flush against his chest. She melted when he placed his fingers under her chin and tilted her head back. His lips hovered a scant breath away from hers, teasing her mercilessly.

"You look enchanting. I want verra much to divest you of

that dress and explore every inch of you," he murmured before he captured her lips and ravaged them. The kiss started slow but quickly turned to a boil. He licked at her, eliciting a gasp. He took advantage when her lips parted and plundered her depths. The feeling of his tongue stroking across hers caused her sex to heat and clench. As their tongues tangled, she thought that in his seven hundred years he had perfected his skill. She wasn't jealous of the women he had used to perfect it on. She almost believed the lie.

He broke the kiss. Both of them were breathing hot and heavy. "There is no other for me, *a ghra*. There never has been," he kissed her one more time before turning her around so her back was to his chest.

He leaned into her ear and his hot breath tickled as he spoke. "Congratulations, my Lady E. You are a remarkable female and the most beautiful in the realm. I have something for you, to recognize your achievement."

He reached around her body and held out several small wrapped boxes. "Zander, what have you done," she whispered and looked over her shoulder into his eyes. The tender emotions she saw there chipped away at more of the wall around her heart. "Those look like jewelry boxes and I can't accept them."

His arms tightened around her and she was reminded of his rigid presence behind her. "You will take them, Elsie. They were made especially for you," he breathed.

She didn't know what to think. He had jewelry made for her. The concept was as foreign to her as giving someone a seventy thousand dollar car. "Mr. Bossy Pants is giving orders again," she grumbled as curiosity won and she picked up the first box. Nervously, she untied the black ribbon and removed the silver wrapping from the little, red box. Inside was a black, leather box. Her hands shook as she lifted the lid to reveal the biggest, most astounding, emerald-cut, diamond earrings she had ever seen.

"You've done it again. These are gorgeous and exquisite, and, way too expensive, I suspect." These supernaturals lived in excess. They not only came from different worlds, but entirely different experiences. But, like any woman, she had always dreamed of owning great, big diamonds. When she looked at him, she saw his emotions on his sleeve and knew in that moment he was as vulnerable as he was ever going to be. For her to accept these gifts was for her to accept him. For him it wasn't about the diamonds, but about her embracing him. She melted for entirely different reasons.

She turned around and cupped his cheeks. She saw him for the vampire he was: loyal, generous, fierce, protective, and loving, even if a bit bossy. "They're perfect. I love them."

She smiled up at him as she handed him the earrings and accepted the next box. She unwrapped it, revealing a stunning bracelet. The design of delicate orchids in platinum was inlaid with diamonds throughout the entire length. She quickly opened the last box and saw that it contained a necklace that matched the bracelet.

"I've never been given more heartfelt gifts. I realize now that it's not the expense of a gift, but the intent behind them. Thank you, I love them!" She wrapped her arms around his neck and embraced him. When she lifted her head and met his eyes, all reason slipped away. She was dangerously close to falling for this vampire.

Cailyn's voice shattered their moment and Elsie blushed all the way to her toes. She blinked and looked over at her sister who was holding the earrings. "And, here I thought I was lucky that John went to Jared," Cailyn remarked, as she looked at the jewelry and lifted her engagement ring, comparing the two. "These are gorgeous, El."

"My *brathair* is ever the romantic one. Och, I hope my Fated Mate is as thoughtful, as well as, someone who can make me laugh," Breslin commented, as she put the necklace on Elsie who was too busy staring at Zander.

"There," Breslin patted her shoulder. "These look great on you, and the orchids above the strapless dress draw the eye to your cleavage," she winked conspiratorially at her.

What did Breslin mean about a Fated Mate? When she lifted her gaze, she saw Zander ogling her breasts, and became caught in his glowing eyes.

"Aye, the look is definitely eye-catching. I could eat you up, *a ghra*," he said hoarsely.

"But, will it hurt?" she asked, as she looked from his eyes to his fangs, peeking out from his lip. Regardless of their differences and her SOVA membership, her body wanted what her body wanted.

"Alright, you two, if you keep this up we're never going to make it to Confetti," Orlando chided and pushed his way between them to give her a hug, earning a feral growl from Zander. Orlando quickly backed away, patting her shoulder.

"You look beautiful, cupcake," Orlando said before informing her he got her a margarita machine so she always had them on tap. The others gave her wonderful gifts, as well, and made her feel special, but none held the meaning Zander's gifts did. She felt truly pampered as Cailyn put the earrings in her ears and clasped the bracelet onto her wrist.

After Dalton died, she'd thought her happy days were over. Her joy now was unexpected, yet welcome. Try as she might, she wasn't able to quash the kernel of hope that blossomed for her future.

CAILYN THREW BACK her fourth drink of the night and rushed back to join Elsie, Zander, Kyran and Breslin on the dance floor. The others had danced with them for a while, but had eventually disappeared to the back area of the club. She smiled as she watched her sister dance freely with the others. It was nice seeing her so full of life, relaxing and having fun. Elsie deserved happiness and Cailyn wanted to see the ghosts of her past lifted. Between Dalton's death and her attack, Elsie had hardened and become cynical, and wasn't the sister she had helped raise.

Cailyn, on the other hand, was wound tight as a drum, and couldn't stop her search for Jace. Ever since she had seen him in Elsie's apartment two months ago, he had not left her thoughts. Why was she unable to keep him out of her mind? Yes, he was sexy, but it was crazy to her how thoughts of him had consumed her. She had been fighting it for weeks.

It had even caused her to have doubts about her engagement to John. She loved him, but thinking incessantly of another man went against her sense of integrity. Still, she wanted to know everything about him. She knew he was a supernatural. Did he have fangs, or turn into an exotic animal? What was he like in bed? Did he have a girlfriend, or wife? Were his lips soft, or firm? Continually her questions returned to the erotic and it was frustrating. She had tried to write her interest off as a by-product of how her mind worked. She was a visual person and that came in handy when designing advertising presentations, but this fascination was fast becoming an obsession.

Shaking off her return to teenage-crushdom, she hip-bumped Breslin as she rejoined the group, and began dancing again. She watched Zander and Elsie together. They were all but making love on the dance floor. Their hands and mouths were all over each other and their bump and grind was on the verge of obscene. She had never seen her sister like this. Elsie and Dalton hadn't been into public displays of affection, but, Zander and Elsie simply couldn't keep their hands off one another. They were like two magnets locked together. It was only a matter of time before they went at it. She heartily approved, the vampire obviously adored her sister.

She felt something pull at her from behind. She danced a slow, sensuous circle and saw thick, black hair in a long braid across the room. She would know that braid anywhere. She had been fantasizing about it for months. It was Jace and she realized that he was kissing a woman. She stood there and gaped at the sight as a heavy stone settled in her gut.

She became incensed at the passionate exchange between the two. She was going to rip that woman's hair out. How could he do such a thing? She took a step toward the couple, driven by Jace's betrayal and her jealousy. But, before she took her second step, she stopped. What the hell was she doing? She was being ridiculous. There was no betrayal, nor was there a reason to be jealous. He could kiss any woman he wanted. Cailyn was nothing to him. She questioned her sanity as she fought back tears, running from the dance floor to the bathroom.

She barged through the door and locked herself in one of the stalls, gritting her teeth against the tears threatening to spill over. None of this made any sense to her. It was as if some unseen force was driving her. She didn't know Jace and she was engaged to a wonderful man. That didn't matter, apparently, as she continued fixating over Jace and what he was doing with the woman.

A rapping on the door brought her head up. "Cai, sweetie, are you ok?" Oh God, it was her sister. Elsie was the last person she wanted to see. She would see right through any lie she attempted to tell her and she had no desire for Elsie to find out what she was thinking. She was ashamed of her behavior.

"I'm fine, needed to go to the bathroom is all." She took a deep breath and cringed at how hoarse her voice was.

"You don't sound fine. You sound upset, and I want to know why. Please let me in." As much as she wanted to hide, it wasn't an option so she unlocked the door and Elsie pushed it open. Elsie took one look at her and drew her into a hug.

"I'm PMSing, I think. Honestly, I don't really know what's wrong with me." That was as close to the truth as she was willing to get. "It's great to see you having fun and I don't want to ruin your night. Don't worry about me, I'm fine now. Hey, you think the bartender could make that Monsterita you talked about?"

She kept her arm around Elsie and guided her out of the bathroom. "Zander is the Vampire King. They will make anything he tells them to." Elsie laughed as they entered the main bar area.

Cailyn vowed she would keep her eyes off Jace and never think about him again. Two steps in and it was torture. Her eyes strayed to the corner to find out if Jace was still making out with that whore. She and Elsie crossed the dance floor and when she didn't see him, she wondered if they'd gone to a private room. "Good, 'cause I need about ten of them right now," she told her sister honestly. She wanted to get blitzed. The mere thought that Jace was in a room with another woman made her want to hunt them down, rip out the bitch's hair extensions, and claw her eyes out for touching what was hers. Now she was staking a claim to Jace? Heaven, help her.

Elsie hugged her close. "You know what? I'm going to ask the others if they want to take this party back to Zeum, while at least one of us can safely drive. We can make drinks there. Zander made sure the kitchen was stocked with energy drinks and tequila for me." That sounded sublime to Cailyn. She didn't want to watch Jace anymore and was grateful Elsie was okay leaving her party. Cailyn looked over and gave her sister a reassuring smile.

JACE BROKE the kiss he had been sharing with a hot, little, feline shifter when he felt a peculiar zing zip through his body. It didn't come from the female in his arms. He'd gone to Confetti to celebrate Zander's mate and had no intention of hooking up with a female. Desire took him over as he watched Zander and the others dancing. This shifter approached him then, and before he knew it, he was kissing her in the corner.

As he looked at the female, he ignored the familiar feeling of nausea and prayed, like he had thousands of times, to complete a sexual encounter. Every time he attempted intimacy of any kind with a female, he became sick. The electricity zipping through his blood was new and arousing. It made him rock-hard and in desperate need of release.

His hormones kicked higher and he returned to kissing the shifter, momentarily losing himself in the uncontrolled passion. He pushed the shifter's panties aside and unzipped his pants, freeing his erection. Unfortunately, as his shaft neared the female's heat, it deflated and bile rose in his throat...Goddess, not again. Before he had an opportunity to think further, Zander's presence entered his mind.

"Where in the hell are you? Bluidy bastard, 'tis my mate's night, and you havena even congratulated her. I know you are here in the club somewhere, but we're leaving now. You will be coming back to Zeum with us, right now. I doona care what, or who, you are doing."

"I'm sorry, Liege, I got side-tracked. I'm right behind you." What he couldn't tell Zander, or anyone else, was that his nightmares had plagued him nightly and he had jumped at the chance with this female when his body had responded.

Thoughts of his nightmares led him to question why he had felt such passion moments before his erection deflated. He had never felt such desire and the shifter hadn't caused it. He could scarcely recall her name, he mused, as he zipped his pants and walked away, ignoring the female's curses.

He hastened his steps, needing fresh air as the bile rose. He spotted his friends and fell into step at the back of the group, needing time to compose himself. He swallowed hard and willed the nausea away. He noticed Cailyn laughing with Elsie and his arousal returned full-force. She was delicate and stunning, her hazel eyes drawing him in.

The ribbing Breslin was giving Zander was a welcomed distraction. *"Brathair,* did you write down your mileage when we came in? I know you were a wee bit distracted by Elsie tonight. We wouldna want you to fuss the whole way home aboot the lads in valet joyriding in your Porsche," Breslin chuckled, as they walked to the exit.

"What are you talking about?" Elsie asked.

"I doona do that," Zander snarled at the same time.

Elsie burst out laughing. "Did you just say goonie-goo-hoo?"

Everyone fell silent. He looked up and his gut hit the cement when he caught sight of an enormous archdemon standing ten feet away, with an army of skirm.

CHAPTER TWENTY-TWO

Eyes wide with horror, Elsie stopped dead in her tracks, unable to grasp what she was seeing. She was mere feet from the ugliest creature she had ever seen. It had gray skin, bright red hair, and sharp black horns on its head. It had to be the devil. Power radiated from his red eyes and he was surrounded by at least fifty kids with fangs and those same eerie eyes. She now had a name for them and it wasn't vampire, they were skirm. Regardless of what they were called, it was a frightening sight, and brought back the terror she had felt that night of her attack. She had to remind herself that she was trained to fight and was surrounded by powerful warriors.

Still, panic crept in. There was no way that the ten or so of them would be able to defeat so many. *Why didn't I feel this?* She wondered if her premonitions had abandoned her. They had always heralded doom for her, and she took that as a sign that no one she loved and cared for was going to be lost this night. She had no room to believe anything else. She withdrew the blade from her thigh sheath and readied for battle.

"Kill the warriors and capture the king, we need him," the huge devil ordered.

Her blood ran cold when she heard the monster order the capture of Zander. No one would take her vampire! She grabbed hold of his jacket, looking around frantically for her sister. Cailyn had no combat skills and was defenseless. She noted with dismay that the skirm had snuck behind them to completely surround them. There was no way to get Cailyn back inside the club.

Zander yelled out, "Bhric, Breslin, protect Cailyn. Orlando, Santiago, doona shift, unless necessary. Elsie, stay close to me." Elsie was grateful Zander could read her mind as he ordered protection for her sister.

The next thing she knew, every warrior had a small knife in their hand, and Breslin had two. Where in that short, tight dress had Breslin hidden the knives? She made a note to ask her later how she managed that one. Flashes of fire erupted all around her as the warriors began killing skirm. Elsie swung out as one rushed her and nicked its arm. The thing howled in outrage. She ducked under his arms and came up right against his chest and plunged her knife home. A quick fire then he was ashes on the wind.

She turned around and saw Zander's tight expression as he fought. "*A ghra*, you are going to be the death of me. Stay close to me where I can keep you safe."

"I won't be safe if I just stand there with a target on my back, Mr. Bossy Pants. I know how to fight. I can fight and I want to fight. Now, shut-up and pay attention."

She didn't miss the slight tilt to his lips. "Aye, Mrs. Bossy Pants."

She was smiling as she took a moment to watch the fluid way these men moved. It spoke to their supernatural nature, and proved how fierce they were. Zander ducked his attackers and parried with such grace and confidence. He never hesitated, but dealt killing blow after killing blow.

She gasped as Zander picked her up and swung around, stabbing his knife into the chest of a skirm, who had made it around their group, and was trying to get to her. She had to pay attention if she wanted to live through this. She kicked a skirm in the gut and felt her spiked heel sink into flesh. Blood poured from the wound as they circled each other. It didn't seem to faze or slow the skirm as he fought with tremendous strength. He caught her arm and she turned to avoid his swing. The hit landed on her shoulder. She thrust her knife into his chest and he turned to ash before she withdrew the blade.

Zander taunted the ugly devil, as he sliced his way toward him. "Another lapdog of Lucifer's? Why doona you come join the fun? My blades are itching for an introduction. Mark my words, you will die for this."

"The name is Kadir, and I will be your downfall, Vampire King."

Her head snapped up. Had Zander lost his mind, provoking that disgusting, evil demon with fangs the size of Santoku Knives? Incredulous, she met Zander's eyes, and saw that his beautiful blues had darkened to an endless black pit. She shivered at the anger emanating from him in vast waves. He was no longer the thoughtful guy who brought her chocolates and gave her a car. He was a ruthless king slaying his enemies.

Momentarily caught up in each other, neither detected the skirm that snuck up behind him. The glint of steel flashed in her peripheral vision. She screamed out when Zander twisted and grunted in pain.

A feral beast erupted inside her. No one was going to

hurt her vampire. These creatures had taken Dalton from her, had attacked her, and now sought to take him. Not gonna happen. A shrill screech burst from her lips as adrenaline was dumped into her system. She shoved Zander aside and lunged at the skirm, driving the blade through its heart. She watched as he flashed, uncaring that her fingers were singed from the intense heat. When the ash form remained in front of her, she savagely hacked at it, covering herself in its dust.

"That was sexy as hell. Take my *sgian dubh*. I have natural weapons," he held up his clawed hands, then dipped his head and met her lips for a sweet kiss that set her on fire. Surely, he was not talking about taking on the creatures with his bare hands? She watched him rip the head off the next attacker. Apparently, he was. And, she couldn't help but admire the walking-talking-lethal-killing-machine.

She looked around for her sister and was relieved to see Breslin and Bhric guarding her. The two stood side by side, wielding fire and ice. If she wasn't seeing it with her own eyes, she wouldn't have believed it. She thought the complementary powers were fitting for the twins. Their moves were synchronized to combat their foes, while they kept Cailyn safe. Bhric immobilized his enemies with ice, and then slashed easily through their hearts. Elsie couldn't decide if Breslin was faster with her fire or her knives. The corpses burning on the ground around her was a gruesome sight. As the horrid smell of putrid flesh scorched her nostrils, bile rose in her throat.

"Die motherfucker!" Elsie twirled around startled at hearing Gerrick's yell so close to her. There was a horrendous wound on his shoulder, but it didn't slow or stop the warrior. He thrust his weapon into a chest, and spun to attack another, without hesitation. A shudder ran up her spine and she felt the rush of more adrenaline. The man was scary calm and had wicked skills.

As she had during so many of her battles, she wondered what Dalton had faced in his last moments. She hoped and prayed he was saved this savage attack, because, if not, he suffered horribly. Suddenly, a war-cry sounded behind her. It was a long, shrill, undulating cry to the heavens that pierced her soul, as the clang of steel on steel raged around her. Looking over her shoulder, she saw it was Jace. He took out enemies with a fevered frenzy. In that moment, it hit her that these men had been protecting humans from these creatures for centuries. They were heroes who should be worshipped for their sacrifice and she was honored to call them friends.

She joined the fight with fervor. At one point she saw that Zander was bleeding profusely and grabbed hold of the back of his jacket, trying to staunch the blood dripping from his wound. A bright light caught her attention. She turned and saw Santiago shift into the biggest wolf she'd ever seen. She watched as he ran in the direction of the demons, only to stop short when they disappeared. They kept teleporting, making it difficult for anyone to land any hits. Elsie saw the danger before he did.

"Santiago, behind you!" She barely had the words out before he had turned and ripped into one skirm, and then slashed his claws across another's throat.

She took stock of their forces and was relieved when she saw that everyone was alive. Orlando was in his animal form as well and was clawing his enemies to pieces. A skirm snuck up behind Orlando, but Kyran was there before she could warn him.

Kyran was wielding two small knives, identical to the ones Zander had handed to her. She recalled Kyran bragging how he was an expert with knives, calling himself "the best in the realm." She prayed he was right about that. Anger and determination splayed across his face, as he suddenly disappeared then reappeared behind another enemy, turning him to ash.

Kyran had simply vanished from where he stood and resurfaced twenty feet away in the blink of an eye. He was quicker than lightning. He was taking out enemies left and right with ease. Determination etched across his harsh features and he was clearly focused on reaching the huge demon.

∾

THUD,

Thud,

Thud,

A menacing laugh followed by a wet, tearing sound, thick, obscene, something out of a nightmare.

A whispered gurgling plea from his mother...

Kyran shook off the horror of his past. Seeing the archdemon had caused the memories to resurface. Witnessing his mother's murder had made him who he was and shaped everything about him. Watching his mother be raped and brutally slaughtered had warped him.

The demon sneered at his brother. Kyran refused to loose anymore family members to this evil scum, not forgetting he had a vendetta to cash-in. Filled with rage, he sifted to the demon's side. Putting all of his hatred and violence into his attack, he thrust one knife into Kadir's side, close to his heart, and ripped it downward. A large, black organ stuck to the end of Kyran's knife as Kadir teleported away. Kyran roared with frustration, knowing the demon had been injured, but not killed. He had an organ to regenerate and would not be returning to the battle. "Fuck," he roared. "Goddess, be damned! Filthy piece of cowardly shit," he cursed, knowing he had lost his opportunity for the revenge he sought.

~

EVERYONE CONTINUED to fight without slowing, but Elsie was tiring. She envied their supernatural strength and stamina. She wasn't going to last much longer. They had made a sizable dent in the skirm, but there were still so many. Silver flashed in her peripheral vision, and she saw a pair of knives flying through the air. They landed in Rhys' hands.

"I don't just attract the ladies," he winked at her when he saw her gaping. He was telekinetic? Now, that was a handy ability to have.

"Come on, Azazel, let's dance, pretty boy. You know you want a piece of this," Rhys curled his fingers toward himself, palms up, egging on the attractive guy. Clearly, they knew each other.

"I'd like to play, cambion," Azazel purred, as he parried Rhys' attack.

"You're not my type. Must suck to have been replaced as the reigning archdemon." Rhys' taunt was the distraction he needed. He feinted left then swung his blades up, severing Azazel's right arm. Azazel merely stumbled back, still smiling, while black blood sprayed the ground around him. How was this demon able to stand there with a smile, when his arm had been cut off?

"This isn't over, cambion," Azazel sneered before disappearing. The remaining skirm kept fighting, regardless that their leaders were gone and there were still so many of them.

Zander gathered Elsie into his chest and she held her body stock-still in his strong arms. She loved the feel of his strength surrounding her. "Form a line and retreat. The Fae is gone. Killian, you, Jace and Gerrick re-establish those protections the moment we have two feet of space between us and them. Everyone, get your arses into the club, now!"

He let go of her waist and grabbed her hand before he began running toward the door of the club. She struggled to keep up with his pace. She searched for her sister and saw that Breslin and a black man had picked up Bhric. She winced at the sight of Bhric's arm dangling by a thread. It looked horridly painful and she wondered if he could recover. This vampire would be severely handicapped if he lost the arm.

Relief swamped her that Cailyn was uninjured and following behind the group. The moment they entered the desolate club, she ran to her sister and held Cailyn tightly as Jace and Zander assessed Bhric's injury.

"We canna remain here. The Fae could come back and break the protections again. We need an exit, now. Can you three create a portal to Zeum, or do you need more power?" Zander asked.

"Gerrick was not injured too badly, and Jace and I are in good shape. I think we may have enough power between the three of us," said a man she was unfamiliar with. He was good-looking with his golden-blond hair and jade-green eyes.

"Do it now, Kill." Zander ordered. "Kyran and I will stay with Bhric while you work."

She was mesmerized by the three men, as they began chanting words in a language she was unable to identify. Their deep voices echoed in unison and threads of power permeated the air around them. The hair on her arms stood on end from the current.

Breslin came up beside her and her sister. "They are verra powerful sorcerers. We'll be back safe and sound at Zeum soon enough."

Elsie nodded but her focus remained on the sorcerers. The air shimmered with lights of the Aurora Borealis as their chant rose to a crescendo. The power was thick and tangible. Within seconds, cool winds were causing her hair to blow across her face. She expected warmth to follow such beauty, but the temperature dropped significantly, causing her to shiver. The colors mixed and swirled until finally coalescing into a mystical doorway. It was breath-taking and she gaped as the crystal chandelier in the foyer of Zeum became visible through the portal. It swayed and tinkled with the breeze created by the magic.

"Everyone, through the portal, now," Zander ordered, as he handed Bhric over to Jace and put his arm around her shoulders then guided her and her sister through the opening to Zeum.

She couldn't help but look back over her shoulder at the desolate club, belatedly wondering what had happened to all the patrons. Jace and Kyran walked through the portal carrying Bhric and they immediately made their way to a door down the hall that led to the kitchen. When the door opened, she saw stairs going down. She remembered someone mentioning a medical clinic on the property and figured it must be in the basement.

She glanced up at Zander as he pulled her closer to his side. She could see his tension lighten as the rest of the warriors hobbled through the portal. As her adrenaline receded, nerves took control, and she started to shake. Her muscles were ready to give way, but she refused to crumble now. Leaning on Zander's strength, she prepared to help the others.

CHAPTER TWENTY-THREE

Zander saw the fatigue in Elsie's eyes and felt the tremble in her body. She may have been shaking, but she didn't dissolve in the wake of the battle. The strength and determination in her thoughts and actions left him in awe. The Goddess had picked well for him, but he feared that this experience would only create a greater distance between them. She had been aware of skirm, but had no knowledge of demons, and she had just come face to face with the war that encompassed his world. He worked tirelessly to protect humans from demons and their minions and the one that mattered most in his universe was smack-dab in the middle.

He held Elsie close, unable to give her the space he knew he should. The mating compulsion would not allow it. He needed to hold her for reassurance that she was unharmed. His heart had yet to settle back into a normal rhythm.

His hands roamed her body, checking her over. Her shoulder was already bruising and she had a cut marring her perfect flesh. He held the small of her back and gathered her close. He'd never been more fearful in his immortal life than he had been for her during the skirmish. He knew that Kadir couldn't have missed the way he had protected her. No doubt, she would now be targeted by the archdemon. He was an idiot for not considering how his actions would bring his Fated Mate more danger.

"Elsie, take your sister upstairs to the last bedroom on the right, to rest, while I go help with Bhric. I'll be up in a wee bit to check on you," he leaned over and kissed her softly.

She looked up into his eyes with her lips scant inches from his. An electric zing raced through his blood. "No, Mr. Bossy Pants," she held his gaze but her usual teasing tone was gone. "Rhys, can you take Cailyn upstairs, please? I'm going with you, Zander. And, you can't stop me, so don't even bother arguing," she said as she raised her hand to halt his reply. "I am not one of your warriors and I don't follow your orders. I am going down there with you."

"Damn, she put you in your place, Liège. You have a feisty one. I like her, already," Nikko laughed, before he sauntered down to the basement.

"I'm not arguing with her. She's scary. Let's go, Cailyn," Rhys chuckled, leading Elsie's sister upstairs. The poor female was in shock and followed the warrior with no complaint or argument.

Zander knew when he was beat. "Alright, *a ghra*, let's go." The guys were absolutely correct and he loved her spirit. She was a natural queen. Consciously, or not, she was embracing her new role, with both arms. Now, he needed to get her to mate with him.

He led her to the medical room in the basement. Bhric lay on one of the two gurneys. Breslin and Killian were assisting Jace, while Kyran was busy patching up Gerrick.

"How are you, *brathair?*" he asked Bhric.

"Good, nothing a little vodka can't cure. Get me that bottle, Ky," Bhric told Kyran.

Zander was hyperaware of Elsie at his side as he kept a firm grip on her waist. He loved the feel of her beneath his fingertips. She belonged at his side. Now, and always.

Shedding the distraction, he scanned the room. "How bad is it, Jace?" he asked.

Jace answered him without stopping his preparations. "Most of us have minor injuries that will heal by morning. But, Bhric will be out of commission a little longer. I cannot heal his arm. He's going to have to heal the old fashioned way."

Elsie tilted her head with a puzzled look. "What do you mean you can't heal Bhric's arm?" she asked curiously.

Jace raised his head from his work on Bhric and addressed Elsie. "As you know, I am a sorcerer, which means I have the ability to cast many types of spells, but there are no spells to heal injuries. Every Dark Warriors has an extra power. Mine is the ability to heal most injuries. I cannot heal mortal injuries or skirm bites because of the venom they leave behind," he glanced back down to Bhric's arm. "Killian, hand me the dissolvable stitches. You see, his arm was bitten and the tissues are now filled with that venom."

"My arm...the venom is why my arm wouldn't heal, right? Does that mean his wound is going to take months to heal, too?"

He placed his hands on her bare shoulders, loving how soft and silky her skin felt, and peered into her lovely, blue eyes. "*A ghra,* Bhric is no' human like you are. Bhric, like the rest of us, has an ability to heal much quicker than mortals. His arm will have a scar, but otherwise, he'll be back to normal in a few days. The rest of us doona need to treat our injuries, since they will be gone by morning."

"That's unbelievable that, that..." Elsie gestured wildly toward Bhric's mangled arm, "will be healed in a few days' time. I mean, it was nearly ripped off! And, your back will be like new by morning?"

"Aye, I will be healed by morning."

"What about the brand on your back. Will you have a scar through it?"

"Nay, I willna have a scar. The weapon wasna silver and no venom entered the wound."

"Well, I'm glad you will be fine by morning, but I'm going to clean the wound anyway. Lord only knows what was on that weapon."

His lips twitched in amusement. It felt like a victory that she worried for him and wanted to tend to him. "Will you put leather on for me, and be my Dr. McYummy?"

Her bark of laughter spurned a round of teasing as she led him to the counter by Orlando. She unbuttoned his shirt with shaking hands. He was shaking as badly as she was. He had longed for her hands on his skin again.

When her fingertips made contact with his pectoral muscles, his body tensed. His erection was instantaneous and only the pain in his back was a bigger distraction. The wound was worse than he realized. When her fingers glided over his mate mark, electricity zinged through his body. The pleasure far exceeded the pain when she placed her palm over the intricate design and he hissed in a breath. Zander was torn between asking her to stop and begging her for more.

Orlando spoke, giving him something else to focus on. "Can we discuss what the hell happened back at the club? Speaking of which, I'm sorry about the loss of Confetti,

Killian. I'll help you in any way I can to get it up and running again."

He didn't know if he wanted to hit Orlando, or kiss him, for interrupting this moment with Elsie. He was one step away from letting his beast loose and feasting on her body before claiming her fully. The loss in Killian's jade-green depths doused some of his ardor, allowing him to maintain control.

"Thanks O, the loss of Confetti will hit the realm hard," Killian replied. "No fears. I'll find another location and be up and running again in no time. If I'm lucky, the bastards didn't destroy the interior. I'd love to salvage my bars and tables. Goddess only knows what they might be doing to the place."

Killian was right, the realm needed a place supernaturals could congregate safely to let off steam and connect. Supernaturals were highly social creatures. In fact, several generations or groups of friends typically lived together. They didn't understand the single family home of humans.

Zander considered their options. They had Bite, but that was a brothel, not a gathering place. Every now and then other realm bars opened up only to be shut down because they didn't have the atmosphere and safeguards Killian provided which was why Killian's club dominated the market.

Santiago changed subjects and asked questions Zander had been asking himself. "How do you think they found us? And, how did they convince the Fae to break your protections? Fae usually stay out of shit because they don't want to take sides."

"When we first walked oot, I saw Azazel cozying up to that Fae bastard. I'm guessing he offered something the Fae couldna resist," Zander answered. "Probably sex, it's the only thing he has. Fae don't need money."

Zander looked over his shoulder to watch Elsie trace his brand with her finger. If she didn't stop touching him like that, he was going to throw her down and fuck her, right there, in front of everyone. She drove him crazy and was oblivious to the effect she had on him. A rumble escaped him, making her start and look up with wide eyes.

Kyran leaned against the wall with his arms crossed over his chest. "Shite, with as many skirm as he had there tonight, you'd think we'd been on holiday, rather than killing those buggers every night for the past few months. I havena seen so many in one place before."

Zander glanced back at the room, his mind in a daze from the contact with Elsie. It was difficult to concentrate and he chastised himself. This was important. The demons and their skirm posed a threat to the realm and his mate and he needed to eliminate them.

Gerrick shrugged his ripped shirt back on and responded. "After Dalton's death, we suspected a new archdemon had stepped in and was leading his skirm differently. Clearly, he has increased his recruitment, their numbers tonight confirm that. I guarantee that he didn't send all of his forces after us. I wouldn't. Goddess only knows how many more were back at his lair. This Kadir seems more strategic than other archdemons we've faced."

Zander hoped Elsie missed the mention of her husband. No such luck. He wanted to knock Gerrick's head off as he felt the tension wrack Elsie's body. He turned, wrapped his arms around her and eased her in front of him. It was natural for him, holding her close. It was all the comfort he could offer her at the moment.

"Why did that devil want my husband dead? He had

nothing to do with this world. He was a good man," Elsie exclaimed.

"A *ghra*, Dalton was in the wrong place at the wrong time. We suspected there was a new demon recruiting in these homes for kids when Dalton was killed. That has been confirmed more than once now. From what we saw tonight, he is obviously targeting large groups of vulnerable young men."

Zander replayed the events of the battle while Elsie digested what he had said. "It seemed that most of his numbers were added recently. They lacked skills and were careless. We easily took oot half his numbers, or more, with the eleven of us. We need to find his lair and develop a counter-attack while his numbers are doon."

His hands gravitated from Elsie's waist to rub circles on her back. The bond calmed them both. She relaxed slightly but his mind touched hers and he had to hold back his wince at her anger over Dalton's death. Every time she encountered skirm it brought her loss close to the surface and hardened the shell around her heart even more.

"I havena any doubt that he has more than what he brought tonight. They need to be eliminated, before they gain better skills. Doona think him desperate, rather he cares little for the humans and is willing to go further than we have seen before," Kyran observed.

Orlando tossed bloodied towels into a nearby laundry basket and cleaned one of the rolling tables. "The hole that piece of shit calls home has to be fairly close to Confetti. Otherwise, there is no way he could have gotten that number of skirm there, and organized, in the few hours we were in the club. We should start looking in areas around Capitol Hill."

"I want to know how that arsehole knew about the club.

For the past seventy-five years, skirm have never come within blocks of the location," Bhric said through gritted teeth. "Goddess, that fucking hurts. Are you no' done?" he asked, glancing at his arm.

"Sorry, buddy, almost there. I wish our scientists had completed development on that antidote to skirm venom. It would make this so much easier on you," Jace continued his suturing, but it seemed to Zander that he was preoccupied, by more than his task. It had been a rough night for everyone.

"Do you think this means the Seelie Queen and Fae have joined with the demons?" Santiago asked as he paced the room like a caged animal, rubbing his bald head as his chocolate-brown eyes glittered with his barely leashed anger. He knew the warrior hated that the demons managed to get the drop on them. Zander did, too. "If they have, we'll be facing a whole new mess of problems."

That was the understatement of a lifetime, Zander thought. "I will be contacting Zanahia to ask aboot that issue. 'Tis likely it was only this one Fae that chose to help Kadir. They are thorny buggers," he sighed as he rested his hands on Elsie's slightly rounded, soft abdomen. He loved her feminine curves. Immediately, his thoughts went to how he wanted to kiss the skin around her belly button then dip lower for another taste of her.

"I think you're right, Zander. I recognized some of the kids from the group home at the fight," Elsie murmured. Zander tightened his hold at his mate's soft-spoken words. "I think this may all be my fault. They must've followed me. Could these kids have hated us that much?" she asked as she stared down at his hands.

With her previous involvement with SOVA, it was easy

for him to forget that she was unaware of the history between the archdemons and the realm.

"There's no way to be certain how they found the club. They've been searching for us from the time the war began, over seven hundred years ago. You canna blame yourself," he said, meeting her worried, blue eyes.

"Wait, that ugly-ass-demon said he wanted you captured, Zander. Why?" While he would rather show her the pleasures of being in his bed, he had to tell her the ugly realities of his world.

CHAPTER TWENTY-FOUR

Elsie squared off with Zander, but he didn't say a word. He wasn't going to answer her. Yeah, that was not going to fly with her. She was getting her answers. Her nerves steeled as she had a stare-down with a seven hundred sixty-five year old vampire king who could squash her like a bug. Good thing she knew he would never hurt her. However, he had no idea how determined she was to get answers.

"Doona fash over the demon and his minions. My warriors and I will keep you safe." Placating her wasn't going to work.

"I have a right to know, Zander," she retorted and waited patiently for him to answer her. Several times he opened his mouth, only to close it again. The connection she felt to him told her he was worried about her and wanted to protect her. That mollified her somewhat.

"Zander, you're too late to protect me. I know all too well how much cruelty and blood-shed is in your world. It took my husband, injured me, and that's not including what happened tonight. I was drug into this against my will. Don't dismiss me outright, I'm stronger than you think. I killed my share of skirm tonight, didn't I?"

He dropped his arms from her, appearing stung by her words. "'Tis my duty to protect you and I will to the day I die." She saw the torment etched into his face and ignored the strong urge she had to comfort him.

Zander turned and paced around the room. She silently watched him until finally he began talking. "Aye, you do have a right to be told. I'll explain what I can. You are familiar with skirm, and know that they are made by archdemons. The reason these demons turn humans is because they want something from me. They are after me because, as the vampire king, I have possession of the Triskele Amulet. There has been a war over the amulet for nearly my entire life. Kadir wants it, so he can free Lucifer from the Ninth Circle of Hell."

"What, exactly, is this amulet, and, what is the Ninth Circle of Hell? And Lucifer? Is he like all the stories and myth say? The Lord of the Underworld?"

He crossed back to her and tucked a strand of hair behind her ear. "You're correct, Lucifer is the Devil, or Satan, or Lord of the Underworld. He created demons, and set them free to wreak havoc on the world. He was cursed for this act. The Goddess Morrigan created the creatures of the Tehrex Realm to combat his evil and protect humans." He paused and rubbed up and down her arms. The motion seemed to calm and center him.

"She gave the first vampire king the Triskele Amulet many millennia ago. It has been passed down through my family, to me. The amulet has many powers and uses, either good or bad, depending on the bearer. Kadir can use this amulet to free Lucifer from where he is frozen in Loch Cocytus," Zander explained.

There was so much for Elsie to take in. "So, your family has been ruling the vampires forever. This is all so hard to wrap my brain around. That does explain why you are so bossy and always telling everyone what to do. You come by your domineering personality naturally." She missed the warmth and comfort of his arms around her and wanted to walk back into his embrace.

He ran his warm hands to her bare shoulders. The tension in her neck and shoulders eased with his heat and nearness. "Aye, lass, I come by it naturally. I come by a great many things naturally. I also inherited a keen intellect, superior strength, incredibly good looks, and a huge...fortune." He winked at her, tracing the blush she felt staining her cheeks with one of his fingers. She was certain he wasn't talking about his fortune, although he certainly had an excess of money.

This man was the most arrogant being she had ever met and yet, she found him sexy and alluring. "You're incorrigible. I have no doubt you come by a lot naturally, like your," she scanned the growing bulge in his pants, "big ego."

Laughing, he pulled her back into his arms and kissed her lips. His tongue traced the outline and he bit her lower lip. She gasped into his mouth and his tongue took advantage, stroking hers in a sensual dance she was coming to savor. Against her lips, he murmured, "You're sassy, lass. I love it. We're no' alone or I would show you my enormous...ego."

Her inner-sex-fiend screamed out, *Show me! Show me! Show me!* Her sane, rational part was glad they weren't alone or she'd be embarrassing herself, at that moment by ripping his clothing off his body.

"Alright, you two, let's simmer it down in here. Can we get back to the matter at hand and begin planning our counter attack, please?" Santiago's full lips twitched as he held back his smirk.

Orlando slapped Santiago on the back. "Let's move this discussion to the war room. I don't like how the demons were watching Zander and Elsie. We need to find that lair ASAP, I have a feeling they may target her."

She wanted to be a part of this discussion and started walking out of the medical clinic with Zander. "I've been in the same danger for several months. Why is it worse now?"

Orlando followed closely behind them as he answered her. "El, the demons have seen you, and you said there were kids there who can identify you. Kadir and that Sidhe bastard will now have no problem finding you. Not to mention, they saw Zander protecting you. They will assume you mean something to him and might try to use you as leverage to obtain the amulet."

She was fuming. She glared at him over her shoulder. "I'm no wilting flower who needs to be locked away and protected. I can help."

"El, you may have some skill with a blade which I admit is impressive as hell, but you can do nothing against the demon. You're just a little female, after all," Orlando teased, but she sensed his worry for her safety.

"Funny, haha. That's like me saying you're just a pussy cat," she countered.

"You know you love my house cat. Well, maybe not, you never did get me a litterbox, just threw my ass out in the cold every time I had to go. That's just cruel," he laughed and ruffled her hair. She reached out and smacked him on the shoulder.

"I swear you are still a stripling. Can you stay focused on the matter at hand?" Gerrick said as he rolled his eyes at their exchange.

Elsie smiled at the surly warrior. "You were a stripper?" she asked Orlando. "Is that what he means?"

Zander laughed and responded, "Nay, lass, he was no' a stripper. A *stripling* is what we call a supernatural who hasna reached sexual maturity. At age twenty-five, we all go through, what you mortals call, puberty. At maturity, we are able to engage in sex and we come into our preternatural abilities."

He nudged her in the direction of the stairs. "Few will also develop their own unique powers. Breslin is the only one in the history of the realm to receive her powers before maturation and I canna tell you the problems she had as a result of gaining her powers so young. Anyway, you know we're immortal. We doona physically age after we transition from a *stripling*."

She began climbing the stairs, more overwhelmed with this new information. "I swear you guys need a handbook, for the newly-initiated into your world. You could call it Tehrex Realm for Dummies," she joked.

"This is a lot to absorb, and right now, the most important thing is that we keep you safe. Och, I'm no' any good to the realm if I think you are in danger. Lass, that means that you must remain here with me at Zeum. Besides, it will be a much shorter commute for your new job, as well." She gaped at the man's audacity.

"Whoa buddy, wait a minute. I can't live here. We aren't in a relationship, and even if we were, I wouldn't be moving in with you so soon. And, I've told you a hundred times that I don't take orders from you, Mr. Bossy Pants." She was going to strangle her inner-sex-fiend as she started packing a suitcase. Shaking her head to deny her body's desire, she continued, "You all have done so much for me. I'm already indebted to you up to my eyeballs and I refuse to be a charity case any longer."

He stopped her at the foot of the main stairs. She easily read the expression on his face and hadn't meant to insult him. She was trying to thank him and say she was going to take care of herself now.

"You havena been a charity case. What I have done has all been because I could do nothing less. For me there is no other choice. I doona think you understand that I *need* to take care of you and ensure your safety. And, Breslin needs your help with Elsie's Hope. We have an office downtown, but she hasna been able to meet any applicants before sundown. We need someone with your degree in Psychology to help these clients."

His fingers sifted through her long, brown tresses. "We canna keep you safe at your apartment any longer. Kadir has enlisted the help of the Fae, which makes securing you in that wee apartment verra dangerous for everyone, especially your neighbors. If the demon decides to attack, he will think nothing of harming innocent humans. Of course, you can have your own suite of rooms upstairs...if you'd like."

She closed her eyes and slapped duct tape across her inner-sex-fiend's mouth before she shouted they'd be sharing his bed. Moving into this mansion was a bad idea. Her vampire drove her insane and pushed every button she had. Yet, she wanted him more than she would ever admit. And, it wasn't simply a desire for his body. Emotions battled and churned in her gut whenever she was near him.

"*Chiquita*, Zander is right. You have to stay here." Santiago's softly spoken words brought her eyes open. "We can move your furniture into your rooms upstairs. In fact, I think it can all fit into the closet. I know you don't want to put anyone else in danger. That's why you do what you do with Mack and SOVA. You may be scared right now, but you know this is right."

She peeked around Zander's large, muscular bicep and narrowed her eyes at Santiago. He knew she would never knowingly place others in danger and was manipulating her with that fact. But, she was astonished that they accepted her for who she was, without judgment or recrimination. That didn't mean it didn't chafe that they were ganging up on her.

"You are a bunch of overbearing men. I am not completely helpless. As Santi pointed out I have fought these creatures nightly for over a year. I get your point that my neighbors would be in danger." She hated the dilemma this posed for her. "If I did stay here a couple of days, and I'm not saying that I'm going to, I would leave my furniture in my apartment. The move wouldn't be permanent and I have no desire to bring my stuff here only to turn right around and move it back."

"*A ghra*, you are staying more than a couple days. End of discussion. You doona fully comprehend the danger."

She stared at Zander with incredulity. She had been attacked and her husband brutally murdered. She understood the danger better than most. Her reply was suddenly cut off when he hefted her over his shoulder. Her stomach hit the wall of muscles as he pounded up the stairs with her.

"What the hell? Put me down! Damn it, Zander, you can't treat me like this. I am not staying," she huffed and hit his back. Her fists hit steel. Nausea struck as her stomach banged his shoulder, jostling the margaritas she had consumed earlier. Ugh. It would serve him right if she threw up all over him.

"You're staying, *a ghra*." He took the stairs two at a time and adjusted her every time she slipped, continuing on with his steady pace. And, he wasn't out of breath in the least, despite the fact that he had fought an epic battle and had a large wound across his back. He was in better shape than she realized. His body may be sigh-worthy but she refused to be treated like a child.

"Stop it, put me down! Listen to me." He ignored her and made his way down the halls. "You are such a caveman!" she screeched, as she was briefly airborne before her backside hit a mattress and bounced.

"You will stay here. I'll be back later," he declared, turning and leaving before locking the door behind him.

"You will regret this, *your Highness!*" she screamed at the wood door. She was fuming. How dare he? She'd never been treated in such a high-handed manner. He needed to join the twenty-first century. Women were not weak-minded possessions in need of direction and protection. He had another thing coming if he thought this would work with her.

And, how are you going to protect yourself from demons? Her rational mind chimed in. *That thing had fangs the size of swords, you need him.*

She sighed, he was right. She knew she couldn't take the demon. That thing would take her life, easy as swatting a fly. Deflated, she sat heavily on the bed. She wasn't going to ignore the danger, but, was it too much to ask that he discuss this issue with her rather than order her around?

Stupid, sexy, Neanderthal vampire.

CHAPTER TWENTY-FIVE

Three bottles of Jameson's Rarest were sitting in front of Bhric when Zander walked into the war room. It took a larger quantity of alcohol to intoxicate supernaturals and apparently Bhric was working his way toward oblivion. Zander debated having a drink himself. He had probably ruined his chance at claiming his mate, but no way in hell was he allowing Elsie to go back to her apartment. It was too fucking dangerous.

"*Brathair*, what are you doing here? You need your rest," Zander barked.

"Och, it hurts like hell, but I need to be here. We have to find that bastard. He almost got your mate," Bhric slurred, raising his bottle to the group. "Besides, Jameson here is helping to take the pain away." His brother tilted the bottle back and finished it off.

Zander didn't have time to lecture his brother. He glanced around the room and noted Orlando pacing restlessly. The movements drove Zander's own anger and anxiety higher.

"Our highest priority right now is finding the lair so we

can get rid of the infestation. That bastard got too close to the only Fated Mate that we know of in the realm. How did that happen?" Orlando asked.

"More important," Kill said, his tone lethally edged, "when did you plan on telling the council that the mating curse has been lifted? I can't believe you kept such important information from us," Killian finished, peering up from a laptop.

Zander pushed aside the guilt he felt. It was huge life-altering news that every member of the realm deserved to know, but he selfishly hadn't wanted to expose his mate until after he had claimed her. He wanted her to be immortal before breaking the news given that he worried the realm would not react well to a human queen. After all, even he hadn't taken her humanity well.

"Och, the whole situation has been a mess from day one. Learning of her existence has been fraught with heartache and trouble."

"It couldn't have all been heartache. You managed to get her into bed and discover what she is to you," Kill pointed out. Killian walked a fine line with Zander's patience. The only thing stopping Zander from taking his head off was the fact that they were equals on the Dark Alliance Council.

"It hasna happened like that at all. I discovered who she was after dreamwalking with her. The encounter wasna real. No' one aspect of our mating has followed how we've been told. I havena been able to feed or ingest any blood for over eighteen months, despite the fact that the mating hasna been completed. My mate has had a husband that was murdered by skirm and she herself was almost killed in a skirm attack. Oh, and my mate runs around at night with a vigilante group killing skirm. Dealing with all of this, it never crossed my mind to tell anyone outside these walls."

"That is an important issue to discuss, but right now we need to focus on the new demon and his ally. What were you able to discover about them on the database?" Santiago questioned as he sat back in his chair with his hands folded across his stomach. It appeared as if Santiago's minor injuries from the battle had already healed. That was good because they needed to be ready to go on the offensive.

Killian's fingers flew across the keyboard so fast human eyes wouldn't be able to track the movements. "You're right. We will discuss it with the entire council, soon. The Fae that assisted Kadir is called Aquiel. He has been connected to Azazel, which isn't all that surprising given his penchant for attractive males."

"He has been associated with Azazel for some time. Despite the risk of iron poisoning here, Aquiel doesn't spend much time in Faerie and is not listed as a member of the royal family. I updated the database on Kadir and what little we know about him, indicating his association to the Fae," Killian shared.

Zander knew that Queen Zanahia was aware of her subjects and kept close tabs on them. The involvement of the Fae complicated matters. Sure they could use iron as a weapon against them, but their magic was still more powerful than the average sorcerer. Not to mention, the queen had knowledge of old magic, spells, and prophecies, something the realm lost track of when the Mystik Grimoire disappeared from the Miakoda family vault four hundred years ago. The leather-bound volume held magical properties few understood, and contained the realm's compilation of spells and prophecies passed from the Goddess to her oracles.

Orlando ran his hands restlessly through his hair making it stick out all over his head. The male was as agitated as he'd ever seen. "Do the Fae have enough power to shield Kadir's lair? That would present a major complication in finding him. We need to change tactics for our patrols. Maybe follow skirm back to the lair, rather than killing them outright. Kadir is aware of Elsie's importance to Zander and will no doubt target her, now. We could use that to our advantage, stake out her apartment."

"No' a bad idea. The problem I see is that they won't go back to the lair if we follow them. They can sense us, like we can them. We stand a chance if you use your animal forms to track them," Zander pointed out, watching his weary warriors.

"Yeah, they can't detect our animals," Santiago added as he stroked his goatee and leaned his chair against the wall.

Kyran walked to the large map of Seattle and looked it over. Zander noticed how his brother favored his right side. They may have been injured and forced to retreat, but they suffered no losses and that was a win in his book.

"This new archdemon has shaken things up for sure. I canna imagine that he would be in most of these neighborhoods," Kyran hypothesized. "Too suburban. We need to concentrate on more urban areas with abandoned warehouses. Downtown, Belltown, Pioneer Square, Denny Triangle or the area around the Seattle Center."

Zander clapped his brother on the back. "Good thinking, *brathair*. Starting now, we focus our patrols on the areas Kyran mentioned. And, Orlando and Santiago will use their animals when possible. Rhys and Gerrick, each of you head up a team and take one of them with you. Bhric and Breslin will remain here to protect Elsie. Orlando and I are taking a trip to Fremont to see Elvis and gain an audience with Queen Zanahia.

"Nikko, you need to fly Cailyn back to San Francisco,"

Zander ordered. His little spitfire of a mate wouldn't like that he was ordering her sister home, but she'd be safer there. The demons were concentrating in Seattle right now. "Have the San Francisco Dark Warriors keep track of and protect her sister. From a distance, of course. The rest of you head to Confetti and follow any trails. Everyone must be on their highest alert, doona take risks until you are fully healed."

"Does Elsie know you are having her sister returned home? She doesn't take orders well, you may want to talk to her first," Orlando suggested.

Zander glared at the warrior. "I've touched her mind and Elsie wants her sister home where she will be safely away from this shite. I assure you, the least of her anger will be aboot my high-handedness with regards to her sister. You walk a fine line, Orlando. Doona ever question me, especially aboot *my* mate! Now, get off your fucking arses and get to work," he snapped.

ELSIE HEARD his thunderous approach before the knock sounded at the door. It was surprisingly gentle compared to the force of his steps. Why was he knocking? It wasn't like she could open the locked door for him. She was still upset about his behavior and refused to respond. Of course, that didn't stop the king. The door opened and he entered with his typical arrogance. Too bad she found that so irresistibly sexy and had to force herself to scowl at the vampire.

"*A ghra,*" he intoned.

Were there brackets of tension around his eyes? He carried the weight of an entire species on his shoulders, and she couldn't help but worry about his obvious stress.

"You don't get to call me that," she hissed and felt bad at the hurt that flashed in his eyes. Well too bad, she wasn't going to be controlled and she had to put her foot down about his behavior now. "You can't order me around. I won't be told what to do, Zander. We need to talk about things before you go around making decisions that affect me."

His countenance softened and he approached her. "I won't apologize, *a ghra*, your safety is the most important thing. I lose all rational thought when I think of you in danger or being hurt. It nearly killed me when I failed to protect you before so you will remain in this house. I must ensure you are protected."

She watched this formidable leader and realized that even when he was giving her orders, he was infinitely gentler with her than he was others. The only thing that saved him at the moment was the fact that he didn't treat her like he did his warriors. Knowing he cared so much deflated her indignant anger. He wasn't human and didn't think like she did which was something she needed to remember. There was no doubt this truly was killing him. The crack in the hard shell around her heart widened and let him in a bit more.

Still, irresistible or not, Zander need to learn that a little please would go a long way.

She didn't want to place anyone in danger. Not these new friends of hers, or her neighbors. Plus, she had to admit that the thought of living in this remarkable home, having her dream job, and cooking in that kitchen was more than tempting.

She smirked and tilted her head, gazing at him. "The best way to get what you want from a human," she placed her hands on her hips, "especially, a woman, is to ask nicely. You know...say please. Since you behaved appallingly, and locked me inside this room alone, I've had time to think things over. First, I'd love to take the job. We can negotiate my salary later. And second, I will only move in here on conditions." She paused and looked him square in the eye. The connection between them took her breath away, causing warmth to flood her chest and surround her black hole.

"One, I will pay you rent, and two, I will be moving out when it's safe again. And, before you ask, yes, I will give up my apartment. I can't imagine I'll be able to afford it, and a room here. Now, I need to check on Cailyn, and then I desperately need rest. There is only so much my wee, mortal brain can handle, and this has been a verra full day," she winked at him.

He let out a breath and grabbed her by the waist, picking her up off the floor. "Are you making fun of the way I talk again, *a ghra*?"

"I would never. But, let's get one thing real clear. If you ever man-handle me and lock me in a room ever again, I will castrate you in your sleep," she threatened.

"Point taken. In my defense, 'tis no' in my nature to ask or use niceties. I promise you I will try, but I ask that you give a caveman a break." He lowered his head and kissed her. It was tender and sweet and it set her ablaze.

He leaned his forehead against hers. "I have made arrangements for your *puithar*. Nikko will fly her home this evening. I'm relieved you will not fight me on staying. I can agree to your conditions, but you will pay me nothing. The thought is preposterous. It is my responsibility to provide for you." He placed her on the sofa behind them and leaned over her. She was trapped by the strong arms bracketing her. Warmth and electricity radiated off his hugely muscled body.

He kissed the tip of her nose and met her gaze. "I have terms of my own. You will never leave the compound at night withoot me and will always have one of my warriors with you during the day. That is non-negotiable. Now, I'll be back shortly. I have to visit a troll about a fairy." He closed the gap and met her lips in a passionate-toe-curling kiss and she melted into him.

He pulled back and his gaze bore into her with its intensity. Between that kiss and the elusive pull she felt toward him, she was a ball of need. "Do you have to leave yet?" she murmured.

She glanced down at the erection that was straining his pants. The sight made her want to explore his luscious body. She cupped his shaft over his pants and squeezed, wanting to give him incentive to stay. A deep, masculine groan escaped his throat. She grinned and ran her hand along his length.

Unsure where the urge was coming from, she suddenly wanted to taste him, but had such little experience with this. She was nervous. She'd only done it a couple times for Dalton and she hadn't enjoyed it. Dalton had always been a gentle, almost tentative lover, until she took him into her mouth and then he grabbed her hair and thrust roughly to the back of her throat, choking her. Like any man, he lost himself in the moment and was unaware of her discomfort. Eventually, she'd stopped doing it altogether.

She licked her lips and reveled in the way Zander's eyes narrowed. She was going to go for it. She pushed against him and he allowed her to stand up. She stepped into his hard body and ran her hands under his shirt and over his chest then down his abdomen to pause at his waist band. His skin was on fire, echoing the fire burning in her core.

Boldly, she slipped her fingertips into the top of his

pants and gasped when she encountered the tip of his shaft. It was already slick from pre-cum. She maneuvered her hand down and grasped his erection where it was confined. For something so hard, the texture of his skin was silky smooth.

"*A ghra.*" His voice was a warning and a plea at the same time.

She went to her knees and looked up into his glowing, sapphire eyes. "I don't have much experience with this and I want to please you, so tell me how you like it," she told him as she unzipped his pants and shoved them to his knees. His cock sprang out, pointing at her. Surprisingly, her mouth watered for his taste.

"I didna come here for this, but I'm no' going to stop you. Your touch alone is enough to make me cum. I'm more worried I will embarrass myself and cum as soon as that hot little mouth closes around me." His erotic words caused an ache in her core.

"I want you to lose that careful control," she murmured and gripped the base of his shaft, overwhelmed at the magnificent size of him. This wasn't going to be easy. "You carry too much on your shoulders. It will do you good to let go."

Her lips parted and her tongue darted out, skimming the pre-cum. She hummed at the flavor of him. It was indescribable. Almost like a full-bodied brandy that she wanted to get drunk on. She wrapped her lips around the head and swirled her tongue around the spongy mass.

He grabbed her hair and thrust involuntarily, hitting the back of her throat. She couldn't breathe around him. Her panic dissipated when he gentled his hold and controlled his movements. "Sorry, you drive me crazy. Doona stop, please. I willna hurt you." His voice had roughened with desire and she could see that he wanted this desperately, but he put her first. His care for her even in the heat of his passion aroused her more.

She stretched her mouth to the limit and took as much of his girth as she could manage. His shaft hardened even more and the sounds of his pleasure had her dropping her inhibitions and reaching up to grasp his balls. She had never been so bold, squeezing the full globes. He cried out and was unable to stop himself from gently thrusting into her mouth. It was not the uncomfortable experience she'd had before and was relieved to find that she didn't mind her mouth being stretched so far.

She sucked him hard and her body responded to his pleasure. Shockingly, her nipples hardened into peaks and her core clenched, echoing how badly she wanted him.

"I can smell your arousal, *a ghra*. Hold on," he murmured before he picked her up and flipped her as he lay down on the nearby sofa. She heard fabric tearing and when she felt his breath against her aching core, she realized he had ripped her panties and she was positioned perfectly over his face. She cried out his name as he began licking, nipping, and sucking her into his mouth. He devoured her like he was a starving man.

"Jesus, Zander...that feels wonderful," she murmured and took him back into her mouth. Elsie reveled in the new experience, loving how this man took her to new heights.

With his gentle thrusting, it took her closer to the edge rather than detracting from the experience. He eased two fingers into her and she arched up. She twisted around and saw her ecstasy reflected back to her. She sucked and stroked him in unison with his ministrations and they reached their peak together, exploding in one another's mouths.

As warm jets of semen spurted down her throat, she set a rhythm of swallowing what he so freely gave her. He didn't let up on her during his orgasm. She had never been so grateful that he was a vampire and his biology gave him long orgasms as he brought her to peak three more times before he was done.

She collapsed onto his groin, breathing heavily. She should have been uncomfortable with her face sitting close to his groin, but she couldn't bring herself to care one iota. That had been incredible and the most intimate act she had ever engaged in. Before she settled her heart, he had flipped her to face him.

"I've never experienced anything like that in my life. While I had only intended to give you pleasure, you took it to the next level and blew my mind. You are very dangerous for me, Zander. Now, I believe you mentioned needing to see a troll about a fairy," she reminded him. She wanted to say goodbye to her sister before she left and neither one of them would get anything done if he didn't leave.

She couldn't ignore the niggle of concern that creeped into her mind about them being from different worlds, literally. She had no idea where this thing between them was going, but it seemed impossible that anything more would develop. After all, he was a vampire and she was a human.

CHAPTER TWENTY-SIX

Zander scrutinized the deserted street under the Aurora Bridge while he thought of how Elsie had initiated intimacy for the first time, giving him the best blow-job he'd ever received. Unfortunately, his mate mark was a painful reminder that they hadn't completed the mating, something he desperately wanted.

He was accustomed to making decisions and having them followed through. He removed obstacles, didn't coddle and tolerate them. But, he wasn't able to announce his mating to the realm, let alone, complete said mating. To say his patience was wearing thin was an understatement. He'd never been closer to the edge of losing his ever-loving mind.

Pushing aside his discomfort, he focused on Elvis, the Fremont Troll. Zander found it comical that the troll was a popular tourist destination for the humans. On the surface, it seemed unlikely to him that the surly troll would tolerate the humans climbing all over him for photo ops. But, he loved it, and was incorrigible as he played pranks on the unknowing. City officials never knew who dressed Elvis up for each of the holidays when in reality,

Elvis did it to attract the women and children. He was, after all, an attention-whore. Not to mention, he physically gained strength by having his image in countless households.

Elvis was an enormous, gray, bridge troll. With his preternatural vision, Zander could make out the tiny scales that covered him. He saw Elvis' huge nose draw in a breath. That was their cue to announce themselves. The troll shifted his massive body and lifted his hand from the dusty, red, VW bug. Zander expected him to move out from under the bridge but he remained hunched over, watching them warily.

Zander reached into his pocket and retrieved the large, emerald pendant that would serve as their toll to the troll. He straightened his red, silk shirt and adjusted his black, leather jacket as he climbed out of Orlando's black Ford Mustang. Belatedly, he acknowledged that he should have worn one of his suits to meet with the infamous Seelie Queen, but he had been too consumed by Elsie's erotic play to think of etiquette.

Zander walked across the street and stopped twenty yards from the troll and spoke the necessary riddle. "When you have me, you want to share me, when you share me, I no longer exist."

The blast of a canon sounded before the ground rolled beneath their feet. Elvis was chuckling. "A secret," boomed Elvis in his deep, bass voice. "Good to see you, Vampire King. Have you brought your toll?"

He lifted the large pendant and held it up so the street light gleamed off the emerald. "Aye, I have." He walked over and dropped the offering into the troll's large hand. "I need to contact her majesty, Zanahia." The Seelie Queen spent most of her time in Faerie, the Fae realm, separated from

Earth by a magical veil only the Fae could cross and Elvis was her gatekeeper in Seattle.

Elvis' fingers closed around the pendant. "It's always a pleasure dealing with you, Zander. Surely, you would rather talk about your *Fated Mate*? I hear she portends change for the realm. That this is a sign that the Goddess is bestowing treasures, once again. Everyone is anxious to see what will come of this. I, for one, am sitting here on pins and needles." The boom echoed again. Elvis was in a jovial mood. "Oh, wait, that's a big boulder. Little to the left, ah, right there. Ahhh, so much better." He shifted to the side, creating a dust storm in the process. He was quite the comedian tonight.

Zander wondered how this creature had heard the news when his council wasn't aware of it yet. "Aye, I have been blessed with my Fated Mate, but I doona know what changes are in store for the realm. I welcome any changes the Goddess brings. It is because of my mate that I need to see Zanahia, right away. There was an altercation earlier this evening at Confetti and a Fae was involved with the archdemons and skirm."

Elvis' grey, scaled eyebrows drew down in a scowl. "I wasn't aware the Fae were involved tonight. Had I known, I would have been there. I enjoy skirm barbeque. Why is it, I am never invited to the parties? I will tell you what I know, if you promise to invite me the next time."

Orlando's expression revealed his amusement. "That would have been interesting news. I can see the headlines, 'The Famous Fremont Troll Traipses Through Town, Skewering Fanged Kids'."

The troll's thunderous laughter echoed and Zander stumbled as the ground rolled. "The photo-ops would be endless. But, next time, bring the party to me. I make a killer crab-dip."

Zander refocused the conversation, needing to get to the matter at hand. Dawn was rapidly approaching. "Can we move along? Time is of the essence," he said glancing at the lightening sky.

"Keep your knickers on, your Highness, she is in Faerie. I will pass on your request for an audience." They watched as the troll's giant, yellow eyes turned shiny silver, resembling two, huge hubcaps from an eighteen-wheeler truck.

A misting fog crept in, obscuring the ground under the Aurora Bridge. Zander brushed the dew off his leather jacket, and looked to check Orlando's reaction to the coming Fae presence. The last thing he needed right now was a lusty, feline shifter losing control with the Seelie Queen.

"I'm okay, Liege." Orlando snapped, clearly annoyed to have his will-power questioned.

As the mist cleared, a bright, white light flashed in the interior of the dirty, old VW. The door creaked open of its own volition, and mist escaped from the inside of the red car. A delicate, white hand reached out to the top of the door. The Seelie Queen attempted to exit the car, but fell to her hands, as her gown snagged on her shoe.

"For the love of Faerie! Elvis, you need a more appropriate contraption for my portal to Seattle. Oh, bother, now look at my gown." She fussed with the torn hem of the see-through, gauzy, white gown, and uttered a spell, repairing the tear. She ran her hand over the bodice, pausing over her pert and visible breasts, while looking at Orlando. "I see you brought me a treat which is always a good idea when you want something, Zander," the queen murmured, finally turning her gaze to him.

He questioned his decision to bring Orlando to this

meeting. It was near impossible for a shifter to deny their desire for a Fae. He had to trust that Orlando would keep the lust at bay.

"Nay, Zanahia, I didna bring him for you, but 'tis good to see you again. Lovely, as always," he said as he approached her, clasped her perfectly, manicured hand, and kissed her big, diamond ring.

He took in Zanahia's long, blond hair with its small braids fastened at her crown. Her intricate, silver crown matched her shiny, silver eyes. She was tall, lean and exceptionally attractive, yet her beauty did nothing for him.

"I need to speak with you aboot an urgent matter, your Majesty."

"Of course, how can I be of assistance?" she smiled.

"Several hours ago, one of your subjects assisted Kadir in taking doon the wards that protect Club Confetti. Then, he, along with two archdemons, and an army of skirm, attacked me, my Fated Mate and my warriors when we left the club."

"Oh, I hadn't been informed that Morrigan was once again playing match-maker. What a momentous occurrence for you. I'm glad to see that you survived the attack. That must've been a bloodbath. It would have been a travesty for you to be lost after just finding your intended."

"Aye, 'twas a bloodbath for them. But, I need to speak with you aboot this subject of yours. I want the threat Aquiel poses eliminated," he ground out.

"Yes, we will get to that, but first, I simply must hear all about this mate of yours. Souls must be singing throughout the realm," she clasped her hands with joy. He had an uneasy feeling in his gut. It couldn't be a good thing that she had such an interest in Elsie.

His brow furrowed, and he ran his hand along his whiskered jaw. She was up to something, but he was unsure what, and didn't have the time to ferret that out. "The Goddess has blessed me with a human for my Fated Mate. She is beyond anything I ever expected. Strong, courageous, loyal, and...beautiful."

Large, silver pools gazed at him, as glittery particles showered from her hair and skin. "Oh, my, that is a great blessing indeed! I can already see your little half-breeds running around that compound of yours." Did he detect something in the tone of her voice? "Now, about this subject of mine. I'm not aware of Aquiel's latest actions. We've been neutral in this war of yours from the beginning, and my subjects are free to consort with whom they choose. I'm sorry that I cannot provide you with more at this time. All I can promise is that I will look into this matter further."

"So, the Fae havena officially allied with Kadir and the demons." That was a relief. "Many feared his involvement meant you'd chosen the wrong side. Do you know where I can find Aquiel? Is he capable of casting a shielding spell on Kadir's lair?"

Zanahia tapped her thin, pale-pink lips with one, long finger as she contemplated. "The one piece of information I will not disclose is his location, since I am aware of your intent to terminate him. That being said, Aquiel is of a lower caste, with limited knowledge, so he's not capable of casting such a strong enchantment. However, if he were to acquire the knowledge, he could cast them. I assure you such information is difficult to come by, especially since the Fae have an oral tradition of passing on spells, unlike the sorcerers of your realm, with their written customs."

He felt a tingle that warned him dawn was imminent. "Thank you for your cooperation. I must take my leave, sunrise approaches. Till next time, then."

"Do keep me updated on your mating ceremony. I wish

you and your human much happiness." He kissed her diamond ring in parting, and watched her awkwardly climb back into the heap of metal.

"She is hiding something. I'm not sure what, but I have a feeling it has to do with....." Orlando cut his commentary short and staggered as Zander blasted into his mind.

"Keep your bluidy mouth shut. Elvis is a servant of the Queen, in case you forgot."

"Run along now, Batman and Robin. I have a sensitive stomach, you know, and don't think I'll be able to keep down that German Sheppard from supper if I had to watch your skin boil and bubble, then fall off your bones, when the sun rises."

SOMETHING WAS wrong and Elsie had no idea what it was. The Dark Warriors surrounded her, tensed and readied for battle. They were standing outside her apartment and she searched fruitlessly for the danger they sensed. Her heart raced like a hummingbird's wings. It was disconcerting to see four powerful men come to attention so abruptly. She wished she had their supernatural senses. It would come in handy when she did her patrols.

"What is it?" she asked in a hushed voice, drawing her blade from the small of her back, ready for battle.

Orlando rolled his eyes as he took a protective stance in front of her, with his body bladed, and his *sgian dubh* ready. "Kadir found you already. I'm sure the Fae helped him locate your home last night because his dimwits have been here. Be on-guard, we could be walking into a trap."

Elsie tensed, suddenly thankful that Zander was a Neanderthal. If she'd had her way last night she and Cailyn would have been at her apartment. She refused to contemplate what would have happened then.

Gerrick joined Orlando in shielding her, keeping his body loose and open. She heard Gerrick mutter in the same language he had used with Jace and Killian the night before.

"What spell are you casting now? Are you doing a portal back to Zeum? Do you think that's wise? Everyone that lives here will see it and ask questions."

Gerrick gazed at her, his exasperation clear. "No, I'm not doing a portal. I'm trying to determine if there are Fae present. I've detected no Fae, but that doesn't mean we aren't in danger. I can't say if there are any skirm still in the apartment."

Santiago looked over at Gerrick then Rhys and Orlando. "On my mark, we go in. You two, follow, and, Elsie, stay in the sunlight until we clear the apartment. On three, one, two," Santiago called, and on three kicked the door open, charging in.

She saw the destruction from where she stood. "Oh, my God! It's all destroyed! I can't believe someone would do this. It can't all be gone," she snarled, her anger taking over. "I will turn every last skirm to dust for this," she vowed as she stumbled into her apartment, not waiting for the all clear. She glanced around and felt completely violated. Everything was ruined. Her entire life had been in that apartment. It might not be much, but it was hers, dammit.

The Mexican blankets that once hung proudly on her walls were in shreds on the floor. She picked up slices of the lime-green throw and felt tears stream down her cheeks, as she surveyed the destruction all around her. Pictures were torn and pottery shards and glass littered the floor. Numbly, she entered her bedroom and fell to her knees by the remains of her photo albums.

She frantically pushed through the coils and foam padding torn from her mattress. She tossed aside desecrated clothing and knickknacks, gathering anything she could salvage. The sound of her friends' boots crunching the debris was like an elephant traipsing through the jungle, destroying everything in its path. She cried harder, every link she had to Dalton and her parents was gone. Her black hole engulfed every fiber of her being as she sobbed.

"Is there something specific you are looking for?" Rhys asked gently. "I can help search. Hey, take a deep breath and try to calm down." She ignored Rhys and continued her frenetic search. She needed to find something to salvage. She couldn't bear it if nothing was left.

"Elsie, you need to stop for a minute. There is broken glass everywhere. Damn it, you're bleeding. Stop!" Orlando squatted next to her and placed his warm hands on her shoulders. She looked up at him, unable to hide her sorrow. He pulled her into his arms, cooing words of comfort to her. They did little to ease the pain that had engulfed her. It felt as if she'd lost Dalton all over again. Her parents, too. Every last picture she had of them was torn.

"There's nothing left. They destroyed it all!" She wailed as she beat her fists against Orlando's broad, muscular chest. It felt as if she were beating her fists against a brick wall. The cuts on her palms were leaving blood on his light-blue shirt. She told herself to stop, but her anger and frustration could not be reined in. Why would they do this?

"We'll pack up everything we can, including the pieces of your pictures and taken them to Killian. He's a computer genius and can put them back together for you," Gerrick promised.

Silently, each of them picked through the debris. They

filled a box with the intact items, along with several pieces of photos.

"Can you guys give me a few moments alone in here?" She watched them exit the apartment and went back to her bedroom. A flash of green flannel caught her eye and she crossed the room. Her eyes misted with tears again as she picked up the pieces of her father's favorite flannel shirt. She had kept it after he'd died and often slept in it. She crouched with her head slumped and noticed Dalton's wedding ring was under the debris of her ruined desk. She picked it up, her breath hitching on a sob as she wiped it off on her pink sweater. She knew better than most that change was an inevitable part of life, but still, she was unprepared for the anguish that resulted from the destruction of everything that meant anything to her.

She stood up and brushed off her knees. She wasn't going to stand by and let this violation go unanswered. Those assholes had taken enough from her. Anger settled like a pit in her chest. They wouldn't know what hit them, she vowed. With that, she turned and left the apartment.

THE STUPID FLOAT drifted away from her again. All Elsie wanted to do was relax in the sun. She had been trying for several minutes to successfully heave her body onto her new float, and not sink, yet the neon-pink contraption was fighting her. She was tempted to grab her blade and slash it to shreds.

Emotionally, she was drained. In an attempt to forget the destruction they had discovered at her apartment yesterday, she had donned a bikini, grabbed a margarita and headed to the pool.

Earlier that morning, she had taken the Jag she loved so much for some shopping therapy. Her trip vetted a new bikini and a great new float. Well, not so great, she amended, when she sank again.

She stood and tugged on the bottom of her new, blue, string-bikini, thinking she may have needed the medium. She was too pale to wear it, but that particular suit had practically jumped off the rack into her cart. The sale price had only clenched the deal.

Dragging the pink, plastic, floating monstrosity back toward her, her thoughts returned to the changes in her life. She had finally graduated from college, gotten a fabulous new job and was dating a sexy vampire. Well, dating was the only term that came to mind. If you asked her inner-sex fiend they were shacking up and planning to elope to Jamaica. They hadn't had "the talk" yet and she was fine with that because she was still on the fence about what she wanted.

Heaving an exasperated sigh, she hefted herself onto the ridiculous contraption. She smiled as she settled onto the float, thinking she had finally won the battle, and laid back to enjoy the sunshine. However, that triumph was short-lived.

"What in the name of Hades are you doing?" Orlando laughed, as he walked into the pool area and saw her being consumed by neon-pink plastic.

"I'm catching some rays on my great, new float. Don't you love it?" She smiled brightly while silently cursing the blasted thing.

"You do realize you aren't floating, you're drowning. I can barely see your beautiful face. Were you waiting for someone else to blow it up for you?" he teased.

She intended to roll off the float gracefully, but ended up

sinking beneath the water. She surged back to the surface, sputtering, and placed her hands on her hips. "Of course, I blew the stupid thing up. I have been fighting it for thirty minutes." She brushed her wet curls out of her face.

"Let me guess, it was an eight dollar special, Ms. Bargain Shopper," he said, dryly. "You have to start shopping somewhere else."

"I'll have you know that it was only five dollars, and I did shop somewhere else. I bought it at the dollar store. I don't know why they call it that. I've never seen anything there for a buck," her lips twitched as she tried not to laugh.

His gaze roved over her. "You were ripped off, but that bikini is a keeper. You should buy it in every color."

She laughed so hard she snorted. "Yeah, right. I'm so round and pale, I look like a snowman with boobs. And, the suit exaggerates that fact."

Their combined laughter echoed off the glass panels that made up the walls and ceiling of the pool's enclosure. She climbed the stairs and crossed to get her towel off the lounge chair, but turned at the last second, and pushed him, fully clothed, toward the water. She screeched as she felt his hand latch onto her arm. Their limbs intertwined as they fell beneath the surface together.

She came up sputtering and hiccupping, as her giggles continued. He splashed her and a water fight of epic proportions ensued. The deck surrounding the pool was soaked and the water was flowing into the covered patio area. This was the therapy she needed.

CHAPTER TWENTY-SEVEN

Zander removed his shoes, so he could enjoy the feel of the dispelled water on his feet. Hidden in the shadows near the patio and kitchen, he watched his mate laugh and play with Orlando. He wished he was able to enjoy the sunshine and pool with her, but contented himself with his view. The predatory male in him wanted to pound Orlando for admiring her, but he was in agreement that she looked fantastic in her suit. He didn't see her as pale, but saw luminescent, peaches-and-cream skin he wanted to devour.

He fantasized about licking the drops of water, which had the luxury of trailing down her shoulders, and under her top. To kiss the clearly erect nipples beneath the fabric. His eyes traveled down further, and he envied the liquid that dripped below the waist of her bottoms. He imagined untying the sides, and baring her glistening flesh to his hungry mouth. With a hiss, his fangs shot down. The ache in his gums was as bad as the ache in his pants. His daydream was cut short, as the plush towel cut off his view when she wrapped it around her torso.

Her soul stirred in his chest and he cherished the warmth that spread through him with each movement. It brought him such love and comfort. Selfish bastard that he was, he wanted to keep her soul where it was, nestled close to his heart, rather than release it to her during their mating.

"Do you want some lunch? The cooks prepared chicken salad," Orlando asked, bringing his attention back to them. His wet t-shirt flew over his head, sopping shoes followed the shirt, and soon there was a pile of wet clothes and a ruined iPhone.

"Sure," Elsie began, but trailed off when she looked over and caught sight of Zander's bright, glowing eyes.

"Oh...Zander, hi." The fact that she was speechless under his heated gaze, further inflamed his lust.

"*A ghra*, you look striking. Orlando," he managed a nod to his warrior, but didn't take his eyes off Elsie. The pain in his mark and the lust from the mating compulsion coupled with his need for Elsie's blood had his emotions all over the place. He was barely keeping himself in check.

He grasped Elsie's hand as soon as she joined him in the shadows. "Do you mind if I join you for lunch? Och, before I forget, Killian said he was able to recreate some of your photos. And, I was able to get your *da's* shirt repaired. It's not perfect, but you can still wear it." He put his jealousy of Dalton aside. There was no reason to hide from her past. It was always going to be a part of her, and thus, him.

He wrapped his arm around her waist and lifted her for his kiss. She molded perfectly to him. His erection nestled against her soft abdomen as he poured his hunger into their kiss.

He paused his kiss, noticing how her eyes remained riveted to the fangs that peeked out from his full lips. His mate was thinking of his bite, wanted his bite. He slid both arms around her back, and tugged her tightly into his chest. He enjoyed her sigh of pleasure, and wished his chest was bare to her breath, instead of encased in a fitted t-shirt.

"There you go again, giving me the perfect gift. I can't believe you had my father's shirt fixed. I was certain it was beyond repair," she said hoarsely. He watched as she shook off her maudlin thoughts and changed the subject. "I'd love for you to join us for lunch. Speaking of eating," she stopped talking and he was tempted even further by the pink that lightened her cheeks. "You're a vampire...do you drink blood? I've never seen you drink blood. You aren't going to bring some woman to the table and feed from her are you?"

He heard the jealousy in her tone and wanted to smile. "Are you volunteering? Because if you are, that would solve my problem." She blushed to the roots of her silky, brown hair. He touched her mind and was floored to realize she wanted it badly, ached for it even.

"No...wait, what problem?" Elsie asked.

"Let's grab some food, and I will explain while we eat," he said as he led her into the kitchen where she saw Santiago eating a sandwich and Orlando reappeared, zipping up a pair of faded jeans.

"Good one, *Chiquita*. I've never been able to get the drop on O," Santiago remarked, taking a bite of his food.

Orlando sliced a croissant and added a generous portion of chicken salad. "That's because I don't trust you. I won't trust Elsie after this, either." He handed the sandwich to Zander. "Here you go, Liege. This will tide you over until you can get some blood from Elsie."

The towel dropped from her body and her eyes were saucers. "Excuse me? I never said I would...that he could," she sputtered then gathered her wits. "Is that why you guys wanted me to stay? To be take-out? I'm not a vampire Slurpee, you know."

He laughed at his mate's humor. "Nay, I didna ask you to stay here for that reason. I know you are no' food. Vampires do need to drink blood for sustenance, but, we survive like any living creature on food, and blood is akin to a necessary vitamin. And, while I want verra much to sink my fangs into your supple flesh and watch you shudder with pleasure, my intent is to keep you safe, lass." He picked up the towel and wrapped it around her shaking shoulders. She had too much exposed skin for him to think straight.

"Vampires are no' ruled by bloodlust. However, there are circumstances where that need is impacted. I have found that since I met you, I canna feed from anyone else. My body rejects it. No one understands why that has happened, but I suspect the connection I feel to you is part of the reason. When Jace took blood from you, it was for me. I ran oot of that blood weeks ago, and I have been feeling the effects of having gone without, for too long. We can have Jace take blood again, if you doona mind. It isna necessary for me to feed directly from you. Either way, I need your blood." He ran his hands up and down her arms, as he kept her close. He hated the idea of drinking her blood from a plastic cup, but would never force her to do anything she wasn't comfortable with.

She chewed her lower lip between her teeth. "Will you die if you don't get blood?"

"Aye, eventually. But, because of my age, it would take a verra long time for me to die from lack of blood. It would be a long and painful process." He ran his fingers across her supple cheek. The blood rushing to the surface was a siren's call.

ELSIE'S BODY zinged when their gazes locked. The thought of him suffering was repellant and she acknowledged that it felt right for her to give him what he needed. The fact that she was the key to Zander's strength and possible survival was outrageous, but his honesty rang through his every word.

"I want you to be strong. It's incomprehensible to me that you have an entire realm that relies on you. So much is on those broad shoulders. Do it. Take my blood."

Breathe, in and out. Repeat. Before she allowed her nerves to resurface, she thrust her wrist to his mouth, closing her eyes to Orlando and Santiago's shocked faces and prepared for the pain to hit.

She heard him inhale deeply and then felt a kiss on her wrist. He placed his hands on her slim hips, and lifted her onto the brown, granite countertop. "Relax, my Lady E, it willna be painful. In fact, a vampire's bite can be verra enjoyable," he lifted her chin and she opened her eyes to meet his glowing gaze, "orgasmic, even," he finished against her lips.

"I guess I'll be the judge of that," she said boldly.

"And, that's our cue to leave, I believe," Santiago quipped as he gathered his plate, and nodded for Orlando to follow. The shifters slipped out of the kitchen, and closed the door, giving them privacy.

Zander searched her countenance. She knew he would sense the raging emotions of fear, repulsion, curiosity and... eagerness. "Are you certain you want to do this?" he asked quietly.

"Yes," she said with more breath than voice. Anticipation

bubbled through her body. She took a moment to memorize every inch of him. She wanted to remember this moment before her life changed forever. She knew that once she crossed this threshold, there was no going back.

His feet were bare and sexy as they peeked out the bottom of his jeans. She followed those tight jeans to the low-rise waist and snagged on the way his t-shirt molded to a heavily muscled chest. His pectoral muscles flexed and her eyes flew to his glowing blue eyes. His desire for her bled from him and her body responded automatically. She looked to his fangs, hoping to dampen her ardor, only to find the sight did anything but. Soon, they would pierce her skin, and he would draw her essence into his body. Was she ready? Hell, yes.

"*A ghra,* your blood has a verra powerful effect on me. I doona want to scare you, but I want to tup you so badly, I canna think straight. I ache for you," he leaned in, and kissed the column of her neck. "I doona know if I can stop myself from claiming you once I take your blood, but I promise I willna harm you."

"I can feel how much you want me. It's prodding my lower belly. I have feelings for you I did not think I ever would again." Would she stop him if he tried for more? Did she want to risk it?

"Just do it," she blurted. All thought ceased, as his attention to the area where her neck met her shoulder, continued. He was going to bite her.

"Doona worry, we willna be tupping on the kitchen counter. When we make love, it will be in our bed, with the finest, silk sheets. You deserve only the best." She didn't know who he was trying to convince, him or her.

He laved her neck over and over before a small prick,

like a bee-sting, below her left ear, surprised her. The sting was quickly replaced by incredible warmth and arousal. She had braced herself for the pain of his bite, but felt her body explode with pleasure, the moment his teeth breached her virginal neck.

She arched to his quaking body and felt the hot liquid of his seed spread across her abdomen and breasts. Her nerve endings fired messages of bliss throughout her body, and she felt tension in her lower abdomen. Her own orgasm exploded before she formed another thought. Twining her legs around his waist, she rode the rigid length of his still erect and spurting cock, unable to stop or control her reaction to his bite. She screamed out his name, as her body shattered and stars blinked behind her eyes. He held her tightly, while his orgasm continued, and he took from her vein.

ZANDER WAS in *Annwn* as he was rocked by an orgasm so intense, he nearly blacked out. Every draw of her blood hit him much as the first sip had, like lightning hitting a rod, re-shaping the sand beneath and creating a beautiful, glass sculpture. She was already integrated into his cellular make-up, but now there was more. He was anxious to claim his mate and had felt her soul reaching out from his chest to her. Her soul was as much a part of him as his was.

Having taken his fill, he gently lapped at her throat, while his orgasm ebbed, and she shuddered against him. His father had shared information about the extended orgasms a vampire garnered after intimate relations with their Fated Mate, but that portrayal was abysmal. There were no words to describe the bliss he experienced.

He licked the twin punctures in her neck, sealing her wounds, and lifted his head to gaze into hot, blue eyes. Her DNA was already altering from his bite. He was desperate to complete their mating. "Are you okay, *a ghra*? Did I hurt you?"

CHAPTER TWENTY-EIGHT

Euphoria was the only word that came to mind. Elsie floated back to her body, slowly blinking at his questions. Had he hurt her? In no way was she hurt. In fact, she felt fantastic. The warmth of his seed on her stomach brought a smile to her face. At least she wasn't the only one who had an orgasm from his feeding. She had almost passed out it was so intense.

"I'm fine, better than fine. Wow, you weren't kidding about your bite being pleasurable. I'm surprised you don't have a line of women begging for you to feed from them." And, why did the thought of him feeding from another woman cause her to become homicidal? She had no idea where this possessiveness was coming from, but shouldn't be all that surprised. After all, he was everything any smart woman wanted in a man. Smart, kind, thoughtful, and giving.

"Och, my Lady E. That was truly realm-shattering. Thank you for your gift. Can you feel how much stronger I am, already? 'Tis magnificent. And, I doona care how many females may beg for my bite, you will be the only one receiving it. We need to clean up before anyone comes in."

"Yeah," she had to stop and clear her throat, "we should clean-up. And, you're right. You look better, and I can feel the energy under your skin."

"'Tis all thanks to you, *a ghra*. Before you, my life was aboot duty and responsibility, and now, there is so much more." She had to admit she was pretty crazy about him, too and may even be falling in love with him.

THREE DAYS HAD PASSED, and Zander was growing increasingly agitated. He had not had any time alone with Elsie since his feeding and he was ready to beat somebody senseless. He has been working night and day to find that bastard, Kadir. Frustrated, he shook his head, as he listened to Rhys and Gerrick tell him that another patrol had yielded zero results on the skirm front. The fact that he had not been able to eliminate the threat to Elsie made his mood worse. He and his Dark Warriors were sitting around the large, maple table in the war room, postulating reasons for the lack of skirm sightings.

His head shifted to the door, as he heard Breslin talking. The alliance council had arrived. Time to suck it up, he had put this off for far too long and knew they were going to be pissed. Finding his Fated Mate was the biggest news in the realm and he had not told them or arranged an announcement for over two months.

His body went rigid as Killian and Nikko sauntered in with Evzen Raziel, the Guild Master for the sorcerers. Evzen's arrogance was evident in the swagger of his tall, lean frame. Dante Tresean, the Cambion Lord, and Hayden Jesaray, the Omega Shifter, followed them into the room. Would they understand why he had withheld information that affected the entire realm? Probably not.

Zander grabbed his tumbler of scotch and took a drink then waited until the chatter in the room quieted. "Welcome everyone. Thank you for coming this evening. I know some of you have traveled far to be here tonight and I appreciate it. Help yourselves to drink and food," Zander gestured with his glass, towards the feast in the middle of the table.

Evzen met his gaze and got right to the point. He'd always been all-business and no-pleasure. "There's no need for formalities. We've been friends longer than we've been allies and I believe it's past time to discuss the attack on Confetti and your Fated Mate."

He perused Evzen's angry countenance. "I sense your anger aboot concealing my mate. You need to understand that she is human and recently experienced a horrendous tragedy at the hand of skirm. They murdered her husband at his place of employment, and since, has become a member of a vigilante group hunting skirm. A few weeks ago, she was also attacked and injured. Because of all this, she wasna in a position to learn of the Tehrex Realm, or that she is my Fated Mate. In fact, she still isna aware of what she is to me."

Dante grabbed a plate and filled it with food before he responded. Zander was glad for his easy mood. "So, the rumors about her husband being murdered are true. I hadn't heard she was a viscous little thing, killing skirm. That does complicate matters, but I am surprised that you kept such important information from your council. We're here to help you through situations like this."

Hayden flexed his enormous biceps where his arms

rested on the table, as his dark-brown eyes remained fixed on his shifters across the table. As the Omega Shifter, it was expected that all shifters were loyal to him, and inform Hayden of everything. Orlando and Santiago had kept him out of the loop on Zander's orders. He knew Hayden would be upset and want someone's ass for it. Zander saw images of the wolf, leopard, and bear waver over Hayden's face and hoped the huge shifter kept control of his animals. He was furious.

"I understand your reasoning for keeping this from the general population, but as Dante pointed out, we have an alliance. We can't advise you, or offer assistance, if we don't know of the issues. And, if you ever force my shifters to dishonor their loyalty to me again," Hayden thundered, showing elongated incisors, "you will not like the outcome."

Zander kept eye contact, aware that he was walking a tightrope. He needed to acknowledge Hayden's dominion over Santiago and Orlando, but at the same time, retain his power over the Dark Warriors. "I meant no disrespect. Your shifter's loyalties are always to you first and their Dark Warrior status second. I've been dealing with one shit-storm after another since I learned of Elsie." He briefly shared the events of the past two months.

Their expressions darkened with their own anger at the circumstances. "It was no' my intent to keep Elsie secret. I know more than anyone the importance of this for the realm, the hope that she represents. We must strengthen our alliance, dark as it is. I need your help to develop a plan to locate the bluidy bastard's lair and keep my mate safe."

Hayden bristled, but Zander knew he was mollified that his position of power over his subjects had not been derided. "It seems unbelievable that the Goddess is once again bestowing her greatest gift. This is something to rejoice over and celebrate, but I understand why you haven't done this given the bold actions of this new archdemon. His behaviors place the realm at a much greater risk of discovery by the humans. Even so, we can't keep this news a secret forever."

Zander grabbed one of the sandwiches Elsie had made for the meeting and refilled his drink. "During the attack at the club, we met the new archdemon. He is a Behemoth demon named Kadir, and the most powerful archdemon I've ever encountered. And, he has enlisted the help of a Fae. Zanahia has assured me the Fae are not aligned with the demons but she refuses to gives us any real aide. Aquiel isna the most powerful Fae, but he is capable enough. The bastard helped them find Elsie's apartment and destroy it."

Hayden ran a hand through his long, brown hair. "We need all the information you can provide about the skirm in your area. I've already issued the order throughout the clan that each pack and pride need to be on the look-out and relay any information they find right away. So, you really think this Kadir's lair is in Seattle?"

"Aye, I do. How else did he get a large number of skirm outside the club in a short time?" Zander asked.

Evzen clasped his long, regal fingers together on the top of the table. "What is most disturbing is how fast they found Elsie's apartment." Zander had also been troubled by that question for days. Thank the Goddess there was no way for the Fae, or any other sorcerer, to trace an individual inside Zeum with its shields in place. It was one of the main reasons he had insisted Elsie stay with him.

"I had stayed at her house for weeks, and there wasn't a sign of skirm," Orlando shared.

"We need to increase our patrols. With the clan involve-ment, we will be able to cover more ground. I think we need to entice Elvis to assist us in locating the demons. He has his ear to the ground and probably has information we need," Hayden said, filling his own plate with food and settling his six-foot-six-inch frame into a chair.

The meeting turned to business, as the council and warriors threw out strategies, plans, and options, but Zander remained half-engaged. His mind kept wandering upstairs, to his lovely mate. It had been too long since he had seen her.

ELSIE FINISHED PUTTING the rest of her new clothes into an antique, Venetian dresser in her bedroom at Zeum. She loved her job and had spent most of the past few days at Elsie's Hope, which was downtown, near the courthouse. To keep her restless mind busy, she threw herself into cleaning, organizing, and adding her personal touch to the office.

Unfortunately, nothing held her attention for long. Her thoughts continuously wandered to Zander and their encounter. Heat coursed through her veins every time she recalled the feel of his lips and fangs on her skin. The walls began closing in on her and she needed to get out of this room. She crossed to the door and almost tripped over a wrapped package that was sitting outside her door. It was rolled foam tied with an enormous, iridescent bow and beside it was a gift-wrapped box. What had that vampire done now? She picked up the card and smiled at the elegant, masculine script.

I thought you may enjoy actually floating in the pool this time. I anxiously await seeing your luminescent skin glistening in the sun. I crave everything about you. Tasting you has irrevocably altered me. Forever yours, Z

"Oh, wow." She gathered the gifts and carried them to the king-sized, canopy bed. She pushed her clothes out of the way and set down her presents. She climbed onto the heirloom quilt and tugged the bow loose. An expensive, pool float unrolled. One that she had dreamed of buying for the past year. She loved that she was living in a house that had a pool that she could use every day if she wanted. She squeezed the thick lime-green foam. No way was she sinking on this puppy. She unwrapped the box and removed a sexy, black, sequined bikini. It was a designer bathing suit and she would bet her next paycheck that Breslin had suggested it. Of course, it was her size, and way too skimpy.

She stood up and looked from the Brazilian-cut of the bottoms to her ass. Not a chance that thing was covering even half of her cheeks. Oh, what the hell, she thought. You only live once and it had been a long time since she had felt so alive. Not allowing second thoughts to stop her, she stripped and put on her new suit. She didn't care that it was nighttime, she was going for a swim. And, she'd grab that hunky vampire on her way to the pool. Excitedly, she grabbed her float and rushed out the door to search for Zander before reason set in.

Her bare feet slapped the wooden floors as she flew down the stairs, only to come to an abrupt halt, at the main landing. Stupefied, she watched about a dozen of the hottest men she had ever seen exit the war room. Apparently, the Goddess Morrigan didn't do ugly.

A hush descended over the group, making her want to crawl back to her room. She found that Zander was staring at her from the middle of the group. As one, the entire group turned to look at her and she was, for all intents and purposes, naked. Self-conscious didn't begin to cover how she felt. Heat blazed over her cheeks, and she searched for an escape or a place to hide.

Okay, don't turn around and run or they will see your butt jiggle. Coming to terms with the fact that she was trapped, she waved nervously, "Hi." Her smile faltered when she was caught by glowing blue sapphires.

CHAPTER TWENTY-NINE

"My Lady E." Zander said, approaching her where she stood, wide-eyed, on the stairs. "I see you received your gifts," his devouring gaze had her stomach tightening with need and heat spreading through her sex. It was unnerving how that man undid her with his mere presence.

"You look truly stunning. Let me introduce you to the council." He took her by the hand and presented her to each council member, explaining their roles. She hastily wrapped the float around her torso as best as she could.

After she had been introduced to everyone and shook their hands, they had all gone down on one knee and lowered their heads, Zander and the Dark Warriors included. Why were they bowing to her? The look in their eyes as they stood was serious and spoke of a deep reverence. Okay...

Zander kissed the back of her hand and murmured, "Are you going for a midnight swim?" She jumped on his change of subject gratefully. His world was foreign to her and there was so much she didn't understand. And, standing in his elegant home in a barely-there bikini was not the time or place to try and figure out what the gesture meant.

"Yes, I was on my way to find you and see if you wanted to join me. I love the float, and the new, uh, bathing suit," she fingered the ties on the side of the bottoms. "I couldn't wait to try this out." She held up the green float and lost her breath with his appraisal. He looked at her in the way that men did when they were totally taken by a woman, like he would die if he didn't have her. Electricity zinged across her skin, leaving chill bumps. And, she enjoyed every second of it.

"El, honey, a plastic bag would be better than that pink nightmare you had before. It was rather funny to watch you heave yourself onto it, though," Orlando laughed, breaking the tension.

She whirled around and smacked Orlando in the shoulder. "You're still upset because I punked you, and you got wet. Poor kitty doesn't like the water."

"Oh, now you've asked for it," Orlando threatened.

She jumped behind Zander and tried to hide, but didn't get very far before he picked her up and threw her over his shoulder, running toward the pool. She couldn't help laughing as she bounced around.

"Skinny-dipping," Rhys whooped, as he tossed his shirt off and undid his pants.

"Put me down, Zander," she pleaded as her stomach bounced on his hard shoulder.

She screeched like a banshee as she was tossed into the pool, but managed to grab onto Zander's shirt sleeve, and they both fell into the still water. They both came to the surface, sputtering and laughing.

"Och, I thought you liked these leather pants, *a ghra*," Zander husked. "Now, you've gone and ruined them. What will you stroke now?" he teased as he shook his head, sending water flying.

"Serves you right. You had my ass bouncing to a room full of strangers. I think they were following the white light, thinking your Goddess was calling them home," she slicked back her wet hair.

Rhys shed his black leathers and charcoal-grey, boxer-briefs in a rapid, graceful sweep. The move was definitely not human, and he wasn't shy about his nudity being on display. "Sweetcakes, watching your ass bounce on Zander's shoulder is indeed like gazing into *Annwyn*," he said, jumping into the pool.

As he floated on his back, his erection stood at attention, a foot above the water, and bobbed like the periscope of a submarine, raised and looking for a target. Elsie chuckled, having become accustomed to the way he operated. He was a sex demon and none of his flirting or arousal was ever really about her.

"Rhys, put some bluidy trunks on. Now. My ma...Elsie doesna want to see your naked arse," Zander snarled, striking out at the warrior. Rhys ducked the punch and swam away.

She waved their exchange off. Rhys didn't bother her with his actions or his words. While Rhys was a gorgeous man, with a hot body, he did nothing to make her blood boil. No, that would be the sexy, brooding vampire looking at her from across the pool. "He's Rhys," she shrugged, as if that explained it all. "And, he's harmless enough. Besides, he isn't the one for me," she quirked a brow at Zander and splashed him.

Zander jumped out and tore off his shirt, shoes and pants, then dove back into the pool in his boxer briefs. He swam up and grabbed her by the legs. She went under and had to catch her breath once she resurfaced. His touch was tantalizing and made her hot with desire. She glanced around to see that all the others had joined them in the pool.

She wished she'd had a chance to grab a margarita from her machine. "What we need now is some Monsteritas. Orlando, can you grab some, please?" She batted her eyelashes at him with a sly smile. "I turned the machine on when I got home from work. That gift was a stroke of genius with so many living in this house."

"Sure, anything else, my Queen?" Orlando asked, sarcasm dripping from every word.

She stuck her tongue out at him. He was her brother from another mother. He brought out the child in her, every time. Despite everything that had happened in her life, she was part of this family now and couldn't be happier.

"I see you have my warriors wrapped around your wee finger." Zander picked up her hand and kissed said wee finger. Goosebumps broke out over her skin.

"That's not true," she objected. "By the way, I didn't mean to interrupt your council meeting, but I can't say I'm sorry." His lips lingered on her fingers, causing her breath to hitch. With everyone around, this was not the time to allow this to go any further and she pulled her hand from his grasp.

Undeterred, he slid his arms around her waist. "Doona ever hesitate to get me if you need me. You will always come first. I've missed you these past few days."

"I have missed you, too," she whispered, finally meeting his eyes.

Orlando broke the moment. "Here is your Monsterita, milady." With a flourish, he handed Elsie a sparkly, pink cup with a straw in the lid. She gratefully grabbed the drink and took a sip, enjoying the tart lime and tequila.

"I loved the margaritas you made for us the last time, Elsie, but this," Santiago said, taking a healthy gulp of his drink, "this recipe of yours, is fantastic."

"Why, thank you, good sir." She tipped an invisible hat to Santiago and yelped when Zander nipped her neck. She liked the nip a little too much. Wanted his fangs to sink into the flesh at the base of her neck, again. Instead of begging him for more, she hefted her body up and onto her float. And, didn't spill a drop of her drink.

"I now understand why people say, you get what you pay for. This float is fabulous! Don't you wish you had one?" She splashed Zander. They both needed to cool down.

"Nay, lass, I plan to share yours." In a surge of motion too quick for her human eyes to follow, she was off the float, then straddling Zander, as he lounged with his hands behind his head. How did he do that? She had not even seen him move. She was dazed. And, this was a dangerous position for her to be in. Especially, since he had a huge erection straining to get inside her. His black boxer-briefs struggled to contain him. Oh my!

She placed a kiss on his lips before she rolled off him and the float, spilling her drink into the pool. When she glanced up, his groin was right next to her face. That position wasn't any better. She attempted to flip him off of the float, but didn't budge him. "Ugh, this was supposed to be easier," she grunted, as she put her shoulder under his back and heaved. "Come on, Orlando, help me dump him."

"It won't do any good, now that he's aware, Elsie. You need the element of surprise for that to work. Otherwise, our reflexes are lightning fast."

To demonstrate that point, Zander was off the float and

she was sputtering as she went under. His body slid against hers. They became entangled and were wrapped around each other. She held him tight and tried not to enjoy the friction of their bodies moving together.

They were momentarily lost in each other, until the waves from an all-out-no-holds-barred-water-fight washed over them. With an evil grin, she turned and pushed Zander's head under the water.

ELSIE GLANCED up from her preparations at the large, granite-topped island, and watched Zander stride into the kitchen. His presence made the huge room seem small and intimate. The sexual tension between them had been steadily rising. She finally admitted to herself that she was falling for him, and it frightened her. Still, she wasn't sure if she was ready for a relationship with him. At least not when she would grow old and he would remain disgustingly handsome.

He did nothing to hide his love and desire for her and did little things to let her know. Just that morning, she entered the kitchen to find Angus, their majordomo, who Elsie had learned was a dragon shifter, directing the staff as they replaced all of the cookware with a brand she had always wanted. Now, the kitchen contained every piece the company ever made. She'd never been lavished upon by anyone, and found that she rather enjoyed it.

Her heart fluttered as she met his sapphire-blue eyes. "Hi. How are you?"

"I'm better now that I'm with you. I doona know my way around the kitchen, but, may I help you cook?" He came up behind her and placed his hands on her hips. She gasped at the electricity the contact elicited, and twirled around to face him. His heated gaze lingered on her breasts. Did he know she had on the lingerie he'd given her?

"Sure, I was about to start making my Vietnamese burgers and egg rolls. I would love your help. I hope you aren't too hungry, because it will take a while."

"I'm rather hungry, actually. I want to lick and nip your body, until you scream my name." She shivered, as waves of arousal rippled through her core from his husky words. The low timbre and lilting accent of his voice evoked provocative fantasies.

"That's good, hungry is good." The ability to put words into a sentence eluded her at the moment. Her eyes ran over him greedily, taking in his powerful stance.

He grabbed her up and sat her on the empty counter. He wedged his legs between hers and touched his lips to hers. With that one touch, fire erupted and their passion quickly whirled out of control.

His lips slid over hers, mimicking what he wanted to do to her. The force of his kiss was bruising. She gasped for breath as he trailed his mouth across her jaw and along her throat, to return to her mouth.

"I need you, *a ghra*," he murmured.

As he licked and sucked her tongue, he removed her top and bra. He caressed her breasts and pinched her nipples. She arched her back, pressing her flesh into his palms. Fire licked over her skin as it heated with his touch. A fluttering caress in her chest enhanced the sensations. This happened every time he was near her and it robbed her of reason.

She grabbed at his chest wanting to touch him. She fumbled at the bottom of his shirt. "Off," she ordered.

He broke the kiss long enough to pull it over his head. He leaned in and began kissing and licking her nipples.

With Zander, there was a connection between her nipples and her core, and at the moment his mouth was making all of her throb. He took one between his teeth and his fangs penetrated the skin around her areola, making her go up in flames. The orgasm hit fast and hard. Stars winked in her vision and she cried out, riding the pleasure. Cool air hit her legs, telling her that he had hiked up her skirt. Moistness flooded her panties.

She ran her hands up and down his chest, exploring his nipples and reactions to her touch. His skin was hot and sweat beaded his brow. He responded to her slightest touch and she loved having the ability to make this strong, alpha shudder with desire.

Her fingers lingered at the band of his pants. He suddenly gripped her panties and ripped them from her body. She had pushed him too far. But, nothing felt as good as his thumb pressed against her, teasing the folds of her flesh.

"Oh God, Zander," she moaned.

She was close again and didn't want him to stop. The sound of a zipper reached her passion-muddled brain, but she didn't realize what it was until his hard cock slid through her slick channel. Back and forth it rubbed against her clit and she soaked him in seconds. The pressure of his shaft at her entrance had her tensing. She knew how big he was and worried about how much he might hurt her, initially.

"Relax, *a ghra,* I willna take you. I just want to find our pleasure like this. We willna go any further, yet," he promised, his cock gliding over the sensitive skin at the apex of her thighs. He set a relenting pace and was careful to keep his promise and not enter her. Slowly, she allowed the pleasure to swamp her. He gripped her tightly, kissed her hotly, and started panting. She didn't doubt she could trust his word and completely let go. She may not be ready for intercourse, but she needed this as much as he did. Her body was going up in flames as his pace increased. He was close and so was she.

He wrapped his arms fully around her and murmured words of affection in her ear. She buried her face in his chest and placed kisses across his flesh. As her muscles tensed with her impending climax, she grabbed his ass and pulled him as close as possible without him entering her. He continued to glide relentlessly through her wet female flesh.

"*A ghra*," he grunted. The moment he called out to her, she came hard. His entire body tensed before his shaft began to convulse against her, releasing his seed.

As their orgasms waned, they stood in each other's embrace, while they caught their breath. Her body was a limp, satisfied noodle. She lifted her head and met his gaze.

"Are you alright?" he asked tentatively.

"Honestly, I have no idea. I don't think I can move. Everything I feel with you is so new and different. Just when I think I have my footing, you do something and sweep me away."

"'Tis how it should be between us. It will always be raw and unhinged and you own every part of me." He picked her up and carried her into the large laundry room. "And, I believe the best is yet to come. Now, I had some of our clothes stored in here. Let's get dressed."

She could only nod her agreement and accept the clean clothing he retrieved for her. After they were dressed, he grabbed her close and kissed her forehead. "I need sustenance, shall we cook?"

"Yes, let's cook." All of a sudden she was starving.

CHAPTER THIRTY

"You said you don't know your way around the kitchen, but can you use a knife?" Elsie asked as she glanced sideways at Zander. His look was comical as he picked up a cutting board, clearly trying to figure out its purpose.

"I can slice a skirm, but no' a vegetable."

"I'm not sure what to say to that, but damn, you'd think after seven hundred years, you'd be well-rounded. Don't tell me you've spent all that time fighting," she said. "I've learned about the realm, but I don't know anything about you. Obviously, you don't cook for yourself. What is your favorite place to eat?" She grabbed a knife and the board, demonstrating how to dice an onion and get her mind off the desire still flooding her system.

"I've spent most of my life leading the alliance, my warriors, and my people. And fighting. After my parents were killed, all responsibilities fell to me. The Goddess made clear her expectations, and I couldna ignore it to pursue my own desires. For immortals, the passage of time is verra different than that of a mortal. We doona experience the pressure to live our lives the same. The only thing I've ever desired outside of fulfilling my duties, was to find my Fated Mate and I didna find her...until recently." He kept his eyes on the chopping block where he attempted to meticulously dice the onion she handed him. She sensed he was avoiding something.

There was that Fated Mate thing, again. Suspicion was snaking through her. "So, tell me about this Fated Mate. You said you finally found her, and I'm guessing she wouldn't be too happy with the...intimacy we have shared."

He looked up and she was hypnotized by the intensity in his eyes. "I hope you're verra happy aboot the intimacy. I know I am. I finally found the keeper of the other half of my soul." His statement unnerved her and confirmed her suspicions. Keeper of his soul? Nervously, she dumped some ground turkey and ground pork into a bowl, along with other ingredients. She began smashing the mixture with her hands, trying to wrap her mind around what he was saying. He remained silent, allowing her time to process.

Had she heard him correctly? The tug in her chest told her what he said was the truth. "Your soul?" she croaked.

"This seems unbelievable, I know. But, *a ghra*, I was born over seven centuries ago with a portion of your soul that I've protected and loved every day since. You were born with a portion of my soul to care for and safeguard, as well."

For the first time, she understood she had been feeling his soul pull to its other half. Words escaped her. Finally, she uttered, "What does this all mean?"

He ignored her question and posed one of his own. "What next, *a ghra?*"

Clearly, he sensed her turmoil and was providing an out by holding up the onions. She felt his anxiety, but he was putting her needs before his own. There was no doubt that he wanted to establish their mating, or relationship, or whatever, but wasn't going to force anything on her. Instinctively, she knew he would never push her to do anything, even if it meant he would suffer. For him, her happiness came first. She realized the idea of him suffering was repellent to her as well.

She was unsure how she felt and needed more information. "Can you get that Nuoc Mam, please? No, it's the fish sauce in that big bottle. I have to tell you that what you are saying sounds crazy, and if I hadn't been fighting vampires for over a year and seen the things I have, I wouldn't believe you. But, I know better. So, what exactly does being a Fated Mate mean? And, grate these carrots, next." She demonstrated what he needed to do, needing the distraction of cooking while she had this conversation.

He moved the carrots gingerly over the grater and she watched him consider his response. "I see you've come to the dark side and embraced giving orders," he winked, earning a smile in return. She liked his sarcasm and had come to realize that he didn't show this side often. Typically, he was all about business.

"It's been centuries since the realm has had a new union between Fated Mates," he continued. "As I mentioned before, the Goddess created the supernaturals of the Tehrex realm. Aside from preternatural senses, she gifted them with a Fated Mate. Each mate keeps and protects half of the other's soul. The souls pull their other half to them. There is also an undeniable compulsion to be physical with one another. This ensures they will procreate and continue the various species."

She grabbed bulbs of garlic and began peeling them. "So I can thank your Goddess for not being able to keep my hands off you. That is very unfair. Does she not believe in free-will?"

"The Goddess has a plan and knows what's best. Think aboot it. If she hadn't made me for you then you would have spent the rest of your life hunting skirm, never really living and would have died too young because of it."

She ignored the truth in his words. It was hard to recognize that her life had become filled with her desire for vengeance. "Why has the Goddess waited so long?"

"After the archdemons first escaped Hell and attacked the realm, new matings ceased. Some have said the Goddess' denial of mates for the past seven hundred years was a curse. I believe she always had a plan, but whatever the reason, that changed when she created you. You were made for me," he explained, pausing to gauge her response.

He gripped her hand and continued, "Being a Fated Mate means that we are destined for one another. For me, there will be no other. Eventually, we will join in a mating ceremony, after which I will claim you, in every way. A blood exchange will bind us for the rest of our immortal lives."

He released her hand to trace the blush she felt stained her cheek. "Both humans and supernaturals go through many changes with a mating. I've already experienced some of those changes. You already know I canna ingest blood from any other source, but you. I also doona desire any other female. In fact, my body refuses to respond to anyone, but you. Typically, these changes only occur after all facets of the mating ceremony are completed."

Her gaze remained on her hands, kneading the meat mixture, while nerves and disbelief warred within her. "So, how do you know that I'm yours? And, what is this ceremony?"

"Mates are distinguished by a Fated Mate mark. Those marks appear after sexual intercourse."

Her head snapped up. "But, we haven't had sex. How can you say that I'm your mate?"

"Nothing aboot our situation has been normal. Not only is my body acting as if the mating has been completed, but my mate mark appeared after I had sex with you in our shared dream. You've seen and touched my mark. It's the cross branded on my back. And, your wee Celtic cross is right here," he grazed his knuckle under her left ear. Suddenly, overwhelming arousal and need coursed through her. "You canna see it until we exchange blood and your DNA alters. After we complete our mating, both of our marks will morph into a tattoo and yours will become visible to humans. I will tell you that my mark becomes more painful the longer we wait."

She shivered with his touch. "You hurt? Why didn't you tell me? Exchange blood how? And, what exactly, do you mean my DNA alters? Will I become a vampire?" The questions left her in rapid succession. It sounded unreal, like something out of a paranormal romance novel.

"Doona worry aboot my discomfort. Nay, you willna become a vampire. Myth has that wrong. Vampires are born, not created. Your DNA will adopt strands of my DNA, so that you become immortal. We will share and enhance each other's powers. You will become stronger and faster, with heightened senses and you will no longer age."

"So, I have this mark that I can't see, and that means that I was made for you? What would have happened if we had met, but my husband was still alive? I don't see how I was made for you."

"'Tis called fate, lass. We were meant to be together. I know you feel it, too. And, while I doona wish, or believe, that Dalton deserved what happened to him, it happened for a reason." He hugged her to him and leaned his forehead against hers.

"The mating ceremony is a ritual much like any joining in your human culture, beginning with ritual vows. Additionally, it involves the blessing of a mating stone, making love, and the exchange of blood. I can see from your face that the idea of a blood exchange is frightening. Trust me. The blood exchange is verra sensual." He released her and leaned his hands on the counter, trapping her in the cage of his arms. "Do you recall when I took your blood last week? How pleasurable we both found it?"

"It was rather unforgettable," she smiled wryly at him. She turned in the cage of his arms and added the cellophane noodles to the meat and shrimp mixture. She felt his warm body close behind her, enjoying the feel of him.

"Now, let me show you how to form an egg roll." She grabbed a wrapper and used a melon-baller to scoop filling into the middle. How long could she ignore the hard length prodding her backside? Especially, when she wanted to take hold and go for a ride. "Are you paying attention, or are you ogling my breasts over my shoulder?"

"I can multi-task verra well. I'm ogling your lush bosom while I watch you roll the food." He reached around her for an empty wrapper, enclosing the cage he had created. She was going to combust from unspent lust. Not even watching him fumble and create a mess doused the flames.

"That looks like a burrito. And, you are invading my bubble. I need space to work, and breathe."

He shamelessly rubbed the hard length of his erection against her ass. "I've got your burrito, *a ghra*." Apparently guys of all species were all the same, always thinking of sex.

"HAVE you had any more specific details on your premonition of impending trouble?" Orlando asked when Elsie rubbed her stomach, again.

She paused, pacing around her desk, and glanced at him. "No I haven't."

"Talk to me El, I can see that something is bothering you," he walked over to her, bumping his shoulder against hers.

She grimaced, in frustration. "I can't seem to figure out who I should warn, or try to protect. I'm not getting the direction that I usually do. And, the feeling of disaster is becoming more urgent, it's annoying," she shook her head and resumed pacing. "I can't think about that right now. I have work to do. My client will be here in forty-five minutes."

Orlando watched as she went back to the paperwork she had been trying to complete for the past hour. He knew when her thoughts strayed to Zander, because her emotions became a tangled mess of arousal, confusion, hope and trepidation. He was not privy to the conversation between them the night before, but given both of their emotions, they had made some progress. He stifled his jealousy. He'd been fighting his attraction to her from day one, but had been unsuccessful. He wanted her beyond what was healthy for him. She belonged to Zander and he needed to remember that. He respected their mating and would never go against their sacred union. Unfortunately, it seemed he had a death wish as he couldn't stop his attraction to the alluring female.

"I can see that you aren't able to work with your worry.

Try not to let it get to you. You have had a lot going on lately. I have a feeling the Goddess has put events into play—"

His words were cut off as his nostrils flared and he sensed skirm. Within seconds, Kadir and Azazel stormed into the small office, followed by a dozen skirm. They were in deep shit. There was no way in hell he'd be able to fight off so many by himself. But, he would die trying before he allowed her to be hurt.

"Very clever, demon, but you won't win." He sprang across the office and flung Elsie behind him, as he slid his titanium *sgian dubh* from his boot. He didn't have time to determine how Kadir had discovered the charity. He had to protect her. "El, stay behind me, and call Santi. Tell him to bring the cavalry, we have an infestation."

"She won't be calling anyone," Kadir said. He teleported behind her and grabbed her by the shoulders. "Tell your king that he can have his *mate* back, in exchange for the amulet." Kadir waved her cell phone in the air. Orlando yelled and shifted mid-leap. He landed on a skirm and tore into its throat. By the time he lifted his head, Elsie was gone, as were the archdemons. He roared to the ceiling. They would all die and he would get her back!

He gave himself over to his rage as he mindlessly clawed and shredded his way through the remaining skirm. He had fucking lost Elsie. He was supposed to protect her, and he had failed, miserably. As he incapacitated the last skirm, he felt Zander's presence enter his mind. He could feel the anger and terror emanating from him.

"What, in the bluidy hell, is happening? I felt her fear, then pain, and now, nothing. I doona feel her at all! I canna get a sense of her location, either!"

"We were ambushed at the office, after sunset. Kadir and Azazel arrived with a dozen skirm. They disappeared with her, Z.

We will get her back. I am so fucking sorry, you can't even imagine."

He shifted back to human form, picked up his blade where he had dropped it, and dispatched the corpses. He contemplated how they could've known where she would be. They had to have had inside help.

He winced as Zander shouted his rage. Orlando was as consumed with fear for Elsie as Zander was. He imagined the havoc Zander was wreaking in the compound, given the spiraling emotions Orlando felt emanating from him. They coalesced into a maelstrom of killing rage.

"Get the FUCK back to Zeum, now. We are going to find my mate! And, you had better start praying to the Goddess that she is found, alive and safe."

ELSIE HAD NEVER TELEPORTED BEFORE and felt like she was on a rollercoaster. She was speeding through a dark tunnel unable to see anything around her then suddenly dropping down a steep hill. Her stomach hollowed out and nausea swamped her. The entire situation was disorienting, to say the least.

She stumbled on shaky limbs as they stopped moving. She blinked and the world took on color and texture again. The demon had a tight hold of her arm, and was dragging her across a dirt floor. In the dim light, she could make out the Fae that she had seen outside Confetti, but little else.

Where had they taken her? She glanced around, taking in her surroundings and realized she was inside a cave, and she was being drug toward a pair of shackles that were set in a stone wall. She thrashed her body, fighting to get free. No way was she going meekly to her death. If he got her shackled, it was over for her.

Kadir laughed. It was an awful sound, like rock scraping metal. "Don't waste your energy trying to get away. There is nowhere for you to run. Your vampire will come for you, soon enough."

Like hell, would she be compliant. She sunk her teeth into his arm and renewed her struggles. "Fuck you," she spat.

"Now you're just turning me on. I may have to rethink my plans for you," Kadir smirked. She cringed and tried to back away when he reached out to stroke her cheek.

A familiar voice interrupted before he made contact. She was grateful for the reprieve, while at the same time, her stomach knotted further. "No, Kadir. Let me handle this. I have longed to silence her from the moment I first saw the whore." She looked for the female who spoke and watched as Lena strode out of thick shadows. Elsie bared her teeth at the woman as she grabbed her by the hair.

"How could you be working with these creatures when you know what they've done to your people? What they did to the man you claim is yours?" Elsie had hated this vampire from the moment she'd met her and knew right away she was evil, but this was beyond. Elsie didn't miss the panic before Lena managed to mask it. The woman was smart to be afraid. Elsie didn't want to be around when Zander found out that one of his own had betrayed him.

"You know nothing, human. I'm not betraying Zander, I'm saving him from your ruin," Lena snarled as she jerked Elsie violently, shoving her into the damp wall of the cave. Her face smashed against the rock, as cold metal clamped around her wrist. Her heart began racing frantically, now she was completely at their mercy. Mack had taught her to fight with everything she had and to use any weapon available to her. She tried to calm her breathing and settle her nerves to develop a plan. After several seconds, she focused enough to scan the objects close to her, looking for anything that she might be able to use. Aside from her body and shoes, she had nothing.

The odd lighting in the cave cast shadows across Lena's face, making her look as hideous as the demon she was standing next to. Elsie forced her fear to the back of her mind before it could debilitate her. She had no idea if these creatures could smell fear, but she refused to allow that vulnerability to show. Confidence was a strong weapon in itself. Let them question why she wasn't cowering in fear. "I know more than you think and I know that Zander will make you pay, traitor. All of you," she declared, standing tall.

"For the record, letting her handle this is a bad idea. Females have a tendency to be more emotional and irrational." She whipped her head around to notice the good-looking demon, Azazel, had joined them in the cave.

"I am more than capable of handling a human," Lena spat in fury then kicked Elsie in the side, connecting with her ribs. Pain rocketed through her, stealing her breath. Gasping, her knees buckled and she fell forward. The cuffs kept Elsie from falling to the floor, but forced her to bend at the waist. She hung there for a moment, struggling for air.

The clack of heels on the dirt floor sounded as Lena paced in front of her, making her stand up, regardless of the pain. No way was she going to be seen as weak. "I made a promise to you both that I could get to Zander and I will," Lena purred as she spoke to the demons. Elsie glared at the vampire through narrowed eyes. "She is the way in. He thinks she is his Fated Mate and would do anything for her. You need to trust me, he will come for her and he will be willing to give you anything you ask for."

"I'll give you leeway to do as you've planned. After all, your information proved accurate. Without it, we wouldn't have been able to get her here," Kadir responded. Elsie was not surprised to hear Lena gave them her location, but she needed to focus her attention on a way out of her predicament. She had no doubt that Zander would find her and she wanted to be alive when he did. She squinted in the dark, searching for an exit. If she could get out of these cuffs she needed to know which direction to run. She'd only have one opportunity and she needed to be fast to stand a chance of escaping.

"You're all mine now, bitch. I want you to die knowing that after you're gone, Zander will come back to me. He has for two hundred years," Lena hissed in Elsie's face. Elsie wiped her cheek on her shoulder, removing the spit. She stood her ground, ignoring Lena's delusional ramblings as she continued her search.

"I understand Zander in ways you will never be able to. I am a vampire like him and know his needs. The Goddess is just waiting to bestow our mate marks until the right moment. I hadn't realized what I needed to do to make that happen, but I do now. No one is better suited to him than I am," Lena said as she resumed her pacing. Delusional much?

Every fiber in Elsie's being protested Lena's declaration and for the first time, Elsie allowed the connection she had with Zander to fill her. A rustling in her chest radiated outward. *He's mine*, her mind screamed. Energy surged through Elsie at her declaration and she embraced Zander's soul. The love that flooded her told her his soul recognized that he was indeed hers. No more denying what she wanted.

She welcomed her feelings for Zander and clung to them like a lifeline. It offered a boldness she'd never possessed and the weapon she needed. No matter what happened, this woman would never be able to take Zander from her. He was hers and she was his, nothing was changing that, ever.

"Somehow," Elsie sneered, certain some of her ribs were cracked, "I doubt the Goddess believes you are what anyone needs. As for Zander, you have never connected with him. You have never seen the real Zander. He reserved that for his Fated Mate...me."

"*Salope*!" Lena screamed, kicking Elsie in the head. Everything went black.

CHAPTER THIRTY-ONE

White powder showered down over Zander's face. His mate had been taken. "Fuck!" he roared. Another chair left his hands, and embedded into the drywall across the room. He was helpless to do anything about it at the moment, and losing his mind. He didn't do helpless. He needed to take action. For all he knew, his mate could be dying.

Angus ducked, as a computer monitor met the door frame. They could be torturing and raping her. It took all of his faculties to remind himself that she wasn't without skill. She had fought and killed dozens of skirm, not that it would do any good against Kadir or Azazel, but it would when facing other enemies. He prayed to the Goddess to help her survive until he reached her.

"I'm going to shred that bastard! He will no' be able to hide! I will go straight to the doors of hell, if I have to!" he thundered.

He heaved the table over his head. As wood shattered and splintered in a hundred directions, he sought another object to take his rage out on. He hoped to vent the worst of his temper, but the destruction was only making it worse. Besides, he reminded himself that he needed to get control, or he wouldn't be of any use in searching for his Elsie. That, of course, was easier said, than done. The sole reason for his existence was in the hands of evil archdemons, undergoing who knew what.

Please, Goddess, watch over her, doona let her die. I need her. I canna live withoot her.

$\sim$

PAIN AND AGONY assailed Elsie as awareness pressed back the darkness. Noise became voices, and memories flooded back. She was in a cave, chained to a wall, and that bitch, Lena, had teamed up with the demons. She had no idea how long she had been unconscious, but not wanting to alert her captors, she kept her eyes closed and remained as still as possible. It was infinitely harder to keep her breathing even and regular.

She wished furtively that she had preternatural hearing, like Zander. He would be able to tell who was in the cave, and exactly where they were. The one thing she had realized before everything went black was that there wasn't a place for her to run should she manage to get free of the steel cuffs.

Wetness dripped from her temple into the corner of her eyes and her head throbbed with a massive headache. Given how hard Lena had kicked her, she figured the wetness was blood and she prayed that she wasn't losing too much. With no escape possible, Elsie was in for a long haul until Zander found her and she needed to keep as much blood in her body as possible.

Wanting to assess her overall condition, she did a quick

mental inventory. Aside from her head, her arms ached from holding up her weight and her chest hurt with each breath, otherwise she was in good shape. None of the voices were near her so she slit her eyes and tried to look around. No matter how hard she tried, she was unable to see anything in the eerie glow let off by candles flickering around the cavern. Footsteps echoed and a shining image wavered in her narrowed vision. Black, over-the-knee boots with mile-high-metal-heels stopped in front of her. Her heart raced, making the pain in her chest worse.

"Ah, you're awake. Good, I was bored," Lena bent down, and purred in her ear. Elsie held back the cry when Lena gripped her hair painfully, but it escaped when she lost a large handful as her head was yanked around. She was forced back at an odd angle and it afforded her a better look at Lena.

Lena's blond hair was pulled back into a tight ponytail high on her head, and she noticed that her eyes had gone black with anger. Elsie fought against Lena's hold, rattling her chains. She kicked out a leg and barely grazed Lena's calf. The laugh that escaped the vampire was infuriating. Elsie wanted to pound her face in and make her bleed all over the dirty cave floor.

"Is that all you've got? This is going to be too easy," Lena taunted. She flipped her ponytail over her shoulder, drawing Elsie's attention to her hair. She reached out trying to grab hold, but the chains stopped her. She cursed under her breath for leaving her dagger at home. She never took the weapon to work with her given that one of the Dark Warriors always accompanied her, but that wasn't a mistake she'd ever make again.

"That's easy for you to say with me chained to the wall.

Unlock these," Elsie rattled the cuffs, "and let's see who is more powerful," she cajoled. The vampire may be able to kick her ass, but she had skills Lena didn't and with free reign of movement, Elsie stood a chance of surviving.

Lena let go of her hair and shook her hand in disgust, trying to dislodge the mound of hair. Elsie laughed as her curly, brown tresses clung to the vampire, like a spider web. That earned her a rough shove against the limestone wall, which abraded her back through her thin blouse. Elsie hadn't been in the supernatural world that long and this served to remind her she wasn't dealing with normal strength. Elsie fought against the helplessness that threatened. Chained and unable to do anything about it, she told herself that no matter what, Lena was going to pay for this.

"Releasing you would only give you a false sense of hope. You won't be living through this. The demons are using you to get the amulet and once they have it they will eliminate you and I will have my Zander free of your influence." Lena backed away from her and prowled the room, like a panther stalking its prey.

"And, what makes you think they are going to allow Zander to live? Or you for that matter? You've made a deal with demons that can't be trusted. That's just confirmation of how stupid you are," Elsie sneered. She could see the wheels turning in Lena's head, but she refused to sit around and wait for her to attack, again. This prey bit back.

She timed her attack to a moment when Lena had lifted her right leg, to avoid a stalagmite and kicked out. A rip, followed by a feminine scream, echoed. She was immediately aware of two things. Her grey, pencil skirt had ripped to her hip, and she had broken Lena's lower leg. A shrill screech filled the cavern. Elsie had pissed off a crazy vampire bent on her destruction. Not the smartest decision, but she refused to go meekly to her death.

It was satisfying to watch as Lena sank to the floor stifling her cries of pain, clutching her leg. She sat glaring at Elsie through narrowed eyes. "That was a mistake," Lena said as she climbed back to her feet and tested her stance and Elsie noticed she didn't show any signs of lingering pain. Elsie hated vampire healing abilities right then.

"You were bested by a weak human. That must sting," she taunted and prepared to kick her again. Lena grabbed her leg as it shot out a second time.

"You're too slow, cow. That's all you are to him, you know, food. He couldn't possibly want you. Not when he has me. You will be quickly forgotten." Lena's fist came down hard on her thigh. The snap of a twig reverberated, and it felt as if a hot poker had been rammed into Elsie's leg. Her vision wavered as she realized her leg was broken. The pain was so intense it trapped her scream in her throat.

She staggered, barely managing to stay upright. Head pounding and ribs protesting, Elsie fought to remain on her feet. The agony made her sick to her stomach. She was forced to rest all of her weight on her good leg. Staggering back against the wall, Elsie fought to remain awake. She was weak and didn't want to be taken off guard.

Taking stock of the scene, she noted that the demons were watching the fight from the back wall and wondered why they weren't attacking. Dizziness washed over her as she contemplated her next moves. She wasn't going to be able to remain conscious long. She wavered and oblivion beckoned, but was pushed off when her stomach finally revolted. The action jostled her broken ribs and breathing became a thing of the past. As the world dipped and blurred, she heard rapid movements and was certain more enemies had joined them.

Her vision cleared long enough for her to see that the space was now full of skirm as well as the two archdemons and Lena. Helplessness set in as she realized there was no way she could fight them off and escape. She prayed to God, and Zander's Goddess, that she lived. She had so much to live for. She may have been uncertain about what was happening between her and Zander, but somewhere along the way she had fallen in love with the vampire and she wanted to tell him.

She regretted not taking the opportunity before. She had been thinking about it all wrong before. It didn't matter that they were two different species any more than it mattered she carried her loss in her heart. Zander had accepted all of her and she hadn't done the same. She would never again allow such emotions to stop her from having a life with him. They had an eternity of passion before them if they completed the mating and there was nothing she wanted more.

The pain intensified and nearly took her under. To escape the sharp edges of her agony, she lost herself in imagining the life they would have together. Zander had already shown her how much he loved her and there was no way this turncoat was taking that from her.

"Nothing you say will make me doubt Zander or how he feels about me. And, mark my words, he's mine, and will always be mine!" At hearing her words, Lena lost it. If the vampire had been mad before she was now a complete lunatic.

Out of control, Lena began hitting her. Elsie tried to duck the blows, but the chains restricted her movements and one after another landed on her head and face. Lena's hands and fists connected next with her broken ribs, sending shooting pain through her torso. It was a blessing when Zander's soul sent warmth through her chest, dulling the intensity.

Elsie refused to give up and twisted and turned with all her might. Sides heaving like a bellows, she smiled at the knowledge that Zander loved her and no matter what, her life had been better for having him in it. The smile threw Lena off and she backed away, staring with narrowed eyes.

"You're so smug because you have his mark on your neck. The mating hasn't been completed and that can be removed before it's inked into your skin. Once removed there's no going back. You will lose him forever." Lena approached her and squeezed her injured leg, making her cry out. Elsie couldn't think through the anguish and wasn't able to fight back. Lena grabbed her neck and panic set in when Lena pulled a knife from her boot.

"This might hurt a little, *ma chere,*" Lena whispered into her ear, before white-hot agony scoured the left side of her neck. Her screams consumed the dank space and black dots winked in her vision as Lena slowly sliced into her skin.

Her soul rose to protect Zander's mark and refused to allow any piece of him to be removed from her body. Her body and both souls had risen to protect what was theirs. Both souls sunk talons into the area and held on with all their might. It warmed her to know she wasn't fighting this battle alone. Further confirmation of what she and Zander shared and proof that Lena was wrong in her assertion. The muscles in Lena's arms stood out as she hacked at the flesh. She began sweating and breathing rapidly as she worked to remove the mark.

Elsie held tight with every slice as her skin was flayed and tissue and tendon was separated from muscle. She hadn't realized what torture was before that moment and as a piece of her soul was sacrificed, she lost all hope of survival. Her heart ached for the loss Zander was going to experience. She knew all too well the pain of losing someone you loved and didn't want him to experience one moment of that misery.

"I stand corrected, Kadir. I love a good cat fight, the bloodier the better," she faintly heard Azazel say as she teetered on unconsciousness.

"Who doesn't love a good blood bath, but that matters naught when the vampire isn't calling. I told you this plan wouldn't work. We've wasted precious time and resources on this," Kadir intoned.

She wanted to rant at the twisted creatures, but blackness consumed her. The last thing she felt was Zander's soul wrapping protectively around her, tethering her to him and the earth.

SANTIAGO'S VOICED intruded in Zander's rampage, spiking his anger. "You may want to hide in your rooms, buddy. He'll rip your head off right now."

Zander gazed past the total destruction of their war room, and saw that Santiago was talking to Orlando. The warrior's face was stricken, and it reminded him all over again of what he had lost. Fear and despair joined his rage and his body coiled once again preparing to let it all go. His previous tirade hadn't helped any and he fought to regain some semblance of the vampire he was, but the monster refused to let go. Several deep breaths didn't do anything to help. The only thing that kept him from descending completely into that pit was holding a vision of Elsie in his mind.

"Get your arse over here," he ordered Orlando as he yanked on his disheveled hair and began pacing. He needed to find her. Save her.

"Have you found a working computer, Killian, or should I be-head you, now? We need that database to go over known locations for archdemons and the Fae. They could have her anywhere in the world, and I still canna connect to her. You," he stabbed a finger into Orlando's chest, "tell me everything that happened."

Orlando took a deep breath, and then recounted everything that happened, and told them what Kadir had said.

"How did they learn aboot our charity? Let alone when Elsie would be there? That could be the link to finding her, if we could figure that oot," Breslin suggested. She dislodged the chair from the wall and set it outside with the pile of growing debris. Normally, he would feel bad about his behavior, but his fear and anger were completely out of his control. And it was only getting worse as the minutes flew by.

"Someone in the realm had to have leaked the information. And, it had to be someone close to one of us. Kadir may be smart, but I doubt he's bright enough to put two and two together. Regardless, there are too many possible leads that will waste precious time. I think we need to focus on your connection to get her back," Hayden clasped Zander's bicep, squeezing with force, "and you need to calm down, so that you can focus, my friend. I can see how hard that is for you, but you are the key to finding your mate."

Hayden held his gaze. "They aren't going to kill her.

They want you to trade the amulet for her." Zander knew that he was right. They wouldn't kill her, but that didnt mean they weren't torturing her.

"That's right, calm down. You can feel her here," Hayden placed his palm on Zander's chest and Elsie's soul jumped in response. He closed his eyes at the proof she still lived. "Okay, now focus on the bond you have with her. You need to use it to guide us to her," Hayden encouraged.

Silence descended in the room while he kept his eyes shut, blocking out the evidence of his anguish. He took several deep breaths, focusing on Elsie's heart-shaped face. He shouted in relief when his connection to her finally sparked. "Thank the Goddess! She's alive. I feel her." He used his blood bond to her to try and determine her exact location. He sensed her within a couple hundred miles. "She isna far from here. No' further than Victoria. I need a map. You have that computer running, Kill?"

Killian waved to the image on the cracked computer screen. "This is the best I can do with the damage. You can still zoom in and out so it should work."

"Och, thank the Goddess." Zander gazed at the computer screen, as he concentrated on the bond he shared with his mate. He knew she was north of his location and he kept zooming in on different areas. After several grueling minutes with her blood acting as a divining rod in his system, he was directed to the Hoh Rainforest. Looking closer at the map on the screen, he realized there would be no easy way to get to her.

They needed buildings that were familiar to the sorcerers to open a portal. She was in the middle of a forest with nothing around for miles. A sense of urgency over-shadowed everything. He had to reach her fast.

"I've found her, but it will take all of us working together to get her back. She is here in the Hoh Rainforest, so we canna portal close to her. Unless one of you," he motioned to Jace, Evzen, Killian, and Gerrick, "has spent time in, and knows of somewhere close to the location. We need to do something, now. I have a verra bad feeling."

Nikko flipped his *sgian dubh,* and then caught it by the hilt. "I can have the Cessna fueled and ready to go in twenty minutes, Liege."

"Bluidy hell, make it fifteen. And, Kill, find an exact location we can use to portal the rest. I'll be taking no chances with my mate's life." He grabbed his weapons from Kyran's arms. The need to annihilate had consumed him. He would tear Kadir and his minions apart, piece by fucking piece.

"Yes, sir," Nikko called from the door, his fingers flying over the keypad of his phone.

"The closest location I found to Hoh is the Misty Valley Inn, a small B&B in Forks, of all places." Killian shook his head and muttered, "Sparkly fucking vampires."

Bhric strapped on his weapons and crossed to the mangled door frame. "Kyran and I are going in the plane, I don't care who else joins us, but I'm not leaving my *brathair's* side. We'll need at least Evzen and Kill to set the portal."

It was a small comfort to him knowing his brother cared so deeply. He called over his shoulder, "Eight of you can come with Nikko and I, but decide quickly. I'm leaving now."

ELSIE FOUGHT against the insistent force that was ripping her from her place of peace and thrusting her back into pain, excruciating, bone-crushing pain. She wanted the peace death would bring her, but she refused to give in when she had yet to discover what it meant to be Zander's other half. She had been created for Zander and he was hers. She was part of something bigger than she'd ever known. Her resolve to live renewed, she was determined to experience every moment of life she could with Zander. Regret flooded her at how much she had already missed out on.

She'd wasted so much precious time questioning what she had clearly felt for the vampire. Her heart skipped several beats and terror hit. She could die without ever experiencing the full scope of his love. And, in return, not have given him all the love she had in her heart for him.

Somewhere between the caramels and the pool float, she had fallen deeply in love with the bossy vampire. She loved him so much, in fact, that it was keeping her alive, giving her the drive to fight. Zander had knocked down the bricks she had erected around her heart, one by one, despite her protests. She had used her guilt as a shield, but Zander had managed his way through. She needed him to manage the impossible right now and save her from these demons and that vile traitor.

Awareness stopped that train of thought as Elsie came to, with a knife at her throat. "Ah, she wants more," Lena whispered in her ear. "Good news for you. I'm happy to oblige."

"Get bent bitch," she spat at Lena, and wrapped her hands around the chains that shackled her to the cave wall. Determined to fight as much as possible, she wrapped her legs, ignoring the pain in the broken one, around Lena's mid-section. In a blur of movement, she twisted and slammed her to the floor with all the strength she could muster. Adrenaline spiked, and her good foot connected with the vampire's head, several times.

Lena screeched and did a back-flip away from her. From

an angle, Lena reached out and slammed Elsie's head against the wall. Her vision blurred around the edges, but this time she remained conscious. Lena moved at her so fast she was a blur and then fire exploded through Elsie's leg. She felt the skin tear and looked down to see her bone sticking out of a gaping wound. That wasn't good.

Lena ripped the chains free of the cave wall and picked Elsie up, throwing her across the space. She hit the ground and rolled.

She stopped when she hit a large boulder. Unable to move a muscle, she lay on the hard, dirt floor, every inch of her body broken or bloodied. As her blood seeped from her veins it took her life force with it. She weakened as the minutes passed. She was going to die in the god-forsaken place and would never see Zander's beautiful face, again.

She pictured his smile, recalled his sexy accent, and everything he had done for her. He hadn't held back, but had showed her how deeply he loved her.

I love you, Zander! Dizziness assailed her, as she felt the blood trickle in a steady, hot stream, down her chilled skin. She was losing too much and was going into shock. Lena stalked toward her, ready to deliver the final blow.

"Lena, desist now!" Kadir roared. "He will give me nothing if I can't prove to him that she lives. If she dies, you will endure far more at my hands!"

Lena paled, her head swinging from Kadir to Elsie's slumped, lifeless form, then back to Kadir, again. "Where is your sidekick? And his Fae? He can heal her, right?"

"No, he can't, you idiot. You know nothing about magic. I'm surrounded by ineptitude," Kadir ranted. "You," he demanded of a nearby skirm, "see if the human is alive, and find Azazel. Hear my words, vampire, you had better start praying to your Goddess that she lives. Otherwise, you will understand why your kind fears demons."

As the demon's words faded away and the tidal wave broke, sweeping her out to sea, her beloved's soul wrapped her in a soothing energy that gave her the strength to hold on. She hoped it wasn't too little, too late.

CHAPTER THIRTY-TWO

After a grueling plane ride, a rough landing and a hike to the Inn, Zander was crawling out of his skin, nerves shot to hell and back. He watched anxiously as the three sorcerers created the portal to Zeum. Not soon enough, Orlando stepped through, followed by the others. *Thank fuck!* No more waiting, now they could proceed. He turned his attention to his brothers and Nikko. "Have you finished? We're wasting time, damn it."

"Aye, *brathair*. The human's memories have been erased, and two of them have kindly given us their SUVs," Kyran informed him.

"Let's go. Something is wrong," he barked, as everyone loaded into the SUVs and they headed out.

He gazed out the window as they drove in silence, praying to the Goddess for the millionth time in the past hour. Bhric's voice echoed in the quietness of the vehicle. "Which direction do we go from here, *brathair*?" he asked after they had crossed into the rainforest. He hadn't realized they were that close. He concentrated on his mate.

The throb of the bond between him and Elsie pulsed

hotter than ever. He nearly collapsed with relief that she was alive, and feeding into their bond. She had accepted him, and her status as his mate. He had been waiting for weeks for this to happen, and now he may never know the joy of claiming her.

"Go east," he ordered. They were not going to arrive too late. He had to believe that.

Orlando's fury seeped from every pore. "Have you tried to communicate with her, Liege?"

"Nay, I havena been able to bring myself to reach out to her. I couldna handle it if I heard her being tortured and could do nothing. I will link with her when we're closer. Through our bond, I have been sending her strength, as well as, every ounce of love I have for her." The car fell silent once again, each consumed with their thoughts of what lay ahead.

He gave Bhric directions when needed and as soon as they were minutes away, he reached out to let her know he hadn't abandoned her. As he linked to her mind, he heard her scream out that she loved him. He lashed out and hit the door frame as their connection was lost before he could respond. Frantically, he repeated his attempts to contact her, but failed. The thrum from her soul was dimming, he was losing her. *Nay, please, Goddess, doona take her.*

"Jace, stay with me. I fear..." his voice broke, as his emotions tightened in his throat. "I fear she may be injured verra badly," he managed past his tears.

As soon as the car slowed, he was out the door and running through the forest, a blur in the night. He had to reach her, before it was too late. Urgency rode him hard as he heard the council members and his warriors close on his heels.

When Hayden gripped his arm, stopping him midstride, he nearly ripped the Omega's head off. The hand signals that followed informed him of two skirm, one archdemon and one Fae, less than a hundred feet ahead. Hayden motioned for Orlando and Santiago to shift. Zander nodded his acknowledgement and continued to Elsie while the shifters ambushed the small group.

On soundless feet, Zander entered the cave first, followed by Jace. His blood boiled when he saw Lena pick Elsie's slack head up by the hair. His worry for Elsie kept his feet moving as the shock of Lena's betrayal hit hard. One of his vampires, one that he knew intimately, had turned against him, and turned his most beloved treasure over to the archdemons. The burn of that treachery was drowned out by his need to get to Elsie.

He ignored the dozen minions that lounged around the edges of the fissure, as he charged toward Lena and his mate. He roared when he saw the blood-soaked cloth around Elsie's neck. Her cheek was swollen and he noticed a bone protruding from one of her leg. This bitch was going to pay for hurting his female. His war-cry drowned out Lena's plea to Kadir.

He was saved the choice between his mate and the archdemon responsible for her torture, when Nikko rushed in and slashed out at the surprised demon. "Not so fast, asshole," Nikko's blade found purchase in the demon's hard, grey chest, but missed his heart. Zander noted the demon was momentarily halted from teleporting away.

"Where is the amulet? I expect that you brought what I require," Kadir brazened, as Nikko ripped the blade from his chest. The demon was trying to buy enough time in order to heal and teleport away, but Nikko didn't pause in his attack. Zander continued on his path to Elsie.

"No, asshole, we didn't, but you won't need to worry

about that after I'm through with you," Nikko reached into his boot, and came up shining, with twin *sgian dubhs.* He sliced at Kadir's neck, missed, and chopped off the demon's right hand, just as the demon teleported away. "Coward!" Nikko shouted.

Killian and Evzen didn't hesitate to attack the skirm that stood between them and Elsie. Evzen muttered a spell, freezing several combatants, while Killian grabbed his titanium blade and dispatched them. Zander reached Elsie's side as four more blades were added to the battle when Bhric and Breslin joined their forces. He ignored the rest of the battle and trusted that his warriors and the council could keep him and his mate safe.

He fell to his knees and gently scooped her to him. Her precious face blurred from his tears as he caressed her soft cheek while he cradled her broken body. She was alive, but barely. Her pulse was sluggish and weak. "Jace, get over here. Heal her, please." The crack in his voice displayed his weakness. He needed to be strong for her. He placed a kiss on her pale lips, and placed her in Jace's arms. He rose to face the evil slime responsible for her capture.

Lena had backed up against the wall and was staring in obvious horror. The treacherous female thought she would get away with this. "You will pay for this, Lena," he spat. Lena spun and attempted to run, but Zander was faster as he lunged and grabbed hold of her throat.

He slammed her down to the hard floor. "No, Zander. You can't, please. You love me. We're meant to be together." She disgusted him with her pleading. The female had misconstrued everything that had ever happened between them. She'd never been anything more than a warm body. She meant nothing to him and he'd never said, or done anything, to give her any other impression.

His fury turned his vision red as she tried to mitigate what she had done. Not going to happen. "You're wrong aboot that. You've never meant shit to me. Nothing more than a body to fuck. The Goddess created me for Elsie, and her for me. I will never belong with you. You will suffer for what you've done."

"No, Zander, please, I did this for us. So we could be together," Lena attempted again.

"You are pitiable and deserve everything you are going to suffer," Zander spat. He was going to enjoy making her pay for what she'd done to Elsie.

"Zander, get over here, Elsie needs you." Jace's words sent ice through his veins and was the only thing that could have reached him at that moment. He didn't have time to torture Lena, as she deserved. Elsie's needs always came before everything.

"Join your demon in hell," he said and with a squeeze of his hand, he ripped Lena's head from her body, tossing it aside. He was at Elsie's side, before Lena's body hit the ground.

"Is she going to be, ok?" he choked out, as he knelt next to them on the floor.

Jace looked up from his mate and held his gaze. The torment he saw reflected there stopped his heart. He couldn't breathe. "She's in bad shape, Liege. She's lost too much blood, I can't heal her," Jace told him.

His stomach hit the floor, and a hollow ache engulfed his chest. The only injuries Jace couldn't heal were those caused by silver or skirm venom...and mortal ones. Seeing his distress, Jace quickly added, "But, you can give her your blood. It's her best chance at survival. In fact, she's going to need a lot of vampire blood. More than you have."

"Will she die?" he forced himself to ask.

Jace exhaled, and reluctantly responded, "I can promise you that she'll die within minutes, if she doesn't receive blood."

He gently cradled Elsie's head in his lap. Her peaches-and-cream complexion was gray, and her normally plump, pink lips were pale, dry and cracked. Blood matted parts of her curly, brown hair. He didn't give it a second thought and with a hiss, his fangs shot down, and he bit deeply into his wrist.

"Open her mouth, Jace." The moment Jace parted her lips Zander placed his bleeding wrist over her mouth. His blood flowed freely and he prayed it would give her what she needed. The wound to his wrist healed over several times, forcing him to bite deeper into his skin. All the while, there was no response from her. Her breathing remained shallow and her heartbeat faint. Eventually, blood no longer flowed from his bite, and when he sliced into his jugular, nothing surged forth. But, Elsie remained unresponsive.

Jace had said she needed more than he had. He looked over his shoulder at his brothers. "She needs more blood. Hurry," he yelled frantically.

As Kyran, Bhric, Nikko and Breslin raced to his side, Orlando ran into the cave, followed by Santiago, and a bloodied Hayden.

"Holy shit..." Orlando breathed.

"Kyran, take Zander's place and open a vein now. Bhric, Nikko, and Breslin, be ready to take over when he runs dry." Jace barked from the other side of Elsie, as he placed pressure on her wounds.

Bhric placed his pierced arm over Elsie's lips. Zander sat beside her, holding her cold hand. She had to live. She was his whole world.

Jace placed his hand on Elsie's neck, and turned his

attention to her leg. He had belted it off, above the open fracture. "Part of the problem is she's still losing blood. Keep pressure on her neck, Zander. If we can get this bleeding to stop, your blood will be able to heal her."

He nodded and removed his t-shirt then went to press the fabric on his mate's neck and went cold. Before the cotton covered her wound, he saw that her mate mark had been cut from her skin. He shook as he held pressure, ensuring no more was lost. He was relieved when he felt the heat of Jace's healing touch.

He held his breath as he watched Elsie's leg heal under Jace's touch. She wasn't out of the woods, yet. Once Bhric had given all he could, Kyran and Nikko each proceeded to give blood to Elsie. Did he feel changes beneath his palm? Was their collective blood really healing Elsie? He refused to lift his hand to see.

He buried his head in her hair, as he waited to see if Elsie survived.

COGNIZANCE RETURNED SUDDENLY and Elsie braced for the pain to follow. She kept still while she assessed her body and surroundings. As she took stock an intoxicating aroma hit her nose. A sliver of recognition floated through her, but drifted away, before she could grasp it.

She finally opened her eyes and looked up at a coffered ceiling. She wasn't in the cave any longer and wondered where she'd been taken. She tried to roll over on the soft mattress, only to bump into a broad, muscular chest.

Zander was asleep next to her. That was the source of the delicious scent. She glanced around and wondered how she got back to Zeum.

She had been kidnapped, tortured, and had been certain she was as good as dead. Her bond with this vampire had given her strength. She loved him with her whole, battered heart. And, she was alive and well and had been given a second chance to be with him.

With that one thought, her body moistened and responded. His scent added to her arousal. She had never noticed the intensity of the fragrance, before. She detected oak, musk, and an indescribable, male essence. It enveloped her and she had trouble not devouring him in his sleep.

He looked unkempt, and there were dark circles under his eyes. She could see strain in the texture of his beautifully, bronzed skin. *Wait, why can I see the texture of his skin?* He opened his eyes, and she lost her train of thought at the joy in his brilliant, sapphire-blue eyes. The wash of his emotions mirrored hers.

"Och, thank the Goddess!" He kissed her fervently and then drew back to stare at her again. "I was so verra worried. I thought I'd lost you. I never want to feel fear like that again. I couldna go on without you, *a ghra*. You are my life, my everything. How do you feel?" He squeezed her tight to his chest and buried his head in her neck.

"I feel surprisingly good given what happened. How long have I been out?"

"You've been unconscious for a little over three days. To think what you went through...and I wasna there to protect you. I will never forgive myself for that."

She held him close, happy she was alive and with him. "It wasn't your fault. I'm here now." Her mouth watered. She was having trouble thinking past her thirst. "I'm thirsty. Can I get a drink, please?"

"Of course, wait here." She watched his muscular back and ass as he stood up and went into the bathroom to get her some water. He had the finest backside she had ever seen. The view of his front was even better. His shaft lifted with awareness as she watched him. He had a beautiful body. She gulped down the water he handed her and fought to recollect everything that had happened.

She only remembered pieces of the puzzle. "I see pictures of the demon and Lena, and remember her torturing me, then pain, but I can't recall all the details. How am I alive? I thought I was dead," she whispered.

He grabbed her and held her so tightly it bordered on painful. She listened, as he told her about how she had been kidnapped from Elsie's Hope, something she hadn't remembered, and how he and his warriors located and saved her. She had been near death when Zander found her so she wasn't surprised that she didn't recall any part of being rescued.

She stretched her leg and rubbed her ribs, then threw her legs over the side of the bed. Gingerly, she tested to see if she could hold her weight. She met his eyes over her shoulder.

He was hot on her heels as she made her way to the bathroom. She grabbed hold of his hand and something settled at the contact. This was where she was always supposed to be.

"Ugh, I need a shower. I can smell the filth. And, I'm hungry...wait, my neck."

She twisted toward the mirror, and was astonished that she could actually see the Celtic cross, below her left ear. She fingered the intricate knots. Her eyes snapped up, as she took in the tribal design that encircled the cross. She grabbed his broad, bare shoulders and turned him around, knowing what she would find. His cross was an exact replica of hers, except that it had no circle around it.

"How can I see it? We haven't mated. And, why doesn't it match yours?"

"You are more realm now than human. And, it matters little that they don't match exactly. You are mine, *a ghra!* The Goddess gave you to me. Nothing will change that. The circle is new, and I canna explain that, but it changes nothing. I can feel your soul right here," he thumped his chest.

He grabbed her roughly into his arms, and brought his lips down on hers. "I need you, now. I love you so much, it hurts." She felt the same way.

She smiled widely. "Yes. You are mine. I claimed you, and will never give you up," she agreed whole-heartedly. "I love you. And, I'm so sorry for not telling you sooner." She cupped his face and looked deeply into his eyes.

"It would kill me to lose you, but nothing will stop me from giving you everything I am. You may not like everything you're going to get, but you're stuck with me, now. I love you," she declared again as she rose up and claimed him in a passionate kiss.

She wanted him and wasn't going to wait anymore. She lifted her sleep-shirt over her head, and dropped it onto the tiled floor. She turned the water on, stepped into the shower, and looked back over her shoulder, with a coy smile. She yelped as he scooped her into his arms. He must not be using vampire speed, since she tracked his every move. She sighed at how he set her on fire.

"The Goddess was shining on my perfect mate."

"You see me through rose colored glasses, Zander, and treat me too good, but you'll never hear a complaint out of me." His lips were soft when they met hers. He set her on her feet inside the shower, but kept ahold of her hips. The warm water at her back was nothing compared to the heat he caused.

"I have to have you. I need to be inside you. Feel you. Och, Goddess, what I want to do to you..." he trailed off, as he kissed a trail down her neck, and lavished attention on her pulse point. She moaned as he picked her up and cradled her against his bare chest. She loved the feel of his body as her breasts mashed against him.

Her nipples hardened with his attention to her neck and chin. Her skin was hyper-sensitive and she dropped her head back as he continued to lick and suck his way across her throat. His lips met her mouth again, and then kissed their way across her face, while he held her bottom tightly. She locked her legs around his waist and was one shift away from impaling herself on his thick shaft. Control, she needed control. She inhaled his heavenly scent and was completely lost.

There would be no going slow.

CHAPTER THIRTY-THREE

Zander was reeling. His mate was alive, she loved him, and he was finally going to make love to her. Life didn't get much better. He gripped her bottom, knowing her intentions, but he refused to pound her against the tile wall their first time together. He hoped she didn't beg him because he had no will-power where she was concerned. "Let me wash you, and then I'm going to take you to bed."

"I don't want to wait. I need you, now," she said against his lips.

He reared back and perused her face. Her eyes were heavy-lidded, her lips swollen from his kisses and her nipples puckered. Slow, he reminded, he wanted to make love to her slowly.

"I have waited so long to hear you say that, but this time, I must make slow, sweet love to you. There will be a time for fast and furious later." He regrettably unlocked her legs, and set her down. Claiming her lips in another kiss, he reached for the shampoo. He lathered her hair and rinsed it, before shifting his attention to her body. He soaped and worshipped her breasts, paying special attention to her pert, pink nipples. Her moans turned desperate. He felt teeth scrape his nipple, and electricity heated his blood. When she sucked his nipple into her mouth, he locked his jaw. Do not pound her into the tile, he scolded himself.

His shaking hands slipped down her abdomen, and slid into heaven. Her core was hot, wet and dripping. His finger teased her sensitive bundle of nerves, and halted at her opening. He turned to shut off the water. He couldn't wait any longer. Not bothering to stop and dry off, he scooped her up, and placed her legs around his waist.

She moaned and writhed against him, sliding deliciously up and down his length. That small amount of friction had his balls drawing up tight, and that telltale tingle set up residence in his spine. Not yet, he gritted his teeth and staved off his orgasm.

"As much as it will hurt to stop, I need to hear you say you want to finish what we seem to keep starting."

She drew in a ragged breath. "Yes, I need you. I want you more than I've ever wanted anything. Make me yours."

He closed his eyes, savoring her words. He set her back on the bed, and took in the splendor of her. "Goddess, there isna a more beautiful sight." He wanted her body and her blood. He'd drained himself when he gave her blood, and hadn't replenished what was lost. He was suddenly rapacious. Dizziness assailed him with thoughts of taking her vein while he took her body.

"I have waited so long for you. Over seven centuries. I can hardly believe this is happening. My life truly began the moment I saw you." He slid his fingers down her moist, feminine flesh.

She moaned, then sat up and licked his nipple, sucking it into her mouth, and then grabbed the base of his erection.

He shook with his desire for her. It worsened when he felt the evidence of her arousal.

"Stop, *a ghra*. You're going to unman me. But, Goddess, you're so ready for me."

"I want you to lose control. Mmmm, baby, you feel so good."

He lowered his head and licked one nipple for several minutes, and then the other, taking his time, causing her to writhe in his arms, as he nipped them with his fangs. He stopped to admire his work, his breaths heating the wet peaks. He gripped her hand, stilling its movement on his shaft.

"I could look at you for centuries, and never get enough."

He stopped her when she reached for him again. If she touched him, at that moment, he would lose all sense and take her like an animal. He ran his hands up her arms and stretched them above her head. "Keep your hands where they are. I want to explore your body."

He was obsessed with her breasts and couldn't get enough of them. He trailed his hands down her chest, watching her face as he worked her nipples between his thumb and forefinger, sucking and licking them. He marveled at how responsive she was to his slightest touch. It was obvious that she liked his teeth on her nipples. What about his fangs? He sank them into her left breast and she detonated in his arms. He took some of her blood as he lost his seed on the bedding. They both shook from head to toe, but he didn't pause in his ministrations. Thanks to his supernatural genes, his shaft remained hard as steel, wanting more.

He toured her abdomen, on his way down. His tongue dipped into her belly button, causing her to giggle. "That tickles, oh...yes, right there. I ache for you." He smiled at her demands, and eased his fingers into her, and cursed in Gaelic. She was close again.

"Your honey is delicious," he whispered, as withdrew his finger, despite her protest, and licked his finger. She tasted so sweet.

"And, it's all yours," she reassured him. He slid his body against hers, continuing the magic of his fingers, between her legs. Her hips lifted and she ground against his hand. He quickened the speed of his fingers, while he settled his body on top of hers. She was a wanton creature, writhing beneath him and he had to have her.

HER HIPS HAD a mind of their own. She wasn't sure how he had her so close again, but she was ready to beg for release. She loved the feel of his strength against her and gasped when his erection nudged her aching core.

"Och, *a ghra,* you drive me wild." His cock gliding over the nub in her slick channel, replaced his hand. His fangs pierced the flesh around her right nipple. Pleasure exploded through her core and stars burst behind her eyelids, as she instantly climaxed.

"Oh, fu..." She lost the ability to respond, as he drew her blood. Removing his fangs, he licked the puncture wounds. Wave, after cresting wave of pleasure, crashed through her and she felt his body shake and heard his groans of release. She would never be the same. She had never truly experienced ecstasy, until that moment.

"You're the most beautiful creature when you orgasm. You roar, like a lioness. It's my new favorite sound." She was surprised at how few inhibitions she seemed to have with him. She felt a freedom and exhilaration she never knew possible. She wanted more and was thrilled that vampires needed no recovery time.

"You're the king of my jungle. And, what those fangs can do...I'm officially addicted to your bite. I have to confess, I'm a bit concerned. I mean, look at your size. What if you don't fit? I ache to have you inside me, Zander."

He licked softly around her belly button. "I'm no' done exploring, my wee lioness. But, rest assured, we were made for each other. We will fit together, seamlessly."

Her eyes widened as he crouched between her legs and spread her wide, gripping her thighs. She moaned loudly when he slid his tongue into her heat, pressing against her clit. He sucked it into his mouth, ran his tongue down to her opening, and inserted his stiff tongue inside her. She involuntarily flexed around his tongue. He withdrew it and moved it back to her nub.

Sex had never been so wild and unfettered. She had already climaxed three times and there was no decrease in her need of him.

"God, yesss." Her eyes snapped open when he slowly sank his fangs into her clit. She left her body as she detonated in his arms.

"Zander," she screamed. The pleasure was so intense she blacked out. She came to and discovered steel arms held her lower body and he was convulsing with his release. The thick, warm ropes of cream hit her calves.

She looked into his glowing, blue eyes and saw he was consumed by lust and had lost his control. He was feral, and gave her no pause. He sat up and crawled over her then thrust his cock into her, in one swift move. He was large and thick and long. He filled and stretched her in the most delicious way. She felt him hit her womb and her erogenous zones were still throbbing from the aphrodisiac of his bite.

Sheer ecstasy.

~

HER CRY of pleasure was his undoing. Lust and need obliterated all other thoughts. The tight, hot sheath tore through his madness. He didn't have the strength to hold still, for her to adjust to his prodigious length, and immediately settled into a punishing rhythm.

"Are you okay? I canna stop. I'm inside you. Goddess, you're so tight and perfect."

"Please, Zander, I need...you have to...give me more." He groaned, as she writhed against him, and her muscles squeezed him painfully.

"Shite, I have waited so long for this. You feel so fucking good." He slowed his pace and withdrew slowly, sliding back in to her channel. He lost his breath. The experience was beyond his imaginings.

"You're so verra wet. I want to make this good for you." Sweat beaded his brow. He held back, wanting this experience to remake her, as it already had him.

"Give me everything you have, I can take it. You may be big and fill me to the point of madness, but only in the best way." She moaned loudly, as he continued his leisurely pace, and cried out when he thumbed her sensitive nipple. His bite had left the area super-charged and caused more ripples of arousal when he tweaked it.

She leaned forward and nibbled his neck. "Yes, *a ghra*. I want your teeth in me." His thrusts increased. She licked, sucked, and kissed her way to his flat, brown nipples. She tentatively suckled, as he pounded into her, increasing his pace. He cried out when she tentatively bit down. He'd never had teeth on his flesh in any way and he loved it.

He pushed her back flat on the bed. "Give me a moment, *a ghra.*" He took her lips in a rough kiss then snuck his thumb between her folds of flesh, to strum her bundle of nerves. He felt her muscles ripple and clench, as she neared orgasm, again.

"I never knew passion like this was possible," she murmured.

Her body was coiled tightly around his massive shaft. He couldn't help the sounds of pleasure, as she bucked wildly. They were lost in passion as their bodies danced together.

"Oh, Zander, yes...faster...harder...MORE!" Her heat threatened to burn his shaft and seconds later, he was squeezed ruthlessly when she climaxed, again.

Spurned by her desires and pleasure, he gave her what she wanted. He kissed her as he bucked relentlessly into her. He felt spasms run down his spine. He growled when her sheath coiled tightly around him. Her nails bit sharply into his shoulders, drawing him closer to her. He wove the fingers of one hand with hers, and caressed her side with the other. He was close to losing his seed again and stroked her body, wanting to bring her with him. Within seconds, another orgasm crested and his seed shot out of his shaft, deep into her womb.

As his release raged on, his emotions flew out of control. He had never loved more deeply, than he loved this female. "I love you, Elsie. So verra much. Och, Goddess..."

"Oh, Zander. I love you more than I've ever loved anyone. And, I never thought I'd ever love, again." Tears glistened in her eyes.

He gazed into her glowing, blue eyes. Glowing? *My blood must still be affecting her.*

"I'm no' done with you yet." He reached between them and pinched her nub.

She was so sensitive that she cried out and peaked again. "Okay, I'm officially addicted to you," she panted.

He shifted inside her. "Hold on, lass. This time, you will feel how a vampire takes his female."

"What? Don't you need a nap? I do." She smiled wickedly, looking anything but tired.

"Nay, I doona need a nap," he nipped her lips. "I need you. This time, I take your body, and your blood." He sank his fangs deep into her neck, and set a fast and furious pace of drawing her blood, while making love to his Fated Mate.

"Is there anything you don't cook well?" Orlando asked, as she finished her second Vietnamese burger. "Damn, girl, I've never seen you eat so much. Do you want me to get you a third burger?"

She blushed, feeling a bit like a pig. She was still hungry and a third burger sounded good. "No, I'd like to go catch some rays in the pool," she said, deciding against eating anymore.

"Sounds good to me. You gonna wear that little black number? Or the blue one?" Rhys asked on a chuckle. She smacked his arm, and he sailed off the barstool. "Shit, that vamp blood juiced you up."

"It sure sprawled you on your ass," she laughed.

An odd look passed between Zander and Jace. Shrugging it off, she jumped down from the barstool, and headed to the pool. "I'm going for a swim," she told Zander and planted a brief kiss on his slightly upturned lips.

She whisked off her cotton dress, revealing her Brazilian

bikini. She enjoyed the widening of Zander's eyes a bit too much. And, put more sway in her hips, as she sauntered off.

"Orlando, go with her. She hasna been conscious long, and, while she seems fine, well, more than fine," Zander conceded, "I worry she hasna healed completely."

She scoffed at Zander's words. She didn't need a babysitter. "I'm great, Zander. Totally healed, stop being overprotective."

"Mate," he barked. She ignored the warning in his tone, and continued to the pool. Of course, he followed. She liked that he would watch her from the shadows as she dove into the cool water.

"Here's your Monsterita, Chiquita," Santiago said, handing her a drink when she surfaced.

She accepted the drink as she settled on her float, holding onto the wall. "Ah, thanks, Santi. Can you pretty please push me into the sun?" She batted her lashes at him and he gave her a shove.

She glided to the middle of the pool and quickly felt heat building under her skin. It became extremely painful and she began to panic, something was seriously wrong. She needed to get out of the pool and have Jace look at her.

"Holy shite," Zander gasped. "Look at your wee fangs. And, your eyes, they're glowing...I was wrong before," Zander said as he stared at her in the middle of the pool.

She was confused by everything happening in her body. He couldn't be talking about her having fangs. Could he? Her skin was turning red and small blisters were forming. She looked back at Zander and heard his heart pounding in fear.

She became distracted by the pounding of his heart. She glanced from his eyes, to the pulse popping enticingly in his throat. Suddenly struck with an urge she didn't understand, she wanted to sink her teeth into his flesh, and drink deeply. That need burned hotly and took over everything else.

Before she knew what was happening, she was wrapped around Zander and had buried those 'wee fangs' in his neck. A climax rocked her body the moment his blood exploded on her tongue. Overcome with bloodlust, she sucked feverishly. When the pain and thirst subsided, she withdrew her fangs, and met his shocked gaze.

Panic struck a chord in her thunderous heart.

ZANDER WATCHED his lovely mate in disbelief. Her skin had burned the moment the sun touched it. Incomprehension had hit when she sifted from the float, into his arms and sank her fangs into his neck. Now, she panted, in obvious discomfort with his blood glistening on her lips and his orgasm still barreling through him. He held her close to his raging body. Thoughts and emotions funneled through him, driven by the hurricane of disbelief. His mate was a vampire!

How did this happen? It shouldn't have happened. In fact, it had never happened in the history of the Tehrex Realm. But, there was no mistaking the fangs, the glow, and the bloodlust.

"*A ghra,* you appear to be a vampire," he whispered.

Wide, hysterical eyes gazed up at him. Her terror slayed him. "What? You're wrong! You told me that vampires were born, not made. Remember?"

She placed her hand over his heated cheek. Of course, his erupting shaft loved the contact, and pulsed again. He needed to reassure and calm his mate, right now. "We will figure this oot—"

"Can someone defrost this pool and get me out? My nuts are getting frost-bite!" Orlando hollered, cutting him off.

Jerking his head, Zander glanced at the frozen pool, and its three, trapped occupants. "Did Bhric do that?" he asked as suspicion slithered through him.

"Nay, brathair," Bhric responded, as he ran into the pool area, followed by the others. "I didna do that to the pool. I was in the kitchen with Kyran and Breslin, when I heard the ruckus. Goddess..."

They gaped at the pool, then at the fangs in Elsie's mouth. His protective instinct roared, and he wrapped his arms around Elsie, shielding her from the scrutiny.

Breslin extended her hand, slowly heating the water, releasing Orlando, Santiago and Rhys.

"Want me to call Jace?" Orlando asked.

"Aye. And the scientists. We have to figure oot what's going on." Seven intense gazes reflected his concern.

"I DON'T UNDERSTAND IT, Liege, but Elsie's blood work shows she has the DNA structure of a vampire. I don't see any human markers left at all. It's not the same changes that are typically seen with a mating. I highly doubt this is a temporary side effect of the vampire blood she imbibed. Somehow, she has become the first turned vampire," Jace related. Elsie gaped at him from where she sat in the war room with the Dark Warriors and the council.

She felt like a bug under a microscope, and rubbed her arms nervously, as they stared at her. She had spent the last couple of evenings with the scientists and Jace while they tried to dissect what had happened to her.

"As disturbing as that is, it makes sense. Ever since I

woke-up, I have experienced the world around me differently. I can hear, see and sense my surroundings better than I ever did before. I was worried I had brain damage. Or, maybe that I was going crazy," she whispered.

"I'd like to repeat testing every few days to see if there are any changes, of course. But, overall, she appears to be a healthy vampire," Jace said.

She leaned into Zander's side, as his arm wound around her waist. His deep baritone echoed loudly in her sensitive ears. "She is no' a test subject, and we willna treat her as such. We need to protect her and figure oot if this is information we share with the realm. I plan to contact the Goddess aboot this, but no' until after we finish the mating ceremony. I doona want anything to stand in the way of completing our bonding. Do you think it's actually possible, to turn humans into vampires?"

"From what I can see of the blood work, I highly doubt it's possible to turn humans. Her earlier samples had different markers from the average human and there is a magical quality present. Under the microscope, I can see purple, blue and green threads woven throughout her blood. I've never seen anything like it, before," Evzen explained, pouring over the printouts.

"I noted that, too. I had previously considered it a side effect of her precognitive ability. I never thought it could mean something more," Jace added.

"She has abilities from each of the four of you. I can't fathom how that happened, given that special powers are not transferred through blood exchanges. Whatever we decide to share with the realm I don't think it's a good idea to share that she has acquired these abilities. Otherwise, we will every greedy sup trying to steal powers from one another, not bothering to stop and think. I'll say this, nothing about your mate is normal, Zander," Hayden pointed out.

Great. One more thing that made her different. At least she no longer saw herself as a freak. She was going to be the Vampire Queen. Excitedly, she turned her thoughts to planning her mating ceremony.

CHAPTER THIRTY-FOUR

Elsie had taken to her new, supernatural, blood-drinking status like a duck to water. She loved her new strength and was anxious to get revenge against the demons. They had disappeared from the cave and had gone radio silent, but they'd be back, and she and the Dark Warriors would be prepared.

She glanced in the full-length mirror as her mind came back to where it needed to be. Her mating ceremony which was going to take place shortly. They hadn't wanted to wait another four weeks for the next full moon, so they were doing it less than a week after she had been turned into a vampire. 'Carpe Diem' was her new motto. Funny, because now that she had eternity stretched out before her, she wasn't wasting a moment.

She shifted her chaplet again, unable to stop wondering if the realm would approve of her. She was an abnormal-unexplainable-phenomenon, and here she stood, about to become the Vampire Queen. This was a powerful position, and she wanted to make Zander proud. She was young and didn't have centuries of life experience, nor did she grow up with knowledge of the realm. She couldn't have been more ill-prepared for the position, but was determined to be the best queen possible.

Cailyn interrupted when she knocked on the doorjamb, "Can I help you with that?"

Elsie smiled tentatively. She was still unsure how Cailyn was taking her new supernatural status. "Yes, please. With these new powers, I keep freezing the fresh flowers in this thing, and can't seem to wrap the chaplet around his family's crown. I'm so nervous and I want this to be perfect."

Cailyn shook her head. "I still can't believe you're a vampire now, but I have to say it suits you. I owe Zander and the others everything for saving you. I don't know what I'd do if I lost you, too." Tears welled in her eyes as her sister crossed the room to her side. Elsie wished Mack could accept her as easily. The fierce SOVA leader hated vampires and Elsie feared would never accept what she had become. It was the reason Elsie hadn't seen her in weeks. She would have to face her eventually, and soon. She missed her friend and was running out of excuses to give her when they spoke on the phone. That was consideration for another day, today she was getting mated!

"I see why you're nervous. Marriage is a nerve-wracking thing, and according to how you've explained this mating, this is a huge deal. You'll be bound to Zander for centuries, if not millennia. I can't even fathom that. Here, give that to me," her sister murmured as she took the crown and arranged fresh flowers on it, then placed it on Elsie's head. "It's obvious how deeply Zander loves you. And, I have to say, I've never seen you happier. You deserve only the best, El."

"Thank you, Cai. I'm so happy you're here with me. I

love him more than life. I never knew it was possible to have what we do."

Cailyn wiped her tears, and then grabbed the gown from the back of the door. "I wonder if I'll ever have even half the love you two share. Okay, it's time, let's get this on you." Elsie wondered what her sister meant. John loved her.

Cailyn held out the dress and Elsie slid into the simple, white, long-sleeved, silk dress. She had chosen an off-shoulder gown with light-gold trim around the collar and cuffs, and a matching belt that sat low on her hips. She loved the feel of the satin against her hyper-sensitive skin.

"You look so beautiful," Cailyn said as she gazed at her with tears brimming in her eyes.

She checked her hair and make-up. "I think I'm ready," she exhaled and headed for the door.

NERVES FROZE her feet at the entryway to the enclosed patio. The room had been cleared of furniture. Not for the first time, Elsie wished Breslin had also given her blood when she was on death's door. It was an awe-inspiring sight, watching her wave a hand and light hundreds of candles. But it paled in comparison to the sight of Zander standing in the center of the room, in traditional, Scottish, formal wear. He took her breath away.

Her feet automatically moved toward her male in his pristine kilt and crisp white shirt. The fabric draped over his shoulder matched his black and gray kilt. His broad shoulders pushed the material of his shirt to its limit. God, he was sexy.

Kyran stepped next to Zander, near the tiled image of the Triskele Amulet, wearing identical clothing. She smiled.

Did they have anything on under those kilts? A laugh bubbled up at the sight of the sporran around their waists, and the tiny flashes holding up their long, white socks.

When Zander first told her that he and his brothers would be wearing kilts with all the Scottish finery, she imagined it being ridiculous. She should have known better. She eyed Zander hungrily as she finished her approach.

"Friends and family please form a circle around the couple," Kyran instructed. Zander removed the amulet from around his neck, and handed it to Kyran. Kyran closed his eyes as he grasped the amulet, clearly overcome by some emotion.

"We have gathered here in this beautiful place, under the eye of the Sun and the glow of the Moon. Let the circle be blessed and consecrated with Fire and Water," Kyran recited.

Bhric and Breslin stepped forward and with a flourish, fire shot forth from Breslin's outstretched palm to flow around the outskirts of the circle. The fire rose from the earth to the heavens, like shooting stars. Bhric raised his hands and water cascaded down in a sheer waterfall, from heaven back to the earth, extinguishing the fire.

Kyran squeezed the amulet. "We call to the Goddess Morrigan, and invoke her to bless this mating."

Smoke and mist filled the room. A bright, white light dispelled her belief that it was caused by the twins' powers. The light was blinding, as strong power buffeted through the room. All the supernaturals of the Tehrex Realm must have recognized the source of the power because they went to their knees with their heads bowed.

Ignorant to what was happening, or why, she and her sister were the only ones who remained standing. They need a class, or book, on supernatural etiquette, she thought, as a shower of fine, silver glitter had her eyes traveling to the ceiling. She sensed the power coalescing, and gaped as a woman of incomparable beauty took form in the fog.

She wore a blood-red, velvet cloak fastened at the neck with a silver broach that looked like the amulet Kyran was clutching. A silver circlet that contained a small, bloodstone in the center of her forehead wound into her silky, black hair. She had soft features with a small nose, full lips, and long, thick lashes framing ice-blue eyes. Her midnight-black gown had an empire-waist, accenting her ample bosom. Elsie noticed her hair had silver streaks and flowed mid-back. She may have been barely over five-feet tall, but Elsie knew she could crush anyone. Her power commanded the entire room.

"I will take over from here, Kyran. Thank you." She extended her hand, and Kyran placed a kiss upon the back of it then he placed the mating stone in her palm. It was a smooth, round, granite rock.

"It has been many centuries since the last mating. I regret the need for such a cessation, but I've always had plans for the realm. Before we continue with the ceremony, I would answer one question that has plagued all of you. Yes, Elsie is the first, and will be the only turned vampire. Now, rise. We have a mating to complete." The Goddess smiled magnificently at Zander and placed the stone into his right hand.

She gasped at the electrical pulses that crawled up her arm when the Goddess grabbed her right hand. She felt power when her hand was laid on top of Zander's hand that was clutching the stone. "We call upon the spirits of the East, of Air, Spring and new beginnings. We call upon the spirits of the South and the inner Fire of the Sun, Summer and personal will. We call upon the spirits of the West, of Water, Autumn, and healing and dreaming. We call upon the spirits of the North, of Earth, Winter, and the time of cleansing and renewal. Join us to bless this couple with your guidance and inspiration," the Goddess chanted. Magic cocooned Elsie and Zander. Emotion choked her while she watched the Goddess.

The Goddess lifted her hand from where she had joined them, leaving theirs clasped together, surrounding the stone. Zander grabbed her left hand and placed it on his chest, over his heart, then placed his left hand over hers.

"I bless this mating under the Sun and the Moon. This circle of love and honour is open and never broken, so may it be," the Goddess' voice resonated with her blessing.

Heat built in the stone as she felt both souls leave her body to enter the stone. She wished fervently to keep a small portion of Zander's as it was the only thing that had kept her alive during her torture. It was selfish yes, but it was such an integral part of her she didn't want to part with it.

A brilliant light flashed between their fingers. Her skin tingled with the magic. The connection she felt to Zander strengthened, and she could now see the bond between them. A thick, golden ribbon wrapped around her heart and ran to his, entwining them. Her soul surged back into her body at that moment, causing her to gasp. Looking up, she saw the joy and astonishment she felt mirrored in Zander's eyes.

She was complete in a way she'd never been before, and knew Zander was experiencing the same. Prodding her newly reformed soul, she discovered her and Zander's soul had been so entwined during the mating that they both resided within her. Wishes do come true, she thought. Her chest may burst from her joy, and she became aware of Zander's every thought and emotion.

She heard the Goddess' voice whisper in her head. *"No power, not even death, can ever sever this bond. Mating stones protect and bless different aspects for different couples. Yours blesses and protects your womb."*

Unable to hold back her curiosity, she raised one of her fingers and gasped. The ordinary-looking, granite rock was now the biggest, most dazzling, blue sapphire she had ever seen. It matched her vampire's eyes.

Zander raised their hands and the stone. "My Queen." Zander reached into his sporran and removed a large, pink diamond ring.

"'Tis the Queen's ring, passed down in my family, and last belonged to my *mamai*. Now, it belongs to you. I am yours, *a ghra*." He slid the exquisite, platinum-gold band with a fifteen-carat, pink diamond onto her slim, left finger. Energy zipped through her skin as the ring sized itself, automatically. She gaped at Zander, in awe. "And, you are mine," he declared.

Kyran nudged her. "Give this one to Zander. 'Tis the King's ring," he whispered into her ear, handing her an intricate, platinum band with a smaller, black diamond.

She raised her lids, meeting Zander's bright, glowing eyes. "I am yours, my King," she said simply, not knowing proper etiquette, and slid the ring onto his finger.

Even in her six-inch heels, she had to go to her tip-toes to reach his mouth. She twined her hands into the hair at his nape. "When is the blood exchange? I need you," she murmured in his ear. The faint, tinkling of laughter told her the Goddess had disappeared. The evening was surreal. And, it wasn't over.

Bluidy hell. I can see her nipples through that silky gown. I am a fully-mated male and my mate wants me. I willna make it two more minutes unless I am inside that sweet body.

She stared at Zander. She had heard him, but his lips hadn't moved. Were those his thoughts?

I agree, love. How do we get out of here? She reached out to him, testing her theory.

The telepathy has already taken effect, mate. Unfortunately, we must greet our subjects. Then, we will make our escape. Or, a quick visit to the pantry.

A quickie will never sate me. Besides, Hayden is approaching, followed by too many others. Let's do this.

Hayden's well-wishes blurred into hundreds of others and her cheeks hurt from smiling. She nearly wept with relief when she saw Rhys was last.

Rhys swore his fealty to the couple and whooped loudly, if irreverently. "Let's partay, warrior style!" He sidled up to Cailyn, "Hey, sweetcakes, want some of my *hey juice?*"

JACE STARED OPENLY at Cailyn while she spoke with Rhys. This was the first time he had seen her face, and he was awed by her soft features and pouty lips. Her light-brown hair was loose around her shoulders, and she looked elegant in her simple, green, silk gown. He was immediately drawn to her. His body came to life and hardened, readying to take her. He braced himself for the nausea and self-hatred that always followed his arousal.

His body zinged and his erection grew out of control. That familiar self-hatred hit, and was compounded by a new level of disgust. Cailyn intruded in his recriminations when she slapped Rhys' shoulder.

"Not in your wildest dreams. However, I want to toast my

sister and it calls for champagne." Cailyn grabbed a flute from the tray of a passing waiter and called out, "To Elsie and Zander."

"Here, here," Elsie responded, as she accepted her glass of bubbly and shared a drink with her sister.

Jace's gaze was riveted on the sight of Cailyn's slender throat, swallowing. It was erotic, and brought images of her sucking and swallowing him. He groaned. Time to think of something else. She had a fiancé. A complication he was glad to avoid. He was damaged goods, anyway.

MILLIONS OF TINY, white lights sparkled in the solarium, around the pool, and in the trees of the backyard. Staff milled about busily, and within minutes, a buffet was on the table and a band, the Night Crawlers, had set up and was playing music.

"Shall we, *a ghra?*" Zander led her to the buffet.

"As much as I want to rush to our bed, we should eat first. You will need your energy later," she squeezed his hand, and felt her heart melting even more for her king. She hadn't believed in fate or destiny before, but she had no doubt that she was *fated* to be Zander's mate. Her place was always meant to be by his side.

Zander filled her plate, and then spent she next few hours eating, drinking and dancing with the Dark Warriors and various council members. All the while, the sexual tension in her body continuously rose as she imagined what the night had in store.

No longer able to wait, she grabbed Zander's hand. "Let's go," she whispered in his ear and hauled him towards the stairs to their bedroom.

Clothing hit the floor as they made their way upstairs. When they reached the rooms they'd been sharing since her rescue, he was bare, but for his socks and Ghillies. Question answered, they don't wear anything under their kilts. And he was a spectacular male specimen!

"Your turn," he rumbled in her ear. She squealed and ran toward the bed. He tackled her mid-leap and twisted, so he took the landing. Somehow, her dress had been ripped off in the process, and lay in tatters on the floor.

"Damn, I liked that dress...mmm." Thoughts scattered as he nipped and nibbled his way down her neck and she gasped as he sliced through her silk panties with his razor-sharp fangs. Before she opened her mouth to admonish him, his fangs had sunk into her intimate flesh and she was climaxing.

"Do...we need...to do...a blood...exchange?" She asked between panting breaths. He was so sexy as he prowled up from between her legs. And, so aroused. His shaft stood up against his stomach.

"Aye, it seals the mating. We take from each other at the same time, while we are joined. Are you ready, *a ghra*?" he asked as he removed her bra.

She fell in love all over again as he poised between her thighs. "Yes, Zander, take me, now," she cried out.

That was all he needed and plunged into her to the hilt, in one swift thrust. She felt her eyes glowing brightly as their gazes locked. She saw their full, happy life together reflected in his depths. Her fangs shot out and she heard him suck in a sharp breath. He enjoyed her bite. She bit into the nape of his neck where it met his broad shoulder while his fangs sunk into her shoulder. Their bodies exploded into the most intense orgasm of her life.

Light exploded through her and her entire body tingled

with magic. She felt him shudder his release and arch his back, pressing his chest into her. The ribbon she had seen earlier binding them together expanded with every draw they took of each other's blood. The golden glow transformed into a million, tiny, gold chains, linking him to her from every point of his body. It formed a cocoon around them and seeped into their pores.

Intense emotions overwhelmed her as she felt the change within and their closeness intensified. She could see how much he loved her, and felt his pleasure, as his orgasm raged on. She was thankful for her new immortality because she never would've survived the night his body was demanding.

THE SORCERY of the mating took hold and irrevocably altered him. He felt their entwined souls swell once again. He took in the bond encompassing them and relished experiencing how she felt about him. He was transformed as new powers surged from his Fated Mate into him. Mates always shared a portion of their abilities, and while he was aware that she had inherited additional powers during her transformation, he didn't think those powers would be bestowed upon him during their mating, but he could feel new magic filling him.

Tingles erupted into flames over his mate mark between his shoulder blades. "My mark. Och, it burns. What does it look like?" He twisted to catch a glimpse of his back.

"Stop moving, let me see," she looked over his shoulder and gasped. "You have the same circle surrounding the body of your cross. We match and now it's inked into your skin. You are mine in every way," she told him fiercely.

"Always." The surge of magic sent his libido skyrocketing. His body took on a mind of its own, and intended to take his little mate in ways she had never dreamed. He groaned, "My mate," and gave himself over to passion.

The night was incredible, his mate was incredible, and he was *truly* complete for the first time in his life. They were two halves of one heart, and shared an intense bond. It went beyond mere love or lust.

After hours of blissful love making, his mate blinked sleepily at him. He would let her rest before he took her again. "Sleep, *a ghra,*" he whispered.

"Mr. Bossy Pants," she muttered as she drifted off to a peaceful, sated sleep.

He pulled her sleeping form closer to his heart. He brushed her brown curls from her beautiful face. She sighed and snuggled closer into his chest. He had never dreamed of being gifted with such a mate. She was flawless.

He lay there for hours gazing at his queen and knew the moment she dreamt. He wondered what was happening in her clever mind. Her eyes roved wildly behind her closed lids, and she tossed and turned. As he was about to join her dream, her eyes flew wide and she sat up, gasping for air.

"Oh my God, Cailyn!"

EXCERPT FROM MYSTIK WARRIOR, DARK WARRIOR ALLIANCE BOOK 2

"**T**hanks for picking me up tonight, especially this late. I owe you," Cailyn murmured as she embraced her best friend on the curb outside baggage claim at San Francisco International airport.

"Anytime, you know that. And thanks for letting me drive your car, I love it. It's the nicest car I'll ever drive," Jessie joked while holding the trunk open for Cailyn to throw in her bags. "So how was the wedding? And more importantly, did you spend *quality* time with the hot Doctor

Jace?" her friend finished as she slammed the trunk closed. Cailyn was still reeling over the fact Zander had placed some of his Dark Warriors in human occupations to keep the supernaturals' existence secret. Jace was one of those undercover supernaturals, a renowned ER physician in Seattle. But he certainly wasn't like any doctor she'd ever been to; he looked more like a model.

Thinking of Jace, a smile crept over Cailyn's mouth. She shook her head and crossed to the driver's door and jumped into the plush leather seat. She thought about the question as she put the car in drive and headed away from the airport. "Surprisingly, the wedding was incredible...magical. Elsie is so happy with her sexy Scot," she finally responded. Jessie would come unglued if she knew Zander was a vampire, let alone the Vampire King. She was dying to tell her, but some things you couldn't even share with your best friend, like how your sister was turned into a vampire to save her life and mated to the Vampire King. "And, you should see the huge house these guys live in. It was a perfect setting, with thousands of twinkling lights...it looked like a scene from a fairytale. How were things here?"

"You didn't miss much. I'm glad your sister is happy, after everything she went through when Dalton was killed. There is no one who deserves it more. But, you, my friend, are avoiding the real issue. You broke off your engagement to John months ago because of your attraction to this doctor. Now, spill it, MacGregor."

Cailyn heaved a breath of exasperation. She loved Jessie, but wished she wasn't so tenacious. She had no desire to talk about Jace. The smallest thoughts about him caused an intense arousal she had never experienced before with anyone else, not even while in the throes of passion. Then, there was this unexplainable pull, drawing her toward him.

His strange, stunning amethyst eyes, and his incredible body all drew her in, like a moth to the flame.

From the moment Jace had entered Elsie's apartment, Cailyn had been captivated by him, which surprised her. Typically, the kind of man who had a long braid, and wore a large, silver cuff wasn't her type. The combination made her think of an effeminate man, but there certainly wasn't anything effeminate about Jace. He was all masculine strength, and a fierce warrior to his core. She would never forget the vicious battle that destroyed Club Confetti, where he had wielded his weapons with expert precision.

She had found herself in the middle of a supernatural war, and had been terrified beyond reason, but the way Jace had moved so fluidly, and fought with confidence and vigor caused her heart to pound for different reasons. She recalled how she'd stood there unable to do anything to help or defend herself. She had been way out of her element. On one hand, she was horrified at the blood and violence, and wanted to run and hide, but on the other hand, she was captivated and enthralled by this mystical warrior. Needless to say, the situation had caused her a whole load of turmoil.

Like Jessie had said, that unrelenting attraction and confusion had made her call off her engagement to John months before. Thoughts of John reared an ugly, yet familiar guilt. He was attractive, caring, loyal, and supportive, everything she wanted in a husband. It was ridiculous to be lusting after Jace. After all, there were plenty of good-looking men in the world. Not to mention that Jace didn't see her as anything other than Elsie's big sister.

She glanced in her rear view mirror at the dark, empty highway behind her, contemplating how to answer Jessie. "I didn't spend any time alone with him. It was a short trip and he was at the hospital nearly the entire time. I sort of danced with him at the reception. Well, we were all together in a big group, but we were so close we touched several times and the heat between us...." Cailyn trailed off as her body shivered in remembrance.

"How are you supposed to figure out your feelings for John versus Jace if you didn't spend any time with him? I thought you were going to get him alone." Jessie waggled her eyebrows at Cailyn, making her chuckle.

"You make it sound so easy. What was I supposed to do, walk up to him and drag him to the nearest closet? Look, you know how confused this whole situation has made me. I was committed to John, and I love him, yet I can't stop thinking about Jace. Honestly, I didn't trust myself to be alone with him. My body tends to have a mind of its own where he is concerned."

"I have got to see this guy. He has to be smokin' to make you, the most faithful person I know, question yourself. Did you at least finally tell your sister that you broke your engagement to John?"

"No, I didn't have the heart to tell her. It was her big day and she has been through so much the past two years that she deserved it to be perfect. If I had told her, she would have spent too much time worrying about me. I will tell her if it becomes necessary. Things may still work out you know." She hated how her voice sounded so uncertain. She typically had no problems making decisions, big or small. This was infuriating.

She meant what she said though. It was possible that things with John would work out. She and John had continued talking since she broke things off, and he continued to try and win her back. She refused to go back to him until she extinguished her desire for Jace though. She kept telling herself that the draw to Jace was a phase, and that it would end. The problem was, her attraction was stronger now than it had been before.

"If you don't want Jace, can I have him? Does he make house calls? I'm suddenly feeling under the weather," Jessie moaned and leaned her head back against the seat, placing the back of her hand over her brown eyes.

Normally, Cailyn would have laughed that off, but jealousy hot and vicious stabbed through her veins. She wanted to punch her best friend in the face, repeatedly. What was wrong with her? This was out of control. She needed to escape the confines of the car. She was close to harming her best friend. The drive to her condo in Potrero Hill was going to be a long one tonight.

"No, you can't have him," she bit out before she could stop herself, immediately regretting her words. "I'm sorry, Jess. I get a bit crazy where Jace is concerned. Remember, I nearly clawed some girl's eyes out for kissing him. If you have any advice about how to resolve this, I'm all ears."

"Cai, you need to stop being so hard on yourself. You did the respectable thing and broke up with John despite the fact that you still love him. I know you would never hurt..."

An engine revving drew Cailyn's attention. Peering into her side and rearview mirrors she noticed a big, dark colored SUV quickly closing in on them. Cailyn got the sense that something was wrong. The aggressive manner of the other driver had panic setting in.

The large SUV loomed closer, and she realized her convertible didn't stand a chance against the beast barreling toward her. And, it was obvious they were gunning right for her car. Her heart sped up as adrenaline dumped into her system.

"What the hell? What's their problem?" She blurted and switched lanes getting out of their way.

"What?"

"That car behind us is all over my ass," she replied, tension lacing her voice.

Jessie turned around in her seat. "They changed lanes with you. Are they following us?"

Cailyn had the ability to read the minds of those around her, and despite the fact that she had come to loathe her power, she lifted the barriers she had in place to protect her mind and opened her telepathy toward the inhabitants in the vehicle behind her.

She recoiled as malevolence and anger coated her mind like slime on a bog in the bayou. Cailyn could read human thoughts like an open book, but it was difficult for her to read supernaturals. The jumbled mess she was picking up on told her that she was being followed by supernaturals. The intentions of the SUV's occupants were tinged with dark malice, causing a shiver to run up her spine. She tried to get enough information to know what they were facing, but it became difficult for Cailyn to concentrate through her growing fear.

EXCERPT FROM PEMA'S STORM, DARK WARRIOR ALLIANCE BOOK 3

A loud crash startled Pema, making her look up from her computer. Cursing echoed from the front of the store, and she cocked her head to the side, catching snippets of the argument raging between her sisters. Apparently, Suvi had dropped a box of fluorite crystals, and Isis was on the verge of going postal. Just a typical day at Black Moon. Shaking her head, Pema ignored them and wound her long blonde hair into a twist at the nape of her neck and went back to the papers she had been reviewing.

She didn't particularly enjoy the bookkeeping portion of their business, but someone had to do it. For two straight years business had boomed, allowing them to pay Cele, their High Priestess, back the money she loaned them. She had given them a loan to start Black Moon Sabbat, and it had taken a mere eighteen months to pay her back. They were proud of that fact, given the economy and Cele's astronomical interest rate.

More quarreling reached her in the back room, and with a sigh, she stood up. Time to play peacemaker. Pema was beginning to rethink her idea of opening earlier in the morning to service more of their human clients. There were too many nights they stayed up late trying to find the perfect martini. Prosperity came at a price, she thought, as she made her way from the office to see what had happened. But it wasn't like they were going to give up their pursuit of the perfect martini any time soon.

Glancing around the shop, she swelled with pride. They had built Black Moon from the ground up. The store was as unique to the Tehrex Realm as Pema and her sisters were. Neither should exist, yet they did and were thriving. Pema and her sisters believed the ignorance of their youth was partially responsible.

They were the youngest witches in the realm, and were impetuous enough to take the risk to create a business that brought humans into close proximity with the realm. They enjoyed interacting with humans, and thrived off of the unique verve for life they had. However, that didn't mean they were completely senseless. They understood the Goddess' edict to maintain secrecy, and would never do anything to risk exposure. But they liked to toe the line.

The pungent odor of lavender and jasmine claimed Pema's attention and almost knocked her over when she entered the front. She glanced around to see Suvi standing amidst a mess of books and various teas, with the pricing stickers in hand. She noticed the decks of tarot cards had already been labeled and set off to the side.

"What are you two bickering about?" Pema asked.

"We are too damn tired to be up and functioning this early, and butterfingers here, dropped a case of fluorite. The entire box is damaged. Thankfully, I managed to save the potions we made last night. Had she broken those, we would be looking at an even bigger mess," Isis griped. "I mean, seriously, those magics, if mixed, would be lethal. When we stay out 'til two or three, it isn't wise to open at ten." Pema pursed her lips at the familiar argument her sisters made to push back her new hours.

"But, you did save the potions, and this," Pema gestured to the mess around Suvi, "is nothing. We're a team, remember? We couldn't run this place without watching each other's backs. And, lest you forget, Suvi sells more crystals and leather pouches than the two of us put together. I'll bet she can sell the damaged ones, just as easy," Pema told Isis as she crossed the room and pulled Suvi into a hug.

"Ugh, whatever. I won't say I'm sorry to her. She needs to try and pay attention for once. All it will take is one serious mishap with our potions to prove Cele right, that mom and dad should have forced us to stay at Callieach Academy all those years ago, and I'll be damned if I prove that witch right about anything." Isis stomped to the big, wood bookshelves that had been in the Rowan family for centuries, irritation in her every step. Isis was easily upset, but Pema shared her disgust about Cailleach Academy. Pema never wanted to be under Cele's thumb again.

"I don't know why you let that female get under your skin. I don't like her, but I'm not going to spend my time worrying about her unnecessarily. I'd rather talk about Confetti Too opening tomorrow night. I wonder if the Dark Warriors will be there," Suvi sang as she flitted about, placing books here and there haphazardly. Pema smiled as she watched her sister, wishing she was more easy-going like Suvi. Everything seemed to roll off Suvi's back, barely ruffling her feathers.

"I'm sure they'll be there. This is Killian's club, I doubt they'd miss the grand opening," Isis offered with a sly grin, her temper finally cooling down.

"On that note, I'm going to change the stone on this wrap to a rose quartz. I want some lovin' in my future," Pema said, waggling her eyebrows as she crossed to the RockCandy Leatherworks display, glad to have the mood lightened. It was her favorite jewelry, and she always wore one of the handcrafted pieces.

"That isn't the right choice of stone if sex is what you want, sister. You need the red jasper. It stimulates vitality," Suvi commented as she walked over to help her pick.

Pema shuddered, Suvi was right. No way did she want love. Love brought nothing but heartache and trouble. "Thank the Goddess you are so much better at remembering that stuff than I am," she replied as she looked through the assortment of stones. "That could have backfired on me," Pema admitted as she unscrewed the rose quartz from the leather band and replaced it with the red jasper.

Being a witch and connected to the earth, Pema felt the power in natural objects like these stones. As the effects of the stone began humming through her system, she turned to the less pleasant task of cleaning the store. "Help me grab the ladder, Suvi. I want to dust the candles on the top shelf. Have you heard anything more about the updates to the club? When we added our protections it was all steel beams and brick, but I've heard it has a whole different feel to it, and that Killian hired additional security. That doesn't surprise me given the skirm attack."

Pema was going against her better judgment in asking Suvi to help her, but her sister needed a boost after the fiasco with the fluorite. As they reached the storage room and gazed at the tall wooden ladder, Pema briefly rethought her decision when she saw the shoes her sister had on. Suvi was always dressed to the nines, no matter what they were doing, and today was no different with her six-inch heels. She sent a silent prayer to the Goddess that they managed without further destruction.

"I heard that Killian had the council members send him their strongest males," Suvi shared as they maneuvered through the halls, "Of course, that means there will be new, highly-mackable males."

Pema released the breath she had been holding when they managed to make it into the open area without breaking anything else.

"Yeah, but can they dance? I'm ready to hit the floor and shake my thang," Isis said as she sashayed over to the stereo and changed the music to a club mix. Pema and Suvi started laughing as Isis began to bump and grind to the sound as she spoke.

"Stop shaking your ass and grab some black candles from the back," Pema told Isis as she climbed up the ladder. "I sold the last we had out here to Camelia a couple hours ago."

Isis winced as she headed to the back. "No telling what crazy Camelia is conjuring with them."

"I heard she was trying to bring her son back from the dead," Suvi said, handing Pema the feather duster.

"You can't believe everything you hear. She may be trying to communicate with him, but she's not crazy enough to believe she can bring him back, resurrection isn't possible." Pema figured Cele was spreading the rumor to discredit Camelia, given the bad blood between them. There was nothing worse than sibling rivalry, and Pema thanked the Goddess that she and her sisters were as close as they were. She reached over and the ladder swayed under her feet, so she quickly muttered a stability spell. It would hurt like a bitch if she fell from the very top.

"I know. It's as insane as what they say about us. I mean, we could never be part of a hostile takeover," Suvi replied from below where she was now rearranging necklaces on the glass counter.

Pema nodded her agreement as she ran the duster over the shelf and candles. "That's the problem with prophecies. They are vague, confusing—" She stopped talking when the tinkling of the wind chimes above the front door signaled they had a customer.

A cool breeze blew through the room, chilling the air. She twisted around to see the most stunning male walk through the door. He was easily six feet tall and had thick, brown hair that fell in soft curls around his ruggedly handsome face. He had a strong, square jaw that she immediately imagined running her tongue over. His warm, brown eyes invited her to share her secrets, and suddenly it wasn't so chilly anymore.

Her gaze traveled over him and she noticed that his jeans were tight in all the right places, and she could easily make out his firmly muscled legs. He took her breath away and she desperately wanted him.

Her sex tightened with need, and arousal flooded her panties as she was overcome with an uncontrollable lust for this stranger, and she couldn't focus on anything but getting him into the office for a quick tryst. She became light-headed when a feathering sensation in her chest set her heart racing. She wondered what was wrong with her. She was no blushing virgin, but she had never responded like this when looking at a male.

Reaching up to wipe the sweat from her brow, she lost her hold on the ladder. As she felt air rush past her, she never once thought to utter a spell. She blamed it on the fact that her brain malfunctioned from hormone overload.

Rather than landing in an ungainly heap on the floor, she was caught by big, strong arms and an electrical current raced across her skin the moment they touched. She wanted to climb to the top of the ladder to have this male catch her again. Then again, that would mean him putting her down, and she had no desire for that to happen.

"Are you okay?" His voice was gruff, and she loved it. The sound sent liquid heat spreading from her abdomen to her core and had her melting into his body.

As much as she didn't want to, she needed to put space between them or she was going to lose control. She pushed against his broad shoulders for him to let her go. She didn't fight it too hard when he refused to release her. "I'm okay. Nice catch, by the way. I'm not usually caught off-guard like that."

She should tell him to let her go. Her lips parted to say the words, but they were trapped in her throat. She breathed in his earthy, pine scent and a new flood of heat traveled through her. She needed to gather her senses, and added more force to her shove until he finally set her down. Her body slid down the hard length of him and she took a couple steps back before acting on impulse to rub against him like a cat in heat.

"I didn't mean to startle you. Are you one of the Rowan sisters?" he asked, holding out his hand. Did he crave contact with her as much as she did him? It seemed like an eternity to Pema since he had touched her, and she would die if he didn't touch her again. Okaaay, she was losing her mind and she needed to stop this behavior.

Her brain and hormones weren't on speaking terms, and she eagerly grabbed his hand and held it tightly. "Yes, I'm Pema and this is my sister, Suvi," she nodded her head in the direction of her sister, keeping hold of his hand. "And you are?"

"My name is Ronan Blackwell," the hunk said, keeping intense gaze into her eyes.

"How can we help you, Ronan?" Suvi asked, awakening Pema from her daydreams of ravishing his body. Realizing how odd it must seem to be holding onto his hand, she pulled from his firm grip and immediately felt a loss. She turned around to face the counter, needing to break eye contact with him.

"I'm not exactly sure. I need to win my female back. I believe her mother forced her to end things between us. I have never believed in this hocus-pocus shit, and I think it made her mother dislike me. I'm a shifter, and I believe in what I see in front of me," Ronan said. Two things happened. For a brief second, Pema wanted to rip this female of his to shreds. She quickly dismissed the notion, reminding herself that she was only fantasizing about the male, nothing more. And, who the hell was he to call their magic hocus-pocus shit? She swiveled and took in this alpha male, and his confident stance amped her body's response, making all other thought flee from her mind.

"I'm not sure what we can do for you. We refuse to make or sell true love potions, so we can't force this female to love you, and we certainly can't create a potion to make you believe in our hocus-pocus shit," Pema said, acid dripping from her tone. "Who is this female anyway?"

Ronan was quiet for several long moments while he stared right through her soul before he answered. "Claire Wells. Surely you have something for me. I was told that the Rowan triplets are supposed to be the most powerful witches in the realm. I want to convince Claire to follow her heart. She has loved me for almost two hundred years, and I don't believe that has changed." He moved closer to Pema as he spoke, angling his body toward her. She wasn't going to be a fool to think that he was as affected by her as she was by him. She was a means to an end for him, and she sure as hell wasn't getting in the middle of his relationship problems.

Still, Pema had to bite her tongue. This magnificent male could not belong to this particular female. She wasn't surprised that he was taken, but why did it have to be with Claire? The male was making Pema crazy with lust, and now disgust. Not a great combination.

She shuddered in revulsion. Claire Wells was Cele's beloved daughter, and Pema hated them both. She didn't have a jealous bone in her body, so why she was so upset over this couple was beyond her. Something had taken over her, and Goddess help her, she may embarrass herself yet.

Suvi jumped right into sales mode. "Of course we are, and if anyone can help you, it's us. We have several truth potions. And, if you want to remind her of the passion you shared, we have pink tourmaline to enhance libido," Suvi winked at him.

Pema watched their interaction, bewitched by his perfection and her desire for him. It had to be the red jasper messing with her. Her libido was working overtime with this male two feet from her. She needed to raise the price on these stones, and order more. This was obviously some powerful mojo.

Pema listened to him talk to Suvi and found herself wondering why he was with Claire. Those thoughts brought up the memory of her last interaction with Claire. It was the day Claire had moved back to Seattle, and Pema and her sisters were making their final payment to the High Priestess.

Claire stood in Cele's office with her hands on her hips, her long mousy-brown hair flying around her shoulders in agitation as she snarled at them. "No matter how much money you make at that store of yours, you three are still just the poor kids in rags. You'll never amount to anything."

Isis sneered back. "This coming from the one who relies on mommy for everything. We may have started in rags, but we aren't in them anymore."

A deep rumble brought her out of the memory. "Bag up whatever crystals or potions you recommend." That quickly, his sexy voice conjured images in Pema's mind of him hovering over her while he slowly thrust into her, driving her to climax.

She clenched her teeth together, telling herself that she *had* to stop thinking about sex. She unclasped the magnet of the wrap around her wrist and dropped the bracelet onto the counter. She walked a few feet away, placing more distance between her and the sexy shifter, and pretended to organize the tarot cards.

Ronan inched closer to her then stopped. He ran his hands through his hair, ruffling his curls and shuffling from foot to foot. His gaze returned to Pema's face again and again. Something in Pema stirred at the way he was staring at her. She couldn't decipher the look in his chocolate brown depths, but it was intense.

Suvi bagged several items for Ronan, telling him how to use each one as she took his payment. Pema didn't think Ronan heard a word her sister had said, given that his gaze never once wavered from her face. For someone who was so hot to win his girlfriend back, he sure didn't seem too concerned about it at the moment. That was *not* wishful thinking, Pema assured herself.

"I need to get to work, but thank you for the help. See you around?" Ronan asked, but didn't move to leave.

"If you are ever at Confetti Too then you'll see me plenty," Pema replied, hoping her invitation wasn't too blatant.

"I guess I'll see you often, since I've just been hired as part of the new security. Will you be there tomorrow night?"

"Yes," she nodded. "We wouldn't miss the grand opening."

"Save me a dance?" he husked.

"Dancing with me is certainly not the way to win back another female," she responded.

"You're right," he said. They stood staring at each other for what seemed like forever before he turned and exited the store. He gazed back at her from the street then hopped into a large truck. There was something about a male in a truck, Pema thought.

"That is some heat you two were throwing off. I need a walk-in freezer to cool down," Suvi broke the silence, fanning her face.

"Shut it, Suvi," Pema mumbled, staring out the window, captivated by glowing, brown eyes.

AUTHORS' NOTE

With new digital download trends, authors rely on readers to spread the word more than ever. I'd love it if you can leave me a review!

Every author asks their readers to take five minutes and let others know how much you enjoyed their work. Here's the reason why. It's a virtual hug for us. Plus, they help your favorite authors become visible. It's simple and easy to do. Visit your favorite retailer and leave a brief review.

Don't forget to visit my website: www.trimandjulka.com and sign up for my newsletter, which is jam-packed with exciting news and monthly giveaways. Also, be sure to visit and like my Facebook page https://www.facebook.com/TrimAndJulka to see hot guys, drink recipes and book teasers.

Trust your journey and remember that the future is yours and it's filled with endless possibilities!

DREAM BIG!

XOXO,

Brenda

OTHER WORKS BY BRENDA TRIM

THE DARK WARRIOR ALLIANCE

Guild Master (Dark Alliance Book 19)
Maven Warrior (Dark Alliance Book 20)
Sentinel of Khoth (Dark Alliance Book 21)

Dark Warrior Alliance Boxsets:
Dark Warrior Alliance Boxset Books 1-4
Dark Warrior Alliance Boxset Books 5-8
Dark Warrior Alliance Boxset Books 9-12
Dark Warrior Alliance Boxset Books 13-16

Hollow Rock Shifters:
Captivity, Hollow Rock Shifters Book 1
Safe Haven, Hollow Rock Shifters Book 2
Alpha, Hollow Rock Shifters Book 3
Ravin, Hollow Rock Shifters Book 4
Impeached, Hollow Rock Shifters Book 5

DON'T MISS OUT!

Don't miss out!
Click the button below and you can sign up to receive a FREE copy of Heat in the Bayou plus emails from me about new releases, fantastic giveaways, and my latest laser engraved creation. There's no charge and no obligation.

Made in the USA
Monee, IL
26 April 2020